Muckross Folly

Also by J.L. Austgen

Keyser Run

Muckross Folly

J.L. Austgen

Dreampipe Publishing, Inc.

Muckross Folly

Copyright © 2013 by J.L. Austgen. All rights reserved. Printed in the United States of America. No part of this work may be reproduced or transmitted in any form or by any means, either electronically or mechanically, including photocopying, recording, or by any information retrieval system, without the express written permission of the publisher. For information, please contact Dreampipe Publishing.

All characters in this work are fictitious. Any resemblance to real persons, living or dead, is purely coincidental.

Published in the United States of America by:

Dreampipe Publishing, Inc.

info@dreampipepublishing.com

http://www.dreampipepublishing.com

Cover design by Jennifer Austgen

Cover photograph by Jennifer Austgen

ISBN: 978-0-9850630-2-3

For Kaleb and Logan

"Music can name the unnameable and communicate the unknowable"

-- Leonard Bernstein

Prologue

With a grim determination, she safed the rifle, leaving his lifeless body in the distance, and began to belly crawl backwards, her eyes scanning the hillside in front of her. The sage and dry alfalfa hid her movement as she slid into the tree line, but she did not feel comfortable rising into a crouch until she was fifty yards in the thick, dark timber of lodge pole pine and evergreen. When she did finally stand all the way up, over a hundred yards behind the line of trees, she would have been lucky to see fifteen yards in any direction. The trees were so dense they cast a pall across the forest, lengthening the shadows and making her surprisingly claustrophobic.

She spent many days of her youth in the woods of Colorado, growing up hunting and fishing in the high country, surrounded by dark timber like this. It was different this morning. The trees stared down, and while she did not feel judged, they seemed closer than normal. Taking a deep breath, she closed her eyes and clutched her rifle, a beautiful seven millimeter Remington Magnum with a silver barrel, and a black, synthetic stock. Justice was finally done. She opened her eyes and was enveloped by the sounds of the forest. Things could go back to normal. There was no longer any reason to keep looking over her shoulder. With a purposeful stride, she stepped off towards her car.

The path back to her SUV, while not marked, was well known. The entire forest, its sounds, its scent, its presence, was as familiar as her dorm at the Air Force Academy. She hunted these woods before, and while she had not been here in many years, she felt safe. The other hunters in her target's party would not miss him for several hours, until he did not report at their next scheduled rendezvous. With luck, he would not be missed until later that evening when the party met for dinner.

She had left her ten year old Wrangler on the side of a forest road some distance away. Covering the ground quickly, she was driving north on Colorado 131 a little over two hours after she shot her target. A gas station and convenience store sat outside of the tiny town of Yampa, and she pulled up to the pump. There was only one other vehicle there that afternoon, a pickup truck, and she could feel its owner's eyes on her as she got out of her SUV and filled the tank.

The thought of being ogled no longer bothered her, and so long as it was not overt or blatant, she found it rather flattering. Tall, trim, young, and athletic with shoulder-length brunette hair and dark green eyes, she knew she was attractive. The physical fitness regimen prescribed by the Academy kept her in excellent physical shape, so it was only natural men would admire her.

Replacing the gas cap on the Wrangler, she walked into the attached convenience store and paid the cashier for the gas. With a nod and a small smile, she went back outside and stopped at the pay phone. She dropped several quarters in the slot and dialed a number. It was answered after the second ring.

"Thomas," she said into the handset, "it's Eve. Is my Dad there?"

"Yes. One second please, Ms. Morgan."

It didn't take long, and she idly scanned the store before a gruff voice came on the line. "Eve! I didn't know when I'd hear back from you. I'm glad you called."

"It's good to talk to you, Dad. I got your message." She was staying at a small motel just outside of town. The rooms did not have phones. When the receptionist handed her the message that morning, before she set out, she was a little surprised to learn her father knew where she was. Though, in retrospect, she should not have been.

"I need to talk to you," he said, "and it would be better in person. As soon as possible. Don't you need to report to the Academy soon? Your leave of absence should be just about up, right?"

"Yes," she said, glancing down at her now-normal stomach. "But I don't need to report for a couple of days. I needed some time to myself, so I drove up to the Flattops."

"I was a little surprised to learn you were up there," he replied, an edge to his voice. "Cold time of the year for backpacking."

"I know, but it was worth it. I needed to clear my head, you know?"

"I can imagine," he said. "Why don't we meet for drinks at the Ore House? It would be comfortable."

"How about Fish Creek falls?" she countered. "It was on my list of places to hit while I'm up here. Say in about an hour?"

"Ok," he said. "See you soon."

"Thanks," she said, replacing the handset. She climbed back into her Wrangler, but did not drive off. She sat there and tried to collect her thoughts. Even that brief reference to her son, given up for adoption barely six weeks ago, brought all the painful memories and emotions boiling to the surface. The Academy offered her a year's leave of absence to figure out what she wanted to do. She made the decision, shortly after discovering she was pregnant, to carry the baby to term and give him up for adoption. She was not in a position to care for a child, and she knew, no matter how difficult it would be, that the child would do far better with adoptive parents.

With a sigh, she wiped a tear from her eye and started the SUV. Her father, while she did not see him that often, was supportive through the whole ordeal, offering to cover all of the expenses. Not that the expenses were a burden for him. The problem was that she had not told him how the child was actually conceived, and she worried about the consequences if he found out.

The drive to the small parking lot above Fish Creek Falls was uneventful, though her mind would not stop turning over the brief phone call with her father. What did he want? She arrived early and found the parking lot deserted. Stepping from the SUV, she could hear the falls in the distance. They were barely a quarter mile down the trail, and she took her time walking. The air was crisp, the sun barely floating above the western line of mountains.

A steep hill rose to her left, and as she followed the trail, it began to cut into the hill's side. After a few steps, the right side dropped dramatically to the river as it cut a gorge down the mountain. The trail, like the parking lot, was deserted. It was wide and well traveled, and before long she picked out a large wooden bridge crossing the river. The falls, a gushing torrent of water during the spring thaw, were still magnificent as a steady stream cascading nearly three hundred feet to the river below.

Stepping onto the bridge, she leaned against the rail and watched the water pour over the cliff. The steady noise from the falls, combined with the peaceful serenity of the forest, tugged at her mind. It wandered, but not to the scene she just left in the forests outside of Yampa. Instead, it travelled to happier times, to a smiling teenage boy, the warmth of his hand enveloping hers, the honesty behind his smile, and the love behind his eyes. It had all been hers, not that long ago, and sometimes she wondered if it would ever happen again.

Footsteps on the bridge brought her mind around to reality, and she glanced to her left. Her father, stocky and muscular with thinning gray hair, strode towards her. Behind him, his assistant stopped at the edge of the bridge, maintaining a discrete distance.

"An odd place for a meeting," her father called as he approached. "Especially in December."

With a nod, she acknowledged his statement and turned back to the falls. She knew he would have preferred to meet while relaxing in an armchair in a quiet room, sipping a glass of scotch.

"Do you remember coming here when you were a little girl?" he asked, stopping next to her and leaning over the rail.

"I do," she said. "Mom would stay down in town."

"She was kind enough to let me have a little time with you, however briefly."

"It's too bad she never made it up here."

He grunted.

"So," she said. "What did you want to talk about?"

"Do you remember when you told me you were pregnant?"

"Yes," she replied carefully.

"And when I asked how it happened, you just told me it was one of those things?"

"Yes."

"That wasn't exactly the truth, was it?"

She studied him, crossing her arms over her chest, but her heart caught in her throat. "I'm not sure what we're talking about."

"I did some digging," he explained, still watching the waterfall. "You declined to name the father on your son's birth certificate."

"Not all that unusual."

"Perhaps," he shrugged. "I also spoke with your boyfriend."

"My ex-boyfriend, you mean."

Wogan waved his hand in the air, signifying his indifference. "He said something interesting. Something you told him."

She knew what was coming, and her heart sank. Despite everything, her father discovered the truth. It killed her keeping it welled up inside for nine months, but she knew she must keep it from this man as long as possible.

He turned towards her, and his eyes were suddenly cold and distant. "I've done a great deal for you over the years. I've supported you and your mother, made sure you were comfortable, provided the best schools, the best education money can buy. I covered all of your bills during the pregnancy. I offered the best doctors, the best of everything to ensure you were comfortable and successful. To ensure you delivered a healthy child."

As he spoke, he stepped closer until he was within inches of her face. She was pressed against the guard rail on the bridge, the rapids' whitewater crashing beneath her feet. "You have not been entirely truthful about several things."

"Are you pissed because I gave him up for adoption," she asked, the wooden guardrail cold against her back, "or because I wasn't entirely honest?"

His anger rose as he stared at her, the defiance in her eyes feeding his temper. "Where is my grandson?"

"Gone."

"I know that" he said, his voice menacing. "I thought we had a deal. The father's name is missing from the birth certificate."

"It was obvious what you wanted the minute you proposed that deal. The birth certificate didn't display the father's name on purpose. It's sealed. The entire process was finished an hour after I gave birth. My son is out of your reach. You won't use him."

His hands balled into fists at his side, he asked, "He's my grandson! Do you know what this could do to me? Did you even think for two seconds before you spread your legs what this might lead to?"

"What do you mean?" she asked, feeling the first tear swell at the edge of her eyes. "Of course! I love you!"

"Then how the hell did this happen?" he screamed, inches from her face. "How could you do this to me?"

"Do this to you?" she cried. "I did it for my son! I gave him up so he might have a life! I gave him up so he could not be tied to you! To protect you!"

"To protect me? You didn't think about that when you were fucking your boyfriend's best friend, did you?"

She shrunk back against the rail as though he struck her. It took all of her strength, all of the resolve she built over the last nine months, to remain standing, to not collapse. "Is that what you think happened?" she asked in a whisper. "Is that what he told you?"

"Yes."

Shaking her head slowly, her eyes closed, she could scarcely believe this was happening. This was her father. The man was supposed to protect her. "I was raped."

"What?" he asked. The sound of the rushing water over the rocks drowned her whispered words.

"I was raped, you son of a bitch!" she spat, looking up, meeting his eyes.

It was as though all of the sound, the crashing of the water, the birds flying through the air, the wind blowing through the trees, ceased to exist. It was sucked from her consciousness, replaced by a vacuum of sound devastating in its stillness. What was more disturbing, though, was how long it lasted. An eternity passed before everything rushed back in, pounding her senses with a symphony of noise.

Through all of it, she heard him ask, "Who? Your boyfriend's best friend? What was his name? Greg?"

"Yes."

He pursed his lips and stared at her, his brow furrowed. "Why didn't you tell me this earlier? I could have done something about it, about Greg."

She knew it was coming. "You don't need to worry about him."

"You don't need to protect him."

"Is that what you think I'm doing?" she asked, wanting to laugh and cry at the same time. She met his blue eyes, but it was impossible to tell what thoughts were flying around behind them. The man was always an enigma to her, despite the fact he was her father. It did not help that her mother allowed only brief visits, sometimes not for months on end.

"I have a pretty good idea what you're doing," he said.

"What?"

"Protecting your son. Why? Are you afraid I might do something to him?"

"Yes."

"Begotten through rape," he spat, disgusted.

"That was not my son's fault."

"Do you know what this could do to me?" he asked, turning back to the waterfall, his fists resting on the bridge's rail.

And there it was. The other reason why he never pushed very hard to be near her, to be involved in her life, other than the presents at Christmas, and the insistence that he pay for whatever college she wished to attend. She was the illegitimate daughter of an affair he regretted to this day.

"I love you, Dad," she said, trying to get a grip on the emotions coursing through her, "but I won't tell you his name. I won't give up my son so you can use him."

"What if this gets out?"

She continued to stare at the side of his face. "You don't need to worry about that. I've taken care of it."

It was as though he never heard her. "This could hurt me badly. If someone uses your son to get to me...."

"I was raped, and all you care about is your precious reputation? Or the reputation of your precious company?"

"I care about taking care of my family."

"Including my sister and your wife?"

"They're none of your concern."

"They're family."

"My family."

She took a deep breath. "I see."

"Do you?" he asked, still not looking at her. "Because what you've just said could ruin everything I've worked for. If you go to the police --"

"I haven't said a word to them," she interrupted. "You know that or you wouldn't have asked me here today. Do you think I would worry about it now?"

He shrugged. "And the Academy?"

"They know I was pregnant, and that's all."

She watched as he turned it over in his mind.

"I want to know who it was. Which organization did you use for the adoption? Who set it up?"

"No."

"And if your son discovers who your father is?"

"The adoption is sealed. I've taken care of everything. He will never know who I am, who his real parents are. My son will grow up thinking his adopted parents are his biological parents."

"And Greg?"

A shadow passed over her eyes, though it did little to diminish the fire behind them. "I already told you it's been taken care of."

"What if Greg finds out who I am? Who your real father is? What I own?" He looked at her with disdain. "What if he learns about all of that and suddenly decides that his son should be a part of it? What if he realizes what could be gained? In the name of his son?" He stared at her. "Because you brought him to term."

She shuddered, wrapping her arms around herself. This was her father. This was the man who brought her into the world, who supposedly loved her. "Is that what you're worried about?" she finally asked. "Is that really what bothers you?"

"You bet your ass."

She nodded, hugging herself tighter as he stepped back.

"Give me a name," he demanded. "Tell me which organization you used!"

She looked at her shoes. "No."

"I'll find out," he threatened. "You know I'll find out."

This time, she was the one that smiled. "No. I don't think you ever will."

He matched her stare for several minutes, the sound of the waterfall cascading like a thunderstorm behind them. "Then we're done," he said finally, turning on his heel and marching down the bridge, motioning for his assistant to follow.

Chapter 1

If she knew this was the night she would be murdered, she might not have ventured out. Hindsight was a luxury she was afforded throughout her young life, but in this instance, even if she could look back, it would not have done any good. Events beyond her control tumbled over themselves, consuming her in the process.

She was young, just starting her sophomore year at St. John's, and a night out, after five days of lecture, was exactly what she needed. Brushing her blonde hair, she laid her comb down, walked out of the bathroom, and stepped into the single apartment's kitchen. She checked her watch and swore, grabbed her purse, and started to root through it when a soft meow, followed by a purr at her elbow, interrupted her.

"Janx," she said, rolling her eyes. "I can't pick you up right now. I just got dressed. I'm going out." She dug through her purse again, looking for something, and the cat pushed against her elbow.

"You're not going to let me out of here unless I pick you up, are you?" she asked, finding what she needed in her purse and finally closing it.

Janx turned in a complete circle, his eyes never leaving hers. Throwing the shoulder strap over her shoulder, she reached down and picked him up. He rewarded her with a loud purr, nuzzling his head against the side of her neck. "I don't know how I'm going to pick somebody up tonight, covered in cat fur."

He purred louder.

"But it's worth it." She gently rubbed his head, then set him down on the counter. "I really have to go, though. All the good seats at the bar will be gone. I love you. See you in a bit."

It was a short walk along Annapolis's well-lit sidewalks to her favorite bar, one she frequented since her freshman year, just past the State House on Main Street. The fresh spring air was damp with that afternoon's rain, and she inhaled deeply as she walked, savoring its crispness. It reminded her of her native Colorado and its summer nights, particularly after an afternoon thunderstorm.

A big part of her missed home, but after everything she endured in the past twelve months, she knew this was where she needed to be. It was a matter of pride that she show her father that she was capable of living on her own, without the need for someone to watch over her all of the time. It was no secret she made some poor decisions in her life, but she had put that behind her. Those demons were gone, and her reward was a furnished apartment where she could concentrate on her degree.

And have some fun, she admitted to herself, pushing the bar's door open.

As she feared, it was crowded. Judging by the number of people jostling around the bar, she figured she was ten or fifteen minutes later than usual. She swore, scanning the long bar for an open seat. There was one, at the end, but judging by the beautiful woman next to it, it was probably already taken.

With nothing to lose, she shrugged her shoulders and walked the length of the bar, stopping just behind the empty chair. The woman sitting next to it was even more stunning than she first thought. Her fine brown hair was combed straight down and cut in a smart pageboy. As she stopped behind the barstool, the woman turned and looked at her with deeply intelligent, dark chocolate eyes.

"Hello," the woman said.

"Hi," she answered, putting her hand on the back of the barstool. "Are you meeting someone? Is this seat taken?"

"No. Help yourself."

"Thank you," she said with a smile, finding it difficult to look away from the woman's eyes.

"Amelia," the woman said, holding out her hand. "Amelia Dyer."

Taking a seat on the barstool, she replied, "Janice Wogan."

Amelia smiled, perfect white teeth flashing through blood-red lips. "What brings you in here tonight, Janice?"

"A good time."

"Are you a student?"

"At St. John's, yes."

"Are you a graduate student?"

Janice smiled, a little uncomfortably. "No. I got a late start. I'm only a sophomore, but I'm an old sophomore."

"Did you take some time off after high school?"

"Something like that," Janice replied, watching as Amelia nodded, then turned back to her drink. "I spent some time at Yale before enrolling at St. John's." It wasn't the complete truth, but it was close enough. The people were one of the main reasons she came back to this bar time and time again, but she was still adjusting to how warm and open this woman seemed, especially given her stunning beauty. Janice's experience with such blindingly attractive women was usually the opposite. Often she found them cold and remote.

One of the bartenders approached as she turned this over in her mind.

"Hey, Janice," he said. "What'll you have tonight?"

"A vanilla stolie, please."

"Coke?"

"Please."

He smiled at her. "Coming right up."

"So you don't come here often enough that they just bring you a drink when you sit down, but you come here often enough that they know your name."

Janice turned in her seat and examined Amelia more closely. She was not young, at least not young enough to be a student, but she did not look nearly old enough to be a professor. There was a keen intelligence behind her eyes, and the tone in her voice suggested she was used to giving orders, and having them obeyed. A naval officer, maybe? They usually did not frequent the bars in Annapolis, preferring either the Officer's Club at the Naval Academy, or something a little further out, to provide more anonymity. Most people were not so forward, though.

"Navy?" Janice asked, intrigued by this woman's personality, and finding herself strangely attracted to her beauty.

Amelia smiled politely. "Does it show that easily?"

"Maybe it was the haircut."

"No, I doubt it. You're a smart young woman."

Feeling herself blush, Janice said, "Thank you."

"But you're right. I am in the Navy. I'm on TDY to the Academy for the next several weeks."

"Are you teaching?"

"Yes," Amelia said. "I've got a class on the role of Japanese women in early feudal Japan. Specifically how they shaped decisions and the political process."

"I thought Japan was ruled by samurai during that period."

"It was."

"I guess I didn't realize there were many female samurai," Janice admitted, confused.

Amelia laughed. "There weren't. In fact, there's very little that's been published or studied on the role of women in feudal Japanese society, other than they were subservient to men."

"No?"

"Well, there's been a lot of study done on women in society, but there's very little information on female leaders during that time. Men ruled women and the country. Little has survived to tell us of female warriors, for example."

"Then how do you know they existed?"

The bartender delivered Janice's drink, and Amelia paused while she tasted it and nodded her appreciation.

"Because some things have survived," she said. "That's what makes it so fascinating. There are stories and tales that have come down through history that detail how some women defied convention and became great warriors. Onna bugeisha were an entire class of women that didn't sit at home and defer to their husbands."

"And your class highlights those women?"

"Among other things."

"Do you look at the role history has played in influencing these stories?" Janice asked. "You mentioned that only some have made it down to us, and it seems like Japan is a very masculine-influenced society."

"We do look at that, because I believe it has played a large role in what did carry through. Japanese culture and society is very interesting in itself, but you take what influences it has placed on the lens of history, and it becomes fascinating, especially in the last ten or twenty years."

"How?"

Amelia took a quick drink of her chardonnay. "Well, as I said, there haven't been too many accounts of true female warriors in Japanese history. There's references everywhere of women picking up arms when necessary -- the defense of castles, that sort of thing. But there's not a whole lot on true female samurai."

"What was that term you used earlier? Onna bugeisha?"

"Yes, but it doesn't translate exactly as female samurai. They were female warriors, yes, and a member of the samurai class, but when I think about the truly special women of Japan, I like to think of them as female samurai."

"Ok."

"One of the most famous female samurai, Tomoe Gozen, might not have actually existed at all, or maybe not under that name. She was supposed to have lived in the thirteenth century, but it's never been proven that she was an actual historical figure."

"You said she could have existed under a different name?"

"Well, the primary story that references her, or rather, the original reference, is a history of the struggle for power between two major Japanese clans during that time period. She's a hugely popular figure in Japanese society, a legend." Amelia's eyes glazed over slightly before refocusing on Janice. It was as though she got lost thousands of years ago before finding her way back to the present. "I'm a believer that there's usually some truth in the legends that make it through the fog of history, and I wonder if she might have been some real person, perhaps elevated through the eye of historical fiction."

"The cultural implications are significant."

"Yes, though it's obvious to see why a male-dominated society would seek some sort of strong female legend." She smiled. "Most men like to think of a strong female counterpart. Someone to test them."

"I've always loved history," Janice said, finishing her drink.

"Is that what you're studying?"

"To be honest, I haven't completely decided. I'm still working through a lot of the required courses. But I'd love to take your course. It sounds fascinating."

"Thanks. I think so," Amelia said. "Can I buy your next round?"

Janice looked at her empty glass. "I'd like that."

She watched, a small smile turning her lips, as Amelia leaned over the bar, caught the bartender's attention, and motioned for another round for both of them. "What rank do you hold in the Navy?" she asked when Amelia sat back down.

"I'm a Lieutenant Commander. Do you know the Navy?"

"No," Janice said, shaking her head. "But my dad's tied into the Department of Defense pretty well, so I picked some stuff up over the years."

"Oh yeah? What does he do?"

"He's a contractor," Janice hedged, not quite sure how much she should divulge. Her dad always told her to be careful. And, really, how well did she know this woman? They just met.

"Which department? Do you know?"

"Uh, I'm not quite sure. I know he spends a lot of time in Washington."

"A lot of them do."

The bartender delivered their next round, and Amelia raised her glass. "Cheers," she said, smiling.

"Cheers," Janice replied, clinking her glass and taking a sip. "How long have you been teaching?"

Amelia thought about it. "Nearly ten years now. Shortly after I got my masters."

"Always history?"

"Always."

"Do you like the Navy?"

"I like the security, and I like teaching. It's allowed me to do both with relative independence."

"How about being a woman in the Navy?"

"What about it?"

Janice caught her chocolate eyes and held them. "Is it hard?"

"It provides some interesting challenges."

"Like what?"

"Like being able to meet people," Amelia said, meeting her eyes. "The right kind of people. Too often, they're too quick to judge."

"What kind of people?" Janice asked, her mouth suddenly dry.

"Can I buy you another drink?"

Glancing down quickly Janice had not realized she finished it. "Yes, please," she said hurriedly, trying to gain some control over her emotions. She had been with a woman before. Well, she corrected herself, more like a girl. It was several years ago, in high school, and they were both very young. It had been... amateurish, she thought. But this. This could be so much more, judging by Amelia's apparent experience. Perhaps it was time to branch out a little more. Certainly men weren't the only ones capable of providing a good time.

The bartender delivered her drink, and she took a tentative sip before asking, "Are you staying somewhere around here?"

"The Academy has me in temporary housing."

"You don't sound too happy about that."

"It leaves much to be desired."

"Too old?"

Amelia smiled. "Too masculine."

Janice took another drink, almost draining the stoli. "I've got a small place not far from here. Just a few blocks away. I'd love to hear more about Japanese history."

"What excited you the most about it?"

Janice took a deep breath. "The women."

Amelia's smile grew, and she said, "Then let's go."

The walk back to her apartment took far less time than she ever remembered, her head overwhelmed with hopeful anticipation. The first time, the only time, she reminded herself, was awkward, with a lot of laughing and giggling. Watching Amelia's purposeful strides, the small lines around her incredible chocolate eyes, expertly covered with makeup, Janice was convinced she was about to have a whole new experience. Her heart skipped another beat, and her pace quickened.

She opened the front door when they arrived at her apartment, neither having said a word since leaving the bar. "Have a seat on the couch. Make yourself at home," she said, the words almost catching in her throat. Forcing herself to take a deep breath, Janice walked into the kitchen and pulled two bottles of beer out of the fridge. She found Amelia on the couch, offered her one of the beers, then sat next to her.

"This is a nice apartment," Amelia said, looking around.

"Beautiful cat," she added, as Janx ran into the room, jumping on Janice's lap.

"His name's Janx," she said, rubbing his head. "He hates it when I have company. I think sometimes he gets jealous."

"How often do you have company?"

Janice looked up. "I've only had this kind of company once."

Amelia nodded, almost imperceptibly, leaned forward, and kissed her, softly at first, delicately.

Closing her eyes, Janice felt the pressure of Amelia's kiss increase. Janx jumped from her lap as Amelia ran one of her hands through Janice's hair. As their kiss deepened, Janice surrendered herself, all of her hopeful anticipation exploding like electricity when Amelia wrapped her hand around the back of Janice's neck, pulling her closer.

Janice felt her mouth open, their tongues touch, and she lost herself in the sensations wracking her body. It was not like the touch of a new lover, or even one she was with for months. It was something else entirely, and it was exquisite, quite unlike anything she ever experienced before.

Surrendering to every suggestion, both verbal and implied, Janice slowly undressed them, Amelia's expert touch unlocking the newly naked flesh in waves of pleasure that steadily advanced until Janice's eyes popped open and she exploded in a climax that left her breathless. But Amelia did not stop there. With a delicate purpose, she leaned Janice back and kissed her again before trailing her mouth down her body. Janice spent the next fifteen minutes writhing, moaning, and sweating, her body wracked in an unending series of climaxes that left her clutching the couch.

Finally, Amelia leaned back, her own body glistening with sweat, her eyes ablaze. "Where's your bedroom?" she asked, huskily.

Janice could only point, still trying to catch her breath, her eyes unfocused, her body spent.

Taking her hand, Amelia helped her from the couch and led her into the bedroom. This was more than Janice ever expected, exactly what she needed after the last week of classes, and she offered no resistance.

As they crossed the threshold, Amelia held back. "Wait, just lay on the bed. I'll be right there. I'll take care of everything."

Janice did as she was told, powerless to resist. She fell on the bed, collapsing on her stomach. No man or drug ever made her feel like this. It was incredible. The crisp white sheets tickled her burning skin like ice, goose bumps exploding all over her body. A faint rustling came from the living room, Amelia going through her purse, and then, as if time did not have any meaning, she felt Amelia's sweet lips caressing her back.

Those same sensations swept over her, and she moaned in expectation, her eyes closed, her head back as Amelia kissed her neck. Wild thoughts flew through her mind when Amelia straddled her and wrapped one arm around her neck. Those thoughts abruptly turned to terror, and her eyes popped open in fear, when Amelia cupped a hand over her mouth and jabbed something sharp into her right thigh.

Her dread passed quickly, though, and she succumbed to the inky darkness invading her mind.

***

There was nothing to drink in her condo, and she desperately needed something, so she stopped at a liquor store on her way back from FBI headquarters. If the clerk thought there was anything strange about the beautiful brunette with piercing green eyes buying a bottle of scotch in the middle of the night, he did not show it. He did not mention the holster on her right hip, either, when she reached inside her trench coat for two twenties. He just took her money, dropped the bottle in a brown paper bag, handed it to her, and turned his attention back to the television blaring behind the bulletproof partition.

"Thanks," she mumbled, trying to be polite, though not really sure why.

She did not get a response.

The short drive back to her condo was lonely, most of the city dark at this late hour, the streetlights the only source of warmth. She pulled into her customary spot, walked to her door, and unlocked it, almost mechanically, her left hand clutching the neck of the bottle. The condo was just as lonely as her drive had been, the parking-lot lights casting strange shadows across the living room as she crossed into the kitchen. There was not much sense in turning on any of the lights inside, she thought, her mind still lost in that week's events.

With the same mechanical motion of the last five days, she reached into a cupboard and took out a glass tumbler. She dropped two ice cubes into the glass and poured herself a generous portion, tossing it down her throat with two quick gulps. Pouring herself another measure, she slowly swilled the scotch in the glass, letting it mix with the ice before she took a long drink, savoring the heat and smoke.

She did not really want to get drunk, she thought to herself, absently spinning the scotch in her drink, but she did not really know what else to do. Everything that needed to be said had been said. Everything that needed to be done had been done over the past five days. There was no sense getting her team up in the middle of the night to work on -- on what? What did she have for them to work on?

Another sip and a slow shake of her head.

The assassin they were tracking, that she was tracking, Omar Ben Iblis, was long gone. His operation to disrupt her investigation, to bring the investigative power of the FBI to its knees, had been a resounding success. Four of her agents were dead, including her lover, murdered by one of their own.

At least she had killed that traitorous son-of-a-bitch.

But did that really matter now? Would it ever matter?

She finished the scotch in her glass and poured more.

"Christ, Eve," she muttered, running a hand over her face. The entire fight with the traitor Baker suddenly flooded her mind, and she saw herself catching his gun hand, smashing his collar bone, and breaking his neck, all in a split second. Just as quickly, though, the scene was replaced by Nichols' broken body, crumpled in a heap where it fell, kicked to the ground by two of Baker's pistol rounds. It was the nightmare that consumed each night since that tragic evening. She saw herself sobbing, swearing, screaming that she should have done something, should have done anything to keep Baker from killing Nichols. But it did not matter. Not now.

The tears came rushing again, despite her every effort to control them. She gripped the edge of the counter and sobbed, trying to take a breath to get control of herself, but every time she tried to stop, she saw his smile, she saw his body, and she was overcome.

It was several minutes before she regained control of herself. With a final sniff, she wiped her nose on the back of her hand and poured herself another drink, adding two more ice cubes and swirling the scotch in the glass. She took a small sip and sniffed again, forcing her emotions back into the depths of her soul.

Nichols was more than a lover. It was foolish to try and argue otherwise. Of course there had been other lovers since the incident in college. If they could be called lovers. But she could not compare those episodes to the night she spent with Nichols. She trusted him, felt safe around him, and those were feelings she was only able to share with one other man.

She took another drink, if only to stop the sobbing again.

Nichols.

"Prost," she said, raising the scotch with a half hearted smile.

"Do you always toast the dead?" a disembodied voice asked from the living room.

She dropped to a crouch behind the counter and drew her gun so quickly she surprised even herself, the years of training taking over and her muscle memory forcing her body to react instinctively.

"If I wanted you dead, it would have happened many days ago," the same voice said with an eerie calm. "Please. Holster your weapon."

"I can have half the FBI here in ten minutes," she boasted, options and choices running through her mind.

"And you'll be dead long before that."

"I'm in good cover here," she said, her mind still frantically trying to piece together all of her options.

"Evelyn. Please. Lower your weapon."

If he was in the living room, she walked right past him in the dark, completely oblivious. He didn't want her dead. At least not yet. This was something else.

"Please," he repeated.

She stood up and holstered her pistol, surprisingly calm for such a situation.

"Will you sit down?" he asked.

An amused smirk formed at the corners of her mouth, though she doubted he could see it in the darkened space. "That seems like an odd offer coming from you. Especially considering this is my home." She watched as a shadow slowly rose from her couch. "Omar Ben Iblis, I presume?" she asked, pouring more scotch into her glass.

"Correct," he said.

"May I offer you a drink?"

"Please."

She reached up, took down another glass, and poured.

"Thank you. Just set it on the coffee table."

"May I turn on a light?" she asked, her eyes darting briefly to the gun in his hand.

"I really don't think that's necessary," he said. "And I must insist that you put your cell phone on the table."

"Alright," she said, dropping her phone on the table before sitting down in a chair opposite him, her drink in her left hand. "I always wondered how this conversation would go," she said, switching to Arabic.

"I'm impressed," he said, a hint of admiration in his voice. "Your Arabic is flawless."

"Thank you."

"Where did you study?"

"At the Academy."

"Which one?"

"The Air Force Academy. In Colorado."

He smiled. "Colorado Springs. I have been there. A beautiful city."

"Yes, it is."

"Where else? Where else have you studied?"

"I've traveled extensively in the Middle East."

"Not easy for a woman."

"No, but well worth the effort."

He picked up his scotch in a gloved hand. "So how did you think this would go? Would it be civil? Have you thought about it for long?"

"My entire professional career," she continued, in Arabic. "And yes, I believed it would be civil. Professional."

"Then it is as I thought."

"What did you think?"

"That you were worth the effort."

"The effort? What effort?"

She caught the gleam of his teeth in the darkness as a smile escaped his lips. "All of this, Evelyn. May I call you Evelyn?"

"You have the weapon, Omar. You're a man of intelligence, and, I think, to some extent, respect. You may call me whatever you wish."

A smile again. "Thank you."

"I was wondering when we'd finally have the chance to meet."

"Honestly, I hoped we never would."

She was surprised. "Then why are you here?"

"For a number of reasons. This is personal, and I knew you would be alone tonight."

"How did you know I'd be alone?"

He cocked his head to one side. "You're always alone."

Not always, she thought, remembering her time with Nichols. Now wasn't the time for those thoughts, though. "I didn't think things were ever personal with you."

"They usually aren't."

She thought about it for a moment. "It's a dangerous position to be in. Very dangerous. Especially in your line of work."

"I know."

"What I still don't understand is why you don't end this. You must know that I'll never stop hunting you, not after this week, not after everything that's happened, not with everything you've done."

Ben Iblis turned it over in his mind. "No, I suppose not."

"He was an innocent man," she said, a sudden hardness entering her voice.

"Nichols?"

"Yes."

"He was a casualty of war, Evelyn."

Aren't we all, she asked herself.

"But," he continued, "since you ask, this was professional courtesy."

"This visit?"

"Yes."

She thought about it, her eyes glancing between the formless shadow and the gun held with rock-steady precision in its hand. "I'm honored," she said after several minutes of silence.

"You should be."

They lapsed into silence again, Morgan trying desperately to concentrate despite the alcohol coursing through her system. "Tell me how you set it up."

"Why?"

"Because you killed him."

"Nichols?" he asked, shaking his head. "I didn't kill him. Baker killed him."

"Through your influence," she countered. "Because of your plan, your set up. You did this. You killed him."

"So innocent," he said, amused. "Did he really mean that much to you?"

"You're damned right he did."

"Why?"

"Because I trusted him."

"Like you trust me?"

"Fuck you!" she exclaimed in English, all of the anger and hatred she'd pushed to the very back of her soul welling up in a single instant. "I know you don't give a shit about him, but I want to know the details. I want to know what happened that night. I want to know about Baker, and how it all led to Nichols' death. And if you kill me when you're done, so be it. I don't care. Nichols and I could have been something. We could have made something. It would be easier that way."

"I'm not going to kill you, Evelyn."

She threw up her hands in disgust and took another drink. "Then why the fuck are you here?"

"Because I do owe you something."

"You're goddamned right you owe me something." She drained her scotch, got up, and refilled it, not even thinking about asking permission.

"Loss is a part of life."

"Is that your mantra? Is that what you tell all those widows whose husbands you killed? Is that what you tell their daughters?"

"I don't believe I've ever told them anything."

It did not surprise her. "Did you love her?" she asked, switching back to Arabic.

"Who?" he asked, confused.

"Astia Baykal."

She sensed, rather than saw, his grip tighten around the pistol.

"I think I did love her," he said. "Not that it matters."

"It does matter. That's what you don't see. That's what you can't see."

"Why?"

She thought back to Nichols' body lying by that briar patch. "Because you know loss. Regardless of what you believe, you lost Astia. You understand."

"You really believe that."

"Yes, I do."

"Then I should kill you now," he said, raising the pistol. "Because you won't stop hunting me."

"Please."

"Are you begging me?"

She snorted, amused. "No."

"Revenge is a dirty business. There's no profit in it."

"I'm not in this business to make money."

"Which is the pity of the world," he said, disappointed. "You would make a fantastic student."

"Morality must exist somewhere."

"Which is why you're not dead," he said simply.

It was an interesting statement, particularly from him, she thought.

"What happened all those years ago?" he asked.

She shifted in the chair, suddenly uncomfortable. "What do you mean?"

"Something happened, some time in your past. Something happened to change you, to set you on this course. It's why you don't date, why you're never with men. I think it's part of why Nichols was so important to you."

She stared at his formless shadow, wishing then, more than any other time of her life, that he would just kill her. It would be less painful. It would be an end. She would not have to relive either of those nights -- the one, fifteen years ago when she found herself broken and bloody, or that night, barely a week ago, her lover dead in her arms because she was not able to save him.

"I think it would be easier if you just shot me," she said.

"But that isn't part of the deal."

"It would be easier."

"Or simpler?"

"Simpler," she agreed. "But no, I'm not going to tell you."

He nodded so slightly she barely caught it. "Because you don't trust men?"

"I don't trust a lot of people," she said, her tone harsh. "Men and women."

"And yet you holstered your weapon here."

"I believe we have a certain understanding."

"After all these years?"

"Call it what you like, but there is a certain amount of trust. Otherwise you wouldn't be here." She cocked her head to one side. "And I'd likely be dead."

"True."

"What happened the other night?"

"With Baker?"

She nodded.

He put his glass down on the coffee table and sat back, the pistol always rock-steady in his hand. "That's actually part of what I wanted to talk to you about tonight. Or, rather, the events leading up to that night."

"Ok," she said, waiting.

"I did set everything up, but it wasn't to have you killed. I couldn't, or rather, I didn't, foresee Baker's actions. I thought I was simply hiring him to fulfill a duty. I just needed him to get me inside, to take care of the surveillance so I could liquidate that terrorist cell. I don't think I ever expected him to take it to such an extent. Obviously, he had his own motives."

"But he did take it that far. Regardless of who pulled that trigger, you put him in the position."

"Part of me regrets his actions."

"Part of you? He cost me three agents."

"Would you rather it have been you?"

She looked at him, pain in her eyes. "I've thought about little else for the last five days, and I still don't have an answer. Part of me, a big part of me, would much rather have taken those bullets. But I don't know if it's because I would rather see those men alive, or if it's because I would rather be dead."

He studied her for several minutes, the diffused light doing little to show her features in any kind of detail. But her emotion, the raw power pulsing from her, told him everything he needed to know. "I see that now," he said, still watching her. "As I said, part of me regrets Baker's actions, but they were out of my hands. I spared you a greater tragedy."

"What?"

"Death."

She closed her eyes. "I would welcome death."

"Don't be so dramatic. It makes you look weak."

"I'm being honest, not dramatic."

He paused, considering. It was obvious she was suffering from Nichols' murder, and he was not unsympathetic. His own mind tortured him regularly with Astia's loss. "What happened to Baker?" She could feel his eyes on her, studying her in the pale glow from the parking lot. "He's dead."

"How?"

"I killed him."

If it surprised him, he didn't show it. "It's for the best."

"I know," she said, almost insulted.

"I'm somewhat surprised he was able to piece together enough of the puzzle to profit from it. How long did Vogel put him in command?"

"Twenty-four hours or so."

"I wouldn't think a man of Baker's intelligence capable of something like that. All I wanted was you to be demoted. You were getting too close. For Baker to manipulate the situation to be placed in command... well, I wouldn't have thought him capable of it."

"Is that why you put the whole operation together?" she asked. "To have me removed?"

"Yes."

"Why not simply kill me?"

"As you said, we've known each other for many years."

"But you knew Astia. You loved her all those years ago, and she's still dead."

"Yes," he said, his voice turning to steel. "I did love her."

"For a long time."

"I wouldn't say that. I knew her for a short time."

"Intimately."

The gun twitched. "Yes."

"And yet you killed her right after you killed her parents. Single shot to the head, if I remember correctly. You'll forgive me, but it I'm going on supposition here. I always assumed you were the one that made those kills. Her father was the mark, right?"

"Yes."

"Did she walk in at the wrong time?"

"Yes."

"And she just wouldn't understand, would she?"

"Would you?"

"Did you even try to make her understand?" she asked. "Did you even give her a chance? She probably loved you. God knows what she might have done, what she might have been capable of."

"No," he replied, his voice softening.

"Love is a powerful thing," she pressed.

"Yes. It is."

"It almost makes you do things you didn't think you were capable of."

"Yes. It does."

They lapsed into silence, Morgan wondering if she would have the capacity to forgive something so heinous. "You mentioned wanting to tell me something earlier."

"I did," he said, collecting his thoughts. "I'm retiring."

She almost choked on her drink. "Retiring? You?"

"Yes."

"How? Is that even possible in this line of work?"

"We shall see."

"Why?"

"It's time."

Morgan considered. "Where will you go?"

"I don't know, to be honest. Somewhere I don't have to constantly worry and watch over my shoulder."

"Do you really believe we'll stop hunting you?"

"No."

"You'll find little sanctuary," she continued. "Not now, not after Bin Laden. There are few places we can't reach."

"I know."

"What will you do then?"

"It's no concern of yours." He stood up. "But consider this a courtesy call. There's no reason to continue your hunt. This is the end, Evelyn. If you pursue me, my retribution won't be so lenient."

"I understand."

He looked at her across the dark room. "Do you?"

"Yes."

Chapter 2

Omar Ben Iblis strode from Morgan's condo, closing the door behind him, her cell phone in his hand. As he crossed the parking lot, he took out the battery and threw it in the bushes. There was a white sedan waiting for him, and just before he stepped inside, he threw the phone's SIM card on the pavement, crushing it with the heel of his boot.

"You took care of the landline, right?" he asked, dropping into the passenger seat and shutting the door. He glanced over at one of the most stunningly beautiful women he had ever known, even more beautiful than Morgan.

"Of course," she said, putting the car in gear and pulling out of the parking lot.

Ben Iblis watched her thin, delicate fingers manipulate the wheel. Her dark Corsican skin was difficult to make out with the muted light from the streetlights, but he could imagine it clearly as she drove towards the interstate.

"And the contract? Did everything go as planned?" he asked.

"Yes," Penelope Morelli said, not taking her brown eyes from the road. "There weren't any problems."

"Good."

"I thought it would be harder."

"Harder?" he asked. "Why?"

"Because of our history."

"You didn't have any history until tonight."

"With her father," Morelli clarified.

"Ah. Yes."

Her brown hair rustled slightly against her jacket as she chanced a glance at him. "And there wasn't much time to prepare. Less than a week. It was a rush job."

"That's true," he reflected. "We were lucky she goes to school in town. I don't think we can expect too many more like this in the future. This contract was born of opportunity."

Morelli didn't respond.

"And it did make you half a million richer."

Still no response.

"Are you alright, Ms. Morelli?" he asked.

She nodded. "I'm usually like this after an operation."

He stared at the flashing streetlights as she accelerated onto the interstate. "Something I'll need to get used to, I suppose."

"I suppose." She paused. "How did things go in there?"

"As expected. Morgan was professional."

They drove through the deserted streets in silence for several minutes before Morelli turned on to the interstate and merged with what little traffic was on the road at that early hour.

"I would like to meet her," she said after settling the car at a comfortable speed.

"You are very much the same in many respects. Your attention to detail, your professionalism... your beauty." He was watching her again, and he caught the faint hint of a smile.

"Our beauty?"

"Yes. You are both attractive."

"It would seem you have good taste in women."

"I have good taste in a great many things." He smiled for the first time in as many days as he could remember. "It may have been foolish, but I wanted to say goodbye. I needed to say goodbye to her."

"Why?"

"I'm not sure."

"I find that surprising, coming from you."

"Why?"

"Because you always know. You always have a plan and a reason. So it's surprising you don't know in this case."

He did know, but he did not need to tell her. "There is a distinct lack of permanence in this business, at least with the living, since we deal so much in the realm of death. I wanted to tell her, in person, about everything that happened over the last week. I also wanted to tell her why."

"Admirable," she said, trying not to roll her eyes.

"You say that as though you either do not believe it, or you do not mean it."

"Perhaps a little of both."

"Evelyn Morgan is one of the few people on this planet who has ever come close to tracking me down. We have history."

"It's that history that makes you blind."

Did it? Ali Khalid, his assistant, thought that, too. "I don't agree. That history and experience has taught me something."

"What?"

"That killing is the easy part."

"I don't understand."

"I know," he said. "Perhaps one day you will."

It was not something he could teach her, even if she had the mindset to look at it openly. In fact, it took him nearly thirty years to reach that conclusion. There was more to the business, more to life, than just cutting it short. Letting Morgan live, continuing to let Morgan live, was something he needed to prove he could do.

"Morgan mentioned something interesting," he said, still staring into the city's glittering lights outside the passenger window. "Something that struck a chord."

"What?"

"Have you ever cared for someone? Loved someone?"

"That's a difficult question to answer."

"Is it?" he asked, turning back towards her. "Why?"

"For me, at least."

"I can think of two, both dead now, both by my hand."

"That you loved?" she asked.

"In one way or another."

A slight nod was her only response.

"As I told Morgan, it is time for me to retire and find something else to do."

"It'll be difficult to find a safe place to go."

"That's what Morgan said."

"Just one more reason to remove her. After all these years, you must know she won't stop hunting you."

"That may be true." He did not want to get into the details with her, though. "Tell me about the operation."

If she was bothered by the change of subject, she did not show it. "It was straightforward."

"No issues?"

"No. The girl was practically begging to be picked up. I was rather disappointed that I didn't need to try a little harder. We left the bar and went back to a little apartment her father keeps for her near the city."

"You should not be disappointed. To be honest, I might have been concerned if you were forced to try harder."

"She was an easy mark," Morelli said, thinking back to earlier that evening.

"They will not always be that simple."

"Still, it makes you wonder what a woman of her background was thinking." Morelli smiled, remembering the girl's soft, yielding flesh. "I would've thought she'd know better. Or, at the least, been taught better. It was entirely too easy."

Ben Iblis remembered his first target. That had not been simple at all, and he knew Morelli would have her fair share of challenges. Plus, he did not need it going to her head. Not yet. She was good, but she had a long way to go.

"Do not get carried away," he said, catching the flush of her cheeks.

"Sorry," she said, trying to focus, slightly embarrassed. "You're right. There's unfinished business that we need to take care of."

"Are we headed there now?"

"Yes, but finishing the job won't be pretty."

"It never is."

***

Colorado's bright sun filtered through the slats in the blinds and poured through his closed eyelids, causing him to grunt and nearly swear. He bit it down at the last second, though, remembering that his wife was lying next to him. Instead, he gently pulled the covers back, stood, and walked into the bathroom.

The mirror greeted him unkindly, enhancing his sagging face, his bald head with wispy white hair, and his pale, sallow skin. Exercise was a luxury he was not afforded this past week. Some sun, a walk, and fresh mountain air would go a long way to help his spirit. He sighed and picked up his toothbrush. He did not have time for a walk.

Running one of the largest defense contractors in the world did not allow him the indulgence of a flexible schedule. Board meetings, share holder meetings, client meetings, political meetings; they all just ran into one another. He needed a break. A vacation. Anything. Some time to get away, turn off his mobile phone, and see his wife without constant interruptions. It was the same with the rest of his family. He would love to have lunch with his daughter without worrying about making it in time for the next meeting.

Hell, he would settle for time with his mistress without constant interruptions, but it was not possible. There was always someone watching, always someone who needed something, always something he had to take care of, and it seemed like he was the only one who was ever capable of taking care of anything.

After showering, he dressed and closed the bedroom door behind him, leaving his wife's sleeping form tucked comfortably under the heavy quilt. Their bedroom was in one wing of his mansion in the Rocky Mountains behind Pike's Peak, and as he walked down a long hall, he afforded himself a long look at the mountain's majesty. The floor to ceiling windows lining the hall offered an unparalleled view, but words often failed him when the early light of dawn lit up the mountain in that purple hue. It was one of his few moments of peaceful solitude, and it passed too quickly every morning.

With a sigh and one last glance, he walked through the living room, the foyer, and into the kitchen. His assistant, Thomas Dean, stood in front of a large butcher block counter, chopping onions.

"Good morning, Mr. Wogan," Dean said, not looking up.

"Good morning."

"Coffee's ready."

"Thank you," Wogan said, walking over to pour himself a cup. "What are you making?"

"A frittata. Spinach, onions, cheese."

"Sounds delicious."

Dean nodded, but did not turn. "Will Mrs. Wogan be joining you?"

"I'm sure. But don't trouble yourself with the dining room table. We can eat in the sun room. It looks like such a pleasant morning."

"A little chilly, but it should be a nice day. Plenty of sunshine."

"Wonderful. Let me know when it's ready."

"Of course."

Wogan took his coffee and walked into his luxuriously appointed office. The furniture and woodworking were a dark cherry, including his massive desk. He powered on his laptop, checked the few voicemails his secretary had not pre-screened, then started to go through the mountain of email. There were several items his secretary marked to his particular attention, but he was happy to see she was able to deal with most of the rest. However, one caught his eye, and he picked up the phone's receiver.

"Senator Bradley's office," he heard after several seconds.

"Marjorie, it's Andy Wogan."

"Mr. Wogan, how are you?" Bradley's personal secretary inquired. "Things are well this morning, I hope?"

"Yes, thank you. And yourself? How's Washington today?"

"The same. Gray. The Senator's been expecting your call. Shall I put you through?"

"If you please."

There was a short pause and Bradley's rather high-pitched voice came on the line. "Andy! Good morning. Thanks for getting back with me so quickly."

"Of course, Senator. I hope something hasn't changed regarding the vote?"

"No, no, nothing like that. Everything is well in hand there. As I said last night, we should have the paperwork complete by the end of the week. The vote for the final endorsement is set for early next week. Once that's done, New York will be able to authorize the PO using the grant money."

"Good. That facial recognition contract is very important to the company. After reading your email, I was a little concerned. You mentioned a troubling development. If it's not the vote, then what's the issue?"

"Well, I'm actually a little hesitant to bring this to your attention."

"Please, Senator," Wogan said, sensing Bradley's embarrassment. "We're old friends. Let's not stand on ceremony. How may I help?"

"Well, it's regarding that personnel director you were so kind to introduce me to the other evening after dinner."

"Ms. Morelli?" Wogan asked, somewhat surprised. He provided the introduction to make it easier for Morelli to take Bradley to bed in the event a little persuasion might be required at some future date. "Has something happened?"

"Well." He cleared his throat. "This is where I am a little embarrassed. We both had a little too much to drink after you and the General left. And, well, one thing led to another, and she joined me in the suite I keep at the Hilton."

"I see," Wogan said with a smile. It was the perfect outcome. The concerns he harbored because he had not heard from Morelli vanished. "Well, these things happen, even to married men."

"Yes, yes," Bradley said, somewhat impatiently. "But the problem is, she's gone. She's not here."

"I'm not in the habit of getting involved in my employees' private lives," Wogan said with a sigh. "So perhaps you can tell me how I may be of service."

"Well, she's gone."

"Yes, you said that. Several times. What exactly is it that you mean? Most women tend to leave at one point or another, especially after situations such as these. I believe there can be feelings of guilt and regret, especially with married men."

"Yes, but I've been trying to contact her and I've not heard a word back. She did leave me her number before we parted ways last night."

"Last night? But we had dinner nearly a week ago." Wogan turned the situation over. Morelli was not supposed to leave. He had instructed her to remain with Bradley, to seduce him, of course, but to implant herself in his life in case they needed additional leverage. His mind raced through possibilities. "Well, Senator. I'm sure you can understand how these things are, especially from a woman's point of view. Perhaps she felt it had been a mistake, and simply came to her senses. I've known it to happen."

"And that would be understandable," Bradley said, "if it weren't for the fact that she left all of her things there."

"Her things?"

"Well, yes," Bradley replied, his embarrassment all too clear. "I've been seeing her all week. All of her clothes are still where she left them. Even her toothbrush. But that's not the strangest part. I remember the phone ringing last night. She left immediately after answering it."

A small knot formed in the pit of Wogan's stomach. "She was with you last night, then?"

"Yes. As I said, we've been spending most of the week together. You, uh, you check your people, right Andy?" His nervous tension was clear across the digital circuit.

"Of course," Wogan replied automatically, but the knot in his stomach did not go away. "Let me make some calls, Senator. I'll look into this."

"Thank you," Bradley said, the relief evident. "I'll wait to hear from you."

"Of course. Goodbye."

"Goodbye."

Wogan dropped the handset onto its base, tapped his fingers idly on his desk, then yelled, "Thomas!"

Dean came racing in, his apron clutched in his hand.

"Morelli's gone," Wogan said.

"Gone? What do you mean, gone?"

"That's what I asked. I just talked to Bradley. She left some time in the middle of the night." He studied Dean closely. "Have you spoken with her?"

"Not since yesterday morning."

Wogan drummed his fingers on his desk. "I haven't heard from her in several days. She was supposed to stay with Bradley. Why would she leave?"

"I don't know."

"We need to track this down immediately. Find out where she went, and find out now!"

Chapter 3

Lying where Morelli left her secured to the bed, hands and feet bound, Janice was still catatonic from the drug injected into her thigh. Together, Ben Iblis and Morelli moved her to the bathtub; not a strenuous effort since Janice was reasonably small and lithe. With a gentle touch, they freed her bindings, and arranged her limbs so she appeared comfortable. Then they doused her with four gallons of bleach.

Morelli's job was done, Ben Iblis thought, and she passed his test with flying colors. The woman was talented. There was no doubt in his mind. But his years of experience would not let him admit it. Not completely, at least. Their arrangement was in its absolute infancy, and there were still several things he needed laid to rest if he were to ever trust her. If, he admitted, that were even possible.

After the bleach was gone, Ben Iblis watched as Morelli put the stopper in the drain and filled the tub with lukewarm water. As the level rose to Janice's neck, she shut off the taps, pulled the plug, and let the water drain out. Once it was gone, she plugged the drain and repeated the process. On the third round, she left the plug in the drain and shut off the taps, leaving Janice mostly submerged, her eyes closed, a small, stupid smile on her face.

"To be honest," Ben Iblis said walking out of the bathroom, "I was not sure you were going to be able to go through with it."

"Why not?" Morelli asked, following him into the bedroom.

"Any number of reasons."

Morelli walked to the other side of the bed and folded her arms across her chest. "You mentioned history in the car earlier when we were leaving Morgan's place. I assume that's one of your reasons?"

"One of several."

"And the others?"

"Inexperience."

She gave him a hard stare. "That's not exactly true."

"In this line of work it is. How many was it before her?" Ben Iblis asked, motioning towards the bathroom. "Two? And she's not even dead yet."

"Don't bother me with trivialities. You know that after the first, it doesn't really matter what the body count is. It's that first one that's the hardest. If you can do that, you can do anything. She wasn't the first. If this arrangement proves fruitful, she won't be the last."

He could sense her determination through the dark room.

"What else?" she asked. "I want to get this over with now. This isn't going to work if you have to second guess every operation. There must be some level of trust. It is a requirement if we're to succeed."

"Trust is elusive in this line of work."

"If this is going to work, there must be a level of trust," she repeated. "What else?"

"Your past."

She took a deep breath and her voice was cold. "What do you know of my past?"

"A good deal."

"Educate me."

"Why?" he said, still looking at her silhouette over the bed. "In the end, it will not change things. Your past built you."

"Poetic."

He shrugged. "If you think so. It's true, and as you mentioned, it really comes down to trust. That is a very rare commodity in this business. Did Wogan trust you?"

"Of course."

"Then you can see my issue. You walked out on him in a heartbeat. The offer of better employ, the idea of moving up, of making something of yourself, something other than a whore, and you fly out of his bed."

His words were having their desired effect. Despite the darkness, broken only by the moon's dim light, he could tell she was growing angry. A simmering energy blossomed from the other side of the room.

"You will need to get that under control," he continued, almost deadpan. "Anger is the last thing you can afford. To survive in this business, you must put it aside. You must put it all aside. It will only cloud your judgment and force you to make stupid decisions. Emotion is your greatest enemy, Ms. Morelli. Do not ever forget that."

He sensed her anger subside as he gathered one of the corners of the bed's sheets in his gloved hands.

"I've never forgotten that," she said, stepping up to the edge of the bed and undoing the opposite corner.

"Not after that first time, you mean."

If she was shocked he knew about the first man she killed, she did not show it. "Andy always said you were one of the most dangerous men alive. Information must make you that way."

"It is as important as keeping your emotions in check."

They rolled the sheets and comforter up towards the head of the bed, taking care to wrap it tightly, keeping the edges up. When they reached the top, they undid those corners and rolled it closed. Morelli carefully dropped the roll into a large garbage bag.

"I was only fifteen when I killed my father," she said, almost conversationally as she sealed the bag with a zip tie. "Though after everything he did, I wish I did it years earlier."

"Did you find it difficult?"

She considered for a moment. "No, not really. One night, after he was done with me, he fell asleep in my bed. I waited until he started snoring, until I knew he was good and out. Then I got up, grabbed my softball bat out of the closet, and beat his face in until it was unrecognizable."

"And then you left."

"Couldn't very well stay," she said, carrying the garbage bag out of the bedroom to the front door. When she returned, she continued, "It didn't make a whole lot of sense to me to hang around. I think, despite everything he'd done to me, I would have at least done a little time in either some kind of mental hospital or juvenile detention. Besides, I'd had it. I wasn't going to let somebody else rule my life. Not anymore."

"Fifteen is young to be setting out on your own."

"You did it at a younger age."

He nodded. "That's true. But Afghanistan is not America."

"And America is not the land of milk and honey everybody thinks it is."

"You would be witness to that."

"I would," she agreed.

Ben Iblis glanced back into the bedroom, looking down at Janice with apparent disinterest. "It wasn't hard?"

"Which?" she asked. "My father, or her?"

"Her."

"No. As I said in the car, I rather enjoyed myself." A small tickle ran up her spine when she remembered her time with Janice, and she shuddered involuntarily.

Ben Iblis watched her carefully, but remained silent.

Morelli glanced down as something brushed across her leg. It was a black and white cat, well-fed, well taken care of. She reached down and picked him up, a small smile creeping across her face as he started to purr in her arms. Gently stroking his head and ears, she asked, "What other doubts do you have about me?"

"Several."

"Why?"

"Because you are inexperienced."

"You mentioned that. How many women do you know have killed their fathers? Of those, how many have gotten away with it? I don't think experience is so much of an issue, at least not when it comes to doing the deed. The logistics of it all, I admit, are new. I never had to worry about that end, but I find it hard to believe the subject is any more difficult to master than taking a life."

"You may be surprised."

She shrugged, unconcerned.

"How many women find it so easy to walk from a lover's bed into another --"

"Arrangement?" Morelli interrupted.

"Yes," he said, matching her stare.

"Your deal was a good one." Her tone turned brittle. "If there's one thing you need to learn, and learn quickly, is my body is my own. I will do whatever I need to do to advance and protect it."

"Even if that means sacrificing it?"

A smirk creased her mouth. "If that's how you see it."

"It is difficult to see it any other way."

"From a man's position, perhaps." She dropped the cat after stroking its head and ears one last time. "It will take time. All these things take time."

He looked at her quizzically.

"Relationships," she clarified.

"I'm surprised you think you know so much about them."

The smile disappeared from her face, and her eyes went cold. "How long has it been since you've been forced to work with someone new?"

"Several years."

"I think it's been longer than that. What happened to your assistant?"

"Why does it matter?"

"Why do you think? You two were in that hotel lobby earlier this week. I saw you as I walked through with Bradley. You were together, drinking coffee." She paused and her eyes narrowed. "Where is he? What happened to him?"

"He is dead."

"How?"

"I killed him."

It was so simple and straightforward it almost caught her off guard, but she had been doing this for a number of years, and she accepted his answer with only a brief nod, her eyes never leaving his. "Why?"

"He outlived his usefulness. He asked too many questions, was unsure of too many of my decisions, and knew too much information."

She cocked her head to one side. "That sounds like the arrangement we've put together, minus the part where I outlive my usefulness."

"It is different."

"If you say so," she said, unconvinced. "Earlier, when we were driving over here, you mentioned that there were two people you cared for in your life, but that they were both gone."

"Yes."

"Your assistant, Khalid," she continued, staring at him, careful to watch his eyes. "He was one of them?"

"Yes."

It made her pause. "It will be the same with me. I intend to ask questions and challenge some decisions. I will know everything about your organization. That's how you presented it when we discussed this arrangement. It's the only way it will work." She continued to watch him carefully. "Is that going to be a problem?"

"No, but there is one key difference. I did not approach you with the idea that you would be subordinate. You're an equal, or soon will be, with a few more operations. Khalid was an assistant. That was always his position. Yes, he was someone that I trusted, for a time, someone I cared for, but also someone expendable. When he outlived his usefulness, when he asked too many questions, and when he doubted my operations...." his voice trailed off.

Morelli watched him, careful to study his eyes as they lost focus and travelled to some distant memory. She noted his mannerisms, wishing she could bore herself into his soul, but it was not any use. His eyes were as cold as hers, used to shutting out anyone with a desire to get close.

After a brief silence, that predatory gleam returned, and he continued. "It was time to move on. But our relationship is different. I did not approach you with the idea of hiring another assistant. I want someone to take over this operation. I am ready to move on to other things."

"So you said."

"And you have done well with your first assignment. You need not worry, Miss Morelli. You will not end up like my late assistant. At least not by my hand."

She pursed her lips and accepted him for his word. "Trust is a funny thing. Especially in relationships. You keep your counsel, Mr. Ben Iblis, and I'll keep mine."

"As you say."

"Is there anything else we need to clean up in here?" she asked, glancing around.

"We have the sheets. They will have the majority of the DNA. I still do not entirely approve of your plan on this. It was reckless. I did not see the point in rolling around in bed with her. It was an unnecessary risk."

Morelli remained silent, but she looked unconvinced.

"It is also dangerous that we returned here. Cleaning up something that should have been taken care of in the first place makes us vulnerable. It is something we will need to address going forward."

"Of course," she said, biting her lip.

If he caught her disapproval, he did not acknowledge it. Instead, he left the bedroom and walked into the apartment's galley kitchen. There was a bottle of olive oil sitting in the cupboard, and he pulled it down with his gloved hand, unscrewing its cap before placing it on the counter.

Morelli came up behind him and stopped just inside the partition between the living room and the kitchen. The cat she picked up earlier jumped up on the partition and started to purr, moving in front of her with longing eyes. She ignored him and concentrated on Ben Iblis.

Moving swiftly, he filled a pot with water and placed it on the gas stove, lighting the burner and setting the stove's dial to high. It wasn't long before small bubbles began to form in the water.

She absently petted the cat while they waited for the stove. After a few more minutes, Ben Iblis casually knocked the open olive oil bottle over and stepped back as its contents splashed into the open flame of the burner and erupted in a small fire. The cat shrieked and ran into the bedroom. Ben Iblis and Morelli walked to the apartment's front door, picking up the garbage bag as they passed.

Just as Morelli shut the door behind her, she heard the cat's cry and turned. He was standing just inside, looking up at her through the small crack between the door and the jamb. She smiled at him, then closed the door quietly, the smoke and flickering flames already licking the drywall behind the cat's black and white tail.

Chapter 4

Morgan thought about calling it in. The man she hunted for her entire career was only miles from her townhouse, but she did not run next door to borrow the neighbor's phone. This was her fight. She wanted Ben Iblis on her own merits. She wanted to find him herself, using her investigative skill, her resources, and her talent. She did not want a gimme. She did not need a gimme, and she suspected that was exactly what he was counting on. He knew she would not do that. She came too far, sacrificed too much to give it all up after a midnight warning.

No, she thought, pushing the bottle of scotch away before collapsing in the same spot on the couch. He could not reasonably expect her to give up the hunt, not after everything he did in the past week. This was not something she could ever let go. Not now.

The liquor burned the back of her throat as she tossed the glass back and closed her eyes. Billings. Sarino. Nichols. Their faces flashed through her mind.

Until she got to Nichols.

His boyish smile, tossled hair, and hazel eyes ravaged her mind, and there was nothing she could do to wash them away. The tears started to form at the corners of her eyes again, but she kept them closed and took a deep breath. She was done crying. Instead, she focused on his smile and the way it warmed every inch of her heart. Her mind cried for more scotch, but she closed her eyes and remembered the softness of his touch on her naked flesh. He made her feel safe in a way only one other man had ever been able to do. But Nichols had not betrayed her. In that, he was alone.

She wanted to mask her pain. It was not the first time such a gash tore open her heart, and reluctantly she admitted it would not be the last. She still wanted to hide it, though. She wanted to make it disappear. He had gotten to her in a way few people had. And while she knew it was Baker who ultimately put the bullets in Nichols' back, Ben Iblis set the entire operation up. The details did not matter. Ben Iblis put Baker forward. Ben Iblis gave Baker the resources.

That made his crime that much more heinous.

It was personal.

She rubbed her weary eyes. It had been a long time since she saw more than four hours of sleep in a single night. The disappearance of the terrorist cell, her demotion, the numerous attempts on her life over the past week all combined to completely drain whatever reserve she possessed.

Nichols' hazel eyes flashed before her again as she tried to force herself up from the couch. She wanted another drink, if only to block the nightmare she knew was coming, but it would not do. Not only was there work, but the alcohol would make those eyes flash more frequently, and that was the last thing she needed. She pressed the backs of her hands harder into her eyelids. The stars that danced in the blackness partially hid the image, but they did not make it disappear.

"Christ," she swore, picking herself up from the couch and pouring another scotch.

She sat back down and sipped the drink slowly in the darkness. It was here, barely a week ago, where she and Nichols spent the night together, and where she divulged one of her deepest secrets. She thought back to that night as they lay in her bed, the rain spitting softly against the windows as she told him how she was raped in college, desperate for him to hold her, but happy when he did not reach out, content when he did not say, "I'm sorry." Because that was not what she wanted. At least not from someone as special as Nichols.

He was different, and she worried what he would do when she told him. But she did not need to worry. He did not hold her. He did not placate her, or her emotions. He cared for her. Loved her, she hoped, and that was what was important. He was the first man she could trust in as long as she could remember. Years.

And now he was dead.

Because of Ben Iblis, and Baker.

Ben Iblis. The man she hunted her entire professional career sitting in her living room. Why hadn't she done something?

It was a foolish notion. What would she have done? What could she have done with that gun pointed at her chest. The alcohol made the memory foggy, despite the fact it was only a short time ago. The counter. She was able to hide behind the counter when he announced himself. Would it have given her enough cover?

No, she thought. He would have killed you, she told herself. She would have been dead before she was able to bring her pistol to bear. That was a certainty. But why not call it in?

Because then someone else would make the kill. Someone else would bring closure.

And that was not what she wanted, not what she needed.

Ben Iblis would be hers. Just like Baker. On her own merits, on her own hunt, she would run him down. She owed that to Nichols. She owed that to herself.

***

They drove north from Baltimore, Morelli at the wheel, passing through Philadelphia before dawn, leaving the small apartment ablaze far behind them. New York was chancy, despite the care they took. American surveillance was excellent, especially there, and they determined it was not worth the risk. The operation just completed would certainly focus more attention than Ben Iblis normally drew, even with his extensive experience. This was something entirely new, a different realm of pursuit, and there was little doubt in his mind that everything the Americans could bring to bear would be focused on the hunt.

He sat back in the passenger seat and closed his eyes as the miles flashed by, trying to determine the best place to get out of the country. Not Boston. Too busy. Something further north. Something smaller where security was not quite so stringent. With the whirlwind they created, they needed to be out of the country within twenty-four hours.

"Is there a smaller airport north of Boston?" he asked.

"Several," Morelli said.

"Know if any handle private charters?"

She thought for several minutes. "For origination? Manchester's probably our best bet. There are several companies that maintain a presence there. I've used them before while travelling for Wogan."

"Head there, then."

"Alright."

"We still need to make arrangements ahead of time. Once we get closer, we will need to find a library or cafe so I can take care of our travel."

"Ok."

"Is there a good deal of foreign travel in and out of Manchester?"

"A fair amount," she said, glancing at him. "I assume you're worried about standing out?"

"It is not as big a deal when you travel on a private charter, but yes. Everybody notices these days. Especially the Americans."

"Manchester's big enough, I don't think it'll be a problem."

"Good."

Ben Iblis dozed off as she drove north and west around Philadelphia and New York. Images of several women drifted in and out of his mind. Some he killed, some he took to bed, some to whom he did both, but the one that came back repeatedly, much more often than the others, was the one he missed the most.

Astia. She was Turkish. Young, with creamy, silky smooth skin not unlike buttermilk. Her lips were a soft red, and he could still vividly remember that day he blundered into her in the market on Cypress. If he concentrated, he could almost taste the sweetness of her lips, even after all these years. Falling in love with her was the single most dangerous and stupid thing he had ever done, but that realization never entered the realm of regret.

He wondered what might have been if he did things differently. Morgan touched a nerve with her questions. Morgan always touched a nerve. Would things have ended differently with Astia? Could they possibly have ended differently? Would she have understood? Or, lacking understanding, was it possible she could have forgiven him?

It was difficult to imagine Astia doing anything other than screaming at the sight of her parents, dead by his hand. Love was an incredible thing, but it was foolish to think she could forgive him after such a heinous act.

Since the beginning of this operation against Morgan, Astia's eyes haunted his dreams. There was no time to try and dissect the reasons why now, of all times, his subconscious wanted to make a point of his profession. And, frankly, his waking mind did not feel it warranted much thought. He loved her, but it did not matter now. The past was then, and he was not a man for self-recrimination or doubt. Hundreds were dead at his hands, and while he was looking forward to retirement, he realized he was not finished yet.

Especially if Morgan did not walk away and let her demons lie.

There was little he could do about that now, though, and little he could do about Astia. His eyes fluttered open, and he yawned. She was long dead. With a silent stretch, he forced her eyes from his conscious mind and looked out the window. It was past dawn, the day's early sun pushing away the last sleepy gray light.

"We should find a library or a café," he said.

"Alright," Morelli agreed.

It took two more exits before they were able to find an area with a public library. As Morelli pulled into the parking lot, Ben Iblis said, "We need to find out about charters from Manchester. I need to get in contact with my people and make the arrangements."

"Do you have some place in mind?"

"International."

"Something more specific?" she asked, putting the car in park and turning off the ignition.

"I've been thinking about Ireland."

"Why?" she asked, somewhat surprised. "Any particular reason?"

"I have a safe house there. It is perfect for your introductions to the organization, and we will need somewhere to lie low for a while. I expect we will see increased efforts to track us down after this past week's activities."

"Especially with you baiting Morgan."

"I warned her," he said. "I didn't bait her."

"You baited her. She doesn't sound like the type of woman to pay much attention to warnings."

"Perhaps."

She nodded and stared out the windshield at the brick facade of the library. "It sounds like Khalid was right. Morgan is a liability."

"And you sound like him," he said, meeting her eyes with a cold stare. "Let Morgan lie. If she comes for me, I will deal with her."

"I'm not sure you're capable."

A malicious smile turned his face. "Then you've grossly underestimated me."

They sat in silence, the car's engine ticking softly as it cooled in the spring air. Did Morgan blind him? He killed Khalid for his continued dissension on how the entire situation was handled. Now

Morelli was expressing the same opinion. Morgan was dangerous. He knew that. But in that same thought, he knew he could not kill her, not while other alternatives existed, and not if she dropped her pursuit. It just was not possible.

"I have made my decision on Morgan," he said. "Is that understood?"

"I understand you've made a decision, but I don't understand the mechanics behind it. She's a threat. It would be easier if she were eliminated."

"If you believe she is an immediate threat, you're welcome to leave and pursue your own agenda."

She studied him. "Fair enough."

"What about Wogan?" he asked, that morning's operation still on his mind.

"Wogan? What do you mean?"

"Do you think he will let this lie?"

"I suppose it depends on whether or not he comes to suspect the poor girl's accident wasn't really an accident at all."

"And will he?"

"Yes," she nodded. "He's a very shrewd, wealthy, and powerful man. Like other such men, he's made a good deal of enemies. I think he'll immediately suspect that it wasn't an accident. He'll demand an investigation."

"He won't buy it as an accident?"

"Would you?"

"No," Ben Iblis said, shaking his head. "He's a dangerous man."

"Yes."

"I do not know if he told you or not, but we met several times. I never considered him much of a threat, at least not directly. I know, though, he is a very dangerous man. That is abundantly clear."

"Yes," she agreed. "He is very capable, and he has a long reach."

He contemplated for a few more minutes. "We will regroup in Shannon."

"Ireland?"

"Yes. Once we're there we can decide on our next steps. As I said, I think you should be introduced to several of my contacts. That way, we can get you involved immediately."

"What about Wogan?" she asked.

"What about him?"

"You just said he was a dangerous man. He may be a threat. Shouldn't he be removed?"

He studied her before responding. "Would you be able to do that?"

"I'm offended you even feel the need to ask," she said, returning his stare with her cold brown eyes.

"Killing strangers is one thing. Killing a former employer is something else, despite your history with your father."

She didn't reply.

"Killing a lover is a whole separate level." Again, he was impressed with her composure. She simply continued to stare at him with those chocolate eyes.

"You're remarkably well informed, Mr. Ben Iblis. That's twice now you've surprised me." She turned and looked out the windshield. "My relationship with Andy Wogan was strictly professional."

"That is an interesting way to put it."

"We covered this earlier in the apartment. What I do with my body, how I use it, is my business. If your notion of how or what a woman should do doesn't include making full use of her gifts and talents, then that's your goddamned problem. I'm comfortable with where I am and how I got here. You can either believe me that my relationship with Wogan was purely professional, or we can go our separate ways right now." She looked back at him and held his stare. "Which will it be?"

"I'm not used to answering ultimatums."

"You're also not used to working with women, training your replacement, or taking the back seat in an operation."

A small smile turned one side of his mouth. "If there is one thing I enjoy about you, Ms. Morelli, it is your spirit."

"Don't patronize me."

"I would not dream of it."

"Do we have an agreement?" she asked.

"For the moment."

She accepted it. "Your contacts. Are you going to introduce me now, or will you make the arrangements for travel to Ireland?"

"I will do it. It will be easier. We will work on integrating you over the next several days. I want you operational as soon as possible, and that includes all of the operational details."

"That's a change from what we discussed earlier this week."

"I know."

She thought about asking him why, but decided now was not the best time. "Alright," she said.

They got out of the car and walked into the library. It was true he admired her spirit. He was also surprised by his lack of real anger. Few dared make demands or present ultimatums, and Morelli's lack of fear spoke well of her ability to handle this job long term, which was exactly what he needed. He was tired, and it was time to hand things over to someone younger. His conversation with Morgan earlier that morning triggered a number of different, mostly uncomfortable feelings. There were other things he needed to do before he got too old to do them.

Chapter 5

Morgan woke early, bolting upright in bed, her sheets drenched in sweat. The last thing she remembered was screaming as the nightmare came to its usual conclusion. She glanced at the bedside table, but her alarm clock did not survive the thrashing it received after its shrill alarm forced her and Nichols from sleep the one night he had spent there. It seemed like an eternity ago.

Without a clock for a frame of reference, she could not tell how long she slept, but judging by how her body felt, it was not nearly enough. She threw her comforter to one side and wearily swung her legs onto the wood floor. Serious doubt invaded her mind, and she wondered how much longer she could keep going like this. Day after day, little to no sleep, the same nightmare, with little to no hope of ever catching Ben Iblis. The chance they had, the chance they built with months of pain-staking investigation was gone, not likely to ever return.

He was out of the country. As she stood and walked into the bathroom, she idly wondered if that was the best decision. What was her fascination with the man? Why did she feel the need to be the one to catch him? Why couldn't she leave it to someone else?

Nichols. She smiled as she turned on the shower and remembered the time they spent under its spray. She scrubbed her skin, pausing briefly at several bruises on her forearms. Those would be from her attack on Baker. They were a dark purple, starting to turn a slight green. The night Nichols died, she used all the force in her lithe frame to block Baker's gun arm from swinging around to bear when she charged. The bruises would heal, though. The physical wounds always knit.

Shutting off the water, she grabbed the only towel and rubbed herself dry. Then she stepped in front of the mirror. A haunted ghost of herself stared back; pale, sallow skin, dark, baggy, nearly sightless green eyes, and colorless lips set in an oval face with high cheekbones and a small chin. She involuntarily shuddered and brushed her dark brown hair.

After replacing the brush in the medicine cabinet, she reached for a small silver chain necklace and held it in her calloused palm. She ran her long, slim fingers over the tarnished silver cross hanging from the chain and smiled slightly. At least that was one memory that was pleasant, she thought, slipping the delicate necklace over her head.

Walking out of the bathroom, she dressed in a nondescript charcoal gray suit and slipped her .40 Sig Sauer P228 in its holster at her side. She picked up her coat, threw it over her shoulders, and walked out of the townhouse. She stopped at her regular coffee shop, ordering a large latte before heading the rest of the way downtown to the Hoover building. It was an uneventful trip, the traffic light that early in the morning. The elevator ride to her boss's office was quick, and she stepped across the threshold a little before 0630.

"Good morning," she said, not surprised at all to see him there that early. He was dressed smartly in a tweed sport coat and dark brown slacks, standing with his back to the door, gazing out his tiny window at the twinkling lights of a waking capital.

"Good morning," he replied, not turning around.

"You didn't sleep much last night."

She saw his eyebrow arch in the window reflection. "I would say you probably got even less."

"That's probably true," she admitted.

Adam Vogel turned and stepped towards the large oak desk which dominated his small office. He was a small man, not at all what she expected when first meeting him after their initial phone interview. His gold-rimmed spectacles perpetually sat halfway down his hawk-like nose, and one often got the impression of being looked down upon when he stared over their tops.

"You look like hell. You didn't head home after you left here?" He motioned for her to take one of the two chairs sitting opposite his desk.

"I did, actually." She sat down. "Ben Iblis paid me a visit."

Her demeanor and voice was so deadpan it temporarily caught him off-guard, a rare feat with Vogel, and she watched, half satisfied, as he paused in the process of settling into his leather executive's chair. "I didn't see an alert."

"I didn't call it in."

"Obviously. Why not?"

"It's complicated."

"You're so full of shit, Eve," he said, running his hand over his face. "I'd really hoped we'd gotten past all this when you finally came clean about having not only his fingerprints, but his picture."

"To be fair, I did come clean."

He stared at her. "After many years."

"But I did come clean. You have the picture and the prints."

"Christ," he said, exasperated. "Tell me what happened last night."

"It's a long story."

"Try me."

"Well, after I left here, I headed home."

"Straight home?"

"No. I stopped and picked up a bottle of scotch."

"Ok. So then you went home?"

"Yes. Ben Iblis was already inside, just sitting in my living room. No idea how long he'd been there. So I poured him a drink, and we chatted."

"You had drinks with him?" Vogel asked, looking at her in disbelief.

"I did."

"With Omar Ben Iblis?"

"Yes."

He shook his head. "What did you discuss?"

"The operation. Baker. Nichols," her voice trailed off before she recovered and was able to meet his eyes again. "His retirement."

"Ben Iblis's retirement? He told you he's going to retire?"

"Supposedly."

Vogel digested that for several minutes. "Do you believe him?"

"I do," she said after some thought. "I don't have anything concrete as to why, but I do believe him. After all these years of studying and hunting him, I think we've both come to an understanding of one another. When he spoke this morning, he didn't sound like a man talking to a complete stranger. There was a familiarity there I doubt he shows too many people. I know I don't."

"And you really believe he was sincere because of this familiarity? Because you two are somehow connected?"

"We are connected," she argued.

Vogel remained dubious. "Is that why you didn't call it in? Or try to arrest him? Because of this connection?"

"I didn't try to arrest him because I'd of been dead before I got off the couch, and I didn't call it in for a number of reasons, one of which was his warning."

"What did he warn you about?"

"Continuing the hunt."

"What did he say?"

"Essentially, that I'd be a dead woman."

"Was it an actual threat?"

"Does it matter?" she asked. "But no, he doesn't operate like that. It was a warning."

"A veiled threat as a warning, maybe. But not just a warning."

She shifted in her seat. "Semantics. I see it as a warning, and that there will be consequences for disregarding it. Consequences which wouldn't be limited to just myself. If I had a family, I can only guess what his retribution would be."

"Hmph," he snorted.

"What I'm trying to say is that you're probably included in whatever list he has in his mind."

"That doesn't worry me."

"It should at least make you pause," she said, watching him. "You know what he's capable of."

"We're not in the business of listening to threats."

"I know that, but you should be aware. Your detail should be aware."

He offered her a rare smile. "Concerned for my welfare, Eve?"

"Who else would put up with me around here?"

"I can't think of a single person in leadership," he said, turning serious, and fixing her with a penetrating stare. "And I mean that. I'm the only lifeline you have."

"Point taken."

"I hope so. Anything else from last night?"

"Not from Ben Iblis, no."

"Ok."

She took a deep breath. "Do you know who's going to be handling Nichols' arrangements? I haven't seen anything official, and it's been several days."

"I haven't heard anything. I assumed it would be his family. I know his parents are both dead, but there's several aunts and uncles."

"He wasn't close to any of them. I doubt he'd appreciate them handling the arrangements."

"I wasn't aware."

"Now you are."

Anger flashed behind his eyes, but he bit it back and tried to look at her kindly. "The Bureau will make the arrangements then, if we're unable to find any immediate family."

"I'd like to be there."

"Of course."

She stood and walked to the door, but before she opened it he said, "One more thing before you go."

"Yes?"

"Two of your agents just hit me for leaves of absence."

"Who?"

"Agents Parker and Borgerten," he said. "I'm going to approve the requests as medical leave."

"Ok," Morgan said, nodding. "They've both been having a hard time with Nichols' death and Baker's betrayal."

"And you?" he asked, studying her.

She offered him a wan smile. "I meant what I said the other night."

"When?"

"After Nichols was killed. About Ben Iblis."

He waited, still watching her. Her bloodshot eyes contrasted starkly with her pale, almost sickly skin. It was obvious she made an effort to put herself together that morning, but he knew there was little to be done. Sleep and rest were the only things that would cure her physically. And mentally... he hoped she would be able to recover emotionally, but he also knew the only possible solution was time.

"I'll kill him," she said. "God damn his warning."

"Look," he said, "I'd love to tell you to go home and get some rest, but we need to run down that dead terrorist cell you discovered. It's the only tie we have to Ben Iblis."

"I know."

"How much sleep did you actually get last night?"

"Two hours."

"Are you even functional?"

She bristled. Choking down her initial reply, she said, "Yes."

"I can have Gebog take over for a few days," he said, referring to one of Morgan's agents. "You've been hitting it really hard. You could use a break."

"She can't handle this, and you know it. She's good, but she doesn't have experience leading a team."

"You need a break."

Closing her eyes, she took a deep breath. When she opened them, she said, "That's probably true. Physically, yes. But what I really need to do now is run down Ben Iblis. This isn't something I can trust to anyone else. I have to see it done."

"For Nichols?"

"For me."

"So where do things stand?"

She thought about it. "Same place as where we left off last night before I went home. The financials are the most promising lead. We'll run those down. We also know now that Ben Iblis was involved, and he's probably not going to stick around the country for long. DHS should hopefully have some information."

"Even if he went with a private charter?"

She shrugged. "We have to try. It's the only way we're going to track him down."

"We're also going through Baker's financials, correct?"

"Yes."

Vogel sighed and looked pensive. "What about Ben Iblis's picture and fingerprints?"

"They're in IAFIS. Charlie put them in last week. I also sent an alert to DHS after Nichols was killed, so they should be keeping an eye out for him."

"Lot of faces to scan."

"He won't take a commercial flight, so it should come down to the charters. Plus, Maryland's now tied into the next generation biometrics database. It may make sense to have any security camera footage run through the system. The program's in its infancy, and it'll tie up resources, but maybe we'll get lucky."

"Do it," he ordered.

"Ok."

"Do you think he'll take a charter from Maryland?"

"No," Morgan said. "He'll find something smaller. One of the regional airports, maybe, and take a charter from there. There's too much security around D.C. to risk it. We could issue an alert to start screening all private charters, but I'm not sure we have the resources, and the backlash would probably be pretty severe."

"Especially since we don't have a specific location to target."

"Exactly," she agreed. "He could have driven anywhere on the eastern seaboard by now. It's not a reasonable demand."

"Alright. Ping DHS again and make sure they're set to do at least extra patrols of the executive terminals. Have their guys keep a sharp lookout for the next twenty-four hours. Somebody might see something, now that we have his picture."

"I'll coordinate with DHS and get some interviews done with the larger charter agencies, too."

"Good idea."

"Thanks," she said. "I'm also going to stop by IT and get a new mobile phone."

"What happened to your old one?"

"Ben Iblis took it last night. I found some of the pieces in the parking lot this morning."

"Ok." He picked up a folder from his desk and scanned the heading. "Did you get some coffee yet this morning?"

"Two cups on the way in. It's the only reason I'm still awake."

Another look of concern clouded his face. "How long are you going to be able to keep this up?"

"Long enough. I hope."

"Me, too. You're one of my only agents with the skills to catch him."

Chapter 6

Wogan tapped his fingers idly on the desk, his eyes closed against the sun streaming in through the large windows. He wanted to close the blinds, but the growing pain behind his left eye made the thought of the effort almost unbearable. In fact, the idea of doing just about anything only increased the sharp pounding in his head. With his eyes still closed, he reached into his desk and took out a pill bottle. Popping one into his mouth, he flushed it back with the remainder of his cold coffee.

Burying his head in his hands, he massaged his temples and thought about that morning. Several hours were gone since Senator Bradley's disturbing call, and they were unable to contact or locate Morelli. It was pretty clear to him she left, despite his desperate hope to the contrary, and God only knew what she might do with the information she took with her.

The fact she left did not hurt him on a personal level, or so he kept telling himself. Few things did. This was business. But business was supposed to be handled professionally, and there was nothing professional about her sudden departure. He expected more from his employees, especially one he handpicked, who was being considered for an executive leadership position. He even gave her a promotion! What the hell was she thinking?

"Another migraine?" Dean asked, walking into the room.

"Yes."

"Do you need something for it?"

"No. I just took a pill," Wogan said, still not looking up. "Any news?"

"Several regular pieces of business for the company."

"What about Morelli?"

"No. Nothing."

They had to find her. "What about Ben Iblis?"

"What do you mean?" Dean asked, confused.

"Anything from him?" Wogan asked. He hired Ben Iblis to deal with a situation at the Capitol over a week ago. "I still haven't heard anything on that contract. I expect it to be fulfilled."

"It's been a very long time," Dean hedged. "You still expect him to act on that?"

"Of course I do!" Wogan thundered. "I paid him handsomely! He has yet to remove any of those Senators, and I'm not in the habit of giving donations to assassins! Send him another message. Find out the status. Find out where he is. This is taking entirely too long."

"A request like that might not be the most prudent move at this point. Let's give him a little more time. It's possible that the operation has already happened."

"There's been nothing on the news. That would be a national event."

"A little more time, Mr. Wogan."

Wogan considered and finally relented. In a softer tone he said, "I appreciate your advice, Thomas."

"Of course."

"It's this damn migraine," he said, trying to relax as he felt the drug go to work on the pain. "Makes it impossible to concentrate effectively."

"Perhaps a vacation would be a good idea? I can start making the arrangements."

Wogan held up his hand. "No, not yet. We must find Morelli. We must know what happened to her, where she went."

"Because of your relationship, or because of what she knows?"

"What was it you said the other day? That young flesh can always be replaced?"

Dean nodded.

"And it's true. From that standpoint, she can always be replaced. There's always young flesh to be had. I'm more concerned about the money the company sank into her and the knowledge she takes away. She was privy to operational details that few others are aware of. There was also the nature of her work. It could generate some very bad press, cause embarrassing questions to be asked."

"Do you think she would do that? To you, I mean?"

Wogan thought about it. "Before this morning, I thought her incapable of betrayal. I suppose I let our relationship blind me to the realities. After all, she doesn't have the most stellar background."

"To be fair, when you hired her, I thought she was ready to put all of that behind her."

"Whatever her motivations, she must be found."

"I don't think she'll last too long on her own. All of her company accounts have been restricted, and I don't know of any personal means for her to support herself for long."

"Have you contacted anyone at ICE?"

"Yes," Dean said. "I've also reached out to our contacts in the Department of Homeland Security. Any hit on one of her passports, and we'll know."

"I hope so."

Dean looked as though he might say something more, but thought better of it.

"What were you going to say?" Wogan asked, catching his expression.

"Nothing, it's not important. One way or another, she'll turn up."

"As much as I hate to say it, I hope she's dead. For her sake."

"I think we shouldn't rush to judgment until we know for certain what's happened to her."

Wogan nodded and turned to a stack of manila folders on his desk, taking little notice as Dean walked out of the room. As his migraine faded and he returned to business, the phone on his desk started to chatter. "Wogan," he answered after two rings.

"Mr. Wogan," his secretary said, "I have Chief Doonigan on the line."

He was surprised. Doonigan ran the police department where his daughter, Janice, kept her apartment. Wogan made a point of introducing himself to the man after Janice left for college and moved to Annapolis. "Put him through, Mary," Wogan told his secretary.

"Yes, sir."

There was a slight pause, then Doonigan's nasally voice rang through the circuit. "Mr. Wogan," he said.

"Chief Doonigan," Wogan replied, "I must be honest in that I'm somewhat surprised to hear from you."

"Yes," he said, his voice somber. "I'm sorry to bother you."

"How can I help you?"

"How soon could you be in Washington?"

"What's happened?" Wogan asked, very softly, his heart suddenly pounding in his ears.

"The sooner you can get here, the better. I'm sure you understand that I wouldn't call you directly like this if it weren't a matter of the utmost importance."

Fear gripped his heart. "Is it Janice?" he asked, afraid of the answer. What else could it be?

"There's been an accident. Please come at once."

"What can you tell me?"

"Sir, I've already said everything I can over this circuit. It's a matter of some urgency. A man of your means," he said, paused, and cleared his throat. "I'm sure you understand my desire for discretion."

Wogan's heart was in his throat, and he feared the worst. His only daughter. His only legitimate daughter, he corrected himself. With some effort, he collected his emotions and said, "Thank you. I will be there as soon as I can. This evening at the latest."

The poor man sounded almost relieved. "Thank you."

Wogan dropped the handset back onto its cradle and called, his voice hoarse, "Thomas!"

Dean walked into the room, took one look at Wogan and stopped short. It was as though he aged ten years in as many minutes. His eyes were sunken, bloodshot, and unseeing. A pale, ghostly sheen covered the normal glow of his skin, and his white mustache appeared to physically droop.

"What's happened?" Dean asked.

"I don't know," Wogan finally managed after two or three false starts.

"What can I do?"

Wogan's eyes came back into focus, and he looked up at his longtime assistant. "Call operations. Get the emergency crew ready, and have them prep the jet. I need to get to Washington immediately."

"Of course. But why? Can you give me any detail?"

"Something's happened to Janice."

"What?"

"I don't know, damnit! Doonigan wouldn't say on the phone. He was very reticent. Just get the jet ready. Have them prep the crew and rush them to Peterson. I need to get to Washington. Let them know we'll need security to be ready to head to St. John's."

"No details?"

"Didn't I already tell you that's all I know?" Wogan snapped, standing and storming towards his bedroom.

"What will you tell Mrs. Wogan?" Dean asked, trailing after him.

Wogan stopped short and whirled around. "Nothing. She won't hear a word about this until I'm able to determine what's going on. From either of us," he emphasized. "Urgent business in Washington is all she needs to know right now."

"Yes, sir."

"Get the jet prepped and the car ready. I want to be in the air in the next hour."

***

After leaving the library, they drove to the next exit and stopped at a café for breakfast. It was a small, family-owned restaurant, popular with the locals judging by the look of the clientele when they walked in. Morelli suggested they keep driving, stopping just long enough to get coffee and breakfast sandwiches from a fast food place, but Ben Iblis insisted they stop.

"They'll have found the body by now," she remarked in French as a blonde teenager showed them to a small table.

"A lot of Americans are fluent in multiple languages," Ben Iblis said, holding her chair. "I'm surprised you're so nonchalant."

"Thank you," she said, ignoring his statement for the moment, and smiling at him as he took his own seat. "It's so rare to find a gentleman these days."

"It may be the company you keep."

"Until now."

He bowed his head. "Until now."

"My apologies for the outburst," she continued. "I'm simply concerned that we're stopping for breakfast. I think it more prudent to leave as soon as possible."

"Normally, you would be correct. I usually have an egress from the country planned as soon after the event as possible. Since this was a last minute job, though, I was unable to follow my usual protocols."

"That in itself is dangerous."

"Yes."

"What can I offer you all?" a waitress asked, stopping at their table.

"Coffee, black, yogurt, and granola," Morelli said in English.

"And you, sir?"

Ben Iblis picked up a menu and quickly scanned it. "Scrambled eggs and hash browns, please."

"Coming right up."

They watched her withdraw. Morelli asked, switching back to French, "Why did you deviate from your normal procedure this time?"

"Some of it was necessity, as I said. There simply was not time to plan."

"And the other part?"

"I wanted to see how you'd react under pressure."

"A test," she said, folding her arms across her chest.

"Yes."

"And have I passed?"

"We are not out of the country yet. We will see."

"You're awfully nonchalant," Morelli quipped. "Do you think they'll catch us?"

"Does that worry you?"

"Of course!"

He smiled patiently. "I think if we were going to be caught, it would have happened by now. It has been several hours. My guess is your plan succeeded. They will initially treat it as an accident."

"But that won't last."

"No," he said, shaking his head. "The toxicology report alone, once they complete the autopsy, will show them some irregularities. The drugs will make them pause."

"She always had problems with drugs."

"Be that as it may, it will make the detectives scrutinize things a bit more closely. It is inevitable when drugs are involved."

"The nature of the business?" Morelli asked.

"Something like that."

The waitress delivered their coffee, and they sipped it appreciatively. They were tired from the long night. Ben Iblis had the luxury of napping in the car while Morelli drove. That, too, was also part of his test. He needed to make sure she had the endurance to carry out some of these operations.

"Do you always use the Internet to communicate with your contacts?" she asked, referring to the time they spent in the library setting up the charter flight to Ireland.

"Yes."

"Why?"

"It's the hardest to intercept, especially when using billboards and forums. Between the security that may be employed, disposable ciphers, rotating code, it makes it very difficult for authorities to track and intercept messages."

"Better than phone and email?"

He laughed. "There's no comparison."

"But aren't they able to track IP addresses?"

"It is possible to set up anonymous VPN connections to mask your IP address."

"VPN?" she asked, confused.

"A virtual private network," Ben Iblis explained. "It is essentially an encrypted connection between two points. It can be used to help mask your true identity."

"So much to learn."

"Wogan handled all the details before?"

She nodded. "Yes. We had encrypted mobile phones that he trusted. We would use those to communicate."

"It helps to have American defense equipment," he said, impressed. "Even so, I am not sure I would trust it completely."

"He didn't either."

"A smart man."

"Yes," she agreed.

Their food arrived, and they began to eat.

"Did you really feel I needed a test?" she asked between mouthfuls.

"Yes. I heard much about you, but some things need to be witnessed firsthand. You have talent, but you are young, inexperienced. I needed to see what areas, specifically, where you need work."

"And?"

"Your emotions may be the end of you."

She cocked an eyebrow and stared at him. "My emotions?"

"Yes. I realize you're a woman --"

"Hey!"

"But that is not an excuse. You must get them under control if you are going to survive."

Putting her fork down, she said, "I believe I've got my emotions under control."

"In certain circumstances, maybe. But you need to learn to control them all of the time. Before, during, and after an operation. So far, you are struggling to control them after the operation's conclusion. I do not doubt you were able to control them during the operation, otherwise we would not be sitting here having this conversation. Someone would have killed you long ago."

"That's a comforting thought."

His tone turned hard. "It should be. With some work, you could really be something, but those emotions must be dealt with."

"I see."

He finished his breakfast, glancing across the table occasionally. By the time he was done, she had only taken four or five bites. It was obvious his criticism was having an effect.

"Not hungry?" he asked.

"Not anymore."

He stood and dropped several bills on the table. "Shall we go?"

"Why not?" she replied, barely able to keep a contemptible sneer from her face.

***

Morgan rode the elevator to her team's space in the Hoover building. There were several empty cubicles and a large conference room set aside in a corner. So many changes in such a short time, she thought to herself as she walked into the conference room and sat down. The night Nichols was killed, he mentioned a promising lead about a deposit that was made into the terrorist cell's account. They spent most of the week trying to run that lead down, and they made progress. When she thought about it, though, she wasn't exactly hopeful. In fact, she was despondent. Part of it was exhaustion, she admitted. She spent a lot of time over the past two days second guessing all of her decisions.

Of course, it did not matter now. Ben Iblis was long gone, and if he already made it out of the country, her odds of finding him were long indeed. Now that his fingerprints were in IAFIS, the FBI's fingerprint database, there was a greater chance of catching him as he tried to leave the country. The increased security patrols would help, too, especially at the executive airport terminals, but it was a long shot at best. If DHS did not come back to her with an arrest notice in the next few hours, she would assume he escaped. He was too savvy to remain in the country any longer than that.

Realistically, he most likely already slipped through the net getting out, which put the burden of the investigation back on her shoulders. The problem was, they did not have anything to go on. The terror cell Ben Iblis set up to remove her was the only tie, and it was tenuous at best. He was too smart to leave any trail that would allow them to track him down from that angle.

So where did that leave her?

She stood and paced the length of the room. The dead suspects were not going to be much help. Their entire purpose was to die.

Ben Iblis would have carefully screened them for any possible ties, however remote, that might lead back to him. She thought for several more minutes, walking back and forth in front of the conference table, forcing her exhausted brain to work through the various possibilities.

The financial trail was the key, especially the recent deposit into the cell's account. It was very odd because most of the initial funding for the group was set up long ago, and they did not have a need for additional funds. Their accounts were well supplied. For a wire transfer to come in this late was strange, so Nichols sent one of her team with a search warrant to get the details. Unclipping her new phone from its holster on her hip, Morgan looked up the agent's number and dialed.

"Gebog," Morgan said after the line connected, "it's Morgan."

"Morning, boss," Agent Joan Gebog replied. She was one of Morgan's senior agents, recently transferred to the team after Nichols' death. "How are you?"

"I've had better mornings."

"Yeah," Gebog said. "I was sorry to hear about Nichols. He was a good man."

"Yes, he was," Morgan replied, clearing her throat. "Where are you?"

"On my way in. I expect most of the team to be there shortly. We've got more work to do on running down the leads. Brad made it back late last night with more information on the wire transfers."

"Is that tied to the deposit Nichols was trying to run down the other day?"

"Yes, but he wouldn't give me any details over the phone. He only said that it was a hell of a thing and that we'd need to go over it first thing in the morning."

"Nothing else?" Morgan asked.

"No, but he sounded surprised. He said he couldn't believe where the transfer originated from. He was really cryptic about it."

"Cryptic?" Morgan asked, confused. That didn't sound like Brad. "How so?"

"Well, usually it doesn't matter all that much, right? I mean, discussing it over a mobile connection. At least, not in general terms. But he said that he couldn't talk about it at all. Almost like he was afraid to mention it."

"So something sensitive, then."

"Yeah, that's what I thought."

Morgan was silent for a moment while she turned that over. "Ok, well, we'll obviously need to wait until Brad gets in to figure out what's going on. Are you close?"

"I'm about twenty minutes out."

"Ok. Make sure Brad's going to be here. I want to hit the ground running this morning. We've got a ton of ground to make up and no time."

"We're ready, boss."

"Good."

Chapter 7

"What the hell is this?" Wogan demanded, stepping out of the car on the tarmac of Peterson Field in Colorado Springs. He was looking at a brand-new business jet, long, sleek, and brilliant in the mid-morning sun. It was silver, with two large turbofans mounted on each side of the towering tail. A beautiful blonde flight attendant stood next to one of his pilots at the bottom of the boarding stairs. "This isn't my usual jet. Where's the usual plane?"

"This is the newest edition to the fleet, Mr. Wogan. A Gulfstream G650," the pilot said, stepping forward and extending his hand. "We just took delivery. I believe you authorized the purchase over six months ago."

Wogan shook it and stood looking along the length of the aircraft. "Now I remember. My apologies. My mind's been elsewhere, lately. Remind me what was the problem with the old one?"

The pilot smiled. "Nothing, sir."

"I just flew on it the other day."

"It's still in service with the company."

Wogan snorted. "I should hope so. It wasn't that old."

"This one will almost reach the speed of sound. It'll do a little over point nine mach for nine thousand kilometers."

"Really?"

"Latest and greatest," the pilot said.

"Just like I like it." Wogan slapped the pilot on the back. "The faster we can get to Washington, the better."

"So I understand. We'll be in the air just as soon as you get aboard."

"Thank you," Wogan said. He smiled warmly at the gorgeous flight attendant before climbing the stairs.

Stepping into the cabin, he was overcome with opulence. It was large, seating eight in the best the industry could provide. There were several recliners and a sofa, all of which looked capable of folding flat for long journeys. Each was covered in a red Moroccan leather, soft and luxurious. As he stepped down the aisle, his feet sunk into the thick carpet, and his eyes were drawn to the dark cherry wood trim.

The Gulfstream G650 held the distinction of being one of the world's fastest private aircraft. At just under the speed of sound, it was capable of travelling from New York to London in less than five hours. At its normal cruise speed, it could carry eight people in luxury thirteen thousand kilometers without refueling. If necessary, Wogan could fly from Tokyo to New York without stopping.

Dean followed him into the cabin carrying an overnight bag and a stoic expression. Their baggage was taken from the car and loaded in the baggage compartment, out of sight. The pilot stepped onto the plane after Wogan was seated, and the flight attendant raised the stairs immediately. The cockpit door was barely closed before they started to taxi on to one of Peterson's active runways. The powerful Rolls Royce turbines pressed Wogan into his seat as they rocketed from the runway and rotated into the air, the Gulfstream pitching into a steep climb towards the east.

Dean walked forward and took the opposite recliner. "We should be in DC in a little over two hours."

"Much faster than the Citation," Wogan observed, remembering the typical flight time of his old Cessna Citation. "I'm a little surprised it's that much faster."

"I instructed the pilots to push it as hard as they could. I know what Janice means to you."

Janice. It was impossible to even contemplate what might await him in Washington.

Dean watched Wogan's expression change. "This is the jet's maiden voyage for the company, at least with passengers. It will be interesting to see how it does. The Board wasn't happy with the purchase. Sixty million for an aircraft was seen as an extravagance."

"The board can go fuck themselves!" Wogan exclaimed. "I believe I made that clear when they first questioned the expense. Most of those idiots don't seem to have a clue how precious my time is. Shaving an hour or two in the air, putting me in front of clients, congressmen, or vendors saves the company money."

"Yes, I know."

Wogan took a deep breath and rubbed his temples. "I'm sorry, Thomas. I don't mean to be angry with you. What's become of my old Citation?"

"Still happily employed. It will remain in the company's fleet for several more years, I'm sure. Some of those same board members will probably make use of it."

"Figures."

The aircraft started to level off as it climbed through 41,000 feet, on its way to a cruising altitude of 52,000 feet, far above any commercial flight paths. Wogan closed his eyes again and pinched the bridge of his nose. "What do we know of the situation with Janice?"

"I wasn't able to get anything more out of Chief Doonigan. He was surprisingly closed-lipped, given our support of his various campaigns over the years."

"Our support?"

"Your support," Dean corrected himself.

Wogan pushed his recliner back, extending the footrest. "Do you think she got into some kind of trouble?"

"I think it's more than likely, given her history."

Wogan grunted. "She's had her fair share of problems, but she put that behind her. You know that. After she dropped out of Yale and did that last stint in rehab, the last couple of years have been very different. She's been different."

"But if something's happened to her, God forbid, you can't ignore her past," Dean argued. "It's possible someone finally caught up with her."

The thought turned Wogan's stomach. "I can't think about that. Not now. She's my only daughter."

"She is not your only daughter."

Wogan opened an eye and turned it towards Dean. "My only legitimate daughter."

"But not your only daughter."

"It's of little consequence in this matter."

"Depending on the outcome, it may have a great deal of consequence. You shouldn't forget you have two. Doonigan's tone was ominous when I spoke with him in the car on the way to the airport. I think you should prepare yourself for the worst."

"I can't contemplate that now," Wogan said, closing his eye and dismissing the thought.

"You need to," Dean persisted. "What's going to happen when we land and you find out she's been in an accident and is in the hospital? Or worse?"

"What do you mean, 'what's going to happen?' I'll deal with it just like I deal with hundreds of crises every year."

"This isn't another company issue. It's not something you're going to be able to sweep under the rug with money or influence. This is your daughter you're talking about."

Turning in his seat, Wogan glared at Dean. "I'm the last man that needs to be reminded about my responsibilities. Why don't you mind your fucking business and get the stewardess to bring me something to drink."

Dean remained seated. In a patient tone, he said, "You pay me to provide advice and guidance."

"I also pay you for your intelligence. You should remember that, and use it to tell yourself when to shut the fuck up!"

"As you wish," Dean said with a heavy sigh. "What would you like to drink?"

Wogan ignored him. "We need more information. This waiting is interminable, and the lack of information from Morelli is only making things worse. This would be the perfect assignment for her, no matter what we learn when we get there. The entire reason I keep an agent on the payroll is circumstances just like this."

"We can start the process to replace her."

Wogan thought about that. "Do you really think she's gone?"

Dean paused. "I think there are a lot of unfortunate coincidences that have all occurred in the last twenty-four hours."

"And it's all tied to Morelli?"

"Perhaps."

"There's too many questions. We'll know more when we arrive. Let's hold off speculation until we have some facts."

***

Morgan walked into the conference room and sat at the head of the table, a cup of steaming black coffee in her hand. Her team was scattered along the table, only four of them now since she killed Baker, and two more were out on leave. She looked down the table at each of them. They were a strong group, handpicked from across the Bureau for their expertise in different areas.

Each of them gazed back at her with something more than caring. It was sympathy. They all lost a brother agent, but they knew she lost so much more. Her relationship with Nichols was not a secret, though no one discussed it publicly. They spent long hours together in cramped quarters for weeks on end. Nothing was secret in that environment. The details of her ordeal with Baker were still private.

She had not shared them with any one, not even Vogel, but the last week of nightmares tore at her mind. Maybe if she told some one, if she shared what happened, her subconscious would be able to rest. Besides, they were a team. They mourned for Nichols, too.

"I know you all are wondering what happened earlier this week, and you've been polite enough not to press me for details. I know you deserve to hear them, but I only want to say this once." She paused and looked at each of them in turn, again. "I think it's time you learned, and I hope it puts a number of things to rest. But don't ask me any questions, and don't ever ask me to repeat it. This will be the one and only time."

Silence was the only response.

"Baker abducted Nichols and I just after lunch. We drove southwest, into Shenandoah National Park. Along the way, he admitted to murdering Sarino and Billings. They were two of our best audio surveillance guys, and I know you all got to know them well over the past several months." She paused and took a sip of her coffee. "Baker had us stop at the end of a country road, and he marched us into the woods. Just before reaching the tree line, Nichols pushed me into the cover and shielded me with his body." She stopped again, and her eyes glassed over as the scene flashed through her mind. "Baker put two rounds into his back. He was probably dead before he hit the ground. I hope so.

"I was able to find a spot in the woods, near a creek, where I could watch Baker's approach under decent cover. He hesitated, but eventually he did come after me. When he was close enough, I broke his neck."

They did not react, at least not immediately. Morgan watched them process the information.

With Baker's departure, Gebog was now the most senior agent. She nodded once, then again, and said, "He got what was coming to him."

"I'm glad he decided to come after you," Brad Kloser said, leaning back in his chair and running a hand through his brown hair. "I'm glad you killed him. It would've been a mess if the Bureau ended up having to track him down wherever he decided to run."

The rest of her team nodded their agreement. If any of them thought it strange that she was still at work after such a traumatic event, they did not voice it. After working so closely, they all knew what Morgan was capable of, and they all admired her for it.

Morgan barely heard their responses. Part of her hoped she might feel something click as she relayed the story, if only to let her know she could dream normally tonight, but she was disappointed. Nothing happened. Nothing changed.

"So what's next?" Gebog asked, clasping her hands on the table.

"Vogel wants Ben Iblis," Morgan said, willing her mind to work on the present.

Kloser whistled, his eyebrows raised in surprise.

"Why now?" Gebog asked.

"After everything we learned about the hit on the terror cell last week, he's convinced it was all orchestrated by Ben Iblis."

"To what end?" Erin Matthews, a middle-aged, larger agent, asked.

"To have me removed," Morgan said, turning her green eyes on Erin.

"Killed?"

"No. At least, according to Ben Iblis, that wasn't the intention."

"Wait," Gebog said. "According to Ben Iblis? What do you mean? How do you know that wasn't his intention?"

"I spoke with him a few hours ago."

"In person?" Kloser asked, shocked.

Morgan nodded. "Yes."

"When?"

"This morning. He broke into my home and was sitting in the living room waiting for me to return. We had a long chat over a glass of scotch."

"You can't be serious," Gebog said, staring at her.

"I am," Morgan replied. "He described the original plan, and his intention to retire."

"I don't suppose he also mentioned where he would be retiring." Morgan smiled. "No, unfortunately not."

"Do you believe him?" Gebog asked

"I do."

"And Vogel finally gave you the green light to hunt him down? To actively hunt him down?"

"Yes."

"How?"

"We're going to start with whatever we have on this terrorist cell. If Ben Iblis put all of this together, then he bankrolled them. I know you all have done a lot of work on the financials. What have you come up with?"

"Squat, boss," Gebog said, shaking her head. "The trail's long cold."

"Except what I came up with last night," Kloser said. "Nichols had me run that warrant out to the bank last week after we picked up a deposit in one of the monitored accounts. So I got all of the information, and we tracked the deposit to its origination."

"And?" Morgan asked.

"Well, it came from within the states."

"From a business?" Gebog asked.

"No. An individual."

"Who?" Morgan asked.

Kloser stared at her. "Senator Bradley."

"That doesn't make any sense," Gebog said, shaking her head. "At all. Maybe he got the account number wrong or something. Sent his transfer to the wrong account, I mean."

Morgan thought about it. She did not know much about the Senator, other than he had been in office for a number terms and was fairly senior in his party. Gebog was right. It did not make sense for a man like that to transfer money to a terrorist organization, unless, of course, he somehow did not realize that was what he was doing.

"Kloser, get a warrant and start backtracking the transfer through Bradley's account. Get the details of where it originated, and how. Was the origination a phone call? Did he do it from a bank branch? If so, where. Get started on that."

"Yes, ma'm," he said.

"Gebog, get started on Bradley."

"Really?" Gebog replied. "A Senator?"

"Get started," Morgan ordered. "Until we know where the money came from, he's a suspect. We all know what Ben Iblis is capable of. We don't know if he might have ties to Bradley or not."

"It's your funeral, Morgan," Gebog muttered.

A smirk turned one side of Morgan's face. "Don't advertise that we're looking into his dealings, but let's see what he's been up to the last couple of years. Something's going on. If it was a bank error, the funds wouldn't have cleared the account, and most people don't tend to get the account numbers wrong when moving... how much money?"

"A little over one hundred thousand dollars," Kloser answered.

"A hundred thousand dollars," Morgan repeated, her eyebrows arched. "Most folks would double check the account number before moving that kind of money."

Gebog threw up her hands in surrender. "Alright. We'll get started on it."

"Good," Morgan said. "I've got to brief Vogel on this wire transfer. Do we have anything on Baker's financials yet?"

"They're extensive," Gebog said. "Our techs have most of Baker's immediate holdings analyzed, but as of last night they were still working through the matching accounts and transfers. It's going to take more time."

Morgan nodded, disappointed. "Time is the one luxury we do not have."

Chapter 8

They left Manchester just before noon, their chartered Bombardier Challenger carrying them north and east over Newfoundland and the Atlantic. Morelli sat back in one of the leather chairs, sipping a glass of club soda. Working for Wogan, she flew on many private jets, but she was still impressed with their speed, efficiency, and luxury. From the time they returned the rental car to wheels up, they spent barely thirty minutes at the airport.

Augustus, Ben Iblis's agent, was also the story of efficiency. From their initial contact, he arranged a charter to Shannon, customs documents and inspection, emigration papers, including forged fingerprints, and all the necessary payments to make their departure seamless. She knew similar efficiency working for Wogan, but he had the resources of a massive corporation behind him. Ben Iblis was a single individual. All of his resources were from private means, developed over a long, lucrative career.

She took another sip of her club soda and smiled. This was where she wanted to be. Finally, after fifteen years on her own, forced to make her own way, she had the opportunity to make something of herself. This arrangement would set her up in the business without being answerable to anyone, and the best part was there was no need to put out to do it. Though, she admitted, she would have to have been both blind and stupid not to recognize some of

Ben Iblis's looks for anything other than what they were. Not that it really concerned her one way or another. He was a man, and, fundamentally, they were all the same.

What concerned her was his relationship with the FBI agent, Morgan. It was obvious there was something there, something more than mutual respect, and she needed to determine exactly how deep this relationship ran.

Glancing at him, dozing peacefully on the couch lining one side of the jet's cabin, she knew it could be worse. He was an attractive man, and she took much worse to bed. The question was whether it would be to her advantage or not. Ben Iblis was unlike any man she ever dealt with. Most of the men she took to bed were dangerous in one way or another. The problem with Ben Iblis was he was dangerous in so many different ways. He was intelligent, cunning, ruthless, and patient.

"You seem lost in thought," Ben Iblis said, his eyes still closed.

"Sorry, I didn't mean to wake you."

"You did not. I was just dozing. What have you been thinking about?"

"Some of the efficiencies in your organization."

"Do you see areas in need of improvement?"

"Quite the opposite, actually. I'm sure I haven't been introduced to everything, but so far I'm quite impressed."

"You cannot substitute good logistics. Not in this business. They are vital."

"How did you find your current man?"

There was a pause as he sat up. "We were in Afghanistan together. That was thirty years ago. After the Russians pulled out, he went to eastern Europe and ran several small-time operations before hiring on with a larger organization."

"Big step from there to running your own shop, especially in that business."

Ben Iblis nodded and motioned for the stewardess. "A glass of champagne, please."

"Of course," the stewardess replied with a slight British accent. "Another club soda, ma'am?"

"Yes, please."

The stewardess nodded and withdrew.

When she was back in the galley, Ben Iblis continued. "He set up and ran a lot of the company's business in Eurasia and sub-Saharan Africa. They made a ton of money in Kosovo, Libya, and the Congo in the nineties."

"I can imagine."

"All during that time, he was working on shoring up his contacts. So in early 2000 or 2001, I cannot remember exactly, he set up his own shop for a small, exclusive set of clients. His services are unparalleled, and, as you saw, he is extremely efficient."

"How did he pull clients away from the larger organization?" Morelli asked, intrigued "Why did they join him, instead of staying?"

"I can only speak for myself, as he keeps his client list strictly confidential. I was uncomfortable with the thought of staying with the larger organization and transitioning to another contact. This man and I did business ever since we turned the Russians out of Afghanistan. It is impossible to replace that kind of trust."

"What was it you called him while we were driving? Augustus?"

He smiled, a bright white line in his swarthy face, "Yes. From our years in Afghanistan. It's expanded to encompass the name of his organization."

"I've not heard of it."

"Few have," he said as the stewardess returned with their drinks. "As I said, he has a select client list."

"You also mentioned he kept it strictly confidential."

"He does. I've only learned of others through third party contacts. Indiscreet individuals at parties, that sort of thing."

"I see." She took another sip of her soda. "Does our arrangement include his services?"

He tasted his champagne, nodding his approval. "Until such time as I'm no longer making direct operational decisions. At that point, all I can promise is the introduction, which will be made in the next day or two. He may or may not agree to take you on as a client. I think your chances are good, though. He is a connoisseur of true talent."

"That sounds fair," she agreed, somewhat begrudgingly.

"Either way, with the direct contacts you will make over the course of our arrangement, you should be able to find someone with a similar skill set to Augustus. I would not worry."

She laughed, amused at the suggestion. "I'm not worried. I was impressed with how the entire business was handled, and it would be great if I could continue to use his organization after you've given up operational control, but I'm not overly concerned."

"I will make the introduction."

She leaned forward in her chair. "Tell me about Morgan."

"No," he said, rolling on to his side, his back towards her.

Morelli shrugged and leaned back in the chair, stretching her long legs across the footrest. It would wait. There was little doubt in her mind that she would learn more about this FBI agent. For some reason, Ben Iblis thought she was something special, and she doubted it was because of past history. Morelli would discover why in due time.

***

Vogel looked up from a stack of papers on his desk when his secretary ushered Morgan in. With a nod of his head, he motioned for her to take a seat and waited for his secretary to withdraw. She closed the door behind her as Morgan sat down and adjusted her pistol on her hip to fit more comfortably against the chair's backrest.

"Seems like I just talked to you," Vogel said, returning his attention to the papers on his desk.

"You did."

"Then why are you back?"

"A new development."

Setting the papers down, he removed his gold-rimmed spectacles and rubbed the bridge of his nose. "Look, Eve, I realize you went through a hell of a lot in the last week. Nobody's going to think any less of you if you take some time to get everything in order. Gebog can run that team for a week or two, or however long it takes for you to set things straight." He paused and set his glasses down on the desk, watching as the smile on her face vanished, replaced by a stone wall. "Losing an agent, let alone someone as close to you as Nichols, isn't something you can bounce back from. Take some time off. Go somewhere, get out of the city. Forget the Bureau for a few weeks so that when you come back, you're a functional team commander again."

"A functional team commander again?" she asked, her anger rising. "What's that supposed to mean?"

He put his glasses back on and fixed her eyes across the desk. "I didn't hire you to run in here every two hours so I could make decisions for you. I need a senior agent and a team lead, not a little girl who needs her hand held while I wipe her nose."

Several seconds passed as she held his stare. Then, in a very cold voice she said, "I didn't come here to ask you for advice or guidance. I came here to give you an update on what the team found this morning, and to inform you that I will be opening a formal investigation on a Senator."

"Christ," he swore, rubbing his temples. "Which one?"

"Bradley."

"He's powerful. Why?"

She shifted in her chair. "Kloser was running down a lead on a bank deposit that hit one of the terror cell's accounts. The transfer came back to one of Bradley's accounts."

He looked at her skeptically.

"I know," she admitted. "I'm not sure I believe it, either, but my team thinks it's legit."

"How much?"

"One hundred thousand."

"Not easily forged," he sighed.

"No, and the money's already cleared, which means that the bank already verified all of the details. Accounts, amounts, everything. So the money came from Bradley's account, and it was supposed to be deposited in the terrorists' account."

"C'mon, though. A Senator? A United States Senator? I know they're capable of some pretty shady things, but funding terrorism?"

"I don't believe it either," she said. "I don't want to, at least, but we wouldn't be doing our jobs if we didn't run this down."

"That will mean notifying Ethics," he said, referring to the U.S. Senate Select Committee on Ethics. "And Treasury. I'm sure they'll want to get the Secret Service involved."

"It's not counterfeit."

"I know, but it is a Senator, and it is a good deal of money. They'll want to be involved in the investigation."

"We can probably keep it under wraps for a bit."

"Maybe, but not for long. You know that. As soon as the warrants are issued, you can bet your ass the good Senator will find out about it. One way or the other. And as soon as he finds out, Treasury will be all over us."

"I'll be careful."

He looked at her dubiously.

"I don't need to deal with an interagency investigation right now," she argued. "Let me get the warrants and execute the search. Then we can deal with Treasury."

He looked at her pointedly. "You want a head start."

"Of course I do. I've brought it this far, and I want to finish it."

"You think this is the break you need?"

Did she? "It stinks to hell, Adam. Either Ben Iblis set Bradley up, or something's going on over there that may give me enough of the puzzle to start putting it together."

"A few hours ago you told me you didn't have anything."

"I told you we didn't have much, but that was before I knew where this money transfer came from. I wouldn't be in here talking to you if we'd traced it to some bank in Pakistan."

He sighed and rubbed his eyes. "Alright."

"I'm ok to open the investigation?"

"I already told you, Eve, I'm not here to wipe your nose. If you think an investigation is necessary, even one involving a Senator, then I trust you to do your job."

"Comforting."

"I'm not here to be comforting," he said, looking at her again. "I'm here to run a division, and you're here to do your job. Either do it, or take some time off while you figure out how to get your life back in order. To be honest, I don't much care either way."

"Thank you for your vote of confidence, sir," she said, emphasizing the last word.

"You're welcome," he replied, his voice dripping with just as much cynicism.

"Is there anything else?"

"You tell me! You're the one that came marching in here."

"Actually, I came in here with a smile on my face and good news that I wanted to tell you. We've made progress. We've got something to look into. I'm more optimistic than I was two hours ago."

"Congratulations," he said dryly. "You've done your job. Keep doing it."

"Yes, sir. Thank you, sir."

As she walked out of his office and closed the door behind her, Vogel's secretary caught her eye.

"He's been like that with everybody for a couple of days now," she said. "You're the first person who's walked out of there today not foaming at the mouth. The last guy looked like somebody just killed his dog."

Morgan stopped halfway across the anteroom and shook her head. "I'm more used to it than most. Why does he get like that?"

"Because he can't stand losing agents, and the last thing he wants to do is lose any more."

"I've caused him nothing but headaches and extra paperwork." She paused. "And three good agents."

His secretary smiled. "I know. But in the end, you get results. That's why he likes you."

***

The Gulfstream landed smoothly, its wheels barely chirping as the pilot touched down on Reagan's long runway. They taxied to the private jet terminal, stopping near a silver Mercedes sedan and an armored, black Chevy SUV. The pilot stepped out of the cockpit as Wogan made his way forward.

"Thank you for such a fast, uneventful flight, Matthew," Wogan said, extending his hand to the pilot.

"My pleasure, sir. I knew you'd enjoy this new bird."

"It's a nice plane. Keep her on standby. I'm not sure how long we'll be here."

"Of course, sir."

Wogan stepped past him and descended the air stairs, Dean just behind him. As they approached the Mercedes, Dean opened the rear door, waiting while Wogan stepped into the luxury sedan and buckled himself in. One of the security men placed their luggage in the trunk, and Dean took the driver's seat. The big sedan fired up immediately with a throaty growl, it's V-12 already warm, eager to whisk them away from the airfield.

Despite Wogan's impatience, Dean maintained some semblance of the speed limit as they sped towards Janice's apartment, the Chevy SUV never straying far from its cover position near their rear bumper. The Mercedes was hardened against most threats, but it would not be able to sustain a prolonged assault, and Wogan's security people knew the key to their principal's survival was the ability to escape and evade.

Wogan sat in the leather seat trying to gain control of his emotions. He knew perfectly well what waited him ahead, despite his own protestations against the inevitable. His Janice, his only daughter, was most likely dead. At this point, the why did not matter. It could have happened for any number of reasons. Perhaps her past finally caught up with her. There wasn't any sense arguing that she had a difficult childhood, but she seemed like a completely different person, after months of therapy, before heading back to the east coast for college. They had no indication that she fell back into her old habits.

What worried him more was that a rival, or, God forbid, an enemy, either got to her directly, or took out a contract. He made an untold number of enemies in his rise to power, but no one dared cross him. Ruthless business dealings were a normal part of his life, and he used less than moral methods in obtaining some of his goals, but he never crossed that line. He never held someone's family hostage to their business concerns. A principal, yes, but never his family.

Could this have been an act of revenge? He steeled himself to the possibility, vowing that he would discover the truth. Whatever happened to Janice, whoever did this to her, he would have his revenge.

Chapter 9

Morgan walked from Vogel's office, caught an elevator, and strode into her team's conference room in their corner of the Hoover building. She was not angry, but Vogel's statements made her pause. If the game she played over the past two weeks was dangerous, it now entered the realm of being deadly, Baker notwithstanding. An investigation into a United States Senator was not something to be undertaken lightly.

Only three agents were there when she walked in. "Gebog," she ordered, "get things going on Bradley."

"What'd Vogel say?" Gebog asked.

Morgan looked at her. Hard. "He said get things moving on Bradley. Any other questions?"

"No, ma'am."

Morgan held her stare until the agent looked down. "Good."

Gebog stood up, pushing her corn-blonde hair to one side as she indicated for the other two agents to follow her. They walked out of the room, leaving Morgan alone. She took a chair, propped her feet up on the table, and thought about that morning. Once they had a better idea on this wire transfer, she would feel more comfortable. Kloser was one of her better agents, extremely good at investigation. She wondered, though, if she could get a head start. Besides, this really was not something she could let go without some sort of heads-up. Politics. It was all about politics.

Picking her mobile phone out of its holster at her side, she dialed a number and waited while the call went through to a mobile on the other side of the city.

"Keller," a tired, rather high-pitched, slightly masculine voice answered after three rings.

"Didn't interrupt your beauty sleep, did I?" she asked.

She heard the rustle of a comforter in the background, and it was several seconds before he said, "No, not at all. What's up?"

"You free for lunch a little later? I've got something I need to run by you."

"Alright," he replied, his voice magnified by the echo of what, she could only assume, was a hotel bathroom. "What did you have in mind?"

"Something quiet. On your dime."

Another pause.

"You still there, Ben?" she asked.

"Yeah," he said, a little quieter. "I'm still here."

"Lunch, then?"

"Alright. Where?"

"Arlington?" she suggested. "About an hour from now?"

"Is it important?"

"More important than that piece of ass you picked up at the bar last night. That I'll guarantee."

"Look, Eve, this normally wouldn't be a problem, but I've got a lot going on today."

"So do I. I wouldn't be calling if it weren't an emergency, believe me."

He sighed. "Ok."

"An hour. Arlington."

She flipped her phone closed and put it back in its holster. She had known Ben for nearly fifteen years, going back to their time at the Air Force Academy in Colorado Springs. They kept in touch over the years, growing closer as they both spent time in Washington. Any question of a romantic connection was lost before it ever started, even while they were at the Academy. Back then, the idea of an openly gay officer in the Air Force was strictly taboo, but everyone that knew Keller had their suspicions. He would show up to balls either alone, or not at all, and invitations for double dates were always politely declined.

It caught up with him in the end, though even that was not publicly discussed. A quiet, honorable discharge was offered and accepted, and Keller went into communications and marketing, eventually landing a job on Senator Kenneth Bradley's staff. Over the last several years, he consolidated his position to become Bradley's chief-of-staff.

If anyone knew what the Senator was up to, it would be Keller, Morgan knew. The problem would be getting it out of him. She hoped he was as good of a friend as she thought. If not, she could always count on him for lunch.

***

"Doonigan," Wogan barked into his mobile phone as Dean maneuvered the Mercedes north of Washington, DC. "It's Andrew Wogan."

"Mr. Wogan," Doonigan replied, his voice very formal. "Are you in town?"

"I just landed at Reagan."

"Are you headed this way?"

"Yes," Wogan said, rubbing his forehead. "Where can we meet?"

"I'm at Janice's apartment."

Wogan's heart sank. This was not going to end well. "Very well. We'll meet you there."

Dean glanced back at him over his shoulder as he merged with traffic.

"Janice's apartment," Wogan repeated, almost to himself, not daring to look up. He felt the car accelerate as they drove through the city towards Annapolis. Taking a deep breath, he resigned himself to the fact that she was dead. If it was merely been an accident, Doonigan would meet them at a hospital, not her apartment. If she was in some kind of legal trouble, they would meet at the jail. No, he sighed, closing his eyes and pushing the pain to the back of his mind. He was a logical man. His Janice was dead.

Dean remained mercifully silent during the thirty mile trip. Wogan downed another pill as the highway passed under Washington, then he closed his eyes and thought back to the limited time he was able to spend with his daughter. Most of the images that flashed before his eyes were happy memories of a small girl with a mischievous smile and blonde pigtails. She would laugh as they went for ice cream in Woodland Park, Colorado, strolling along main street in the brilliant Colorado sunshine. He remembered how he was so proud when she came running into his office that day, several years ago, with her acceptance letter to St. John's. Though she kept it to herself, he knew she harbored real doubts about going back to school after dropping out of Yale and entering rehab.

He also remembered the tears in his wife's eyes as they bid Janice goodbye after dropping her off for her sophomore year. She came a long way from the months she spent in rehab. Too much money and too much freedom, he told himself, but she managed to put her life back together. And for what?

"We're almost there, Mr. Wogan," Dean said.

Wogan could not bring himself to speak. He pushed the memories to the back of his mind and took several deep, cleansing breaths. The last thing he needed was for Doonigan to see him like this. After several moments, he opened his eyes, sat up in the sedan's seat, straightened his coat and tie, and turned to look out the window like any other billionaire: calm, dedicated, and in complete control.

There were two police cruisers in Janice's complex, both parked in 'reserved' spaces in front of her unit. What shocked him to the core, though, overcoming the composure he put together, was the burned hulk of her apartment building. Nothing remained but a single wall, charred and twisted. Dean pulled up behind the police cruisers, and Wogan stepped out, his eyes wide at the sight of the destruction.

A heavy-set, slightly balding man in a police uniform approached. Several men were combing through the still-sopping wreckage, stepping over debris and puddles of water.

"Mr. Wogan," the officer said, extending his hand. "Thank you for coming on such short notice."

"Of course, Chief," Wogan said, absently shaking Doonigan's hand, still staring at the rubble.

"I wish it were under better circumstances."

"Janice?" Wogan asked, turning and focusing on Doonigan's fat, globular face.

"I have a priest on the way."

"I'm not Catholic."

Doonigan looked to Dean for help, but all he received was a cold stare. "I'm sorry, I didn't know. We can find someone else. What religion do you --"

"She was killed in the fire," Wogan said, ignoring Doonigan. He pursed his lips, desperately trying to control himself. "How?"

Doonigan cleared his throat. "The coroner hasn't made his report, yet."

Wogan fixed him with a deadly stare, boring his eyes into the other man. "I'm not interested in the coroner's report, Chief Doonigan. I'm interested in learning how my daughter died."

"It would be premature for me to say."

Taking a step forward, Wogan seethed through clenched teeth. "Tell me how my daughter died."

Doonigan recoiled despite his years of experience. The anger and hostility radiating from Wogan forced him back. "Let's sit down in my car, and we can discuss this. As I said, I have a priest on the way. Maybe you could speak with him."

"Tell me how my daughter died, you fat piece of shit! Tell me now! Not in five minutes. Not in your police cruiser. Now!"

"It's not confirmed," Doonigan hedged, clearly at a loss for words. Despite his many years of experience, Wogan's unchecked anger caught him off guard. "We'll need to wait for the medical examiner's report, of course. I'm sure you understand."

"Just tell me, Doonigan. How did she die?"

"We think it was accidental."

"Accidental?" Wogan parroted, examining him closely.

"Yes. The investigation team found an accelerant near the --"

"Where did you find Janice?" Wogan interrupted.

"In the bathtub."

"Just lying there?"

Doonigan nodded.

"And there weren't... there wasn't anything," he cleared his throat. "There weren't any marks on her?"

"Marks?"

"Signs of trauma? Signs of a struggle?"

"No," Doonigan answered, confused.

Wogan nodded. "What is this business about finding something?"

"An accelerant. The investigators found an accelerant spread all over the stove."

"So the fire was intentionally set?" Wogan asked, a renewed hope filling his voice.

"No. We don't think so. Did Janice have cats?"

Wogan thought for a moment. "Yes. She mentioned something about cats. I think she had one or two."

"We found a carcass in the apartment. We think she went to take a bath while boiling some water on the stove. One of the cats knocked over a jar of cooking oil of some kind, and it started the blaze. That's why we believe it may have been accidental." Doonigan cleared his throat again. "Obviously, the investigation is in its earliest stages, but it's a plausible theory."

"A plausible theory, Chief?" Wogan sneered. "My daughter's dead. My only daughter, and you're standing here feeding me bullshit about a plausible theory? What the fuck happened in there last night? You need to find out!"

"We will," Doonigan assured him. "These things take time."

"Christ!" Wogan swore, running his hand down his face, suddenly very tired.

"I truly am sorry. The few times I met Janice, she seemed like a wonderful young woman."

"She was," Dean agreed, speaking up for the first time. "She was very full of life."

"Wouldn't she have gotten out of the tub?" Wogan asked, not hearing him. It was surreal. He couldn't believe this was happening.

"We don't know."

"Why not?" Wogan pressed, returning to the present.

"Because all of this is preliminary, as I said. They just got the fire under control. We have an entire investigation to complete. There's a lot of evidence and information we still need to gather and put together."

"I don't pay you for preliminary results, Doonigan. I pay you so that I have something to fall back on when the shit hits the fan."

"I'm sorry," Doonigan said, matching Wogan's stare for the first time. "I really am, but there wasn't anything to be done. It went up like a matchbook. She was gone long before the fire department ever arrived. There's nothing that could have been done. Believe me. They tried."

Wogan stared and chewed on his lip. It was not possible. There was always something to be done, something that could be changed, something that could be fixed! "Fuck!" he swore again. "What the hell am I going to tell her mother? What the hell am I going to do? Why the hell didn't she get out of that tub? What the fuck was she thinking?"

"Let's sit down," Doonigan suggested, trying to shuffle Wogan toward his cruiser.

"If I wanted to fucking sit down, I would have done it already."

Doonigan held up his hands. "I'm really sorry. We'll know more once the autopsy and toxicology reports come back. Until everything's complete, though, all we've got is speculation and some good guesses."

Wogan looked at him with loathing. "No one saw anything? No witnesses?"

"No. It was an automated alarm from the building's security system."

"Security cameras?" Dean asked.

"There are several. We're pulling the feeds now, but, again, it'll take time to go through the footage."

Time. Wogan did not have time. He had to find out who did this. "Was anyone else killed?" he asked.

"No. No one else was in the building at the time."

Wogan turned and watched the investigators as they picked through the wreckage. "Not another soul? No one? Seems kind of odd."

"Late on a Friday night? Early Saturday morning?" Doonigan shrugged. "It's student housing. Not too out of the ordinary. Everybody's out late having a good time. I think we were lucky there weren't additional casualties. The place went up like a matchbook."

"Yes, you mentioned that."

They watched for several minutes as the men on the rubble pile sorted through the debris. Wogan was never in law enforcement, so he did not have any sort of grounding in the grisly business of gathering evidence, but he certainly knew all about creating the messes that investigators were later forced to piece through. This bore many of those marks: no witnesses, no other casualties. Just his dead Janice.

He took another deep breath and forced his daughter, and his devastation, to the back of his mind. There was not much he could do to help her memory, or to discover exactly what happened here last night, if he was caught up in emotional baggage. "Tell me, Chief," he said, turning back to Doonigan, lowering his voice. "Would you be opposed to the idea of one of my people going through the evidence on this one? After you've had a chance to pour through it, of course."

Doonigan contemplated for a moment. "You have been extremely generous in the past, Mr. Wogan. And I understand what an utter tragedy this must be for you. It's difficult to comprehend what you, and Mrs. Wogan, must be going through."

"I think we could probably contribute something to your future re-election campaign," Wogan said, looking at Dean. "In recognition of your discretion in this matter."

Dean nodded.

"That would be most appreciated," Doonigan said.

Wogan held out his hand. "Thank you, Chief. One of my people will be in touch shortly. I'm sure they'll have your department's full cooperation?"

"Of course," Doonigan said, shaking Wogan's hand. "We're always happy to assist such a generous benefactor of the police department."

Smiling perfunctorily, Wogan walked back to his waiting sedan.

Dean held the door open for him, then ran back around the front of the car. "The brownstone?" he asked, after he settled into the driver's seat.

"Yes."

Dean put the car in drive and started towards the interstate. "Mrs. Wogan?"

"Later."

"Later?"

"Yes," Wogan said. "I'll tell her later."

"Are you sure?"

Wogan glanced out the window as the houses flashed by. "Now's not the time, Thomas. Please. Later. I need a drink and some time to think. Time is important here. I need to come up with a plan. It's the only way we'll catch those responsible."

"Responsible?" Dean asked, somewhat surprised. "Doonigan said the fire was accidental."

"No," Wogan clarified. "He said the fire was probably accidental."

"You don't believe him?"

Raising an eyebrow, Wogan caught Dean's eyes in the rearview mirror. "Do you?"

Chapter 10

The maître d' greeted her as she opened the door and stepped into the redesigned brick warehouse, an icon from a Confederate Alexandria, Virginia. Taking her coat with a flourish, he said, "Ms. Morgan, how wonderful to see you again!"

"Thank you, Peter," she replied, a slight color flushing her cheeks at the thought of being recognized in so exclusive an establishment.

"Mr. Keller is already here, at your usual table," Peter said, offering her his arm and ushering her into the dining room.

It was beautifully appointed with stuccoed crème walls and an old-growth, wide-plank oak floor. Numerous tables were spread across the large room, placed far enough apart to invite private conversation. Large booths lined the exterior, each paisley floral print backrest nearly six feet tall and more than adequate to lock in any conversation, especially when its occupants spoke quietly to purposely keep it contained.

A thin, rather diminutive man rose from a corner of one such booth as she approached. He was balding, closely cropped brown hair forming a half moon around his ears and the back of his head. The top gleamed despite the muted glow from the dining room's chandeliers. Dressed smartly, he sported a three-piece tailored silk suit, a brilliant purple tie, and an American flag lapel pin. It was one thing she admired about Keller. The man could dress.

Peter stopped at the edge of the table. "Mr. Keller, Ms. Morgan."

Keller smiled and extended his hand, inviting her to sit opposite him. Peter bowed and withdrew.

"Always the showman, Ben," she said, smiling as she sat down.

"I can't look bad in front of so many colleagues," he replied, his award-winning smile still plastered across his face. "Besides, what would they say if I treated one of the FBI's finest without any of the basest civilities?"

She tucked a lock of brunette hair behind one ear and settled into the booth.

"Especially one as beautiful as you are," he added, unfolding his napkin in his lap.

"Stop," she said, her face flushing again. "You'll make me blush."

"I doubt it."

Her smile grew, and she picked up her napkin. "I wish we could do this more often."

"And I wish you'd have married me all those years ago when I asked."

"But then we would both be unhappy, and there'd be one more divorce in the world. You know it wouldn't have worked out. The sex would've been terrible."

"Another divorce wouldn't be nearly as bad as the loss of a friendship," he said, gazing at her across the table.

"You were always a charmer, Ben," she admitted in a rare moment of embarrassment.

"I do believe you're blushing, Eve Morgan!" He laughed, a deep booming sound in direct contrast to his voice and frame. It carried across the dining room, drawing several stares and a few masked smiles.

She recovered, trying to hide some of her lingering emotion by nervously straightening the silverware on the table. "Those were good years," she said, looking up and meeting his eyes.

"They were," he agreed as a waiter approached.

"It's wonderful to see you both again," the waiter, Dennis, said. "Do you have a preference on the water?"

Keller looked at Morgan expectantly.

"Just tap water for me, please," she said.

"The same," Keller said.

"May I offer either of you a cocktail?"

"Not for me," Morgan said.

"A Manhattan, please, Dennis," Keller said, smiling at the waiter.

He withdrew, leaving two placards with that day's lunch menu on the side of the table.

"So why did you turn me down?" Keller asked, reverting his eyes from the waiter's closely cut tuxedo pants.

"You ask me this at least every other time."

"So tell me again."

"Because it never would have worked out. You were on your way to Korea --"

"And you were tied up with your mystery man."

"Among other things," she smiled, humoring him. "Traipsing around the world after you like some camp follower never really appealed to me. Then there's the question that nobody likes to talk about."

"Trivialities."

She smiled. "Besides, I had my own career to look after. You know that."

"Well," he said. "It would've been magical while it lasted."

"Of that I have little doubt, but it would have ended."

He reached over and picked up the menus, offering one to her. "You would've made a lousy homemaker."

"And you would have made a lousy lover. Let alone a husband."

His booming laugh carried through the restaurant again as they looked over that day's selections. The chef changed the menu almost daily, depending on Virginia's season and his own inspirations. They were all Celtic based, the chef having grown up, and later emigrated, from Ireland. His selections were rooted in classical culinary tradition, and he maintained a nightly seven-course service, but his lunch menu was generally more relaxed. It was why Morgan came back again and again when she was interested in something a little nicer than her typical deli fare.

Keller laid his menu to the side as their waiter reappeared and delivered the cocktail. A busboy filled their water glasses from a crystal decanter.

"What may I offer you for lunch?" Dennis asked.

"The halibut, please," Morgan said.

"Pan roasted halibut, new potatoes, and tapenade. Of course, Ms. Morgan," he replied. He turned to Keller. "Mr. Keller?"

"The steak salad, if you please."

"It's a New York Strip from a local farm today, Mr. Keller. Is that alright?"

"That would be lovely."

"And how would you like your steak today?"

"Medium rare, please," Keller answered.

"Right away," Dennis said and withdrew.

Keller took a sip of his cocktail and smacked his lips.

"Good?" Morgan asked.

"As always," he said, looking around. "How long have we been coming here?"

"Years. Ever since you got out and took that job at the Capitol."

"And when were we last here?"

"Two or three months ago. It's been a while."

He nodded. "So then this isn't a personal call, is it?"

"No," she admitted. "It's not."

"I wondered when you called this morning. It sounded like something was going on. What's up?"

She collected her thoughts, folding her hands in her lap. "We found some interesting transfers from one of the Senator's accounts this morning."

That caught him off-guard, but he recovered quickly. "Setting aside the fact that you're obviously investigating a Senator, he makes a number of different financial transactions. So what?"

"While that wouldn't be very out of the ordinary, in and of itself, the recipient account makes things a bit more interesting."

"Why?"

She sipped her water, making him wait. "Did you hear about the multiple homicide over in Reston the other day?"

"Of course. Half the city is talking about it. Something about a home invasion?"

"Not exactly. That was the official line Reston PD fed to the media."

"What's the real line?"

"I was tracking a terrorist cell, and there was an incident."

Keller possessed a keen intelligence, and he followed her immediately. "Something to do with your mystery man?"

"Perhaps, but that's not open for discussion now."

"Ok," he said, taking another sip of his drink.

"We've been tracing the terrorist cell's financial history, all of their accounts, all of the action into and out of the various systems ever since we picked things up over a year ago." She paused. "There was a deposit from one of Bradley's accounts into one of our marked accounts yesterday afternoon."

"Pretty hard to believe," Keller said, deadpan, careful to keep his body position rock-solid. "There could be any number of explanations for that. Erroneous transfer, bank error, stolen check, outright fraud." He shrugged and leaned back in the booth. "Not exactly the first time, I'm sure, that the FBI has run into this with a public official."

She folded her hands together on the table. "Those are all distinct possibilities, and any one of them might be a potential avenue to explore."

He smiled in satisfaction.

"Except that we've already explored them."

"I wouldn't expect anything less," he said, not missing a beat, the smile still etched on his face. "So what did you find?"

"The deposit's already cleared."

"In twenty-four hours?"

"Yes."

A slight hint of surprise flashed briefly behind his eyes. "A very fast turnaround. Transfers typically take much longer, especially between different financial institutions."

"I didn't say they were different institutions."

"That's true, you didn't," he said, quickly. "Were they?"

"They were," she said, watching him closely.

"Twenty-four hours is very fast."

"Yes, it is. Because it cleared, though, it rules out bank error, stolen check, or erroneous transfer. Whoever has access to that account meant to send that money, and they meant to send it to the terrorist cell. Of that, we are positive."

He finished his cocktail. "That's a very serious charge."

"Extremely," she said, then stopped as the waiter delivered their meals.

They ate in silence for several minutes, Morgan finishing half her fish, savoring each bite, before Keller asked, "Do you have any leads on a suspect?"

"No, not right now. We're still in the beginning stages of tracking this down."

"But you're opening an investigation?"

"Yes."

"So this is a courtesy call?"

"Partly."

He took another bite and chewed. Slowly. "And the other part?"

She fixed his eyes, piercing them with her own green stare. "Because I lost someone earlier this week, and whoever was involved killed him."

That penetrated his political stoicism like a lightning bolt. He set down his silverware and looked genuinely concerned. "I'm sorry, Eve."

"Jesus," she said with a loud sigh. "Why is everybody always sorry?"

"What?"

She shook her head and took a deep breath. "It doesn't matter. He's dead."

"How?"

"Christ, Ben. Really? Do you really want to know?"

"If it matters this much to you, yes, of course I want to know."

"One of my agents executed him."

Keller just stared at her, not wanting to believe it. "Were you involved with somebody on the wrong team?"

"No."

"Then I don't understand."

"My agent was the traitor. He killed several members of my team. He even made an attempt on my life."

"And this agent?" Keller asked.

"Dead."

"How?"

She didn't reply.

"You killed him," he continued, realization dawning.

"Yes."

Keller leaned back in the booth and collected his thoughts while Morgan ate her fish. "This... this friend of yours. You two were close?"

"Very."

"Lovers?"

"Yes."

He wiped his mouth with his napkin and looked genuinely contrite. "I'm sorry, Eve. Truly."

"So you said."

Fumbling with his napkin, he asked, "You think Bradley's involved?"

"We know he's involved." She swallowed and reached for her water. "We just haven't gotten into how far, yet. I lost three agents over five days. We're coming for him."

"Fair enough."

"Did you hear what I just said? He may have directly funded a terrorist organization."

"I heard you."

"And that's all you have to say?"

Keller wiped his mouth with his napkin again, studying her. "Bradley has been around a very long time. He's one of the most senior senators in the legislature, and he's cultivated powerful alliances. This isn't going to be a straight-forward case, and I think you probably realize that, or you wouldn't have called me."

"I'm not going to ask you to help."

"Good, because I'd tell you to piss up a rope."

She gave him a bored look. "You know me better than that."

"So what do you want?" he asked.

She pushed her empty plate forward and crossed her arms on the table. "Just a free lunch."

"You are a piece of work, Evelyn Morgan."

"I know," she said, shooting him a devastating smile.

***

Dean set a large ceramic mug brimming with coffee in front of Wogan. Thankfully, the man had not asked for scotch. They stood in the kitchen of Wogan's brownstone in Washington, and Dean watched Wogan carefully. The man had aged before his eyes. In the twenty minutes it took to drive from Annapolis, Wogan physically shrunk. He seemed frail, as though he could not bear the weight of his daughter's death.

"Thanks," Wogan said, accepting the mug.

"Are you ok?" Dean asked, pouring himself a cup.

"We need Morelli," Wogan said, turning the situation over in his mind for the twentieth time.

"She's gone."

"Nothing?"

Dean shook his head. "No."

Wogan took a long drink, savoring the dark flavors of the expensive coffee on the back of his tongue. "I suppose I shouldn't be surprised. She was always one to look out for number one. Do you think she found a better offer?"

"Yes, I do."

"We don't have enough information. I can't run an operation blind."

"I'm not sure we have much choice at the moment."

"You could get me some goddamned information," Wogan barked, staring at him.

Dean ignored the outburst. "And Janice?"

"Janice is dead."

"I'm surprised."

"That she's dead?"

Dean shook his head. "No, that you're rolling over on it."

Wogan looked at his assistant sharply. "Careful. You forget who you're talking to."

"Do I?" Dean asked reasonably. "Or am I merely pointing out the obvious? You're too emotionally involved in --"

"She's my daughter!"

"Was your daughter," Dean corrected. "She's dead."

"Because I didn't protect her. I couldn't keep her safe. I should've insisted she have someone live with her, someone to watch over her. They could've done something about the fire. They could've saved her."

"Maybe, or they might be dead right alongside her."

"How?"

"What if there wasn't any way she could have escaped that apartment last night? What if somebody designed it so she couldn't leave."

"What do you mean?"

"The timing of all of this is awfully convenient."

"You think they're connected. Morrelli's disappearance and Janice's," Wogan paused, almost choking out the word, "demise."

"I think it would be a hell of a coincidence."

"Do you think she's capable of that? Morelli? Do you think she could do something like that to me, after all the years she spent here?" He looked helpless. "And why? Why would she do that?"

"I think she's capable of anything. She is an extremely dangerous operative. Independent, autonomous, smart, crafty, and ruthless. Absolutely ruthless. Morelli is capable of anything. I've warned you about that before."

"I know, but it's those same qualities which make her such a successful employee. Those are the reasons I hired her."

"It's a difficult proposition, at best, to tame a wild animal."

Wogan looked across the kitchen. "But even a wild animal may be leashed."

"Perhaps," Dean said. "But never tamed."

"If you say so."

"If she's truly gone," Dean continued, "it poses many problems."

"Yes, I know."

Dean nodded. "What about your wife? Mrs. Wogan must be told about Janice."

"I know."

"Soon," Dean insisted.

"I know."

"Will you do it in person?"

"Of course I'll do it in person," Wogan said.

Dean finished his coffee and set his mug down on the counter. "I'll get the jet prepped."

"Have them make it a quick turnaround."

"What do you mean?"

"In Colorado Springs," Wogan said. "I want to be back in Washington tonight."

"You're joking."

Wogan fixed him with a cold stare. "Have you ever known me to joke?"

Dean looked down. "No."

"Have them prep the jet and file a flight plan back to Washington for tonight. Arrange for our minister and a counselor to meet us at the house. Mrs. Wogan will need help. A lot of help. I expect to be back here tonight."

"Why?"

"You said it yourself. There's too many coincidences. As much as I don't want to admit it, Morelli was involved."

"You think so? Why?"

Wogan stood up from the table and walked towards his office. "Too many coincidences," he repeated, stopping in the threshold. "It doesn't add up. We lose track of Morelli and Janice is murdered?"

"You don't know she was murdered."

"You were the one trying to convince me otherwise just a few minutes ago!"

"I just want you to look at all the options," Dean replied, trying to keep his voice reasonable. "I'm not saying she was murdered."

"But you said there were an awful lot of coincidences. The more I think about it, the more I agree with you. There's too much going on to not be suspicious. Janice was a fighter. All her life, she was a fighter. She beat addiction, she beat those stereotypes. She made a life for herself. She got into St. John's. Despite the press wanting it to be my influence, she got into that school on her own merits." Wogan paused and closed his eyes. When he opened them, they were filled with purpose. "She was murdered. The question is the origin. Was it a contract to get at me? Was it random? Was she in the wrong place at the wrong time?"

Dean didn't respond.

Wogan continued, "Whatever the reason, she wouldn't have just sat in that bathtub and died. Something happened last night. She was murdered."

"How are you going to prove that?"

"That's why I need Morelli. That's why I need an operative. Baker's gone. Dead, according to the papers. With luck, he really is dead and not in some government interrogation complex. Morelli's gone. God knows where, but she's gone." He shook his head. "Maybe Morelli isn't even the best choice at this point with everything that's happened. It sounds more and more like she may be involved."

"We can always find and hire another one."

"Too much time, Thomas. That's not a luxury I can afford at the moment. I need somebody now."

Dean looked helpless, not a position he found himself in often.

"What do you think we should do?" Wogan asked.

"I don't know."

Wogan raised an eyebrow. "Not the response I expected. You always have an opinion, an option, something we should run down or try."

"We could use contractors to keep an eye on the key international airports. That would give us some visibility on the international routes when Morelli or Ben Iblis try to get out of the country."

Wogan shook his head. "No good. They won't use commercial carriers."

"Then it may be a little easier, actually. If they're using charters, there are only a handful of airports that offer pre-screening into the States. Ben Iblis seems like a man of habit. Let's try and find him by posting agents at some of the easiest crossing points."

Wogan thought about it before nodding his agreement. "Alright. That makes sense."

"With Morelli gone," Dean continued, "it will take time to rebuild the organization. She was Baker's replacement. We hadn't yet identified any one to back fill her position because she was so new." Dean looked at him. "You just marked her for advancement last week."

"I know," Wogan sighed. "This isn't your failure, Thomas. I need you to know that. I want you to believe it. This failure is mine, and we'll need to revisit our policies once we've got everything sorted out. But for the moment, we have a bigger issue. Janice's death wasn't an accident, despite what they're going to eventually find in the coroner's report. She wouldn't have stayed in that bathtub. She wouldn't allow herself to succumb to a fire. She would've fought. She would've moved. She would've done something! She wouldn't have gone out like that. Not in a bathtub, not without a fight. I could see her falling through rafters trying to get out a window, or maybe succumbing on the stairs getting to the door. But in the bathtub?" He shook his head again. "No. Not Janice."

"Neither of your daughters," Dean added, making a point to catch Wogan's eye.

"That's right," Wogan agreed.

"Are you going to call her?"

"Do I have a choice?"

"No."

"Then I'll call her."

"When?"

"When we get back from Colorado. Right now, though, my wife needs me."

Chapter 11

They left the restaurant together, Morgan giving Keller a perfunctory hug outside as they stood on the sidewalk, the lunch crowd moving around them.

"Where's your car?" she asked, pulling away.

"Up the street a bit. I got here early, so parking wasn't too bad."

"Mine's the other way," she lied. Her car was in the same direction. "I'd forgotten what a pain it can be finding somewhere close when you're running late."

"And you're always running late," he said with a smile.

"One of the privileges of being a woman."

"I'm sorry about your... friend," he said, trying a weak smile. "I'm sure he was a good man."

"Thanks," she replied. It took some effort to keep her face impassive.

"Alright," he said, "well I need to get back to the office. Give me a call when you want to do this again. I always enjoy seeing you."

"You bet," she said, and turned to walk away.

"Thanks again for the heads-up!" he called, half turned.

She smiled and nodded, waving as he went around a corner and was lost from view. After walking another block, she crossed the street and rounded a corner, headed in the opposite direction. After she walked another two blocks, she stopped, found a bench, and sat down.

It was hard for her to imagine Keller being involved in something as sinister as this, but after their conversation, she could not come up with any other conclusion. At a minimum, he knew of the money transfer, if he did not conduct the transaction himself. Despite being a consummate politician, he was a terrible liar, at least in her experience. Of course, that could be because she'd known him for so many years. They went through basic together, becoming friends when others shunned him for his unconvincingly concealed tendencies.

Keller was a patriot, though, she reminded herself. He served his country. He put in his time. What the hell was he doing mixed up in this?

Burying her head in her hands, she leaned forward and closed her eyes. Could it be the discharge? She knew he wasn't happy about having to take it, and she knew it wasn't right, but would it cause him to betray his country? Would it drive him to get mixed up in something like this?

Not only did she not want to believe it, but she could not believe it. She could not force her mind to buy it. There were too many things that did not add up, too many things that did not make sense.

Could it be money?

Her head came up, and she stared across the street.

Money was always an issue. The discharge was offered after a particularly nasty investigation into gambling within the service. Though she never participated, she knew Keller was neck deep in it, and they wanted to make an example of several officers. Plus, it was just the excuse they needed to take care of another of Keller's 'issues.'

Money. That made sense. It was at least plausible.

Fishing her phone from its holster, she found Gebog's number and hit the speed dial. It rang several times before she answered.

"Gebog, it's Morgan. I want a tag put on Keller."
"Bradley's Keller?" Gebog asked, surprised. "His chief of staff?"
"Yes."
"Ok, I'll get it done. Any particular reason?"
"Call it an educated guess."
"Will do. Can you fill me in?"
"When I get back to the office. I'm out in the open right now. I should be back in about thirty minutes."
"Sounds good. I'll see you then."

Morgan flipped her phone closed and replaced it on her hip. God help Keller if he was involved.

***

Their flight landed without incident in Shannon, the lush Irish fields a muted emerald green in the fading evening light as the jet dropped effortlessly onto the runway. Customs and immigration cleared them without issue, most of the details having been arranged by Augustus several hours ago, shortly after they left the States.

Morelli preceded Ben Iblis out of the cabin, stepping onto the tarmac in the fading light of dusk. Stopping at the bottom of the stairs, she looked up. Several stars twinkled in the cloudless sky, and she took a deep breath, happy to take in humid, non-recycled air. It was a pleasant evening, warm enough that she did not feel chilled, and still, despite the occasional roar of turbofans rocketing a plane into the sky. As Ben Iblis came down the stairs and stood next to her, she took his proffered arm and smiled. "A gentleman."

"Who wouldn't want to be seen strolling arm-in-arm with you?"

"Careful," she said, flushing. "You don't know what flattery does to a woman."

"Shall we?"

She nodded, and they walked towards the small private jet terminal. An impish, non-descript man in a poorly tailored suit stood just outside the door. He looked at them expectantly as they approached, calling out, "Mrs. Colton?"

"Yes?" Morelli replied, studying him.

"We've taken the liberty of pulling your car hire around the front. I believe your luggage will be transferred shortly. Would you care to follow me?"

"Of course," Morelli said.

Ben Iblis studied the little man and, in his accented English, said, "I'm sorry, Monsieur, I didn't catch your name."

"It's somewhat different," the man replied, "but my friends call me Carrier."

"Like a schlemiel."

"But only when duty calls," the man said, finishing the sequence.

Ben Iblis nodded. "Please, lead on," he said, and they followed the man at a discreet distance.

"I'm amazed how effortless this whole trip was," Morelli said in French, still holding on to his arm. "I know I mentioned it in the plane, but it's still surprising. Leaving the States, clearing customs, not having to worry about security... even when I was travelling with Wogan, I don't remember it ever being quite this effortless."

"Shannon is one of the few airports in Europe with U.S. Customs pre-clearance status." Ben Iblis replied in the same language. "While I would never fly commercial in and out of the United States, pre-clearance makes it so much easier to get in and out of the country."

"So do you usually travel through Shannon?"

"When I go anywhere in North America, I do. It is extremely convenient. I do not know how it's all handled on the backend, but I've never run into a problem coming through here."

"Your man is very good."

"The best, but we covered that."

She patted his arm with her free hand and said, "I do hope you'll introduce us."

"I already said I would."

They passed through the terminal's front doors back into the early twilight of Ireland's spring. She'd only been to Ireland twice, but she swore there was a distinct sweetness to the air she never encountered elsewhere in Europe, or the world, for that matter.

"Is there anywhere you haven't been?" she asked.

"No," he replied as they stopped in front of a silver Volkswagen. "Though it has gotten much harder to move about in the last ten years. There is a good deal more scrutiny."

Carrier motioned at the car and asked, "Will this do? Your luggage has already been loaded in the boot."

Ben Iblis took one glance at the sedan and said, simply, "No."

"I'm sorry," Carrier apologized, his embarrassment evident. "I'll have another car brought around immediately."

"Do you have something larger?" Morelli asked. "Maybe a Land Rover? We may head off the paved roads."

"I'm sure we can arrange something," Carrier said, pulling a mobile phone from his pocket.

They watched him as he walked to a pillar several feet away. "You know," she said, switching back to French, "with surveillance equipment these days, we could request ten different cars and they would simply bug each one."

"I know," Ben Iblis replied, trying to do his best not to look at their contact. "But it was a good thought. We'll simply have to continue to trust Augustus."

"How close were you in Afghanistan?"

"Very. I trusted him with my life on numerous occasions. He is an old, dear friend. I have no reason not to trust him now."

"Is that wise?"

He looked at her, his eyes turning cold. "You spoke of trust earlier. Our friendship spans many decades, far longer than I have known you, and in much more dangerous circumstances. He has done many things to earn my trust. Do not question it again."

It felt like an eternity, holding his stare, before she finally tore her eyes away. "You're right. My apologies."

Carrier dropped his phone back into his pocket and approached them. "It's all set. A Discovery has just become available. It should be here shortly."

"Thank you," Ben Iblis said.

They stood silently on the sidewalk, Morelli marveling at the serenity of the evening. The sun was low over the horizon, casting muted shadows across the orange light. A light breeze tickled the fields on the other side of the road, pushing that crisp sweetness through the air. If she were Ben Iblis, she would retire in Ireland.

After fifteen minutes, a green Land Rover Discovery rolled to the curb and stopped, its driver running around the front of the SUV to open the passenger door for Morelli. She nodded her appreciation, traced his steps around the front of the car, and stepped in. Ben Iblis ensured their bags were transferred and took the driver's seat on the right side.

They drove east in silence, picking up the main carriageway to Limerick. She kept silent as the Irish countryside faded to blackness, the kilometers passing like highway markers under the Land Rover's tires. The entire enterprise depended on trust. And despite what Ben Iblis said earlier that morning in the apartment in Annapolis, she knew it was already growing between them.

The sticking point was this FBI agent, Morgan, and his absolute refusal in discussing anything to do with her. The meaning behind his curt reply on the plane was very clear. Morelli knew little of the woman, but it was apparent she held some sort of special place in Ben Iblis's heart. But who was she and why was she there? Why did he care so much for her? Was it really simply a matter of admiration, or was there something deeper? The fact that he insisted on meeting her, face to face, to say goodbye was particularly disconcerting.

It was something best left for another time, Morelli admitted, clasping her hands in her lap and closing her eyes. They could discuss it later.

"You know," he said, his hands on the wheel, "adjusting to a new partner is challenging. It's been so long, I'd quite forgotten just how challenging it can be."

"Why is that?" she asked.

"Just trying to get used to someone's personality."

"I've never had a partner," she said.

"I guess I've never had a real partner, either. I've worked with several people. Khalid was my assistant for many, many years, but I've never worked with someone who I would call my partner."

She laughed. "Then how do you know it's so hard?"

"Working with Khalid was never easy, and judging by the past five or six days, working with you is not going to be any better."

"Thanks for the vote of confidence," she said. "Adjusting to any new working environment is a challenge. Perhaps that's a more appropriate way of putting it."

"Perhaps."

She shifted in her seat, trying to get a little more comfortable. "You never told me the plan, now that we're here."

"I have a safe house near Killarney."

"How far is that?"

"Not far. A couple of hours at the most."

She stared out her window, watching the last of the daylight fade slowly away. "You never told me about your arrangement with Wogan."

"You never asked."

"And if I asked now?"

"What makes you think I had any sort of arrangement with Wogan?"

She sighed tiredly, "You must know by now that I'm not stupid. Don't be obtuse. Sitting in that coffee shop last week, your questions about Bradley, your ultimate proposal to me, and your questions about Wogan earlier suggest to even the most naive of operatives that you've had some sort of business arrangement with him, if you don't have one currently."

"I did have an arrangement with him."

"In what context?"

"He hired me to fulfill a contract."

"Who was the contract for?"

"Actually," he explained, "it was for any one of a dozen Senators on a committee."

"Which committee? What was he ultimately after?"

"A guarantee for an upcoming grant, I believe."

"That seems somewhat excessive."

"I understand it was a large contract. He wanted to make sure it went through."

She thought for a moment. "The facial recognition software! He's been after that for years. It will be huge for WGI Systems. No wonder he hired you. That was one of the few contracts that had to succeed. The company invested too much money in R&D to see it fail."

Ben Iblis shrugged. "All I know is Bradley was on the list."

"So you targeted him."

"Yes, of course. Wogan specifically mentioned Bradley when we met."

"Is that why you targeted him?"

"No," he said, shaking his head, "but he was one of our primary targets. I sent my assistant to do some of the preliminary research while I completed another job."

"Your assistant thought it would be best to target Bradley?"

"Yes," Ben Iblis lied, remembering the conversation he had with Wogan in Colorado Springs two weeks ago. "We determined he would be one of the less challenging targets to prosecute."

She considered everything he said, not quite sure she believed it. The removal of Bradley may have hurt Wogan's case more than help, unless he was going to threaten the rest of the committee. "You've had a hell of a week."

He stifled a yawn. "We will be there in a little while. Try to get some rest. You did not sleep at all on the flight over. You look exhausted."

"That's a good idea," she said, leaning her seat back and closing her eyes. The last thing she did was fall asleep, though. There was too much to think about.

***

Closing the door behind him as he entered his office in the Capitol, Keller walked around his desk and sat down. Years of experience operating within Washington's political minefield taught him to be cautious, so he was not a man to make rash decisions. Morgan's warning scared him, and despite his desperate attempts to keep his face impassive during the conversation, he knew she picked up on something.

If that were the case, friend or not, she would hit him with everything she had. The question was what to do about it.

He worked for Wogan for many years, and while he held no illusions about the benefits Wogan received from the deal, it also made Keller a reasonably wealthy man. When Dean called to arrange this latest wire transfer, it seemed like any of hundreds Keller arranged over the years. He learned long ago not to ask too many questions. There was not any profit in it.

With an FBI investigation, though, there would not be any more profit, either. It would be a long, drawn-out process, probably taking years. Bradley would use his influence to protect his people, potentially derailing the entire process, but how would Wogan react, Keller asked himself. Would the man have any use for him after the fact?

There were many details he still needed to work out, including where he stood with Morgan. They had been good friends for many, many years, but the energy behind her conviction at lunch surprised him. It was clear losing her lover caused a dramatic change, and that worried him the most. She would be relentless in her pursuit, and while he did not have anything to do with her lover's death, he doubted that distinction would be so clear in her eyes. He was involved in the scheme. Maybe not directly, but involved nonetheless.

What value did she place on their friendship?

***

Morgan sat at a desk in a tiny cubicle in the Hoover building, staring into space. The meeting with Keller was troubling. It would be interesting to watch the fallout. Either Keller would tell his boss, and she would hear about it through Vogel, or he wouldn't, and the investigation would come as a complete surprise. In the end, though, it really did not matter. They had more than enough to start looking at Bradley. If he filed a formal complaint, and she was sure he would, regardless of how he learned about the investigation, she didn't really give a damn.

Keller's reaction would be important. If he knew about the wire transfer, it was one thing, but if he was in league with Bradley, she expected to hear about it. They could not very well run. There was too much visibility. The best they could hope for would be to cover it up somehow.

Everything ran into one bucket. She needed to find Nichols' killer. She needed to find Ben Iblis. Blowing a long, slow sigh, she stretched in tired exasperation. Baker may have pulled the trigger that sent those bullets into Nichols' back last week, but Ben Iblis put it all together. He was the one she needed to find, and she was prepared to go through whoever she needed to in order to see justice done. Even a United States Senator.

"Boss."

Morgan turned in her chair and looked at Gebog. "Yeah?"

"Warrants are piling in. We're in business."

"You sound surprised," Morgan said, examining her.

"Bradley plays in a big pond," Gebog said with a shrug.

"With lots of fish."

"But he's one of the bigger fish."

Morgan scratched her head. "You've been with the Bureau a long time, right?"

"Yes, nearly ten years."

"I really don't understand your hesitation, then."

"I wouldn't say it's hesitation."

"Then what?" Morgan asked. "You questioned my orders earlier this morning, you've been moping around here since lunch, and you've got this air of reluctance just hanging all over you." She held up her hand when Gebog was about to interrupt. "I don't mind questions, when they're legitimate, but what you did this morning in the conference room was more destructive than anything. The rest of the team looks up to you, despite the fact that you've been here barely a week, and I expect you to display a little more support for my decisions."

"What if I don't agree with your decisions?"

Morgan pursed her lips and leaned back in her chair. "Then disagree professionally. Don't sit there and spout stupid questions just because we're talking about a Senator."

"Is that what you think I did?"

"C'mon, that's exactly what you did!" Morgan exclaimed, trying to control her temper. "This team needs a senior agent, especially after everything that's happened. They're going to be looking to you for advice and support. Sitting in there and asking stupid questions isn't the way to go about it. You know that. That's why I brought you onboard."

"I hear Nichols used to be pretty good at that."

He did. He used to be good at a lot of things, Morgan thought, fighting that constriction in her chest. "Yes, he was."

"Look, boss, I'm sorry, but this is just a hell of a lot to take on at once."

"I know that. Believe me. But I need somebody that can lead them through this. This is going to be a huge investigation. You can put it together. Bradley's just any other bent crook trying to beat the system. You've done this investigation a hundred times."

"But this is a huge pond."

"It's the World Series, there's no doubt," Morgan admitted. "Now where do we stand?"

Gebog took a deep breath and closed her eyes, collecting her thoughts. "The warrants are in. We can start the financial traces through Bradley's bank and confirm the origination, though I don't think there's much question to that at this point, at least not with a transfer of that amount. The banks would certainly catch an error."

"Makes our job easier."

Gebog nodded, tossing her blonde hair.

"We need to coordinate the rest of the warrants on Bradley's offices, houses… everything. Do we even have a list of everything we need to hit?"

"Kloser's working on it. I asked him to get started right after the meeting this morning. I figured the warrants would start coming through about lunchtime."

Morgan smiled. "So you are on top of it."

"I do try, ma'am."

"Let me know if he needs any help. I may be able to call in a few favors."

"Will do."

"While he's building that list, let's get somebody on the financial trail. That's a solid lead. There's an entire bank trail there. Destination to source and whatever may be tied on at the end." Morgan paused while she thought about it some more. "It really doesn't make sense that it would be tied up so neat and tidy. The transfer, I mean. There's something else going on there, and we need to keep digging."

"We'll run with it," Gebog said, her confidence returning. "Somebody screwed up somewhere. We just need to run it down and figure out where and why."

"Exactly."

"One other question."

"Yes?"

"Keller," Gebog asked. "What's the deal? The word is you two are friends. Pretty good friends."

"We are, which is why I requested the tail. I had lunch with him, mostly to feel him out on the whole Bradley thing."

"Ok," Gebog said, unconvinced.

"He tried to hide it pretty well, but what I was telling him took a toll. It was written all over his face. At a minimum, he's aware of what Bradley's up to. The question is whether or not he's in on it somehow."

"Well, we've got resources on him now, so if something turns up, they'll let us know."

"Just make sure they don't lose him," Morgan said. "If we need to pick him up, I don't want him to slip through the cracks."

"I'll make sure they know how critical it is."

Morgan nodded as Gebog turned to leave. Before she took two steps, though, she turned and leaned back into the cube. "Oh, and thanks, boss."

"Thanks?" Morgan asked, confused. "For?"

Gebog smiled. "The pep talk."

"Anytime."

Chapter 12

They passed through Portland Park, Ireland and turned south after going through the industrial sections of Limerick. Morelli turned and glanced in the left-side mirror after they made the turn south, her eyes focused on the same pair of headlights. "How long have they been following us?"

"I thought you were going to take a nap."

"For somebody who's being followed, you're awfully glib."

He shrugged.

"How long have they been back there?" Morelli asked.

"The past five or six kilometers."

"I assume they're not part of your normal security procedures here?"

"No."

Ben Iblis pushed the accelerator down, and Morelli felt the surge of the big V-8 as the car rushed forward, its three hundred and seventy horses pounding underneath the hood. As she glanced in the mirror, the headlights stayed perfectly positioned behind them, not deviating even a meter. The engine roared as he pushed the throttle even further, driving the big SUV past 140 kph.

Morelli tried to control her breathing, her heart pounding in her chest, her eyes darting between her mirror and the road speeding away in front of them. Most people, she knew, in a situation like that would be thinking of little else but their own lives. It excited her, though. Everything about the situation flooded her system with adrenaline, and she felt that familiar rush, that rush she hadn't been able to find in anything else.

Chancing a glance at Ben Iblis, she noted his serenity. Both of his hands were on the wheel, his breathing was steady, and there was a calmness to his features that forced her to reevaluate her own emotions. She lived for these moments. The only thing holding her to her seat was the seatbelt.

"There may be some rational explanation," he said, sensing her gaze as he kept his eyes focused on the road ahead.

"Do you really believe that?"

"No," he admitted, glancing at the pursuing headlights in the rearview mirror.

They continued on for several more kilometers before another exit appeared. Ben Iblis took it at the last possible moment, careening the big Land Rover across the ramp, its tires squealing in the quiet Irish night.

The headlights swerved momentarily behind them, then steadied along the exit, following their path.

"Reach under your seat," Ben Iblis said. "There should be a pistol and something heavier."

Morelli did as she was told, reaching between her legs. Her fingers wrapped around the familiar grip of a Glock 23, and she pulled it up and handed it to Ben Iblis. It was a favorite of police agencies around the world, especially in the United States. Chambered in forty caliber, it was brutally efficient in its singular purpose: to put people down quickly and easily.

Reaching under the seat again, she felt around until her fingers found the muzzle of something much longer and heavier. As she brought the barrel forward, she ran into the front grip and trigger assembly of a Steyr AUG, a bullpup-style assault rifle chambered in the standard NATO five five six caliber. It was an older weapon, but its ease of procurement, due to the large number produced, as well as its use of standard ammunition, made it a favorite amongst rogue military and other clandestine organizations. The fact that it was compact and lethal made Morelli's smile grow that much more as she detached the magazine, checked its capacity, and chambered a round.

"There should be spare magazines under there, too," Ben Iblis said, his eyes darting to the lights in the rearview mirror.

She reached under the seat once more and found the three spare thirty round magazines taped to the bottom of the seat, just behind the holster for the Glock. "Nothing more for the pistol, I'm afraid."

"It's of little consequence."

"Is this a standard arrangement for you?

"The guns?" he asked.

"Yes."

Looking in the mirror again, he nodded. "Yes."

"Augustus?"

"Yes."

She was impressed. "How do you want to do this?"

"I've been thinking about it," he said, his eyes focused ahead as another deserted industrial section flashed by. "I'm going to put some space between us, drop you off, and then move ahead and make the second left. When they come by, spray them with the Steyr."

"Isn't it semi-auto?"

He shook his head. "No, it should be triggered for full-auto. It's one of the stipulations I make when I book travel through Augustus."

"Have you ever had to test that?"

"No," he admitted, pursing his lips.

"I guess now's a good a time as any," she said, her smile growing. It didn't bother her. It never bothered her.

Glancing over at her with a look of real concern, he asked, "Have you ever fired an automatic weapon before?"

She laughed, tossing her head back and tucking a section of her hair behind an ear. "Of course. What a silly question. You looked concerned."

He did not look amused. "For my own skin, I am sure."

They passed through the last section of light industrial, the streetlights ending abruptly and casting the country-side into darkness. In the distance, a faint glow could be seen near the horizon, but for the moment they were completely dark and alone. Ben Iblis killed the Discovery's lights and gunned the engine. As the speedometer blew past 160 kph, Morelli gripped the bullpup Steyr and gauged the distance to the lights glowing in her mirror. They'd fallen behind, growing smaller, maybe confused by the disappearance of the Discovery's tail lights.

"Another minute," Ben Iblis said. "I will slow down, you jump out, and I will continue on for another mile. If they make it through your fire, I will take them."

"They won't," she stated, already taking slow, even breaths to still her heart and nerves.

The minute passed slowly, and it seemed like an eternity before Ben Iblis began to slow the car, barely bringing it to a rolling stop. It was over in a second. Jumping, the throaty roar of the Land Rover's big V-8 erupting behind her, then silence, the still darkness covering her like a blanket.

As her eyes adjusted to the dark, the muted glow of Limerick's southern houses lit the horizon to her left. Taking a quick survey of her surroundings, she picked up several lights in front of her, across the inky blackness of Ireland's lush fields. It was hard to judge the distance at night, but she felt the lights were far enough away to not pose an immediate hazard. They would hear the gunfire, but she planned to be long gone by the time anyone arrived.

There was nothing to use for cover, unfortunately. She was standing in a shallow ditch running along the road. Wire fences lined the field behind her, and she imagined it was the same on the other side of the road. A rock, a tree, or something with some mass would have been her preferred shooting platform, but there was nothing in sight. So she waited, the Steyr in her left hand, as the twinkling headlights grew brighter. They were moving very fast, faster than even Ben Iblis dare press the Land Rover, now they knew their quarry was bent on escape or, at the very least, evasion.

When she judged they were only five or six hundred meters away, she dropped to one knee, brought the Steyr up, and held it at the ready. She was in the ditch, her head and shoulders even with the road. At two hundred yards, she tucked the assault rifle's hard composite stock into her shoulder and released the safety. As the car, it was a large sedan she now thought, came into the peripheral vision of her left eye, she began to match its movement across her body, leading it by several inches. Just as it was about to cross immediately in front of her, she gently squeezed the trigger, controlling the rifle's recoil as it kicked back into her shoulder, the first round erupting from the barrel.

Within seconds, she sent four more controlled bursts into the sedan. Nearly deafened by the automatic fire, she didn't hear the rounds plow into the thin body of the sedan, but she watched as they wrecked their deadly havoc. The driver, his unprotected body directly across from her, took the brunt of the assault. The sedan drifted to the right as the first rounds hit, then corrected violently to the left, leaving the roadway and careening across the dark expanse of grass. She watched its lights for a brief second before dropping the magazine from the rifle and refreshing it with a full one.

The sedan stopped abruptly with a loud crump which reached her a moment later, followed by the mournful sound of its horn. Morelli jogged to her left, covering the sedan with the rifle. Crossing the roadway, she approached from the passenger's side. The interior of the car was dark, and she could not hear anything over the blare of the horn. All of the doors were closed, and it wasn't until she was almost on top of it that she saw the passenger sitting upright in his seat. She stayed out of his line of sight, walking silently on the soft green grass, until she got close enough to pick out the details of the wreck. The sedan had plowed into a stone wall, its mass crushing the front of the car, pushing the engine block back into the passenger compartment.

The passenger turned his head to look at her, his legs destroyed, a twisted, mangled mess of flesh, bone, and metal. He was pale, almost ghostly, deep in shock, and she knew he would not survive long. She chanced a glance at the driver over the top of the assault rifle. His eyes stared forward, unseeing, his chest crushed by the steering column.

"How did you find us?" she asked, stopping five feet from the side of the car.

The passenger just stared at her.

"Who hired you?"

He coughed, blood seeping from his lips, but he remained silent.

Morelli shot him twice in the chest, his body jerking from the hits, followed by a bullet through the side of his head. The fourth round went through the driver's head, and she walked back to the road. The Land Rover stopped and she climbed in, tucking the Steyr under her seat.

"How many were there?" Ben Iblis asked.

"Two."

"Get anything out of them?"

"No."

***

Morgan resigned herself and leaned back in her chair. It was a waiting game. They were tracing the financial data, and the warrants were ready. Keller was under surveillance. Now she needed to wait before she could continue her hunt for Ben Iblis.

How long would they search, she asked herself. Their resources were finite, and if Ben Iblis really did intend to retire and disappear, the Bureau would not spend extra money trying to track him down. If additional hits did not pop up with his MO, then there would not be much point actively hunting him. She rubbed her hands over her tired eyes, puffy and black from lack of sleep.

The computer screen in front of her stared dumbly back. No alerts from DHS, which meant they had not picked him up. It also meant that he got out of the country safely, probably on fake emigration documents. That did not come as a surprise. A man operating in that space for over thirty years would have numerous ways of slipping in and out of countries without the trivialities of border controls. Even the United States.

But was that even possible at a moment's notice? They introduced ever more stringent controls since 9/11. Was it possible to get out of the country that quickly, with little to no planning? She thought about it. Even the private charters were required to file extensive paperwork, the pilot verifying and guaranteeing his passengers and manifest.

Was there some way around that, though?

She idly tapped her fingers on top of the desk. Of course it was possible. Anything was possible with enough time and resources.

It was getting late. Her team was busy around her, and what little sunlight remained struggled to make it to her cubicle. Exhaustion threatened to consume her as she forced her mind to focus. The human element. There was always the human element. No matter how many systems they put in place to make the process more automated, there was always the human element.

She leaned forward and tapped several keys on the keyboard. How many private charters left the United States for foreign destinations in the last twelve hours? The computer spit back a staggering number: nearly ten thousand.

Not helpful.

It was possible someone could have entered false information, someone on either Ben Iblis's payroll or an organization he employed to handle his logistics. If it was an organization, they would not have a lot of lead time on his travel plans. That was particularly true if he did not know how long his latest operation would take. Even if he triggered the 911 call last week which forced them to raid the terrorists' apartment, he was still in the country as of this morning. Assuming he left right after speaking with her in her townhouse, twelve hours was probably generous. She hit several more keys on the keyboard and waited for the computer. Unfortunately, it still spat back over five thousand flights.

"Want me to get you something from the cafeteria?" Gebog asked as she passed by.

"Would you mind?" Morgan asked, tearing her eyes from the computer screen.

"What do you want?"

"Corned beef on rye, Swiss cheese, slathered in brown mustard."

Gebog nodded and walked towards the elevators.

He would not fly out of D.C., that much Morgan was certain as she turned back to the computer. He would drive, and she doubted he would drive to a major airport. Not if he was taking a charter. They could fly in and out of just about anywhere. A smaller, regional airport would be less conspicuous, easier to get in and out of without all the hassle and scrutiny of a major hub. That removed Boston, New York, Philly, Atlanta… her mind trailed off as she thought about heading west. Would he head west? How far was realistic? Two hours? Four hours? Six?

"Christ," she swore, shaking her head and rubbing her eyes again.

He could have flown from just about anywhere along the eastern seaboard west to Kentucky, Ohio, or Tennessee. It was an impossible number if she took the regional airports into account. Any mid-sized town in the middle of nowhere held a landing strip that could handle a charter aircraft. But it was something to run down. It had to be run down. They could not disregard any potential lead.

"Got anything solid?" Vogel asked suddenly, startling her.

"No," she said, surprised he got that close without her noticing. She must be more tired than she thought. "We ran the financial trail into Bradley's account, and the team's starting to pick apart the rest of his holdings, but we haven't come across anything that sticks out yet. Gebog's still working on the wire transfer, trying to trace where it originated."

"I thought we knew that."

"Well, we know the account, but she's trying to trace the origin. Where did the order come from? Was it local? Did it originate from one of Bradley's offices? That kind of thing. The bank should have the IP address of the originating computer."

"Which will give us a location."

"Right."

"Ok," Vogel said, pushing his wire-rimmed glasses back up his nose and leaning forward to get a better look of her computer screen. "What are you working on?"

She leaned back in her chair. "Well, we haven't gotten anything from DHS, and it's getting late. I think he's already gone."

"Makes sense. He wouldn't stick around after talking to you."

"No. But why did he stick around in the first place? Why didn't he have something set up a week ago to get out? Why now? Why wait? What happened last night?"

"Nothing that I know of," Vogel said. "At least not on a national level."

"He stayed for some reason," she mused. "Why? And how did he get out of the country? A flight seems like the most logical choice. Probably a charter. He wouldn't risk a commercial charter. I doubt he knows we have his fingerprints, but after all these years he must at least be wary of a picture, however grainy. It's too much of a risk. Somebody from DHS might recognize him, or at least question him."

"Ok."

"He wouldn't take something out of Dulles or Reagan. Too much scrutiny, even for a charter, especially with the alerts we've put out. So I think he drove somewhere, probably a regional airport. The question is how far he would've gone before calling it safe. If he goes too far, it actually makes it harder for him to get out. There's a sweet spot he targeted, somewhere four to six hours away, by car."

"Four or six hours puts him just about anywhere. There must be hundreds of airports and thousands of flights, even if you restrict it just to charters."

"Yeah," she agreed. "An impossible number to run down in any reasonable time. I can cut that number down pretty good if I only include flights with flight plans that were filed within twelve hours of departure."

"But if he wasn't planning on leaving until this morning, he had a week to put a plan together. That means his charter could file a flight plan any time over the past forty-eight hours." Vogel stood up straight and continued, "Not that it really even matters. Most flight plans are filed shortly before takeoff by third party companies."

"How do you know?" she asked, unable to contain her surprise as she turned to look at him.

"I'm a pilot."

"Great."

Vogel grunted and asked, "Were you ever able to find anything on his logistics network?"

"No."

"So you're going to run all these flights down?" he asked, looking back at the screen. "That's a good number, and I'm not sure it'll gain us anything."

"Yeah. I think we have to. We'll start tonight. Hopefully we'll run across a bogus set of fingerprints, or falsified records. Something has to pop that'll give us an edge. We're due for a little luck after these past two weeks."

He studied the top of her head as she stared at the screen. "And if you don't?"

"Then I hope the financial data gives us something." She was about to go on, but the thought of not finding Ben Iblis was too hard to even contemplate.

"We'll track him down, Eve."

"Yeah," she smiled, wanting to believe it. Needing to believe it.

"I understand you put Keller under surveillance."

"Yes."

"Why?"

"What do you mean?"

"I mean, why Keller specifically?" Vogel asked. "There's forty or fifty people on Bradley's staff. Why pick Keller?"

"I had lunch with him today."

"Oh, Jesus," Vogel said, rolling his eyes and staring at the ceiling. "Do I need to sit down for this?"

"I talked to him about Bradley."

"I am going to need to sit down."

"He knows about it," she said. "One way or another, he knows."

"Every time I talk to you, Eve, every goddamn time, I've got to down antacid. What the hell are you doing warning him? You know sure as hell he's going to talk to Bradley about it, and you're still sitting here trying to track down the data!"

"One of them will screw up," she explained. "Somebody over there will do something that'll give us what we want."

"How do you know?"

"Trust me."

"Trust you? Really? That's your answer?" He stared at her. "I'm having a hell of a time not relieving you and ordering you to see a shrink."

"If that were the case, you'd of already done it."

Vogel shook his head. "Twelve hours, Eve. You've got twelve hours."

Watching him walk away, she smiled. That was plenty of time.

Chapter 13

Wogan clutched the glass tumbler in his right hand as the Gulfstream's engines thundered, rotating the sleek jet into the air. As the jet climbed, he rested his bald head on the back of the seat and closed his eyes. The scene he just left was one of the ugliest he ever saw, which was a big part of why this was his second drink in a little over an hour. His wife, quickly switching from wild hysteria to uncontrolled sobbing, was more than he could bear.

People died. He saw that in Vietnam. He saw it while building his business. It was a part of life. He made hundreds of millions of dollars on that fact. But the sight of his wife, his daughter's mother, inconsolable, was devastating. After all their years together, after all the support she offered him, he could not keep her from this uncontrollable grief.

His Janice. Gone.

He took another long gulp from the glass. Hopefully they could manage to keep his wife's mind in one piece through this. The pills her therapist prescribed would help, he knew. At least she would be able to sleep and start to heal. He paid the therapist a fortune, but it would be worth every penny over the next several days. At least until he could get back to Colorado. Then, maybe, a vacation. A month or two somewhere with a secluded beach. They could pick up the pieces. Put things back together. Move on.

Another drink.

Move on. They had to move on.

The ice in his glass clattered against its empty sides as he set it back on the small table next to his chair. The drone of the engines changed pitch, and his ear told him that they had leveled off.

"Another drink, Mr. Wogan?" Dean asked, coming down the aisle.

"Please," Wogan answered, opening his eyes.

Dean took his glass. "We should be in Washington in a few hours."

"Fastest jet in the fleet, right?"

"Yes."

Wogan watched as he walked back to the galley and poured more of the amber liquid in his glass, adding several more ice cubes. "Thank you," he said as Dean returned. "Lot of ice. Oban?"

"No," Dean replied. He added extra ice to this round, knowing Wogan would need it at the pace he was downing the drinks. "Macallan."

"Hard to go wrong with either one."

"It is." Dean sat down in the opposite seat, leaned forward, and rested his elbows on his knees. "There's been news."

"Morelli?"

Dean nodded. "And Ben Iblis."

"They're together," Wogan said, not missing a beat.

"Yes. They're together."

"Where?" Wogan hissed, his anger radiating an almost palpable aura.

Dean considered him for a moment. "Ireland."

"Where in Ireland?"

"Shannon. One of our contacts saw them arrive in Shannon. He alerted us, and we were able to get a surveillance team on them before they left the airport."

"Can we divert?"

"Divert?" Dean asked, surprised. "To Ireland?"

"Yes," Wogan said, sitting up. This was the best news he had in several days. "Refuel somewhere if we need to and fly on to Ireland."

"It's not that simple."

"Why the hell not?"

Dean looked away, folding his hands in his lap.

"Sweet Jesus. They lost them. They found them and then they lost them. Is that what you're telling me? How the hell is that possible?"

"Not exactly."

"Then what?"

"They're dead."

Wogan collapsed, deflated. He took another long drink, nearly draining the glass, and looked out one of the jet's windows. It was several minutes before he regained enough of his composure to continue. "They're dead? Who's dead? Morelli?"

"No, the surveillance team."

"How?"

"The secondary team reported the police were investigating reports of a car off the road south of Limerick."

"A car accident?" Wogan asked, surprised.

"No. The police are keeping the investigation under wraps, but we were able to learn the original team was shot multiple times. From the reports, the car was riddled with gunfire."

Wogan nodded, still looking out the window. "And no leads on Morelli or Ben Iblis? No idea where they ended up? Where they were headed?"

"They could be anywhere in the country by now, or headed anywhere in Europe."

"My orders were clear that they should be shadowed but not approached? Reports on their movements only?"

"Yes."

"Then what the hell happened?" Wogan demanded, turning back to Dean.

"I can only surmise their surveillance was detected."

"You can only surmise?" Wogan asked, his eyes wide. "And what? Ben Iblis took the team out? Jesus Christ! Find out!"

"I will."

"And they're sure they were together? Morelli was with Ben Iblis?"

"Yes."

"Shit!" Wogan swore. He shook his head and rubbed his mustache with his hand. "So she did leave. She ended up with Ben Iblis."

Dean took a deep breath and nodded. "I know you want them."

"You bet your ass I want them! I've spent a million dollars on a contract that wasn't fulfilled. I've spent countless millions on an operative that leaves the company on a whim, on what I can only assume was probably 'the next best offer,' without even consulting me! Without even giving me the chance to counter-offer! A woman I shared my bed with!"

"Maybe he made her an offer she couldn't refuse."

"What, like he kidnapped her?"

Dean shrugged and held up his hands. "I don't know. Until we speak with her, I wouldn't rule it out. She's capable of anything."

"Hmph," Wogan snorted. He wanted to believe it. Desperately. But his rational being would not let him. There was too much at stake.

"What will you tell your daughter?"

"My daughter is dead," Wogan replied, looking him in the eye.

"What will you tell Morgan?"

"I don't know."

"Do you think she'll help?" Dean asked.

"Would you?"

"No."

***

Ben Iblis pulled the Land Rover on to a small lane outside of Killarney. Its headlights cast shadows on either side of the narrow track, and Morelli was surprised to find that the surrounding fields were so much lower. The lane narrowed, dropping steeply on each side, the headlights barely flirting with the tops of shrubs and grasses. After a few minutes, they made a sharp turn, and the lane dropped. The headlights picked out the shutters and windows of a small house. Ben Iblis made a wide circle around the front, drove along the side, and parked the SUV in a large barn.

Darkness enveloped them when he shut off the engine and killed the headlights. The only sound for several minutes was the occasional ticking of the cooling motor.

"You did very well back there," Ben Iblis finally said after running the events over in his mind.

"Thank you."

"Any idea who they were?"

"No."

"We need to find out."

"Obviously."

He peered at her in the darkness. "Is there something wrong?"

"No. But it's disconcerting to know we were identified."

"Yes," he agreed. "And you didn't recognize them?"

"I already answered that," she said, turning and matching his stare. "Why do you keep asking me?"

"Wogan's one of the few men with the resources to actively search for us. If those were his men, I thought you might recognize them."

"He doesn't keep many people on the direct payroll. He prefers contractors."

Ben Iblis folded his hands in his lap and stared out the windshield. "Do you think they were Wogan's men?"

"They could be anybody's men. You're one of the most wanted assassins in the world, and I just walked away from one of its most powerful organizations." She tried to pick out his features in the dark. "I would guess we both have a number of enemies."

"Do you consider Wogan an enemy?"

"No, but I can't speak for him. He may feel very differently."

"A difficult proposition," he said, opening his door, flooding the interior with light.

"But certainly one you've faced before," she replied, stepping out of the SUV and joining him in the barn. It reeked of damp earth, dust, and grass. Moonlight filtered through many holes in the roof, lighting the interior with an unearthly glow. Several empty stalls lined one wall, and a ladder led to a hay loft at one end. It was good-sized, with ample room for the tools and animals needed to maintain a large property.

"What is this place?" she asked.

"My sanctuary," he said, coming around the back of the SUV. "I bought it many years ago. I usually come here to recover after an operation."

"Only here? You don't move around?"

"Sometimes."

"But you always come back here. Eventually."

"Usually."

"That seems short-sighted."

"Perhaps," he said, "but it has been nearly two years since I was last here. I have several locations spread throughout the globe. I have bought and sold many properties in the past thirty years. This is the only one I kept for any length of time."

She picked her bag out of the trunk and threw it over her shoulder. "Why?"

"A lot of reasons. The serenity is unparalleled."

"It was a long drive from Shannon. Are there closer airports?"

"There are, but Shannon is the most convenient when I'm coming from the States. It is large enough that their security forces do not scrutinize flights too closely."

"Have you used the other airports, though?"

He nodded and said, "Please," motioning for her to precede him. They walked out of the barn into the still spring night. "There's over a hundred acres here. We're about twenty minutes from Killarney."

"Who takes care of the place?"

"An older woman who's lived here since she was a child."

"On this property?"

"Yes. I bought it from her husband. He ran into some financial difficulties years ago, and the bank was preparing to evict them. I purchased the property, cleared their remaining debts, and agreed to let them stay in the caretaker's cottage."

"Where is that?" she asked, looking around. Only the barn and the house were visible. "I don't see any other buildings."

"Down by the highway, just as you turn on to the property."

"I didn't see it."

"It's set back from the road," he explained.

"What happened to her husband?"

"He died four or five years ago."

They walked towards the house, Morelli inhaling deeply, savoring the taste of the air. "What do they think you do?"

"I'm a businessman. I have never offered more than that, and she is polite enough not to ask. I simply let her know when I will be arriving, and when I plan to leave. She takes care of the rest of the details, including the groceries."

They approached the front door, and as they got closer, Morelli saw the house was built out of a beautiful blue and gray stone. Two large windows flanked the solid wood door, and the faint glow of a dying fire sparkled through the glass.

"You spoke of trust earlier," he said, not turning to face her, his hand resting on the door handle.

"I did."

"You trusted that I would return after I dropped you on the highway earlier this evening."

"Yes."

"I think you appreciate what a large step I'm making here, introducing you to this place." He looked at her. "We are building a relationship, which, as you said, will be required if this is to work. In time, I may show you more."

If his words had any emotional impact, she didn't show it. "I understand."

The door opened without a sound, and Morelli sensed they were stepping into a large room, the embers she saw moments before provided the only light. Ben Iblis walked forward and switched on a small lamp next to a large leather recliner. It was a living room, centered around a stone fireplace and decorated in a distinctly masculine fashion. Two recliners, a couch, and a coffee table sat in front of the fireplace.

"That little action on the road cost us more time than I thought," he said, looking at the remains of the fire. "She was kind enough to light us a fire. I will get it going again in a few minutes." He turned and looked at her. "Your room is down this hall, third door on the left. Your bathroom is attached. Despite the exterior, I have redone most of everything inside."

"From what I could see of the exterior, it looked to be in very good shape."

"Thank you. They take excellent care of the place," he said, adding wood to the fire. "Take some time and freshen up. You should find everything you need in your room. I will prepare us something for dinner."

"Thank you," she said.

As she walked through the living room and entered the hall, he turned and called, "I store most of my library in there."

"Your library?" she asked, pausing at the threshold.

"Yes. My books. It's a small collection."

"I look forward to viewing it."

"Do you like books?" he asked, somewhat surprised.

"I appreciate many fine things."

He smiled. "It's at your disposal, then. Please make yourself at home."

"Thank you," she repeated, continuing down the hall.

She flipped the light switch as she stepped into the room. It was appointed in the same luxury as the living room, and, she started to guess, the rest of the small house. The dark wood floors continued through the hall into the room where a large, wood-framed bed stood against the far wall. A small desk, chair, and a built-in bookcase completed the arrangement.

Morelli closed the door behind her, dropped her bag on the bed, and examined the books lining the shelves. There were numerous classics ranging from ancient Greek to Chaucer and on, covering both fiction and non-fiction. The collection was not large, but she guessed there were probably close to a hundred books on its shelves.

Several looked brand new as she picked some at random and flipped through them. Others, though, were well used. There was a copy of Dumas's *The Count of Monte Cristo*, in the original French, with several loose pages. They nearly fell out as she gently read through the first several chapters, translating the text easily. It was one of her favorites, the epitome of complicated relationships and revenge. She smiled. There was always revenge.

She put the book back in its slot on the shelf and walked into the bathroom. It was large, probably an addition to the original structure, done tastefully in a beige tile and accented with marble. Modern and functional, there was a large shower, two vanities, and a porcelain tub.

Morelli stripped, dropping her clothes on the floor, and turned on the shower. After the last few minutes exploring the house, she was not surprised to find digital controls to modify the temperature and spray. She adjusted the settings using the keypad, turned the two showerheads on, and stepped into their spray. A decent assortment of scented washes and shampoos sat in a small niche cut in the crème-colored marble, and she selected several, washing both her body and her hair multiple times, lingering under the warmth of the spray and the steam.

As the water pounded her tired muscles and washed over her shoulders, she considered her current situation. The last five days were a whirlwind; the last two weeks the most tumultuous of her young life. She killed three people, but that was not the issue. She had killed people before. The girl in the apartment was routine. Part of the job.

However, the two men in the sedan tonight were worrisome for other reasons. Who found her after so short a time? When were they picked up? At the airport? Were they being targeted? It bore some consideration. Before she joined Ben Iblis, she was afforded the luxury of shielding. Wogan could use his influence to protect her. Now, though, that influence was gone. She read the intelligence. She saw the briefings. The FBI was interested in Ben Iblis. They kept him from the public top ten lists, but they wanted him. Badly.

Now they would want her, once they discovered she was involved in the latest contract. How long would that take? How long before they put it all together?

She considered, letting the spray run down her brown hair, her mind lost in the cascade of sound as it splattered against the marble under her feet. After all of these years, despite her age, she held few illusions about whether or not the FBI would put it together. They would. Eventually, they would recognize the act for what it was. Of that, she had no doubt.

And how did she feel about killing her lover's daughter? The thought was amusing, and her smile grew under the spray. It was a silly question. She didn't feel much of anything, if anything at all. It was a job. It was a profession.

She looked back at the shampoo and thought about washing her hair one more time. Whoever the caretaker was, she knew her business. Closing her eyes, she dipped her head back under one nozzle's spray and relished the droplets as they caressed her forehead, dribbled down her neck, and finally trailed along her back.

Could those men on the highway have been Interpol? Or even FBI? Could they have traced them to Ireland? The thought chilled her to the bone despite the hot spray. They were very cautious, but Ben Iblis was not in the States on a holiday. Did he do a job? He mentioned meeting with Wogan and targeting Bradley, but could he have been there doing something else? Could it have something to do with Morgan? Is that why he felt the need to visit her that morning?

She turned it over in her mind, looking at it from different angles. In the end she reached one conclusion: she needed to find out more about Morgan, and what, exactly, was her relationship with Ben Iblis.

Chapter 14

Keller propped his feet up on his desk and unbuttoned his suit coat. Washington lay spread out before him. He sat in the growing darkness, his eyes closed, an instrumental soundtrack playing softly through his computer speakers. The nature of his position afforded him a relatively spacious office in the confines of the Capitol complex, comfortable and well furnished, but the nature of the job caused him considerable mental and physical problems which, while curable, were not easily resolved at the end of a fifth of scotch. While he had not reached the bottom, the bottle did sit solitary and desolate on the far corner of his desk. He placed it there in the vain hope of making it harder to reach as he sat in the darkness, reminiscing about his friendship with Morgan, and the trouble she put him in.

He leaned forward and grabbed the bottle, pouring himself another generous measure before replacing the cork and pushing the bottle as far as his slender fingers would reach. The Scotch went down smoothly as he took a sip and set the glass back on his desk.

Morgan.

It was not a question of if she would come for the Senator, but when. The only person he was fooling was himself. Yes, Bradley's influence might delay things, but it would not hold up long. There was nothing to be done. Morgan would come for them, and the longer he put off asking for help, the harder it would be.

"Shit," he said, fumbling for the phone on his desk, knocking the receiver off the cradle before he was able to get a hold of it. With infinite patience, he dialed a number from memory.

"Yes," came a voice after several clicks and buzzes.

"Dean," Keller said, clutching the handset to his ear with a sweaty hand, "we need to meet."

There was a pause, then, "When?"

"Now."

"And if I'm in Colorado?"

"You're not," Keller objected. "I got Wogan's request to meet with the Senator tomorrow morning for breakfast. Don't bullshit me. I have the itinerary right here. You're at the brownstone now. The flight landed hours ago."

"Is it important?"

"Christ!" Keller blurted, exasperated. "Of course it's important."

"And it has to be in person?"

"Yes."

There was a loud sigh, crystal clear over the digital circuit. "When?"

"Now," Keller said, gripping the phone even tighter. "Our usual spot."

"Give me an hour," and the phone went dead in his ear.

Keller replaced the handset. An hour, he thought, settling back into his chair. Plenty of time to have another drink. He drained what was left of his glass and reached for the bottle. As he poured himself another measure, he hit the speed dial on the phone and requested a cab. He might be drunk, but he wasn't stupid.

***

Morgan drove home, struggling to keep her eyes open on the nearly deserted beltway. It was the last thing she wanted to be doing, but she knew she was barely functional. There were too many days without enough sleep, and if she did not get some soon, she would collapse. A shower, a few hours in bed, and she would head back into the office.

Her phone chirped as she pulled off the highway on to the boulevard that would take her to her townhome. "Morgan," she muttered, holding it to her ear.

"Hey, it's Gebog. Sorry to bother you this late."

"What's up?" Morgan asked, more chipper than she could have ever possibly felt at that moment, her arms guiding her home on muscle memory alone.

"We got the trace back from the wire transfer. It originated on a computer at the Capitol."

"So either the good Senator or one of his staff."

"Looks that way."

"Are we sure?" Morgan asked. "You've double checked?"

"We've got the IP and the MAC address."

"Mac address?" Morgan asked, confused.

"According to the tech guys, it's a unique address assigned to each computer's network card. The card the computer uses to connect to the internet."

"And they're unique?"

"Supposedly," Gebog said. "Though I guess it's possible for them to be spoofed."

"How likely is that?"

"Your guess is as good as mine. The tech pukes sounded pretty confident, though, so I'm guessing we can trace it down to one of those boxes without too much effort."

Morgan parked the car and concentrated on the conversation, her brain re-engaging, desperately trying to shrug off the overwhelming blanket of exhaustion. "Get a warrant for Bradley's capitol offices. I want those computers."

"We may have problems with immunity."

"I don't really give a shit about his Senatorial immunity," Morgan said. "Besides, it doesn't protect him, or his office, from searches authorized by the courts. I'm not arresting him, I'm just confiscating and searching his computers. The judge should be able to see the difference."

"Alright, we'll get started on it."

"Expedite. It took us most of the day to trace that financial transaction back to one of those computers. I don't want to end up empty handed. Not now."

"Will do."

"I'm going to try for three or four hours of sleep, then I'll be back." Morgan stifled a yawn. "I want those computers locked up before Congress returns for work in the morning. We can't risk that whoever sent those funds will come back and delete whatever evidence is on the hard drive."

"If they haven't done so already."

"Exactly. Three or four hours, and I'll be back."

"Will do, boss. Do you want me to call Vogel?"

"No. No sense bothering him with this until we've got something a little more concrete. Work on the search warrant and get a team over to the offices to seize the equipment. Work with Homeland Security and Treasury if you need to, but it get done."

"What about the press?"

"Try to do it quietly."

Gebog laughed. "Right."

***

The cab dropped Keller at the curb of a bar a few blocks from downtown Alexandria, the Indian driver eyeing him carefully as he handed over a crisp Benjamin. "Keep the change," he muttered, slurring every syllable while opening the cab door and staggering onto the sidewalk. He waited until the cab pulled away, trying to get his bearings in the chilly evening. The bar was up a short flight of stairs, discreetly located above a fish and chips restaurant, shuttered and dark this time of night.

Keller climbed the stairs, grasping the handrail for support. Before pulling open the door, he paused on the landing and caught his breath, a blue light casting a sallow pallor over his face. This was getting to be too much, he thought to himself, stifling a belch and swallowing the bile that accompanied it. He fought the urge to retch over the railing and forced himself to open the door.

It was a small affair, styled as an early twentieth century speakeasy with comfortable chairs and lounges. Several private rooms lined the back wall. Much to his happiness, it was virtually deserted, and he smiled drunkenly as he passed the well-dressed hostess and picked his way to one of the private rooms, settling on a blue suede couch.

The hostess followed him, waited until he was seated, then said, as politely as she could, "Mr. Keller, we'll be closing soon."

"I know," he said. "And I apologize for the late hour, but I simply must have some time to meet with Mr. Dean."

She considered him for a moment, but all she could manage through her anger was a simple, "I see."

"I'm sure something can be arranged," he continued, pulling out an American Express. "If you would be so kind as to bring a bottle of the Glenlivet twenty-one year?"

She took the credit card, but didn't leave.

"Please show Mr. Dean in when he arrives," Keller continued, trying to focus on her features. "I'm sure Mr. Wogan will appreciate your hospitality."

"Of course," she said, finally relenting at Wogan's name. "And you won't be long? We're near closing."

"Not too long."

She did not look happy, but she left the room, closing the doors behind her.

Keller sat back and closed his eyes. It did not feel like long, but suddenly something kicked the side of his foot hard enough to make him wince, and he realized with some shame that he fell asleep. Opening an eye, he licked his lips, smacking his tongue against the cottonmouth dryness.

Dean was dressed well in grey slacks, a baby blue shirt open at the collar, and a matching sport coat. "Can I pour you a drink?" he asked, in total control, as he walked in front of Keller and picked up the bottle of scotch.

"Please," Keller croaked, sitting up and rubbing his hands over his face.

Dean opened the bottle, poured two glasses, and sat in a leather armchair.

Keller nodded his thanks and added a large dose of water from a glass carafe on the table. "Thank you," he said after taking a sip.

"What did you need to discuss?" Dean asked, crossing one leg over the other and assuming a bored expression. "You said it was important."

"It is."

"What is it?"

"An FBI agent came to see me today."

"About what?"

"Bradley."

Dean looked pensive. "In what context?"

"They're starting an investigation."

"Why?"

"They found the money transfer."

Dean turned it over in his mind, though he already had some notion of why Keller requested the meeting. It was really only a matter of time before the FBI discovered the funds transfer. Wogan planned on it, but Keller obviously did not know that. "What did you tell them?"

"Nothing," Keller said, shifting on the couch. "It wasn't a them. It was a her, and it wasn't so much an official investigation as a friendly tip, with a bit of fact finding mixed in to assuage her conscience."

"Who was the agent?"

"Evelyn Morgan."

"One of their best," Dean said, sipping his Scotch, feigning disinterest.

"Yes," Keller agreed. "Do you think they know?"

"Know what?"

"Know that Wogan had me transfer that money from Bradley's account."

"I doubt it," Dean said, still looking bored. "My guess is they're fishing. They found the wire transfer, but they don't know who initiated it."

"What if they know it's me?" Keller blurted.

"Calm yourself, Mr. Keller. This isn't the time for rash decisions." He picked a piece of lint off his pants. "You went to school with Morgan, as I recall."

"Yes, I did."

"At the Academy, correct?"

"Yes."

Dean nodded, thoughtfully. "Then this might work to our advantage."

"I don't see how."

"She obviously trusts you."

"That won't stop her once they discover who made that wire transfer!" Keller protested.

"And how will they find that?" Dean asked patiently. "There are hundreds of staffers under Bradley's thumb."

"Who have access to his personal accounts?"

Dean still looked unconcerned. "I wouldn't worry. If you keep your head, you stand to gain from this little inconvenience."

"Inconvenience? Is that what you're calling it?"

Dean shrugged.

"Is that what Wogan's calling it?"

Dean's eyes turned cold. "Mr. Wogan has no knowledge of this affair. You should know that by now. He has no knowledge of any of these affairs, regardless of whether or not he ordered you directly."

"Right," Keller said, rolling his eyes.

Leaning forward, Dean pierced Keller's bloodshot eyes. "I suggest you learn how to say that. Except that you might substitute 'I' for 'Mr. Wogan.' I doubt he'll look upon any indiscretion favorably."

"I am the Senator's Chief of Staff!"

"You're a poor, ill-used, overworked gay man, Mr. Keller," Dean said in a calm, measured tone. "I'm sure I don't need to illustrate the position that puts you in, especially as the Senator's Chief of Staff."

Keller looked like he might say something, but he sank back into the couch, deflated, burying his head in his hands and mumbling incoherently.

"I wouldn't concern yourself with the FBI," Dean continued, draining the last of his scotch. "Morgan will do her job, but there's little to tie you to this whole business. Especially if you keep your mouth shut."

With a shaky hand, Keller reached for the bottle and poured himself another glass, knocking it back in one large gulp. He poured himself another and looked like he might toss that back, too, but thought better of it and sat clutching the glass, staring into the liquid.

"Are you still friends?" Dean asked.

"What?" Keller asked, not taking his eyes from his drink.

"You and Morgan. Are you still friends?"

"Yes, we are."

"Good friends?"

"How do you know who your friends are in this town?" Keller's eyes drooped. "But yes. We have lunch every month or two. I think we're still good friends. As good as you can get in this miserable shithole of a town."

"Then that creates a conflict of interest. I certainly wouldn't worry about this investigation."

Keller looked up. "That's easy for you to say."

"Please," Dean said. "Between the Senator's influence and this potential conflict of interest, once it comes to light, you don't have anything to worry about. Blame it on some nameless zealot Bradley keeps around as a volunteer. I'm sure there are three or four you could choose from."

"You have all the answers."

"Yes, I do."

"So Wogan won't help me?"

"Mr. Wogan's an extremely busy man. Besides, I don't see what sort of help he may be able to provide."

"So that's it, then?"

"What's it?"

"You're hanging me out to dry."

"Don't be so dramatic, Mr. Keller." Dean set his empty glass back on the table. "You're not in any immediate danger. Now, if you'll excuse me, I have other business to attend to. If something does come up, please let me know."

Keller watched him walk from the room. It was not a question of how dangerous a game this would eventually become when he accepted Wogan's offer of employ. He knew it could potentially turn deadly, but that was the risk he accepted in return for Wogan's lucrative rewards. What he did not foresee was being completely abandoned. Upon consideration, though, that was naive. This was a dangerous game, and it was clear Wogan was not going to help. Perhaps, though, if he put his trust in Morgan, he might still make it out with his life.

Chapter 15

Morgan bolted awake at the sound of her phone rattling on the bedside table. The nightmare did not have enough time to run its full course last night. They were still in the car, driving down the road, Baker laughing maniacally in the backseat when she was forced awake. Rubbing her weary eyes, she swung her long legs from under the comforter and picked it up. Three and a half hours, she thought. Not nearly long enough. With several cups of coffee, she would survive another day.

"Morgan," she said, rubbing her eyes.

"Boss, it's Gebog," the blonde said. "I've got some news."

"About the search at the Capitol?"

"No, we're on our way there now, actually. I should be able to give you something on that in a couple of hours."

"Ok, then what?"

"I just heard from the team tailing Keller. Apparently, he's on his way to the Capitol in a taxi."

"So?" Morgan asked. "He works there."

"Right, I know. That's not the interesting part. They called because of where he just came from, and who he met with."

"Who?"

"Thomas Dean."

Morgan racked her tired brain, and it took her a minute to put it together. "Wogan's man?"

"Yes."

"That's interesting." She did not know of any official link between Dean and Keller, especially not at two or three in the morning. What the hell were they doing together?

"I thought it was a little odd, too," Gebog said. "Figured I'd better give you a call."

"Yeah, thanks. I appreciate it. Call the surveillance team and make sure they stick on him, especially with the execution of the search warrant."

"Will do."

Morgan flipped her phone closed, and sat on the edge of the bed turning it over in her head. Keller probably worked with Wogan a good deal because of Senator Bradley's ties to the defense industry. If that were the reason for this meeting, though, she would expect Wogan to appear personally and the business to be conducted at a more reasonable hour. Something was going on, but whether or not it was related to her investigation, she had no idea.

There were too many moving pieces, she thought, glancing at her phone. Maybe a quick jog would be a good idea. It had been a while since she got any meaningful exercise, and it would help clear her head, forcing her body to wake up. She stood, put on a pair of athletic shorts, an old t-shirt with 'Air Force' stenciled across the front, and wrapped her jogging pack around her waist. It held two water bottles and a discreet pocket for her forty caliber Sig Sauer P224, her concealed carry weapon of choice.

The first flecks of light tickled the eastern horizon as she turned left out of her townhouse, jogging lightly along the sidewalk until she hit the street. Once on the blacktop, she picked up her pace and let her mind wander, trying to think of something other than Nichols and their failure to catch Ben Iblis.

A mile went by before she really even noticed, her mind so absorbed in reliving those last awful minutes of Nichols' life, trying desperately to come up with some solution, some answer, some way she could have gotten them out of it. But it was not any use, and she ran harder when her mind kept coming to the same conclusion regardless of how she approached the situation. The only solution would have been to discover Baker's duplicity earlier.

Sweat poured from her body as she pushed herself harder, passing two miles in a little over fifteen minutes. The only thing she could do for Nichols was to get Ben Iblis, but that trail was growing colder by the minute. Maybe there was something on the computer in Bradley's office that would get them closer. A communications medium, a digital trail, something that would give them an edge. There was also Baker's financial records. That analysis was not yet complete.

Her townhouse appeared in the distance as she closed in on the end of her typical five mile loop. A silver Jaguar, parked in front of her townhouse, caught her eye when she got closer, and her pace slowed. There were two occupants, one in the driver's seat, one in the back, sitting serenely in the early morning air. She approached them from the right, on the passenger's side, keeping as many vehicles as possible between her and the Jaguar. It was not a sense of danger that caused her caution, but the need to confirm who was waiting for her.

Before she crossed the last manicured divider, its mulch, ferns, and evergreens perfectly trimmed, she paused, catching the last of her breath and resting her hands on her hips. If she had any lingering doubt, it was dispelled by that hawk nose as the Jaguar's passenger turned his head to his right.

"Christ," she swore, picking at the mulch under her right shoe.

The security team would not be far away. She took a quick glance at the parking lot and found them almost immediately: a black SUV, two rows back and to the left. They spotted her, the man in the passenger seat busy punching numbers on his mobile phone. As she glanced back at the Jaguar, she saw its driver answer his mobile, nod twice, then say something to his passenger.

"Christ," she swore again and shook her head. She knew exactly who was in the back of the Jag. What she did not know was why.

She passed between two ferns and walked towards her front door with long, purposeful strides. Hawk-nose opened his door and stepped out when she was still twenty feet away. He was dressed in a superbly tailored three-piece black suit with silver pinstripes. A miniaturized Naval Academy ring tie-pin held his tie exactly centered, and the early morning dawn made his bald head glow with an almost simmering fire.

Morgan stopped in the middle of the parking lot, a row of spaces separating her from the Jag. There was an inevitability to this, she knew, but it really did not make it easier.

"Andrew," she said as a way of greeting, crossing that final twenty feet.

He offered his hand and said, "Hello, Eve."

She looked at it, hanging there in the air, well manicured, moisturized, soft, few liver spots to denote his true age, but she did not take it. Instead, she arched an eyebrow and met his eyes with a cold stare. "I was going to make some scrambled eggs. Want to come inside?"

"Is that an invitation to breakfast?" he asked, a half-hearted attempt at a smile curving one side of his mouth.

"No."

He withdrew his hand and pursed his lips. "I see."

"A little extra security this trip?" she asked, nodding at the black SUV in the distance.

"A little."

"Dean wasn't up to the task?"

"Just a routine precaution."

"Right," she said, not believing it in the least.

He walked around her and opened the trunk. "I brought some groceries."

She closed her eyes, her back to him, and said, "Groceries." She tried to control her temper. "Why are you here?"

"Can't a man see his daughter?"

She turned and faced him, a fire growing behind her eyes. "Not in your case. When have you ever stopped by just to see me? Or even called just to talk? All these years, Andy, and not a damn thing other than some fucked up version of an obligation."

"I'm sorry."

It took her by surprise, which was rare, especially with this man. She thought she figured out their relationship years ago. "What did you say?"

He looked up from staring into the trunk. "I said I'm sorry. It's something I should have said years ago."

The regret choking his voice shocked her to her core.

"Look, Eve," he said, still looking at the trunk as she gripped one edge of the Jaguar, trying to process a sudden rush of emotions, "I know I didn't do everything right at the Falls, and I know it's not something I can fix overnight."

A biting reproof was perched on the edge of her tongue, but she bit it back and waited.

"But I'd like to start. I'd like to try."

He reached into the trunk and tried to pick up three paper bags full of groceries. The first two bags were easy, but he struggled holding them while lifting the third. Morgan watched him dispassionately for a while, trying to cope with the blast of emotions that threatened to overwhelm her exhausted mind.

"Here, let me help you," she finally said, taking one of the bags and leading the way to her townhouse.

It was still dark inside, the pale light of dawn desperate to penetrate her wooden-slat blinds. She set the grocery bag on the kitchen counter and flipped on the lights. "Have a seat."

"Thanks."

"I'd offer you a cup of coffee, but I don't think I have any."

"There's some in one of the bags," he said, taking a quick survey of her modest kitchen. It was efficient. A stove, refrigerator, and microwave sat galley-style, with a small bar doubling as the serving and eating area. Wogan took one of the bar stools and sat with his hands folded on the laminate counter.

"I have a hard time functioning without at least a pot in the morning," he said.

"So you knew I was going to invite you in?"

"No," he admitted, "but I'm glad you did."

She cut open the vacuum-sealed bag and filled her coffee maker, carefully measuring both the grounds and the liquid before turning the machine on. The whole situation was bewildering. It had been over a decade since she last saw her father in person, and he made it perfectly clear then that she was on her own, that he did everything he was ever going to do.

"So why are you here?" she asked, carefully sealing the opened coffee grounds in a plastic bag.

"I can't just want to have breakfast with my daughter?"

Morgan pierced him again with that green-eyed stare. "Like how you wanted to have breakfast with your daughter last week? Or last month? Or that time you invited your daughter over for breakfast last year? Or any time in the last fifteen years?"

He moved his hands from the counter to his lap, but he did not look away.

"How about the time you showed up for my latest promotion celebration? Or that time you were there to congratulate me on graduating from Quantico? Or fuck Quantico. What about that time you gave me a big hug and said how proud you were that I graduated from the Academy in the top ten percent of my class? Or when mom died?" She stared at him, anger flaring behind her eyes. "Where were you then, Andy?"

"I'm sorry."

"You said that already."

"I am."

"It's a little late now."

"That's what I'm afraid of."

Morgan took a carton of eggs from the refrigerator, cracked two in a bowl, and started to whisk them with a little milk.

"I like mine over medium," Wogan said.

"Congratulations."

She cooked them quickly, then put them on a plate. Standing in the middle of the kitchen, the bar separating her from her father, she silently ate her eggs and tried everything she could come up with to not think about the man sitting in front of her.

"Look, Eve...," he started, but either the words failed him, or he did not know how to continue.

"Just go," she said, almost inaudibly, the last of her eggs nearly gone.

He stared at her, his face impassive.

"You need to go," she repeated.

He pursed his lips, shrugged, stood up, and pushed his stool back under the bar. "Janice is dead."

She closed her eyes and took a deep breath. The lack of emotion in his voice was in stark contrast to the naked sorrow when he apologized in the parking lot. "How?"

"A fire."

Setting her plate down on the counter, she said, "You should go." She did not need to deal with that. Not now. Not after everything that happened that week, not when her own problems threatened to consume her.

"Alright," he said with a nod, and let himself out.

She stood in the kitchen shaking with rage. Was it grief, she asked herself, leaning back against the fridge. No protest, no fight, no argument. Just resignation at her dismissal. It was a far cry from the man she remembered; from the man she read about in the papers. He was a shadow of the man she thought she knew.

***

Sitting on the porch with a cup of coffee steaming on the table beside him, Ben Iblis stared across the wide green fields. The sun rose several hours ago, lighting the countryside through a beautiful blue sky, but it did not bring him any warmth. He wondered if it ever would again. It was a stupid sentiment, one that caught him off guard, but as he sat on the porch surrounded by the serenity of the countryside, he could not help but wonder.

No one was more successful in his profession, and that success afforded him a lucrative lifestyle that would make many wantonly jealous. If he retired now, he could live a handsome lifestyle on any continent in the world, flying between large estates when he needed a change of scenery. He completed every goal he ever set down for himself, and yet something was missing.

Days ago, when he recruited Morelli, he told himself that he needed a student. After working with her, though, he was not convinced. As he surmised, she was a gifted operative, but he deceived himself in just how gifted. There were no illusions in just what Morelli was after. She was ambitious. She wanted the business, and he would give it to her, eventually, but he doubted that would fulfill that growing emptiness he felt in his soul.

Maybe it was the episode last night, but something was different. Something changed. The serenity he longed for, when he decided to retire, but before he decided to accept Morelli as a student, tugged at his soul. This business would destroy him, he was convinced, if he did not get out.

"Good morning," he said, catching sight of Morelli in the doorway as she stepped onto the porch.

"Good morning," she replied. "This is an exquisite view."

He took a sip of his coffee, his brown eyes gazing across the open fields. "Yes, it is."

They spent several minutes in silence, each lost in their own thoughts, nearly mesmerized by the way the breeze danced across the lush green grass. Ben Iblis was grateful she did not feel the need to fill the silence with needless chatter. After the last several weeks, a peaceful silence was the only thing he needed.

"You're up early," he finally said, breaking their reverie.

"A hard habit to break. How long have you been awake?"

"A while."

"Trouble sleeping?"

"A little," he admitted. "There is coffee. The machine is by the refrigerator. There are mugs in the cabinet above it."

"Thank you."

"I also made some eggs and potatoes. I covered them and put them in the oven to keep warm."

"Thank you."

He studied her. She was dressed simply in a sweater and green cargo pants. "I meant what I said last night about making yourself at home. Please feel free to use whatever you need."

She turned and looked at him. "I appreciate it. Your hospitality has been wonderful."

He nodded his acknowledgement.

"When will we meet your contacts?" she asked.

His eyes narrowed, and he studied her. "So anxious."

"There's much to learn."

"All in good time. We'll meet with them soon."

With a reluctant nod, she turned and went back into the house.

It was difficult to get mad at her. He remembered being that age, just starting out, very anxious to make a name for himself. That first hit now haunted him every night. Astia's uncomprehending face at the sight of her parent's bodies came to him again and again. Before that night, before he shot them, he remembered being excited at the prospect of that first contract, of traveling to Cyprus, of the planning and detail that went into the hit. Now, he wondered what he might tell that same kid, knowing the outcome.

Chapter 16

Wogan walked down the concrete sidewalk and paused just in front of Dean as he stood holding the rear passenger door open. The sun was trying to creep over the eastern horizon, but it did little to increase Wogan's spirits. The discussion with Morgan did not go well, but, upon reflection, he was not surprised.

"How'd it go?" Dean asked.

"About as I expected," Wogan replied.

"So, not well."

"No, not at all," Wogan said, turning his back and looking away. "I'm not sure why I thought it might go differently."

"She wasn't happy to see us here this morning," Dean said, watching the back of Wogan's head.

"Of course not. She's an obstinate woman."

"Like her father."

Wogan turned sharply, but bit down his initial harsh reply. Instead, he said, "It runs in the family."

Dean nodded. "So what do you want to do?"

"I need to think about it." He sat down in the Jaguar's opulent leather, letting Dean close the door behind him.

"Where do you want to go?" Dean asked after he climbed into the driver's seat.

Wogan thought for a moment. "The Capitol. I want to talk to Bradley."

"Do you think he'll be in the office this early?"
"Perhaps. It'll take a while to get down there. We may be able to speak with Keller if Bradley's not in yet."

Nodding, Dean put the car in gear and used his mobile phone to call the security detail and update them on their destination. "What are you going to do about Morgan?" he asked, setting the phone down.

"Asking her directly didn't work. She didn't even let me get far enough into an explanation to even ask the question. So we'll simply need to exert a bit of influence on the overall situation."

"What do you mean?"

"I'll call the Director on the way to the Capitol," Wogan said. "I'm sure he'll find some use for my talented daughter. Letting Janice go without an investigation would be a mistake. Morgan may not like it, but she needs to know who's in charge." He sank deeper into his seat with a heavy sigh. Even if he had been paying attention, it was doubtful he would have seen Morgan's head in her kitchen window, watching with a distracted interest as they pulled out of the parking lot.

***

Turning away from the window, Morgan leaned against the counter and folded her arms across her chest. She never met her half-sister, never spoke to her, even over the phone, but the news of her death made her pause. For it to have shaken Wogan so severely made her reconsider everything she knew about him. After the episode at the falls, and her mother's death, she was on her own. Which made his actions that morning much harder to associate with the man she knew, she thought, rubbing her tired eyes. Was it remorse? Did he really want to try and repair their relationship because she was the only daughter he had left?

That would be more like the man she knew.

Regardless, it was not something she could spend much time contemplating. She had an investigation to run, and she needed to get back downtown. She stripped off her jogging attire on her way to the bathroom and showered quickly. When she came back into the bedroom, she found her phone chirping a subtle reminder that she had a new voicemail. She picked it up and listened to the message, smiling when she heard Gebog report the successful execution of the search warrant.

She dressed in her typical gray pantsuit and hurried out to her car, dialing Gebog's number on her mobile.

"Gebog," the agent answered after two rings.

"It's Morgan."

"Long time no talk."

"Yeah. Listen, I got your voicemail. The search warrant went well?"

"About as well as we could expect. The good Senator wasn't there, and his staff only put up a light protest."

"And the press?"

"Haven't gotten wind of it yet, to my knowledge. Apparently, even they take some kind of a break at four in the morning."

"It's only a matter of time, I'm sure," Morgan said.

"I'm sure."

"Anything from the computers yet?"

"No. The lab is working on them, though. Vogel cleared the docket for several of the techs and made this one a priority. I think he's worried about what may happen once Bradley's lawyers get their hands on the search warrant."

"Smart man."

"One of the best," Gebog agreed.

"I'm on my way in," Morgan said, putting her car in gear. "Should be there in a little while. I'll relieve you when I get there. Sounds like you could use some sleep."

"I could use a lot of sleep," Gebog joked.

"Couldn't we all?"

"I'll give you a call if I get anything before you get here, but I'd guess it'll be a while until we hear something."

"Yep, thanks," Morgan said, then flipped the phone closed.

She was glad that the execution of the warrant went so well. The longer they could keep it under wraps, the better off they would be. Including Bradley, she thought to herself. He would want to keep the press at bay as long as possible while his lawyers worked on getting in front of everything.

Her phone rang. "Morgan," she answered.

"Your agents were very professional this morning, Eve," Ben Keller said, his high-pitched voice clear through the digital circuit.

"I'm glad to hear it," she hedged.

"Efficient, too," he continued. "They stripped the offices of everything electronic. I think one of them even grabbed my graphing calculator."

"Can't be too careful these days."

"Apparently. You sound tired."

"It was a long night."

"Get any sleep?" he asked.

"A little."

"Must be hard coordinating all of those searches," Keller said in a thoughtful, musing tone.

"All of what searches?"

"You were obviously looking for something specific. I've gotten calls from two other offices. You hit several locations at the same time."

"More efficient that way," she replied, her eyes narrowing. "No need to track down things that might've been misplaced."

"So it would seem."

"What were you doing there this morning, Ben?"

"My job," he countered. "But don't worry. I didn't mention a word to the Senator or any other staff."

She wanted to throw the phone through the windshield. "Do you have any idea how that looks? People know we're friends, Ben. They know we went to school together. Most folks know we even have lunch on occasion."

"Relax, Eve."

"Relax?" she asked, incredulous. "I told you how important this was, not only to me, but to the country. I'm not hunting a burglar or some white-collar baby boomer wanted for tax evasion."

"I know."

"You're into something way over your head, but you haven't said a damn thing to me about it."

He didn't respond.

"Does it have something to do with Wogan? Is that why you met with Dean last night?"

"What?" he blurted, a sense of panic coming through the digital circuit.

"You met last night with Thomas Dean," she repeated, knowing she had him. "Why don't you meet me somewhere? We can talk about it."

"You've got me under surveillance?" he asked, his voice rising even higher.

"Let's meet. I'll buy you a cup of coffee."

"I don't think that's a good idea."

She tried a different approach. "Are you free for lunch?"

"Not today."

"Tomorrow?"

"Probably not for a long time."

It was a strange answer, and it took her a few seconds to process it. "Because of this investigation?"

"Look," he said, ignoring her question, "I want to ask you something before this goes any further. At lunch yesterday you mentioned losing someone very close to you."

"Yes," she replied, wary.

"Have you read the Post this morning?"

"No, why?"

"There was an article in there, way back, about two FBI agents who were killed in the line of duty last week." He paused. "Your friend. Arnon Nichols --"

"And Timothy Baker," she bit out. The press did not yet know about Baker's treason. Vogel was working on that release still, she knew.

"Nichols was close to you?"

"Extremely," she said, fighting the constriction in her chest.

There was a long pause, and Morgan thought she might have lost the connection. "Ben?" she asked. "Are you still there?"

"Yeah, I'm still here," he replied, his voice different. Somber. "Listen, I came to a conclusion last night."

"About?" she asked, confused by the entire string of the conversation.

"Are your men still around? Are they still following me?"

"Yes. What decision did you come to last night?"

He sighed. "Do you remember, back at the Academy, when you backed me up all those times... all those parties we ended up at in the Springs?"

"I remember a lot about those years, Ben."

"But when we'd get back and you'd cover my ass? You were one of the few that ever cared, Eve."

"We were friends," she said, her brow furrowed trying to figure out where this conversation was going. "Of course I cared."

"I know. We still are friends. Trust me. I've got to go, though."

The finality of the statement scared her, and she stared at the phone before flipping it closed. This was not the Ben she knew. In all their years, nothing like this ever happened. The conversation was all over the place. She was convinced, more than ever, he was directly involved.

The car's tires chirped as she sped into the underground garage, squealing into the first available space. She picked up her mobile and ran for the elevators, dialing on her way.

"Gebog," the agent answered.

"It's Morgan," she said, punching the elevator call button.

"What's up? You sound out of breath."

Morgan ignored her. "The team that's on Keller, they're still there, right?"

"Yeah, Kloser's over there with several agents. Why?"

"Have him pick up Keller for questioning."

"Really?" Gebog asked, surprised. "Why?"

"I'll tell you in a minute, I'm just downstairs." She stepped on to the elevator. "Call Kloser and have him do it. If you can't get a hold of him, call everybody on the surveillance detail until you get a hold of someone, but either way bring Keller down here for questioning."

"Yes, ma'am."

Morgan flipped her phone closed and replaced it on her hip. How involved was Keller? What the hell was he talking about when he asked about Nichols? Did he wire that money to the terrorist cell? She racked her brain. Why would he do that, though? Following Bradley's orders?

No, she thought. Not Keller.

She stepped on the elevator and punched the button for her desired floor. The doors closed and she rode in silence, lost in her thoughts. She had known Keller for nearly fifteen years. It was impossible for her to grasp that he might be wrapped up in all of this.

The doors parted, and she walked down a long, narrow hall. Cheap, white linoleum masked the sound of her black shoes. She stopped in the doorway of a tiny closet of an office, not daring to enter for fear of stumbling on the piles of books, manuscripts, documents, and technical manuals piled like monoliths on every free surface, including the floor. Shelves bolted to the walls sagged like fat women, overburdened and overworked for far too many years. Buried in the middle of this bedlam was a small pressboard desk, almost completely obscured by papers, magazines, and documents. Behind the desk sat a tall, very thin man, his face buried in a trade magazine. What little hair left on his head was so grey it was almost white. A pair of black-rimmed reading glasses sat perched on his dwarfish nose, a beaded chain running from their ear pieces, and around his neck.

"If you're not here to congratulate me," he said without looking up, "just turn around and get the hell out."

"Congratulate you?" she asked, puzzled. "For what?"

Charles Runfo gazed up over the top of his reading glasses. "You haven't heard?"

"Heard what?"

"That idiot FBI director promoted me to head the lab down in Quantico."

Morgan's eyes nearly burst from their sockets. "Are you serious?"

"Yes," Runfo said, whipping off his reading glasses and letting them fall to his chest, held there by the beaded chain. "I've got the damn memo here somewhere." He sifted through several piles of paper before coming to the right one. Pulling it out, he offered it to her.

Picking her way through the piles on the floor, she took the paper and scanned it quickly. "Charlie, this is wonderful! Congratulations!"

"I don't see how," he harrumphed. "Do you have any idea what a pain in the ass it's gonna be to get down to Quantico every day?"

She smiled kindly. "You could just rent something down there."

"What, and give up my house here?" He shook his head. "Jeanne's gonna throw a damn fit. We just got that brownstone how we want it."

Morgan leaned forward and kissed him gently on his mostly bald head. "I think it's incredible news. And, knowing Jeanne, she's going to say the same thing. It's incredible news! She'll be so proud of you."

"Hmph," he sighed, looking at the memo one more time before throwing it on top of a pile. "So if you're not here to congratulate me, you must be here to ruin my day."

"Why would you say something like that?"

"Because that's what you always do, Eve. Ever since I first met you. Remember that stint you pulled here as a cadet? I've never seen so many ruined experiments in my entire career."

"That's not fair," she protested. "Some of those tests were rigged."

"Right, and you figured out most of them."

"I figured out every one but one, and you know it."

"You were one of the best," he admitted with a small smile. "So, I'll ask you again. How are you going to ruin my day today?"

"I'm still working that terror case for Vogel."

"Yeah, your name's all over the forensic requests from the search warrants that came flooding in this morning."

"I need to know where they pulled a computer, which location in the Capitol."

"Location?"

"Whose office," she clarified.

"Shouldn't be too hard if you know which computer you're looking for."

"Gebog was saying something about a unique address that's tied to each network card in a computer. The manufacturers embed it in the network card, and it can be used to identify a machine on a network."

"Computers aren't my strong suit, but I think you're talking about the MAC address. Every computer on a network has one, even modems. They can be used to identify and trace a machine, so long as the card with the embedded address stays in one computer."

"Are they easy to move?"

"The cards?" he asked. "Yes, if it's separate from the motherboard. It's simply a matter of removing a card and plugging it into another computer."

"Do most people know how to do that?"

"I doubt it."

"What about the machines pulled out of Bradley's senate office? Do they have this motherboard thing?"

He chuckled. "Every computer has a motherboard. The question is whether or not the network cards are separate, or built into the motherboard."

"Ok, and the machines from Bradley's Capitol office?"

"I don't know offhand, I'd have to check. Do you have the address you want to look up?"

"Yeah," Morgan answered, pulling out her phone. "Gebog emailed it to me earlier." She tapped away for a few seconds, then handed it to Runfo. "That one, but I also want to look through the records and pull any machines that came from Ben Keller's office."

"One of the perks of this new job is a secretary." He picked up the phone on his desk and punched several buttons. "Lynn," he said after a brief pause, "it's Charlie Runfo."

Morgan could hear his secretary's garbled voice through the phone.

"What?" Runfo asked his secretary.

Morgan remained silent as another jumbled mass of noise came through the handset.

"I know you know who I am," Runfo continued. "Saying my name... it's a habit, ok? That's all. Listen, do you know if they've got all of the evidence from the Bradley warrant inventoried yet?"

Another pause. "Yeah? Great. Hey, would you mind running something down for me? I need to know if a computer got picked up. I've got the MAC address here." He read it off and waited. "Two minutes? You want me to hold? Yeah, great."

Morgan waved her arms, trying to get his attention.

"Wait, one second, Lynn."

"The machines from Keller's office," Morgan reminded him.

"Right!" he said. "Lynn, find out how many machines they pulled from Keller's office, too. Thanks."

Morgan looked around the room. Ever since her days at the FBI Academy, Runfo took a special interest in her, mentoring and tutoring her in the art of investigation and forensic analysis. After she decided to become an agent, Runfo offered what guidance and support he could, staying in touch and checking on her often. Of all the men that passed through her life, this dusty old gentleman was one of the few she was ever able to extend some measure of trust.

Several minutes of silence passed before she heard his secretary's voice chirp through the handset again. Morgan listened to the conversation, that now-familiar, dreadful knot forming in the pit of her stomach as he hung up the phone.

"They don't have it," he said. "No computer with that address was inventoried for evidence."

"And they pulled every computer?"

He nodded. "Yes."

"What about the computers from Keller's office?"

"There weren't any."

"Shit!" she swore. She picked up her phone and dialed Gebog's number.

"Gebog."

"It's Morgan," she said. "Do they have Keller?"

"I was about to call you. Kloser didn't have to track him down. Keller approached our team. He said he had a confession."

The knot in Morgan's stomach tightened. "A confession?"

"Yes, ma'am."

"Ok. Have Kloser bring him down here."

"Will do," Gebog said.

Morgan hung up and looked at Runfo.

"Bad news?" he asked.

"One of my agents traced a funds transfer to one of the terrorist cell's bank accounts using the computer with that address I gave you. It came from a machine in Bradley's Senate offices. That's what we were after with these search warrants."

"And now it's missing."

"Yeah, but the guy I'm afraid might be mixed up in all of this just surrendered to one of my agents."

"Isn't that good news?"

Morgan bit her lower lip. "I'm not sure."

Chapter 17

Wogan walked in the congressional entrance of the Capitol administration building, Dean trailing at his heels. As they approached Bradley's Senate offices, a Capitol security guard and a young man with closely cropped hair sporting a poorly tailored suit stopped them.

"Do you have identification, sir?" the guard asked.

Wogan reached into the jacket of his Savile Row suit and pulled out his Department of Defense ID. "We already went through security. I'm here to see Senator Bradley."

The guard examined the identification closely before he handed it to the young man in the suit.

"Is there a problem?" Wogan asked politely. There were far more uniformed and plainclothes officers than normal. "I haven't seen this place so full of security since 9/11."

"Just a routine security matter, Mr. Wogan," the guard replied.

"I doubt it."

"Just wait here, please."

Wogan and Dean waited while the man in the suit took their IDs and disappeared down the hall. "Will this take long?" Wogan asked.

"Not long," the guard said.

It was five minutes, which seemed like an eternity to a man of Wogan's standing, used to being ushered right through slight inconveniences such as routine security checks. The young man finally returned and handed the identification back to the security guard with a nod.

"Sorry about the inconvenience," the guard said, returning Wogan's ID.

"I'm sure."

They walked past the two men into Bradley's offices, which were in absolute disarray. The normally cheerful, bouncy blonde receptionist was beside herself reorganizing three massive piles of paper. Aides and interns scurried around like ants whose nest was just kicked over by the neighborhood bully.

"Mr. Wogan!" the blonde called, spotting them in the middle of the small lobby.

"Michelle," Wogan replied, walking up to her desk. "What the hell's going on? What happened?"

"Oh, it was awful!" she cried. "The FBI came in here with a search warrant earlier this morning and tore the place apart! They've taken everything. It was just terrible!"

"Why?"

"I don't know!" she said, throwing her hands up in exasperation. "I guess they must've been looking for something."

"What?" Wogan asked. "Did they say anything?"

"I don't know! All of my papers were just strewn about all over the place. It's going to take me ages to get it all back together again. Ages! And they took the computers! Can you believe that? All of them! How are we supposed to do anything without our computers? The poor Senator's schedule is completely up in the air! I don't have any idea what's going on!" She looked back up at him, a sudden, horrified expression on her face. "Did you have an appointment with the Senator this morning?"

"No, I didn't," Wogan said, somewhat sympathetically. He did not give a rat's ass how the FBI made Michelle's life harder, but he could sympathize with any kind of government intrusion or scrutiny. "I'd hoped he might have ten minutes to spare me, just for a brief chat. It won't take long at all."

Her face fell. "I'm sorry, Mr. Wogan, but the Senator's not in at the moment."

"I see. He called me yesterday about a personal matter, and I hoped to be able to speak with him about it today. I have some information which he may find helpful."

"Oh, I'm sure he'll be sorry to have missed you."

"Yes, I'm sure. When do you expect him back?"

"This afternoon. He will be available then. I know what close friends you two are."

"That's very kind. Thank you," Wogan said with a smile. "What about his Chief of Staff? Mr. Keller? Is he available? I'm sure he could handle this as well, or pass on the information, at least."

She looked down at the desk and said, "I'm afraid not. He left about half an hour ago."

"When will he be back?"

"Well, I don't know," she said, somewhat embarrassed.

"Where did he go? Perhaps I could find him there."

Glancing nervously around, she leaned forward and said, "We're not really sure where he went. He just took off. Sort of disappeared."

"He didn't tell you where he was going?" Wogan asked. "Or when he would be back?"

"No," she said. "I'm afraid not."

"That's a bit unusual," Dean said, speaking for the first time.

"Yes, it is. Especially for Mr. Keller," the receptionist said.

"Well," Wogan said, "please tell Senator Bradley that we were here, and we will try to find him at a more convenient time this afternoon."

"I will!" she said, blossoming again. "And I apologize for the inconvenience."

Wogan nodded, and they left. As they walked down the stairs and out into the chilly Washington spring, he said, "Odd."

"Extremely," Dean agreed.

"Did Keller give you any indication? Any notice that the FBI had Bradley under investigation?"

"Yes. I spoke with him early this morning while you were asleep. There wasn't any mention of the FBI having him under surveillance, but he did mention a conversation he had with your daughter yesterday."

"A conversation? What conversation?" Wogan asked, walking down the sidewalk that surrounded the Senate office buildings. They crossed Constitution and headed towards the Capitol building, mixing with the throng of tourists and lawmakers. He nodded to several as he passed.

"Over lunch," Dean said. "The FBI was investigating Bradley over the wire transfer."

"So they did find it."

Dean nodded. "Though as you feared, it was far too late for them to have any hope of catching Ben Iblis."

"What did you tell Keller?"

"That he was fine and not to worry. Between Bradley's influence, his position as Chief of Staff, and his conversation with Morgan, he was fine. The investigation alone will probably take months, and that's only if Bradley's lawyers sit on their thumbs. I doubt they'll be that reluctant to slow the legal process."

"Did he ask for help? Does he expect us to take care of him?"

"Not in as many words. I think he was fishing."

"Fishing for support. As if he honestly expects me to help him." Wogan shook his head. "The man never ceases to amaze me."

"Yes."

"You didn't promise anything?"

Dean looked insulted. "No. Of course not."

Pursing his lips, Wogan gazed at the expanse of the Capitol. "I think Mr. Keller's outlived his usefulness."

"It may be that he realizes that, too."

"Yes. Bradley's receptionist seemed rather perplexed that Keller took off so suddenly."

"What do you want to do?" Dean asked.

"I want to find him. He's got a lot of information stored in that tiny head of his. In the wrong hands, he could do serious damage. Now that we don't have further use for him, there's little need to risk that information getting out."

"You want to find him?" Dean asked, puzzled. "To speak with him?"

"No," Wogan said, shaking his head. "Let's have someone find him for us. They can deal with the problem. Permanently."

***

They were still sitting on the porch, savoring the peace of the Irish morning when Ben Iblis finished his coffee and asked, "Do you want another cup?"

"Please."

He took her mug and walked into the house, leaving her alone with the sounds of the birds. Idly, she wondered if the sun could ever break through a mist like this, low and dense over the fields. It seemed like an impossible task, and part of her hoped it would never happen. It rolled across the land thirty minutes ago, covering everything like a blanket. It was peaceful, but it did not get her any closer to Ben Iblis's contacts, or to his business.

"We should go into town today," Ben Iblis said, returning with two steaming mugs of coffee.

She took hers. "Thanks."

"There are some things we need to follow up on."

"From last night, you mean?"

Leaning against one of the wood railings surrounding the porch, he nodded. "Yes, among other things. I also want to confirm payment for the contract yesterday morning. It was a neat little package, and I want to make sure we are paid the full amount. You did good work."

A puzzled look furrowed her brow. "Do you have any reason to think they won't fulfill their end of the contract?"

"No," he said, shaking his head. "I have worked with this contact in the past, and he has always been prompt with his payments."

"Then why the concern?"

"This was the daughter of a prominent American businessman."

"So?" she asked. "And he's not just a businessman. He's a global figure, really. It was a big job, despite its simplicity."

"Yes," he agreed, "and it doesn't hurt to make sure that the details have worked themselves out, as expected."

"Have you ever had any one refuse payment before?"

He thought back, his eyes focused on some piece of stone above her head. "Only once. In nearly thirty years, only once."

"What did you do?" she asked, intrigued.

"I forced him to pay me."

"Forced?"

"Yes."

"How?"

"I slit his daughter's throat and threatened to do the same to his son and his wife, one by one, unless he wired the money."

"In front of him?"

He tried to judge if she was serious. "How else do you make a point like that?"

"And you never had problems after that?"

"No," he said, turning his back to her and gazing out across the fields. "No, there were not any other problems."

"And this man," Morelli said, "he was obviously powerful and rich to be able to afford a contract with you. What did he do after all of this?"

"I don't know," he replied, unconcerned. "I assume he made love to his wife, or one of his mistresses, and replaced that daughter."

"He never came after you?"

"Would you?" he asked looking at her over his shoulder, bemused.

"Did you ever work with him again?"

"No."

"Why not?"

"A man who can't pay his debts isn't to be trusted."

"Do you always pay your debts?"

"Yes, always."

"I admire a man who pays his debts."

"What about a woman?" he asked.

"What about them?"

"Do you admire them? Those that pay their debts?"

"Of course."

Ben Iblis nodded. "And you? Do you always pay yours?"

"Would you have invited me on this adventure if you didn't already know the answer to that?"

"No."

"Then what more do you need to know?"

He smiled again, flashing brilliant white teeth under two days of stubble. "Everything. Information is king, especially when you're working with someone."

"In good time."

He turned back to the green fields and inhaled deeply. "Sometimes I forget how peaceful Ireland can be. I regret not being able to come here more often."

"You're serious about retiring, right?"

"Yes," he said, staring across the open land in front of them.

"I'm not sure I believed that until now," she said after studying his back for several moments.

"Why not?"

"Can you really ever retire from this business? Willfully, I mean? It all seems so impossible. So far away."

"I used to believe the same thing," he said. "In Afghanistan, back when the Russians were doing everything in their power to control the country, an end seemed like an impossible dream. I never thought for an instant that I would make it through alive. But I did. Somehow." His voice took on a chill that almost froze the mist. "When I started this business, I knew I would eventually reach the end. I would be successful. I would build a reputation, and when I was done, I would retire. Back then, I felt invulnerable. Untouchable. Those first contracts aside, things went off without a hitch. I was invincible in my twenties. Every contract I took was an unequivocal success. No problems, no hang-ups, no need for contingency plans. They were golden years."

"What happened?"

"It all went to hell," he admitted. "There was one operation that shocked me back into reality, that made me realize this was not something where you could afford to take a break. You could not afford to let your guard down, or else you would never see retirement."

"A bad operation?"

He nodded. "It was here, actually. In Dublin. Security was nearly impenetrable, almost as good as good can be." He turned and looked at her. "Almost like a government operation."

"What happened?"

"I created a diversion. Rather, I set up a diversion to be created. Hired it out, through my old assistant. It was supposed to be a traffic accident. The diversionary car would take out one of the security cars in the convoy."

"Why not have them simply take out the principal?"

He looked at her patiently. "Two reasons. One, I could not trust that they would actually be able to ensure the termination of the principal, and two, I do not leave anything to chance. I wanted the diversion to make my escape easier. Removing any lightly armored target with a HEAT round is a relative piece of cake. The devil is getting out of the engagement area alive and undetected. That is why I needed the diversion. Without it, I was sure the security people would stand a reasonable chance of tracking me down."

"So what went wrong?"

"Everything," he said, his eyes glazing over as he remembered that night. "The contractors did not hit the security car. They hit the principal. They did not hit him from the left, though, which would have been ideal, but from the right, completely obscuring my target."

"Why not target the accident site?"

"I did. I sent the missile right into the middle of the two cars and blew them both to hell."

"So you fulfilled the contract."

"Yes," he said. "But it is little comfort if you are not able to collect the payment, or enjoy it."

"Security lit you up like a firecracker," she said, watching as he relived that night behind his eyes.

"Yes. They knew exactly where that missile came from. It was impossible to hide its flight path in the middle of the night. They came hard."

"But you escaped."

"Barely. There was a running gun battle through the outskirts of Dublin. My assistant and I were both hit before we managed to get out."

"Badly?"

"Yes," he said, remembering the agony of the rifle rounds as they tore through the thin aluminum of the car, its upholstery, his Kevlar vest, and, finally, his side. "There was at least one assault rifle, Swiss, by the sound of it, and its handler was deadly accurate. Khalid and I were both hit."

"Khalid?" she asked, puzzled for a second, then, "Ah, yes. Your assistant."

"Yes," he said, a brief shadow passing over his eyes as he recalled plunging the syringe into his assistant's arm.

"How'd you get away?" she asked, ignoring the almost imperceptible change, gone just as quickly as it appeared.

"Smoke grenades," Ben Iblis said. "Our contingency plan. We lined three boulevards with them, set to remote detonate. As we drove through, we set them off. It blinded the security forces, and slowed them long enough for us to get enough distance that we were able to change cars and head to a safe house."

"Here?"

"No. I am not sure I would have used this place even if I owned it then. Not for an operation, at least. Too much at stake."

"For the operation or for this place?" she asked.

"For this place. I wouldn't risk it on a contract."

Looking out across the fields, she smiled. "It really is almost magical."

"Yes."

The stillness enveloped them again. Finally, Morelli finished her coffee and stood up. "How do you want to handle today?"

"There are several shops in town that offer internet access for the tourists. We will drive into Killarney and check on things. As I said, at a minimum, I want to confirm payment on the last contract."

"What about new assignments?"

"No, not right away. I have given considerable thought to last night's incident, and I think it would be best to lay low for a while. Several months, perhaps. There is much we can start on along the operational side -- travel, customs, planning, that sort of thing."

"Ok," she said, trying to mask her disappointment.

"Think of the bright side, once the payment from the Wogan contract clears, your share alone will allow you to live a comfortable life almost anywhere in the world."

"After we've found out who's responsible for the incident on the road last night," she reminded him. "Let's not forget that."

He smiled, a wolfish gleam in his eye. "I hoped you might say that."

Chapter 18

"Come on," Vogel growled, stopping next to her desk in the Hoover building. "You send me an email saying the warrant went well, and, by the way, you arrested a Senatorial Chief of Staff? Are you kidding me? Where's the Evelyn Morgan I know? Where's the woman that would've marched into my office proudly boasting you violated protocol, Congressional immunity, and common sense?"

Morgan looked up from her computer and frowned. "Where's the boss that would've demanded I come to his office so he could chew my ass out for thirty minutes on proper procedures?"

"You really arrested Keller?"

She nodded. "Yes. My team's bringing him down here now."

"What about the rest of your people?"

"I sent Gebog home to get some sleep. She was up working all night."

"Do you think you'll get anything out of Keller?"

"We better. He's the one good lead we have, and my time's running out. I want to talk to him as soon as I can. Probably after lunch."

"Speaking of which, I'm buying you lunch."

She was instantly on guard, her frown growing. "You've never bought me lunch. In the ten years I've been here, you've never once offered to buy me lunch."

"I thought you could use some company after what's happened the last couple of days. Especially with this morning," he said, looking at her carefully. "With your sister."

"Bullshit," she countered, ignoring the bait, ignoring the issue completely. She did not even want to know how he found out about Janice. "What's the real reason?"

"I have an assignment for you."

"I already have an assignment," she said, leaning back in her chair and folding her arms across her chest. "That you gave me. Remember? Time's ticking, and I don't have a hell of a lot to show for it."

"I need you for something else."

"Why?"

"Let's discuss it over lunch."

"And what happens to this investigation?" she asked, not at all happy about the potential change. "What happens to Ben Iblis?"

"Gebog can handle it."

"I like Gebog," Morgan sighed. "She's a good agent, but she isn't ready to handle all of this, and you know it."

"She can take most of it and send you highlights."

"So you want me to handle two investigations?"

"Let's talk about it over lunch," he insisted. "Do you like sushi?"

"This is a setup."

"Don't you trust me?"

She looked dubious. "Ten years. You haven't invited me to lunch in ten years."

"We finally have something to discuss."

"You're so full of shit."

"So, sushi?"

"Fine."

***

It was a tiny Japanese restaurant, marked only in kanji, set back in Alexandria, its front door a nondescript, semi-rusted affair that led to a basement immaculately clean and smelling sweetly of incense. A small waterfall cascaded in a corner behind the cute receptionist as Vogel led Morgan and two agents from his security detail across the tiny waiting area.

"Good afternoon," the demure woman greeted them, bowing slightly over her podium.

"Two for lunch, please, and a separate table for these gentlemen," Vogel said, motioning to his security detail.

"Right this way."

She led them to a dark cherry table, set for four, in one of the quieter corners of the tiny dining room. Vogel held Morgan's chair for her, then sat opposite. Morgan nodded her appreciation and looked around the restaurant. There were only ten or twelve other tables, all set identically with thick white linen tablecloths and heavy silverware.

"This is one of my favorite restaurants," she said, folding her napkin in her lap.

"I know."

She looked at him curiously. The usual gruff, all-business exterior was gone, and his attitude caught her off guard, which only served to make her more uneasy. It was a side of Vogel she saw only once before, the night Nichols died, when they shared a bottle of bourbon in his office.

A young Japanese woman, dressed in a beautiful silk kimono, approached, bowed, and asked if she could bring them something to drink.

"Saki," Morgan said. "Warm. Please."

"The same," Vogel said.

The waitress nodded and withdrew.

"Not going to give me a hard time about drinking on the job?" Morgan asked.

"Not until it affects your job performance."

"I've known you to bust people for less."

"Director's prerogative."

She leaned forward and contemplated the bookish deputy director, resting her hands on the table. "That's two lies in less than an hour."

"Is there a question in there somewhere?"

"No. Just that it's rare even for a man with your political connections," she paused and took a sip of her water. "And ambitions."

"That's a low blow," he said, his eyes turning cold. "Even for you."

"Then tell me what the hell's going on."

He took a deep breath, but she got the feeling he was not quite ready to play his hand. Not yet. "You and Nichols were lovers, right?"

"I already told you that."

"Then why are you here?"

Morgan stared at him, a rush of emotions flooding her body. Was that really why he asked her to lunch? Did he want to hear, again, why she needed to keep working? Why, if she stopped, she was afraid she'd collapse? And if she collapsed and actually thought about that night, thought about Nichols, thought about what he meant to her, she was afraid she might never get back up again? She might never be able to crawl out of that black pit? Is that what he wanted to hear? What he wanted to know?

She looked across the table at him for what seemed like an eternity, afraid to answer, afraid to tell him the truth. They had known each other for years, and she knew she could trust him. Maybe that was why he asked her to lunch. Maybe it would be easier to get her to open up away from the office, away from her colleagues and those surroundings. Maybe that was his angle.

"Is that why you asked me to have lunch?" she finally asked. "To figure out why I'm pushing to see this through?"

"No," he replied, shaking his head. "As I said, I have another assignment for you."

"Then why do you keep asking me whether or not I should be here?"

Vogel leaned back in his chair. "I need you to be at your best, especially given what I'm about to ask you to do."

"Are you suggesting I may not be at my best?"

"Not directly, no."

"Then what?"

"I just want to make sure there aren't any lingering issues which may be blinding you to the realities of the situation."

"And what are the realities of the situation?" she asked, folding her arms across her chest.

"That you just lost someone very close to you."

"I'm not blind to that. What else?"

"Why are you protecting Keller?"

She was not happy at all about the course of this conversation. "Who says I'm protecting Keller? I just ordered his arrest."

One of his eyebrows went up. "You warned him yesterday."

"No," she said. "Well, yes, and no. I did warn him about the investigation into Bradley's finances, but I didn't say a word that he might be included because we didn't know he was involved at that point. That lunch was actually very productive. Without it, we wouldn't of known that we should be watching him."

"Maybe that was a lucky call."

"Hey! I covered his ass. An entire team was watching him shortly after that lunch. It's how we know he talked to Thomas Dean early this morning."

"You didn't tell me that," he said, surprised. "Wogan's man?"

"Yes."

"Do you think Wogan's involved somehow?"

She thought about it. "Let's just say it wouldn't surprise me."

"Do you have anything concrete?"

"Not yet."

"That's going to make things interesting."

Confused, she asked, "What do you mean?"

"You'll see."

Morgan was still staring at him when the waitress arrived bearing two small, ceramic carafes of sake. With a delicate hand borne from years of practice, she poured the wine into small cups and placed them before her guests.

"Thank you," Morgan said, taking a sip and smiling with pleasure.

"May I ask what you would like to enjoy for lunch?" the waitress asked.

Vogel cleared his throat. "Actually, we're waiting for one more."

"Oh! My apologies. I wasn't aware," the waitress said, withdrawing with a silent swish of her kimono.

"You didn't mention a third," Morgan said. "Who are you expecting?"

"Your father."

It was as though a stone hand suddenly gripped her heart, squeezing it with a cold, merciless force that knocked the breath from her lungs.

"Have a drink," he said, pouring more rice wine from the carafe.

She swallowed it down, barley registering the warmth as it spread from her stomach. "You could have warned me."

"Would you have come?"

"No."

"Then I couldn't have warned you."

"I don't like being ambushed."

"Who does?" he asked. "But you can see it was the only way."

"Why are we having lunch with him?"

"Because the Director asked me to set it up."

"You mean because Wogan asked the Director to set it up." Vogel shrugged.

"And you condone his actions?" Morgan asked, disgust dripping from every syllable. "You work with him? Facilitate his control of this town? Help him run down whatever little errands he needs done?"

"Careful, Eve," Vogel warned, anger flashing in his eyes.

"And yet we're here."

His eyes hardened. "Of course we're here. We have a job to do."

"Jesus," she said, shaking her head. "How long have you known him?"

"Wogan? Many years."

"And your relationship?"

"Purely professional."

She looked at him with a hate she did not think she could ever feel for the man. "And you get things done for him, I assume? That's why I'm here? Something that he needs done, so he calls in the FBI because his own people aren't able to handle it?"

"Something like that," Vogel said, watching her.

"What do you know of our relationship?" she asked, trying to control her temper. "Between my father and myself?"

"Strained, is the word that comes to mind."

"That doesn't begin to describe it."

"Then enlighten me."

"Until this morning, I hadn't seen him in over ten years. He walked out of my life years ago. He would send money and gifts at Christmas, but never anything more than that. When I was little, he was never around. Not much, at any rate. My mother taught me to ride a bike, running behind me, trying to balance everything by holding on to the back of the seat. It was the same with soccer, and volleyball, and a million other things that kids do while they're growing up. My mother was always there, but he could never be bothered."

"And now you hate him for it."

That was not why she hated him, but the real reason was not something she wanted to discuss with Vogel. "Wouldn't you?"

"Perhaps."

"Then why did you sucker me into this lunch?" she asked.

"Several reasons. You need to hear what we discuss, and because the FBI believes this is the best use of your time and skills."

"I don't believe this."

"Believe it."

"And if I refuse?"

"Then you can discharge yourself for a psychiatric evaluation. Put something in your resignation letter about stress, coupled with Nichols' death and the pressure to find Ben Iblis. I'll get medical to sign off on the evaluation, and you can have six months of leave."

"And push a desk for the rest of my life."

Vogel shrugged. "I'm sure some consideration would be allowed for the conditions in which you left."

"Right."

"It's your choice, Eve."

"If I quit, you're out an expert."

"On Ben Iblis?" he asked. "We'll just have to find somebody else."

"There isn't anybody else."

He leaned forward and made a point to catch, and hold, her eyes. "Despite whatever illusions you may have, no one is irreplaceable." He held her stare for several seconds. "Just listen to what Wogan has to say. That's all. Just listen."

Wogan walked into the dining room, and Vogel stood to greet him.

"You owe me," she seethed, glancing behind her as Wogan caught sight of them.

Vogel looked down and a cold, hard ice froze his voice. "No, Eve. Not this time."

***

Ben Iblis was silent on the drive into Killarney, which suited Morelli just fine. She crossed her long legs in the Land Rover and closed her eyes. The drive was quiet and peaceful, and while she would glance in the side-view mirror frequently, she was not too worried about being followed. Whoever she killed last night likely did not have time to relay too many details to their handlers, so it was doubtful another team would be able to find them and set up surveillance so quickly.

Regardless, they agreed to take a round-about route into town, following sparsely travelled country roads and circling back several times. The typical ten minute drive took nearly an hour before they were satisfied they were not under active surveillance, and Ben Iblis pulled into town and parked the SUV on a side street.

"Ready?" he asked, switching off the engine.

She caught his dark eyes as he glanced over at her. They were colder that morning. "Yes," she said, opening her door.

They stepped from the Land Rover, and she waited on the sidewalk as he rounded the front of the SUV. With an offer of his arm, which she accepted, they strolled slowly towards Main Street, making a left amid the bustle of a surprisingly large crowd of people.

"It's usually not this busy," he said.

Morelli glanced at both sides of the street, taking in the architecture of the row buildings, but also the breaks in their structure. If they needed to get off the street, one of those breaks would be their best bet for immediate cover. She also noted the alleys, to be used or avoided, depending on any one particular need.

Ben Iblis seemed unconcerned, the muscles in his arm relaxed, just walking along the street, stopping occasionally to peer into the glass of the shops lining its front. She would, of course, stop with him, pretending to be interested in whatever was displayed, but it was hard to forget her training. When they were stationary, she scanned and made mental notes of the faces passing in the glass store-fronts, paying particular attention to those on the other side of the street.

"I do not think we have much to worry about here," Ben Iblis said, after the third or fourth stop. "But I am glad you are keeping an eye out."

"I wouldn't worry so much either, but for the incident last night."

"Do you think we are being followed?"

"No, but I think your beautiful FBI agent would be foolish to give up the hunt now."

He turned to look at her. "You think it was the Americans last night?"

"I don't know who it was last night, but you've mentioned her several times. That fact alone makes me wonder."

He smiled and said, "I do believe you are jealous."

"No, just cautious."

"If you say so," he said, still smiling.

They resumed their stroll, turning at the next side street, cutting through an alley before stepping onto another sidewalk. It was less crowded than the first, but both sides of the street were still lined with shops and cafes.

"There is an internet café a little further down the street," he said.

She stopped and withdrew her arm. "You check the messages. There are some things I need to take care of."

"What do you need to take care of?"

"I want to check our tail, for one," she said, glancing back down the alley. "And I need to pick up a few things. I noticed two or three clothing stores on that other street."

He studied her, his eyes flashing back and forth between hers. "Alright. The café's just down the street, on the left. Meet me there in forty-five minutes? Will that give you enough time?"

"Let's make it an hour."

"Fair enough," he agreed. "Do you have some money?"

"Enough."

He nodded, and without another word, turned on his heel and started towards the café. She watched until he opened the door, then turned and headed back down the alley. It was true what she said. She needed to pick up a few things, and there were several clothing stores on High Street, but it was not the complete truth. She needed to make her own inquiries, and she saw a quiet internet café where she could casually observe anyone coming and going, including anyone trying to keep an eye on her.

Chapter 19

After greeting Vogel, Wogan looked down at Morgan and extended his hand. She shook it perfunctorily, without a smile. Vogel might be her boss, and she would do as he asked, within reason, but it did not mean she had to like it, and it certainly did not mean she had to be polite. Especially not to this man.

They sat and their waitress reappeared. With another bow, she asked their guest what he would like to drink.

"Scotch, please," Wogan said. "Neat."

"Do you prefer a particular distillery?" she asked. "Or region?"

"Do you have an Oban? Or something from the Highlands?"

"Yes, sir. Of course."

Wogan nodded his appreciation and said, "Please."

"So nice of you to arrange time from your busy schedule to have lunch with us," Morgan said dryly as the waitress withdrew.

"It's important to me," Wogan replied.

She cast a disgusted look at Vogel before taking another sip of her drink. "I'm sure. I know how busy you must be, running the company, keeping tabs on all the politicians in your pocket."

Wogan glanced at Vogel before saying, "To be fair, Mr. Vogel isn't in my pocket."

"I'm not sure I believe that."

"I'm hurt," Vogel feigned.

"Now that I wish I could believe," she said.

Wogan cleared his throat. "To be honest, Mr. Vogel is here at the instruction of the Director. At my personal request."

"So it is your personal political wish," she quipped.

"But I'm not the one at the end of the puppet strings," Vogel said. "Despite your apparent ardent desire."

"Well," she said. "I'm glad I wasn't completely wrong in my judgment."

"Your judgment?" Wogan asked.

"Or rather my faith," she said. "In people. I can understand following orders, so long as those orders aren't held by a billionaire with his own political agenda."

"Politics are the furthest thing from my mind at the moment," Wogan said.

"Then what's the issue?" she asked.

"I'm surprised you don't know," Wogan said.

"Janice," she said. Unless he was here to explain his involvement with Bradley, which she doubted, it was the only thing which made sense.

"You wouldn't agree to it this morning when I asked, so I decided to try different cards. The Director owes me a favor or two, and I believe Janice was murdered."

"This is the assignment you were referring to?" Morgan asked, looking at Vogel.

He nodded.

"And if I refuse?"

"We already discussed that. There are alternatives."

"Hardball," she said.

"It's the only game in this town," Wogan interjected before Vogel could respond. "You should know that by now, Eve. You've been here long enough."

The waitress reappeared, setting down Wogan's drink, then taking their orders. It gave Morgan a chance to think, however brief.

It was not a good position. As much as she wanted justice, she really did not give a shit for Janice, half-sister or not. They never met, were never introduced, and never spoke. It was sad, but the only thing she wanted to do was find Ben Iblis. That was what mattered.

"Why do you want me?" Morgan asked after the waitress withdrew.

"Because you're the best," Wogan said.

"The Bureau has a lot of good agents," she countered.

"Because she was your sister."

Morgan leaned forward. "Only in blood. Let's get something straight. Unless you want an outright refusal, we play with my rules. No bullshit. No games. No tricks." She bored her green eyes right into him. "I didn't know Janice, and I haven't seen you in over ten years. I have no illusions or dreams of some fantastic reunion for a family that never was. If you want me to do this because I'm damn good at what I do, fine. But don't try to feed me some bullshit line about how she was family, or blood, or some crap like that, because I really don't give a shit. I'll do this to keep my job. That's the only reason."

It was a struggle, but Wogan did his best to keep his temper under control. "You always did tell it like it was."

"That's right, and the first whiff I get of you not playing straight, of withholding something, of making my job even the least bit difficult, I walk. There are half a dozen private security firms that will take me in an instant where the hours are less, the stress is more manageable, and the pay is a hell of a lot better."

"Is it a matter of money?" Wogan asked.

She just stared at him, for a full minute, taking slow measured breaths to try and control her rising anger. Finally, she turned to Vogel. "You can relay that to the Director. If he wants me to do this, fine. I don't agree with it, and the fact that he," she nodded towards Wogan, "has enough weight to throw around to force this kind of assignment makes me sick. But I meant what I said. I will walk at the first hint of this son of a bitch stabbing me in the back." She looked at Wogan. "Because it will happen."

"I'm not used to women talking to me like that," Wogan said, his face red.

"Women? Or people in general?" Morgan asked. "And in the interest of full disclosure, I really don't give a fuck. You are a miserable piece of shit who walks all over people. You abandoned my mother. You abandoned me. Why should I expect anything different this time around?"

"Did you ever want for anything?"

"I wanted for a father."

It went home. The color drained from Wogan's face and he downed the rest of his Scotch.

Vogel cleared his throat and stood. "I'll check on our meal," he said, straightening his suit coat before walking to the hostess station.

"I would apologize," Wogan said softly, trying to regain his composure, watching the hurt in her eyes, "but I don't think it would help."

"You're right."

He nodded, slowly, multiple times. "For what it's worth, I regret some of the choices I made earlier in my life, including that day in Steamboat, at the waterfall."

Like me, Morgan thought, because I was born out of wedlock. Not that it mattered. There was nothing she could say that would influence the man in any meaningful way. That much was clear. Wogan lost one daughter, but he really did not give a shit about Morgan, other than to use her to find Janice's killer. She was an asset, an investment he spent hundreds of thousands of dollars on over the years, and now he wanted to cash in.

She thought back to that day on the bridge under Fish Creek Falls when she finally realized how little he actually cared about her, or her mother. There was no real concern for her welfare, or for the fact that she was raped. He was only concerned for his own reputation.

"That day in Steamboat." She searched his eyes. "When I told you how my son was conceived?"

He watched her carefully. "Yes?"

"You remember how you walked away?"

"Yes."

She nodded and looked down at her hands before raising her head and meeting his eyes. "I want to stand up, tell you to go fuck yourself, and walk out the door." She leaned forward and her voice turned even colder. "I want to do that knowing what it will do to you, knowing you'll never discover the truth of what happened to Janice, regardless of whether she was murdered or not. You'll go to your grave wondering."

He took a deep breath. "So why don't you?"

"Because I'm not you." She fell back in her chair and ran a hand through her hair. It was true. She wanted to walk away. Desperately. But she could not, and it made her sick to her stomach.

Vogel left the hostess and walked back to their table, not at all surprised by the hatred radiating from Morgan. "Lunch will be here shortly."

"Good," she said.

"So," Vogel continued, sitting down. "Where will you start?"

"Actually," Morgan said, trying to suppress some of her emotions, "I'm curious why he thinks she was murdered."

"Because she wouldn't be so careless as to fall asleep in the tub," Wogan said, motioning for another drink.

"Is that where they found her?" Morgan asked.

"What was left of her," Wogan said.

"Burned?"

"That's right."

"Was that the cause of death?" Morgan asked.

"The coroner hasn't released the results of his autopsy," Vogel said.

Morgan scoffed and looked pointedly at Wogan. "I find that hard to believe."

"Smoke inhalation," Wogan said, ignoring her stare. "We got the results an hour ago."

"But that hasn't even posted to the database!" Vogel protested. "I checked half an hour ago, before lunch."

"See what I mean?" Morgan asked.

"The point is," Wogan said, "she wouldn't have sat in that tub. She wouldn't have just sat there and died. Not Janice."

"Toxicology?" Morgan asked.

Vogel shook his head. "Too soon."

"I've asked the Director to see what can be done in that area," Wogan said, nodding his appreciation as the waitress delivered another drink. "He indicated the lab in Quantico would start working on it immediately. They just need to get the sample."

"I've already dispatched a tech to pick it up," Vogel said.

Morgan sighed and shook her head, resigning herself to the inevitability of it all. "I'll check with Runfo when we get finished with lunch, then. He should have an answer by tonight if it has an executive priority on it."

"What will that tell us?" Wogan asked.

"Whether or not she was drugged. Maybe that's why she didn't get out of the tub."

"So you believe me?"

"No," she said. "I believe that somebody thinks the government's resources are best used to confirm whether or not one of its citizens died in an ordinary house fire, or if she was murdered for reasons yet unknown."

"Do you believe me or not?" Wogan asked, exasperated, his frustration boiling over.

"It's irrelevant," Morgan said.

"Why?"

"It has no bearing on the facts. As much as you want it to, the science will tell us what happened to Janice."

"She was murdered."

"Why? Because she didn't get up?" Morgan shook her head. "C'mon. As much as you hate the idea, it happens all the time. She's dead. It's entirely possible it was an accident."

"I don't believe it," Wogan said.

"Obviously."

Wogan frowned and sipped at his drink.

"What's been done so far?" she asked. "Do you know what the local police have looked at?"

"They've been going through some of the surveillance video," he replied. "I guess Janice went to a bar that night."

"Did she meet someone?"

"They think she may have, but they were going to look into it further."

"Did she take him home?" she asked.

"They haven't said."

"What about where she went?" Vogel asked, speaking for the first time in several minutes. "Have the police tried to talk to people that may have been at the bar that night?"

"I don't know," Wogan replied.

Morgan sat back in her chair and turned it over in her mind. If Janice went home with someone that night, then they obviously needed to find that person. It also lent credibility to Wogan's theory that she was murdered. The timing was just too neat for Janice to have brought someone home, and then have her house burn down around her ears.

"So that's settled?" Vogel asked, watching Morgan as she thought about the possibilities. He'd seen that look before.

"Sure," she said. "It's settled." As if there were any question about the outcome.

***

Morelli signed off the web browser at the internet café in downtown Killarney, rose from the plastic chair, and approached the cashier. It took her a moment, fumbling in her handbag, to find the correct amount of Euros to pay her bill, all while carefully watching the pedestrians outside. No one appeared to be paying particular attention to the café, but a good surveillance team would not need to. They would simply pick her up as she left, trading personnel at frequent intervals. It would be nearly impossible to pick them up, which made her little act of finding the correct change futile, but she did it anyway.

She paid the pimply-faced cashier, shot him a dazzling smile, and stepped out of the building onto the sidewalk. Several large clouds drifted lazily through the blue sky, and she wrapped a black scarf around her head, making sure to cover all of her hair. She fought the urge to look around, to try to find the eyes she knew must be there. The hair on the back of her neck told her all she needed to know. Someone was watching.

Mixing with the throng of people on the sidewalk, she moved down the street, through the alley, and stopped when she caught sight of Ben Iblis's café. Instead of going in, she crossed the street and waited, busying herself with the storefronts, trying to pick up the surveillance in the windows' reflections. Despite her efforts, though, she wasn't able to pick anyone out of the crowd.

Of course, she could be imagining it, but she did not really believe that. She had been in the business long enough to cultivate that sixth sense, and it was screaming at her. The good news was she was on a crowded avenue. There was little to be gained by making a scene here, and while it was possible they simply wanted her dead, she doubted that was the case. It would have been simpler to remove her when she walked out of the café.

There was another possibility. Maybe she was not the primary target. They needed her to lead them to Ben Iblis. Then they might make their move, take them together with little chance for one to escape. They could also just sit back and wait, following them to the safe house. There would be few to witness any action on the farm, as far out as it was in the Irish countryside.

Too many possibilities, she thought, turning away from the storefront and merging with a small group of women. She bundled her coat more tightly around her slim waist and watched her feet, keeping pace with the group. As she closed the distance with Ben Iblis's café, she chanced surreptitious glances, hoping to spot the surveillance, but it was useless. So she kept walking, staying with the group long after they passed that simple glass door, his silhouette visible in her peripheral vision, backlit by the dim glow of the computer monitor.

The group of women, their shopping bags slung over their arms, deep in conversation, either ignorant or dismissive of the stranger in their ranks, turned at the next corner and continued down the sidewalk. Morelli stayed with them, embedded in the middle, her mind working on the problem. There was an alternate rendezvous, one they set up as a precaution, two hours from now. That was not her primary concern, though. She needed to know who was after her.

Or them.

As they crossed the street in front of St. Mary's, a large cathedral on the outskirts of Killarney, steps away from Killarney National Park, Morelli broke away and crossed the small parking lot under its towering spire. She moved quickly, opening one of the cathedral's massive doors, solid wood creaking slightly against ancient iron hinges.

The mustiness of an old Catholic cathedral washed over her as she stood in the atrium. It was almost dark inside, and it took her eyes some time to adjust to the dim light. The door creaked closed behind her, and she dipped two fingers in the brass stoup, crossing herself involuntarily with the holy water dripping from her fingertips. Nearly a decade had passed since she last stepped into a church, but the old habits, beaten into her for years, were impossible to forget.

An inner calm, unexplainable in her current situation, overcame her, and she gently stepped down one of the cathedral's aisles, genuflecting at the end of a straight back, wooden pew near the altar. As she sat down, she marveled at the simplicity of the bench. It was a basic wooden pew, duplicated in hundreds of churches across the world, designed to make the worshipper uncomfortable.

She shifted her black scarf, pulling it from her hair and tucking it into a pocket in her jacket. Reaching down, she brought the pew's small, padded knee rest onto the floor. Crossing herself again, she leaned forward until her knees hit the soft leather of the rest, and she could rest her folded hands on the back of the next pew. Memories, most from when she was a little girl, flashed through her mind. She spent hours every week in church, a chore her parents forced her into when she was young, but something that became a refuge as she grew older.

Under her breath, her lips barely moving, she recited the Hail Mary. She proceeded to the Lord's Prayer before she heard the ominous creak of one of the cathedral's heavy wooden doors. It almost did not register, and her sub-conscious was screaming as she recited the final words, "For thine is the Kingdom, the Power, and the Glory, forever and ever."

At the final "Amen," Morelli stood, picked the knee rest up with one foot, and slowly shuffled along the deserted pew to the aisle. There were two sets of eyes on her back, which surprised her. She honestly expected more. In fact, she thought, they would need more. Two was not a problem.

Stopping at the end of the pew, her back to her pursuers, she stared at the sacristy door, just to the right of the altar, only a few short steps away. Before sprinting across, she turned and looked at the back of the church, her eyes cold and distant. There were two of them, both good sized, coming down the center aisle. One wore gray slacks and a blue pea coat, buttoned across the front. The other was dressed in tennis shoes, khakis, and a blue sweater. Despite the fact they outweighed her, she was not concerned.

Turning back around, she ran to the sacristy door, bursting through and slamming it behind her. There was no lock, but it did not matter. Not now. The advantage was hers. It was foolish for them to follow her into the cathedral when they had the upper hand outside.

She ran down a stone passageway, lit by only a few dim bulbs, before she ducked into an alcove behind a large statue of Mary. Sinking back as far as she could, deep in the shadows, she waited, her muscles taught, her mind focused. She withdrew a Walther PPK from her handbag and screwed on its silencer, watching the door at the end of the passageway. It seemed like an eternity before it slowly began to open, and she idly wondered if they would both come through.

No, only one. Pea Coat.

She watched from behind the Virgin Mary as he used the door for cover, staying behind it as long as possible, a small pistol extended in front of him. When he was not immediately confronted with shots, he moved forward, growing cautious again at the first alcove, pausing in front of a bust of St. Peter.

The PPK spit twice, in quick succession, sending two rounds into the side of the man's head. She was moving before his body hit the floor, walking quickly, keeping her back to one side of the hall, the pistol at her side. An exit sign directed her to the right, and she crouched down, slowly pushing open the door, the PPK in front of her.

The lush greenery of Killarney National Park was visible on the opposite side of the nearly deserted parking lot. She scanned the area, but did not see anyone. Looking behind her, down the corridor, she did not see any sign of the guy in the sweater. Tucking the pistol back into her handbag, she glanced left and right again, searching, then stood and walked towards the park, leaving behind any thought of the man she just killed in the church.

Chapter 20

Morgan sat in silence as Vogel drove downtown. As the buildings flashed by, she was reminded of a Christmas, over twenty years ago, when her mother drove them through Des Moines, in a hurry to get to Chicago for a new job opportunity. It was something Wogan set up for her mother, but it had not made Morgan very happy. She was forced to leave good friends behind.

"You're angry," Vogel said.

"No," she replied. "I'm not angry. I'm just tired of being in the middle."

"I didn't know he was your father until he called me."

"He called you?"

"Yes, after he spoke with the Director."

"I'm surprised he told you. I can probably count the number of people that know on one hand."

"The Director doesn't know."

Morgan nodded, looking out her window. "He doesn't like to share that little mistake he made all those years ago."

"Is that what you think you are?"

"No, but that's what he thinks I am."

"Does that really matter to you?"

She looked at him and considered. Did it? It was not a question she spent much time reflecting on in the last several days, not with everything else that happened. It should not matter, but every time she thought about it, she grew angry.

"Look at all you've accomplished in spite of him," Vogel continued. "Youngest team lead in generations, and one of the Bureau's top investigators. You've got character, spirit, and a sense of morality and justice that is distinctly lacking in this day and age."

"Thank you," she said, taken back by his sincerity. She knew Vogel to be kind, and even caring on occasion, but the directness of his compliment surprised her. "I suppose that's why I'm going to go along with this little investigation. Do you agree with the Director's decision?"

"It's irrelevant."

"That's not an answer."

"No, it's not," Vogel said. "Wogan's an extremely powerful and influential man. I'm sure what he said is true. The Director probably owes him several favors."

"Would you have made the same choice?"

"That's also irrelevant."

"But still a valid question."

"Politics will always play a role in this town," he sighed, "especially with government agencies. You know that." He turned into the parking garage. "I wasn't there when Wogan met with the Director. I just got the order after they were finished. Would I have made the same decision? I don't know. I may not be privy to all of the details. I like to think it would depend on a number of things."

"Like what?"

"Like what kind of a plea Wogan made, and what I knew of the man in prior personal dealings. It would also depend on if I were ultimately in charge. There may be things that the Director sees that I do not."

"I find that hard to believe."

"He's a politician," Vogel said. "That alone gives him access to information kept from me."

"Wogan's a shell of his former self," Morgan said, remembering the ghostly shadow she saw in Wogan's eyes over lunch. "He's no longer the man that built WGI Systems."

"I know losing a child can be devastating, but it's difficult to watch in a man of Wogan's stature."

"Do you think she could have been murdered?"

"Wogan obviously believes that. I think he's well within his rights to insist that it be investigated."

"But to demand FBI involvement?"

"As I said, he's a very wealthy and powerful man. Would you leave the investigation into the death of your child in the hands of local police if you could involve the FBI?"

"No," she admitted.

They got out of the car and walked to the elevator. "It shouldn't take you too long, once you get the tox results. Just get it wrapped up and get back on the terror cell. I'll let Gebog know what's going on, and I'll make sure she stays in contact with you. You're still in charge, and you still have your team. Any developments or big questions, she'll come to you. Fair enough?"

Morgan nodded. "Fair enough."

Vogel took off his spectacles and wiped them with a cloth. "I meant what I said earlier. The whole reason you're still here is because you're one of the best. Remember that when you start down this rabbit hole."

A puzzled look crossed her face. "What do you mean?"

"I mean, be careful."

"Why? Do you know something I don't?"

He replaced the spectacles on his nose and looked at her. The elevator dinged its arrival, and the doors opened. "When you play in the majors, and something like this comes across your desk, nine times out of ten, it's not exactly as it appears. Janice died under suspicious circumstances, and Wogan calls in a favor to have his other daughter put in charge of the case?"

Morgan watched him, but didn't reply.

"Just be careful. Something isn't right, and coming on the heels of everything you've gone through in the past several days, it really starts to smell funny. The fact that Dean met with Bradley's man, Keller, this morning, only makes things worse. There's too many coincidences."

"Do you think Ben Iblis is involved somehow?"

"I don't know, but you need to watch your ass. We don't have all the pieces to the puzzle, and I'll bet you a week's worth of lattes that Wogan hasn't shown his full hand."

She nodded and watched as he got on the elevator.

"Are you coming up?" he asked.

"No," she said, her mind turning over the problem. "I need to run out to Annapolis and talk to the local cops. I want to know if they were able to run anybody down from that bar Janice visited. They may be able to give me some leads. I also need to give Charlie a call. He may have that toxicology report by now."

"Good luck," Vogel said, punching the button for his floor.

Morgan watched the doors close before turning away and walking to her own car. Vogel was right. She could not trust Wogan, father or not. But she knew that. She might be the only daughter he had left, but he never showed any inclination in recognizing her as his blood. That could pose problems, if push came to shove. On the other hand, it might be beneficial. A small smile creased her lips. Emotional attachment would not be an issue.

***

Morelli tried to relax as she followed the dirt and gravel path along the Deenagh River in Killarney National Park. It was little more than a stream at that point, just a slow channel cutting through the Irish countryside, flanked by lush trees, flowers, and dark green grass. The clouds burned off as she walked, and the sun shone through the trees, casting moving shadows as a light breeze sang through their leaves. It was a stark contrast to the adrenaline still pumping through her system, and she did not allow herself a deep breath until she put nearly a mile between her and the cathedral.

As she rounded a bend, she slowed her pace and took several more deep breaths, trying to shake the tension from her limbs. What she desperately wanted was a bottle of water, but she had not thought to put one in her hand bag before they left the farm that morning. She continued down the path, thinking about the last thirty minutes. The man in the cathedral, the man she shot, Pea Coat, was new, but she thought she recognized his partner. He was one of Wogan's men, one of his supervisory agents, which meant Wogan was hunting them, not the FBI.

It also meant that he was probably hunting her, not Ben Iblis. She was the one attracting danger.

Did they know about the farm?

Thinking back through that morning, she doubted it. There was no sign of surveillance on the drive in to town, and they were not there when she split up with Ben Iblis. No, they picked her up either in the internet café, or somewhere else in town. It was reasonable to assume the farm was still safe. At least, for the moment. But it also meant they were covering all of the major cities, and probably some of the towns, throughout Ireland.

The path forked and she veered left back towards town. Her first pre-arranged rendezvous with Ben Iblis was fifteen minutes away, and she guessed it would take her almost that to get there. Idly, she wondered if she would hear sirens before she met Ben Iblis. It would have been impossible for anyone outside of that hallway to hear her shots, the PPK was far too quiet with the suppressor, but the body would not go undiscovered for long.

She continued up the path, cresting a small hill before crossing back into town. Their rendezvous was five minutes up a side street, on a corner in the southern part of the city, but as she passed a pharmacy she was surprised by the squeal of tires behind her. In an instant, she was down on one knee turning to face the threat, her right hand buried in her handbag, her hand curled around the PPK's familiar grip. Her grip relaxed when she recognized their Land Rover.

It jerked to a stop next to her. "Get in!" Ben Iblis ordered from the driver's seat.

Catching her heart in her throat, she ran around the front and climbed in. Ben Iblis took off in a shot. She barely closed her door before they rocketed down the small drive.

"Intelligence?" he asked, making a hard right at the next intersection and stomping down on the accelerator.

"No."

"Americans?"

Morelli tried to collect her thoughts. "No," she said, "and not intelligence. I got a good look at one of the guys."

"And?" Ben Iblis asked, slowing the big SUV as they neared the center of town. It was the fastest route out of the city.

"I think it's Wogan."

"Wogan?"

"Yes."

His knuckles tightened on the wheel. "Tell me what happened."

"I picked them up about an hour ago, on my way back to meet you at the café. I didn't see them, or couldn't pick out individuals, but I knew they were there. Somebody was watching me on that street."

"And?"

"I headed for the cathedral and removed one of them there."

"Dead?" he asked, turning on the carriageway that would lead them to the farm.

"Yes."

"How many did you see?"

"Just two."

"What happened to the other one?"

"I don't know," she said. "There was only one guy who pursued me through the cathedral. After I got out, I didn't see his partner. He must have terminated the pursuit."

"Why?"

"I don't know," she said, honestly. She was still trying to figure it out.

"He was the one you recognized?"

"Yes."

"Are you sure?"

"Yes."

"Such a brief glance...."

"I'm sure," she said, piercing him with a hard glare. "I got a good look. The one that survived was one of his supervisory agents. He knows we're here, or he'll know soon." Morelli turned and looked out her window, staring at the countryside as it sped away on her left. The ferocity of Wogan's hunt did make her pause, especially given the brief period she was gone. Was her departure really what was driving him? Did she really mean that much?

Of course not, she thought. He simply could not afford to leave a loose end. But to spend these kind of resources? An entire country under surveillance?

"Do you think he's really after me?" she asked.

"No."

"Then why?"

Ben Iblis turned on to a rural road. "I think he's hunting me."

It surprised her. "Why?"

"Because of your good Senator -- Bradley. He is not dead, and I did not fulfill my end of the contract. Really, though, it is a moot point. The contract is void because he put you on the same target."

"I doubt he sees it like that."

"I agree."

"They keep locating me, though," she said. "Not you."

"You are much easier to find. They have figured out by now that you have run, and given the fact that I disappeared about the same time, they think you ran with me. You are more easily recognizable. They do not need to run me down."

"Why?"

"Because you are visible. You are known. Pictures, fingerprints, DNA. You are everywhere. They can pinpoint you."

"But you said you met Wogan," she protested. "They know what you look like, too."

"That does not mean I gave him the opportunity for a photograph. He might be able to put together some kind of sketch, but he does not have a picture, and he certainly does not know my habits."

"He does not know my habits, either!"

"You can learn a lot about a woman after spending several nights with her," he replied, amused. "How many nights did you two spend together?"

She stared at him, loathing in her eyes.

"I'm sure he has you pretty well pegged at this point, professional or not."

I doubt it, she thought, but did not voice her opinion. "What now?" she asked instead.

"We will go back to the farm after driving around for a couple of hours, just to make sure we have not picked up a tail coming out of town. I doubt even Wogan has access to satellites."

"And then?"

"If we're clear, we will lay low, then move."

"And if we're not?" she asked.

"Then we move and deal with the threat on the way."

"Like after the airport?"

"Exactly," he said, a predatory gleam in his eyes.

***

Morgan leaned against the hood of her car, her arms folded across her chest, and stared at the remains of her sister's apartment building. The emergency equipment was long gone. All that remained was a pile of blackened debris surrounded by crime scene tape and warning placards. Coming here really did not serve any purpose, other than the fact she felt she should see it with her own eyes. Some crime scenes provided an emotional stimulus, which could be either good or bad. This one, though, did not leave her feeling anything. It was simply a burned out pile of rubble where her sister died.

An unmarked police car, nearly identical to her own, pulled up alongside. She stood as Captain Doonigan stepped out and walked towards her, maneuvering his bulk in the small space between the cars.

"Agent Morgan?" he asked, extending his hand.

She accepted it with a smile. "That's right. I appreciate you taking the time to meet with me on such short notice, Chief."

"My pleasure. Anything I can do to help Mr. Wogan and the FBI."

That explained why the chief of police was meeting her instead of a desk sergeant, she thought. "Yes, I'm sure," she said, her smile fading. "The FBI's been asked to take a look into this. I got a chance to briefly glance through what the arson investigators have put together so far, but I wanted to talk to you directly to see what you thought about the whole thing."

"Personally, I think it was an accident."

"So you don't agree with Wogan?" she asked, watching him closely.

"I think Mr. Wogan's upset, which is understandable given this tragedy." He looked at the rubble. "Do you have children Agent Morgan?"

"No."

"I couldn't imagine losing one of mine."

Morgan knew exactly what it felt like, but this was not the time, or the place. "What are the arson people going to come away with?"

"I spoke with them a while ago. Most likely accidental, unless something comes up, but they don't anticipate that."

"Wogan said something about a bar."

"Yes," Doonigan nodded. "We've got some security footage of Janice leaving the bar with a woman the night the apartment went up."

"A woman?" Morgan asked, surprised.

"Apparently."

"And they came back here?"

"Yes." He turned around and pointed to a security camera on a building across the street. "That camera picked them up walking down the sidewalk towards the apartment. We believe they went in together."

"But this mystery woman came out."

"We haven't found her remains inside, at least."

Morgan's brow furrowed. "You don't have her on camera coming out?"

"No. Something happened to the camera a few hours later. The feed died."

"Odd."

He shrugged. "Technical problems come up all the time."

It was something to keep in mind. Security cameras were very simple, from a technical point of view. A camera, a data stream, and a recorder were all that were necessary, and they could run indefinitely. "Have you identified the woman?"

"No. We've asked around, even sent her image to the local news stations and posted signs at the Naval Academy, but we haven't gotten anything concrete."

"It's a pretty close-knit community out here," Morgan remarked. "Even the people coming through the Academy are generally known by someone else."

"Not this woman. One of my guys went down to the bar and questioned the staff on duty last night. They were all pretty broken up about Janice. I guess she was a regular, but nobody had ever seen this mystery woman before."

"That doesn't strike you as odd?"

He hedged. "It piques my curiosity, but it's a pretty far stretch from there to murder, especially given Janice was alive when the fire started."

"Yes, so I heard. Any thoughts on why she stayed in the bathtub?"

"Perhaps she was overcome by the smoke."

"So quickly?" Morgan shook her head. "It would be hard to believe. She would have had some warning, some time to get to the ground and stay under it." It bothered her. No one in their right mind would simply sit in the tub and die from smoke inhalation. There must be an explanation.

"Do you have a picture of this woman?" Morgan asked.

"Sure," he said, walking back to his car and pulling out a copy.

She examined the grainy picture, but did not recognize the woman. "Thanks."

"Of course. What're your next steps?"

Dropping the picture into a pocket in her coat, she said, "We're still waiting on the toxicology report. That should give us a better idea of what happened."

"Do you think she was murdered?"

"I think there are a number of things we don't know," Morgan said after a brief pause. "If we could find out who this mystery woman is, I'd rest easier. Wogan's a high-profile individual."

"You think she could be a hitman?" Doonigan asked, not able to mask his surprise.

Morgan extended her hand. "I like to keep my options open. Thank you for your time, Chief."

Chapter 21

Morgan stepped into the interrogation room's antechamber. Kloser rose from a stool when she walked into the room. Through a one-way mirror, Morgan saw Ben Keller sitting calmly on a folding chair, his hands resting on the metal table in front of him. The interrogation room was small and brightly lit. As she stood looking at Keller, he looked up at the mirror and squinted. It appeared to her that he did not have a care in the world. It was a surprising shift from the disjointed conversation they shared that morning.

"Has he said anything?" she asked Kloser.

"Not a word."

"Did you have any issues arresting him?"

"No. In fact, he surrendered to us."

"He didn't resist or protest?"

"No," Kloser said. "He walked up to us and asked if we were FBI agents. After I said yes, he introduced himself and asked to speak with you."

"Nothing else?"

"He had a laptop with him."

Morgan turned from the mirror. "Where is it?"

"I gave it to the tech pukes."

"What'd they say?"

He shrugged. "It's the one we're looking for. Other than that, though, nothing. It's encrypted. They can't get into it without a password."

"They can't get anything out of it?"

"No data. Not without the password."

She nodded, biting down the bitter frustration that rose like bile in her throat. "Has he had anything to drink? Anything to eat?"

"No."

"Why not?"

Kloser caught the anger in her tone, but did not shrink from her withering stare. "To be honest, I haven't thought about it. You just wanted him arrested and brought down here for questioning."

"Did you think he might be a tad more cooperative if he were shown some basic courtesies?"

"Is he a suspect, or a guest?"

"Both," she said, shaking her head. "I'll be right back." Turning on her heel, she left the anteroom and walked down the hall to a small break room. Inside, she fished several quarters from her pocket and fed them into a vending machine. Returning to the anteroom with a bottle of water, she did not stop to glance at Kloser. She pushed open the door to the interrogation room and stepped inside.

"I was beginning to wonder if you'd ever show up," Keller said, looking up as she closed the door behind her.

"You look like you're working on a six alarm hangover."

He nodded and licked his lips. "Too much Scotch."

"Long night?" she asked, taking a seat opposite him.

"Yes. What time is it?"

"After lunch."

He closed his eyes and exhaled slowly. "You let me rot in here all morning."

"Here," Morgan said, pushing the bottle of water across the table. "You look like you could use that."

"What I could use is something much stronger." He took the bottle, though, and drank greedily.

"Tell me about the laptop."

"No," he said, shaking his head, setting the bottle back on the table. "Let me speak with my lawyer."

She cast an amused smile across the table. "That laptop, which you held in your possession at the time of your detention, is directly tied to an ongoing investigation into illegal financial transactions with known terrorist organizations. That makes you subject to the National Defense Authorization Act, which means we can hold you until the cows come home."

"That law was challenged and an injunction issued," he said, his voice measured. "You may not hold United States citizens without due process."

With a shrug, she stood. "Let me know how that works out for you. Nobody knows you're here."

"Eve, please."

"Please, what?" she snarled, suddenly leaning over the table, her face inches from his. "That laptop, your laptop, initiated a sizable fund transfer to a terrorist cell put together by Omar Ben Iblis. That same operation saw my friend killed -- butchered, saving me."

"I didn't kill him!"

"Do you think I give a fuck?" Her eyes narrowed. "You were involved. It's your laptop, you either made the transfer, or know who did."

He recoiled in his chair as if she slapped him. The look in his eyes was one of sheer terror, and they flew around the room, hoping for a way out, but the only thing he could focus on was the burning anger behind Morgan's eyes.

"I will let them butcher you," she continued. "Whoever your handler is. Whoever pulls the strings won't let you breathe for long, once they learn you're in custody. There's too much in your head,

Ben. I can see it behind those beady little eyes. Tell me about the laptop. Tell me how to get the data from it."

"It's encrypted," he managed, wiping a hand absently across his chin.

"I know it's encrypted!" Her fist thundered down on the table as her anger finally overcame whatever restraint she had left. "That's why I'm in here! I need the password to get into the system!"

"No."

Deflated, she leaned against the table and took several deep breaths in an effort to get her temper under control. The man knew everything. It was written all over his face. Keller was the key. Despite her threats, she could not hold him indefinitely. They would eventually have to allow him access to his lawyer. It was only a matter of time.

With a sigh, she sat back down and watched him for several minutes. The room was silent except for the slight noise from the building's climate systems. "Why did you approach my agents? Why did you surrender?"

"Because I'm out of options," he said. "You are the last one I can trust to do the right thing."

"The right thing, Ben?"

"Yes."

"I don't know what you mean, and I can't help you without access to that laptop. We must have that data."

"I can't give you that."

"Why not?"

"I just can't."

Shaking her head, she said, "Then we have nothing left to discuss."

***

The afternoon sun cast muted, brooding shadows across the office's dark cherry floor, mixed with spires of sunshine not obscured by the half-open blinds. Wogan sat behind his desk, his feet propped on its surface, a cigar clamped between his lips, its smoke rising lazily to the vaulted ceiling.

Time did not hold much meaning as the cigar slowly burned. His eyes glazed over, and his mind wandered across the events of the past thirty-six hours: a daughter dead, a wife disconsolate, an investigation finished, but not yet begun. The conversation with Chief Doonigan was a blurred dream; his discussion with the director of the FBI a faded memory. Even lunch with Morgan was nothing more than a hazy cloud.

Then there was Morelli. A vivid memory of their last night together, distinct in its clarity and passion, almost brought focus to his exhausted eyes. A sharp image of her lithe, dark body moving rhythmically above him, her head tossed back in ecstasy, her muscles taught, centered itself in his mind and while he wanted to look away, he could not. She abandoned him. Deserted him. But despite all of that, despite the fact it broke his heart, he could not tear the image from his mind.

She was loose, though. She ran, and it was pretty evident she was not coming back.

He took a long, slow drag on the cigar, sending a large cloud of smoke rising to the ceiling. Running his company, doing what was right for the country, protecting the freedoms they all enjoyed, called for numerous tough decisions and unpleasant choices. Those choices sometimes caused the deaths of innocent people, but it was always clear what needed to be done.

Not this time. Not now. Now the answer was not clear at all.

As Wogan drained the last of his scotch, Dean walked into the room. "I have news," he said.

"Pour me another drink first," Wogan ordered, holding up his empty tumbler. "Will you join me?"

"Please," Dean said, taking Wogan's glass. He walked over to a small bureau. "I've heard from our man in Ireland," he said as he poured.

"And?"

Dean handed Wogan's glass back. "It's not good news."

"How bad?"

"We lost another man in Killarney."

"How?" Wogan asked, his eyes going wide.

"Two nine millimeter slugs to the side of the head."

"Christ."

"It gets worse."

Wogan looked at him expectantly.

"Morelli shot our man."

Wogan struggled to keep his face impassive. "How do you know?"

"They were trailing her through Killarney after they picked her up coming out of an internet café."

"She spotted them?"

"He doesn't think so, but something spooked her. She started to evade and eventually ended up running into a cathedral."

"A church?" Wogan asked in disbelief.

"Yes."

"Jesus. So she did pick them up."

"Probably."

"What happened?"

"They went after her into the church."

"Then why aren't they both dead?"

"Morelli bolted into the sacristy as they approached. Our man knew there was only one way out, so he went around the building to a spot where he could watch the exit. She came out a few minutes later and headed into the park. When his partner didn't come out after her, our man abandoned the surveillance and went back in the cathedral."

"And?"

"He found the body in the hallway to the sacristy."

Wogan shook his head, his face hanging, and his eyes dropping to the top of his desk. His frustration was palpable. "My instructions were not to approach her. They were only supposed to observe so we could bring in a team to deal with the situation. A team which could handle her!"

"I know."

"Could they have misunderstood?"

"I doubt it," Dean replied. "I was very clear."

"Remove him," Wogan said, looking up and meeting Dean's eyes in the fading light. "Find somebody competent to run that operation."

"Alright," Dean said, not willing to argue.

"Any sign of Ben Iblis?"

"No."

"Do you think Morelli's still in the area?"

"Yes."

"Why?"

"A couple of reasons," Dean said, picking a piece of lint from his trousers. "She hasn't moved since the first incident on the highway, when she obviously knew she was being followed, so she must feel like she is safe there. Or maybe he does."

Wogan leaned forward. "But they haven't seen him, right? Do we know for sure if he's there?"

"No, we don't."

"So she could still be acting on her own."

"She could, but I don't believe that's realistic, as we've already discussed. It would be too much of a coincidence."

Wogan chomped on his cigar as his eyes glazed over and lost focus.

"The fact that she spooked, though, tells us something," Dean continued.

"What?" Wogan asked. "What does it tell us?"

"That she may be hiding him, or protecting him somehow. Our agents didn't pick them up on their way into town. They reported that it looked like she was in town for some time before they spotted her. So it's reasonable to assume that Ben Iblis may be there, and they simply split up for whatever reason."

"Hmph," Wogan snorted.

"They were in Washington when Janice was killed."

Wogan looked at him sharply. "What?"

Dean nodded. "We traced their charter from Shannon. They flew in from Manchester after dropping off a rental car. That rental originated from one of the car agencies at Reagan."

Wogan closed his eyes and slowly shook his head. This wasn't happening. Not to him. Not after all these years. "You think I should have her killed."

"Absolutely," Dean said. "I wonder why you haven't given the order already."

"But we don't know! I don't know if she actually made that hit on Janice."

"Does it matter?"

"What do you mean?" Wogan asked.

"She left. She's a liability. Regardless of the fact they were in Washington the night Janice died!"

"She's an expensive asset!"

"She's no longer an asset! She's hiding in Ireland!" Dean shook his head in exasperation. How could it be any plainer? "Why hide? Because she knows you'd come after her with every resource, every available man. She's running because she made that hit! There's no other explanation."

"There must be!" Wogan exploded, jumping from his chair. "She wouldn't do that to me! Not Pen! Not now! Not after the last year we spent together. No!"

Even Dean was somewhat surprised by the outburst. He finished his drink and set it on the end table while he waited for Wogan to regain control of himself. It took several deep breaths and the rest of the scotch in his glass, but he eventually calmed down.

"I'm sorry, Thomas," he said, smoothing his tie and sitting back down. "I don't mean to yell at you."

"I understand."

"It's just that after all these years, I can't make this simple decision. I can't make this call." He met Dean's eyes again with a sad, tired, dejected look. "She meant so much to this organization. To me. Of all the principal agents I've hired and trained, she really could have been special."

"She could have replaced me," Dean said, realization finally dawning across his face.

Wogan nodded, just once.

Dean cleared his throat, but it was several minutes before he found his voice. "What instructions should I send the new director of the Ireland operations?"

"Capture her."

"Capture?"

"Yes," Wogan said, some light hint of his usual steely resolve etching his words. "Capture her. I want to question her personally. No harm is to come to her until we've had a chance to speak. I must ask her face to face. I must know."

"Janice was murdered."

"But did Pen do it?"

"It shouldn't matter."

Wogan thought about it, nearly finishing his cigar before he replied. "It could change everything."

Dean stared at him before slowly shaking his head. "This is foolish."

"Perhaps, but I must know."

The phone on Wogan's desk began to ring, and Dean leaned over to pick it up. "It's Morgan," he said after a brief exchange. "Do you want to speak with her?"

"Yes, of course," Wogan said, taking the phone. "Evelyn, I didn't expect to hear from you so soon."

"Lucky me," she quipped over the digital circuit.

"Have you heard anything?" Wogan asked.

"I just spoke with Doonigan. He was most helpful."

"Did he have something new?"

"No, he was just filling me in on some of the specifics."

"Oh," Wogan sighed, his disappointment palpable.

"I wanted to ask you about Janice's medical history."

"Her medical history?" Wogan asked, looking across his desk at Dean. "Why?"

"Some of the things Doonigan mentioned, plus what I've learned reading the preliminary arson report. Like you said, she never got out of that tub. It made me wonder what would have kept her there."

"Well, as I said, she wasn't the type to take something like that sitting down. I have no idea why she would have stayed in that tub."

"There isn't an easy way to ask this, so I'll just come out and say it," Morgan said. "Did she ever have a problem with drugs?"

Wogan swallowed hard and sat down. "No," he lied. "Why do you ask?"

"I'm just exploring all the options. An overdose would have kept her in that tub. She didn't take any sleep aids?"

"No, not that I'm aware of."

"What about a prescription?" she asked. "Something legal that might've helped her on those nights she couldn't get to bed?"

Wogan paused before he said, "Again, I don't think so."

"Are you sure?"

He didn't know if she could sense his hesitation, but Janice's rehab was something he worked very hard to keep secret. "As I said, not that I know of."

"Ok, then, next question. Did she have a lot of friends in Annapolis?"

"There were a few she spoke about," Wogan said, still looking at Dean, a question on his face. Had Morgan found something?

"Did she ever mention a woman in her late twenties or early thirties? Brown hair? Attractive?"

"It doesn't ring any bells," Wogan said. "The friends she mentioned were classmates, people she knew at school."

"And that's what I would expect."

"Was there someone older?" Wogan asked, clutching the handset. "Did you find something?"

"No, just curious. She went to a local bar the night she died, and the bartender mentioned that she spent a lot of time talking to a woman there."

"Hold on one second, please," Wogan said, pressing the mute button on the phone's base. Still looking at Dean, he said, "Morgan's asking about a woman, older, late twenties, early thirties, attractive, brown hair. Do you know if Janice ran around with someone like that?"

Dean stared at him, his mouth slightly open. "She just described Morelli."

"No."

Dean's eyebrows arched, but he didn't say anything.

Wogan looked down at the phone's base. Morelli would not do that to him, he repeated to himself. He unmuted the phone. "I just asked Dean," he said into the handset. "He's not aware of anyone that matches that description, either. Did you get the toxicology results back?"

"No, not yet. They should be ready soon. I was going to head down there and check after I got off the phone with you."

"Please let me know as soon as you hear."

"Of course," Morgan said.

The phone went dead in his ear and he placed it in its cradle.

"Drugs?" Dean asked.

"She was throwing out ideas. Fishing."

"You don't think she could have fallen back in the habit, do you?"

Wogan shook his head and rubbed his temples. "I don't know what to think anymore."

***

Morgan stepped off the elevator and walked to Runfo's office. In the few hours since she was last there, a complete change overcame the place. The cheap shelves, nearly buckling under the weight of countless tomes on every conceivable forensic subject, were gone, replaced by bare, albeit dirty, white walls. The floor was clear for the first time in Morgan's memory. The stacks of books, folders, magazines, and papers were packed away, on their way to Runfo's new office.

The entire room was nearly bare, save for the worn-down, battered old desk and chair. Runfo sat there, his head buried in a report, the white wisps of his hair floating lazily in the breeze from the air conditioning.

"Hey, Eve," he said as she crossed the threshold.

"I'm amazed."

"Why?" he asked, not looking up from the report.

"I can actually walk in here without fear for my life."

He glanced up and tilted his head to one side, a look of supreme boredom plastered on his face. "Really? After ten years, that's the best you can do? What happened to that stinging wit I've grown to love?"

"It's been a long couple of weeks." A small smile crossed her lips. "I'm going to miss you."

"Yeah, me too. I've grown used to everything around here. It's going to be a shock going down to Quantico."

"I'm sure you'll be fine."

He laughed. "Of course I'll be fine, my dear. I'm in charge of the damn place."

She looked around. "You know, there still isn't anywhere for guests to sit."

"Wouldn't want them to think they can stay too long."

"Is your new office going to have the same policy?"

He shook his head, those white wisps dancing harder. "No. My new secretary informed me that a conference table is standard fare for my new office."

"Ouch."

"Yes. Quite the change."

Her smile grew. "I'm happy for you."

"I know. And thank you. I don't know how reasonable it'll be for you to visit, but I hope you'll make the effort from time to time. It would mean a lot to me."

"I'll try."

"I hope so. You're what little beauty that keeps this place bearable."

She flushed, smiled with obvious embarrassment, and mumbled, "Thank you."

"I mean it, Eve," he said. "Come visit. Please."

"I will try," she assured him. "What girl can refuse an offer like that?"

"It's difficult, I'm sure."

"So," she said, obviously changing the subject. "What about my tox report? Have you got anything?"

He cleared his throat and rubbed the stubble on his chin. "I've been reading it, actually," he said, tapping the folder on his desk.

"And?"

"It's interesting."

"How so?"

"You know a decent bit about forensics, I know, especially ballistics, since I taught you everything. But what about forensic pathology?"

"Not as much as I should," she admitted.

"But you know enough to request the toxicology report and read the autopsy that Wogan ordered done on his daughter's body?"

She nodded. "Of course I do. This is my job. That promotion going to your head, Charlie? Give me a little credit."

He ignored her. "It's very interesting to read, and there are a number of details that, I would guess, the good Mr. Wogan is unaware of."

"Such as?"

"Indications of habitual drug use."

"What?" she asked, surprised.

"Indications of intravenous drug use," he said again, reading directly from the report.

"No, I heard you. Recent? Or did the track marks show up post mortem?

"Well, both, actually."

"That son of a bitch."

"Excuse me?"

She waved her hand in the air. "Nothing. I'm just remembering the conversation I had with Wogan five minutes ago."

"And?"

"I asked him specifically about Janice's medical history and any possible drug use. He said he wasn't aware of any."

"Do you believe him?"

"Not anymore," she said, her anger growing. "What else?"

"Early indications of cirrhosis of the liver."

"If she was an addict, I'm not surprised."

Runfo nodded. "But here's where it gets interesting. Do you know if she was seeing anybody for insomnia?"

"Like treatment?" Morgan shook her head. "No. Again, I asked Wogan about it directly. The information I got indicated she was a pretty run of the mill kid. My...." She almost said 'sister,' but she caught herself at the last moment. "Janice was either a fantastic actor, or her parents had absolutely no clue what she was up to."

"Given her family history, do you think either of those is reasonable?"

"I don't have any idea," she admitted. "I'm sure Wogan would have kept pretty good tabs on her growing up. He seems like the protective sort."

"Hiding a habitual IV habit isn't something that's easy to do. Even if you manage to keep the injections secret, those drugs will eventually wreck their havoc physically. The stupidest parents in the world should be able to tell something's going on."

"Exactly, but when I questioned Wogan about it, he didn't mention a thing."

Runfo pursed his lips but did not pursue it. "According to the report, her body was chock full of hypnotics."

"Hypnotics?"

"A lot of the drugs used today to treat insomnia fall into that classification. In your sister's case, her system was saturated with a nonbenzodiazepine hypnotic. Zolpidem."

"My sister?" Morgan asked, feigning ignorance.

"It's all over the office. Everybody knows Janice was your sister."

"Shit," she said, hanging her head.

"It's really not a big deal."

"The hell it isn't. Tell me about these hypnotics."

He watched her, then shrugged. "It's better known as Ambien, though there are several other manufacturers that sell it under generic brands."

Morgan paced back and forth in front of his desk, turning the discovery over in her mind. "It would certainly support the hypothesis that she was killed accidentally." She crossed her arms and continued to pace. "Let's say she meets someone at the bar, they head back to her place for a good time, inject some drugs, and she collapses in the bathtub. Her friend makes sure she's still breathing and goes on her merry way. What was the cause of death, by the way?"

"Smoke inhalation."

"They're ruling it accidental?"

Runfo nodded.

"Ok," Morgan said. "What about a prescription? Were they able to dig up anything in the databases?"

"No," he said, shaking his head.

"Fuck," Morgan swore, shaking her head. "So she's full of illegal drugs, passes out in the tub, leaves the stove on, the place catches fire, and she's too bonkers to get up out of the tub and leave the apartment."

"So it would seem."

Her anger rising, Morgan swore again and paced in front of his desk. "And they've got me trying to drum up some fantastic story as to why daddy's little girl died in a fire, when the evidence really is pretty cut and dry, despite Wogan's insistence that his daughter didn't have anything to do with drugs."

"C'mon, Eve," Runfo said, amused. "You know how this town works. Of course they're going to do everything they can to placate a man as powerful as Wogan. He's got far too many people in his pocket. It's how the game's played. You just happened to draw the short straw this time around."

"That and the fact that I'm on the Director's shit list."

"That probably doesn't help."

"What else?" she asked, jutting her chin at the folder.

"Not much, I'm afraid. The report's very thorough and complete, but really there's not a whole lot to support the theory that she's been murdered. The toxicology report isn't that abnormal, not for an addict anyway, and the rest of the evidence points to an accidental fire, tragic as it is. I don't really see how this can be seen as anything other than a horrible tragedy."

"Ok, Charlie," she said. "Thank you, as always."

"You'll come see me in Quantico?"

She grinned sweetly, despite the anger flaring in her gut. "I will," she said, flashing a broad smile that grew the longer she looked down at her old mentor.

Chapter 22

Morgan rode the elevator down to the garage, her mind still boiling at the thought of an entire afternoon wasted on this useless fool's errand. Keller surrendered, but would not cooperate. They were dead in the water on the financial trail, and Ben Iblis was only moving further from her reach. On top of that, her sister was dead because she was stupid, and her father would rather lie about Janice's past than help the very people he demanded be brought in to lead the investigation.

It was that simple. There wasn't anything sinister about it. Janice was stupid, and she paid for it with her life. There were far more pressing matters she needed to address, far more important people she needed to find. But none of that could happen until she either convinced the director, or Wogan, to drop the investigation and move on. Given the state of affairs with her career, she thought she would have a far better chance with Wogan, so she got into her car and drove fifteen minutes until she was parked outside his expansive brownstone.

The setting sun lit the dark dash of her car with a splash of color that brought a smile to her face. It was absurd. The last thing she should be was content, and, in fact, she was simmering at the thought of the wasted hours chasing down the false hope that Janice was not responsible for her own death. But that single beam of sunlight, filtered through the walnuts and oaks that lined the lane, put everything in perspective. Yes, it was an almost unbearably painful week. Her lover murdered, three agents under her command killed, and the only real chance they ever had at the world's foremost assassin fading with each passing hour. But she was still there. She could still fight.

The beam of sunlight danced with the shadows on her dashboard. More opportunities awaited. She could still catch Ben Iblis. It was an achievable goal because she fought, and she won. She was alive. While the news she was about to deliver was not good, she knew Wogan would take her for her word. He would make a rational decision. Wogan's marked decline shocked even her, but despite the crushing loss of a child, and Morgan could sympathize, she knew there was enough left in the man to come to a reasonable conclusion.

Getting out of the car, she strode up the sidewalk and stopped in front of the large wooden front door. She would do her duty and inform Wogan of the details of the autopsy, but that was the end. There was no longer any reason to continue this investigation. She needed to get back to Nichols' killer. She needed to get back to Ben Iblis.

Dean answered the door several short seconds after her knock. "Agent Morgan," he said.

"May I come in?" she asked.

"I assume you would like to see Mr. Wogan?"

"Yes." Who else would she want to see, she asked herself, trying not to look at him too strangely.

He motioned with his left hand and said, "Please."

She stepped into a marble covered foyer, bright even in the setting sun, the last hints of its warmth bouncing from the white stone. A dark mahogany staircase rose away to her left, dwarfing the rest of the entryway.

Dean shut the door behind her. "He's in the office. This way."

Following him, she was led through a comfortable living room and a gourmet kitchen before Dean knocked softly on two solid cherry doors. A muffled voice called from within, and Dean stepped forward, opening the doors, ushering her into Wogan's office.

The splendor of the floor to ceiling solid wood bookshelves, ornate cherry desk, and wood floors surprised her, but she kept her emotions cloaked behind a mask of indifference, her piercing green eyes meeting her father's across that broad expanse of wood. He rose slowly from his seat, and she could feel his eyes as they passed over her, taking in every detail, judging every nuance.

"Evelyn," he said.

"Andy," she replied.

They stood there staring at each other for several moments before he finally waved his hand and called over her shoulder, "That will be all, Thomas."

Dean withdrew, closing the doors behind him.

"May I offer you a drink?"

"Bourbon," she said. "Please."

"Aren't you on duty?" Wogan asked, a little taken back by her request.

"Does it matter? Why would you offer me a drink and then question whether or not I should drink it?"

He shrugged, walked over to the bureau and poured a large measure from one of the crystal decanters.

"Thank you," she said, accepting the tumbler.

Wogan walked back around his desk and picked up his own glass. "To fallen friends."

"And strangers," she added, raising her glass before taking a slow sip, relishing the amber liquid as it burned the back of her throat.

Draining his glass, he walked back to the bureau and poured himself another. "I'd wondered when I'd see you again. Please," he said, motioning to one of the chairs in front of his desk. "Have a seat."

"Thank you," she said, settling into one of the plush leather chairs.

"Did I ever tell you the story of how your mother and I met?"

"Well, no," she said, unsure how to respond, shifting uncomfortably in her chair. It was not the beginning she expected.

He crossed one leg over the other and leaned back, a small smile creasing his white mustache. "She was radiant. Basically the only thing in the entire bar with any kind of grace or light. I was in Vegas for a conference. Just a couple of days." He glanced over at her. "You look displeased."

"You'll forgive me if I'm not overjoyed at the prospect of being the love child of some fling that started in a bar in Las Vegas."

His reflective smile grew into a patient gaze, and he continued. "I had a couple of drinks at the bar, and I couldn't help but notice that she just kept sitting there, in a booth, all alone. It had to have been twenty minutes or so, and I really couldn't figure out why she was still sitting there all alone." He chuckled at the memory. "So I finally walked over to her --"

"Why are you telling me this?" Morgan asked, interrupting.

"I thought you might want to know."

"Why?"

He shrugged. "I guess I just figured everybody wanted to know how their parents met."

"Did Janice?"

The blue in his eyes turned to ice, and he stared at her. "I didn't get the opportunity."

"What a shame."

He sniffed and licked his lips. "Are you bitter because I wasn't there, or because Janice was?"

"I wouldn't say I was bitter either way."

"Then what is it?"

"I think you're a despicable piece of shit."

The ensuing silence was haunting in its utter stillness. They sat there as the last light of evening faded, twilight finally filtering through the slatted blinds. After what seemed like an eternity, Wogan switched on his desktop lamp, bathing their faces in soft, yellow light.

"Why?" he asked. "Because I wasn't there when you were growing up?"

"Does it matter why?"

He took another drink from his glass. "I suppose not."

"Were you there for Janice?"

"As often as I could be."

"That wasn't my question."

"But that was my answer."

She held his stare. "Were you there for her?"

"Yes."

"Then why is she dead?"

"You tell me!"

Morgan shook her head and sighed. "Were you there for her rehab?"

Standing up, he walked back to the bureau and poured himself another drink. "I'm not sure I like your tone."

"We found the track marks," she said to his back. "What we didn't find is the records. Was that painful? Writing that check to have everything disappear as if it didn't happen? How much did it cost?" She felt him stiffen. "Was it worth it?"

"I was the one that forced her into the hospital. Her mother..." his voice trailed off, and he drained the tumbler he just poured. "Her mother thought we could treat her at home."

"I find that hard to believe."

"To be honest, I don't really care."

"You didn't believe she could be treated at home?"

He shook his head.

"Why not?"

"It was beyond that. She was too far gone."

Morgan caught something in his tone. It was not sorrow. It was resignation. He was ready to talk. Finally. "She relapsed after the inpatient treatment."

He sighed, poured himself more scotch, and sat back down behind his desk. "Yes."

"Heroin?"

"Among other things," he said. "Alcohol, then cocaine, then on into the heavier narcotics."

"Why didn't you think you could handle it at home?"

"She needed the best." He made a point to look at her. "My daughters deserve the best. That wasn't possible at home, regardless of what I was willing to pay. The doctors simply weren't able to relocate to Woodland Park for the time necessary to treat her."

"Not everyone can be bought."

He ignored the jab. "The best treatment was at a facility."

"And the relapse?"

Wogan studied her for a moment, then asked, "Have you ever had to support a loved one in the throes of addiction?"

"No."

"It's a fate I wouldn't wish on anyone. There's nothing worse than wanting to help someone you love that much, especially your child, but not being able to do anything but sit back and watch. It's terrible."

"Kinda like losing her for good?"

He cleared his throat. "Something like that."

So why did you abandon me, she wanted to scream. Instead, she just swallowed and asked, "What happened?"

Wogan shrugged. "We did what we could. Sent her back to rehab, got her more treatment, supported her through it all. When she came out of it the second time, after dropping out of school, she was different, and I hoped this time it might stick, this time she beat it. There wouldn't be another trip to the emergency room, and she wouldn't need to go back to the hospital. She fought, and she got past it."

"When was the last time you saw her?"

"Several weeks ago," he said, thinking back. "We had lunch when I was in Washington for meetings."

"Did you see her arms?"

"No," he said, shaking his head. "She was wearing a sweater her mother gave her for Christmas. Why?"

"You said she was a fighter."

"She was."

"Yet she kept slipping back into old habits."

"But she always fought to get past them. She always went back to rehab with the attitude that she would beat it. That it would be different. That this time she'd stay clean."

"But she slipped back."

"No," he said, his fist banging the desk. "No. Not this last time."

Morgan looked at him patiently, even with a hint of sympathy. "There were track marks on her arms and thighs when she died."

"Old scars, I'm sure. Maybe something that came out in the fire."

"No," Morgan said, shaking he head. "Some were recent."

"I find that hard to believe. There weren't any signs three weeks ago."

"But you just said you didn't see her arms. More lies?"

"She didn't look like she'd been using again. She didn't look like she relapsed. Believe me, I'd know. Those years nearly killed me. She wasn't using again. No."

"There's more," Morgan said, leaning back in the chair. "There were trace amounts of heroin in her system."

Wogan pursed his lips and took another drink. "What else?"

"Zolpidem."

He looked at her blankly.

"It's better known as Ambien."

"She's always had trouble sleeping," he said, latching on to that bit of hope. "Ever since that first stint in rehab. She's got a prescription."

"It's not in any of the files. There's no record."

He just looked at her.

"Who was her doctor?" she asked with a deep sigh.

"I don't know. Dean will, though," he said, walking around the desk and opening the doors. "It was a private deal. I didn't want it to be too visible. Thomas!" he yelled. "Please come here a moment."

He sat back down behind his desk as Dean walked into the room and stood behind the second leather chair.

"Who was Janice's doctor?" Wogan asked.

"Jenson," Dean said. "Dr. Jenson."

Morgan wrote it down in a small notebook.

"Thomas," Wogan asked. "You sometimes went to help Janice run errands. Did you ever go by the pharmacy?"

"Yes," he said. "On a few occasions."

"Would you please tell Evelyn, then," Wogan said, "that Janice did have a prescription for Ambien? For her insomnia?"

Dean looked puzzled. "Well, yes. She did have insomnia, and I believe Dr. Jenson was treating her for it, but she didn't have a prescription for Ambien, and it wasn't in her name. When I went to pick up her prescription last month, the drug was Lunesta, not Ambien. I suppose the name's irrelevant."

"Why would she take Ambien if she had a script for Lunesta?" Morgan asked.

"I don't know," Wogan said. "If she wanted to get high, why not just take the prescription?"

"Get high?" Morgan asked.

"That's what she was always interested in. Escaping reality, her therapist always told us. For some reason she found it, or rather me, to be overbearing."

"I can only imagine," Morgan said, raising an eyebrow.

"So I'm sure if she wanted to get high, to escape, she could have just used her prescription somehow."

"The interesting thing about Ambien is the distinct difference it produces when injected," Morgan explained, "rather than taken as prescribed, which is orally."

"Difference?" Dean asked. "What kind of a difference?"

"Well, when ingested orally, it is slowly absorbed, the capsule dissolved over many hours, trickling the drug into the blood stream to gently put the host to sleep. In some cases, people who take the drug don't remember the past eight to ten hours."

"And intravenously?" Wogan asked.

"It hits you like a freight train," she said, "if you dose it large enough. If you cook just the regular oral dose, you're not going to get that big of a hit, but when you pop enough, the trip will take you out for a while."

"Take you out how?" Wogan asked.

"Knock you flat on your ass," she said, placing her empty glass on the edge of Wogan's desk. "Sit back, close your eyes, and nod off. You won't remember a damn thing when you wake up. Problem is, it hits people differently. There's no guarantee it'll knock you flat out, and there's no guarantee at what dose it'll really have a lasting effect."

"Doesn't seem like a real good drug to use when you're trying to kill someone," Dean said.

Morgan looked at him. "Unless you're trying very hard to mask the death as something else. If you can get the dose right, get out without being seen, and stage the murder as an accident, then you're really on to something."

"Is that what you think happened?" Wogan asked.

"No," Morgan said, shaking her head. "It's an interesting point, but it doesn't indicate foul play. Given her history, it simply adds fuel to the theory that she died accidentally. That's why she didn't get out of the bathtub. She couldn't. She was flat on her ass riding that Ambien high. Based on everything we've learned, I really don't think she was murdered."

"But you just said her body was full of Zolpidem," Dean protested. "Her prescription was for a different drug."

Morgan shrugged. "She was an addict. Who knows. Maybe she decided to shoot something different that night. Maybe she got tired of taking the prescription orally and decided to shoot something similar instead."

"But in the bathtub?" Dean asked. "She knew the affects of those drugs, regardless if she took one or the other. She would've known to be careful and not take it before climbing into the bath with something on the stove."

"What was the cause of death?" Wogan asked, almost afraid of what the answer might be.

"Smoke inhalation."

His face fell, and he shrunk even further into his seat.

"Which means she was alive when that fire started," Dean said.

"Yes," Morgan said.

"And the Ambien?" Wogan asked, very softly.

"I don't think it signifies anything in this case, other than to offer an explanation as to why she didn't get out of the tub. She was a known drug abuser. The Ambien was taken for one reason or another, and it prevented her being able to get out before she was overcome by the smoke."

"Closed case, then?" Wogan asked, resigned.

"I don't know how to make it any clearer."

Wogan glanced over at Dean before turning back to Morgan. "On the phone you were asking me about a woman. Is she a suspect?"

Morgan watched him carefully, conscious of the picture still in her jacket pocket. "No, not at this time. No one's been able to bring anything forward that would indicate she had anything to do with this."

"Other than she was probably the last person to see my daughter alive."

"Perhaps."

Glancing over at Dean one more time, Wogan reached into a desk drawer and withdrew a piece of photo paper. "As I said, my daughter mentioned several friends she was close with at college, but none of them matched her description."

Morgan nodded. "Yes, I remember."

"She had mentioned one individual, who she was somewhat leery of."

Wogan pushed the picture across the desk. Picking it up, Morgan was surprised to see it was a black and white picture of the same woman caught in the surveillance camera outside of Janice's apartment.

"Janice didn't know who she was," Dean said, "but she was concerned, so she asked me to snap that picture. It was the best shot I could get, taken at some distance, I'm afraid."

They watched as Morgan stared at the picture.

"Is it the woman in the surveillance photo?" Wogan asked.

"No," Morgan lied, shaking her head. She met Wogan's eyes. "I'm sorry."

He nodded, almost painfully.

"Who is this woman?" Morgan asked.

Dean, ever cautious about protecting Wogan, said, "We ran her down, but didn't come up with a whole lot. We believe she's a drifter, maybe somebody that was stalking Janice to steal her identity."

"I see," Morgan said, not believing it. It was one more piece of the puzzle, though. Wogan knew the woman caught on the surveillance picture. "You'll call the Director?" she asked. "Now that I think we have this somewhat settled?"

"Thomas?" Wogan asked.

"I'll make the call," Dean said.

"Thank you," Morgan said, standing.

"Will you stay for dinner?" Dean asked.

"No, I won't," she said, and walked to the door.

"I appreciate you looking into this personally, Eve," Wogan choked from behind his desk.

She turned in the doorway. He aged ten years in less than a few minutes; thinner, paler, a haunted, gaunt expression hanging from his face. Whatever life there was in his eyes faded completely as she stared at him. It was hard for her to feel anything but pity for this shell of a man, despite the anger that burned like fire in her gut. She bit back her original rebuke. "Good day," she said with a slight nod.

The front door closed quietly behind her as she showed herself out, leaving the two men staring at her shadow in the office. She never suffered fools, and there was not any love lost between her and her father. What troubled her, though, was the picture they handed her matched the surveillance photo exactly. Wogan knew the woman, or at least he had an idea.

Who was this woman?

Her phone jingled impatiently as she opened her car door, and she made a mental note to run the woman's picture through the FBI database. "Morgan," she barked, trying to ignore the increasing exhaustion.

"It's Kloser."

Her heart almost stopped. She dropped into the car and shut the door. "Do you have something from Keller?" She left him in the interrogation room with the slim hope that time alone might change his mind.

"Two things, actually. You're gonna need to sit down for one of them."

"Ok," she said, a cold hand gripping her heart.

"Keller wants to see you. Now."

"I'll come down," she said. "But that's not why you wanted me to sit down, is it?"

"No."

"Tell me."

"The team finished tracing Baker's financial records," he said, his voice heavy. "We found something."

"What?"

"There was an offshore account with several very large deposits spread over many, many years. We traced them back to their originations. All of them were sent through one shell company or another, but tracing those records back we found they all came from one corporation."

"Which one?"

"Odyssey Systems."

"That doesn't ring any bells," she said, suddenly confused. Where was he going with this?

"Right. But if you run down Odyssey Systems, the CEO is listed as one Janice Wogan."

Chapter 23

Wogan dropped into his chair thoroughly deflated. Massaging his temples, he closed his eyes and sighed. He wanted to be angry at Morgan, but it did not matter now. Janice was gone, and there wasn't even the possibility of revenge. She was simply gone.

"Would you like another drink?" Dean asked.

"How many have I had?"

"A lot." Wogan was deteriorating before his eyes. He who was always in control of his emotions and destiny appeared unable to make the simplest decision.

"Then one more won't hurt."

Dean nodded and walked to the bureau. Filling two glasses with the last of the scotch, he asked, "Do you believe her?"

"Does it matter?"

"I think so."

"Then yes," Wogan said. "I do believe her."

"I'm rather surprised, to be honest."

"Why?" Wogan asked, accepting the proffered glass.

"That toxicology report came back very quickly. I could see confirmation of drugs in her system in such a short span of time, but isolating the individual compounds?" Dean shook his head. "It's hard to believe."

"So?"

Dean sat down in one of the leather chairs and took a sip of his drink. "Even for the FBI, it was damn quick. It's not like television."

"I'd say, 'it's not,' but I don't really give a shit anymore."

"There's a lot of tests that must be run in order to separate the compounds, at the molecular level, from the victim's blood," Dean continued, not really caring if Wogan was listening or not. "It takes time."

"You don't trust her?"

"I don't trust them," Dean clarified.

"It's amazing what can happen, or what can be made to happen, when the correct leverage is applied. You know that as well as I do. The fact that they had that autopsy done, and a preliminary report, doesn't surprise me all that much. The toxicology report could have been completed faster if they dedicated a number of resources towards its completion."

"I think it was too quick."

"What do they have to gain by falsifying the report?" Wogan asked.

"To mollify you."

"You give me too much credit. I doubt even the FBI would go to such lengths to placate me. No, not after everything I've done for the Director. They're good people. They do their job."

"And Evelyn?" Dean asked.

"Evelyn's their best. Of all the people, she would be the last to sacrifice her character simply for my gratification. Quite the opposite, actually. She would see it to the bitter end just to spite me." He remembered the hate burning in her eyes. "No. That one will honor her duty above anything."

"Even you?"

"Especially me. I'm surprised you didn't see it."

"Oh, I did. I just wanted to emphasize the point."

Wogan contemplated his assistant. "You still believe Janice was murdered?"

"What I believe is rather irrelevant at the moment. She wasn't my daughter."

"But you would continue to pursue this?" Wogan asked, watching him closely.

"I would simply be cautious before accepting the FBI's word at face value."

"Even Evelyn's word?"

Dean thought carefully before replying. "Even Evelyn has been known to make mistakes. Ben Iblis alluded to that."

"Through no fault of her own. He was out to ruin her, no matter the cost."

"And to her credit, she recovered. But it doesn't diminish the fact that she screwed up. No one's infallible. Not in this line of work."

Wogan leaned back and folded his hands in his lap. What Dean was saying made sense, and he wanted to believe it more than anything else, but he knew what Evelyn was capable of. He watched her grow up, from afar, yes, but he watched her, which was why he also knew he should give up any hope for Janice. The sad truth was that she had not been murdered. She died in a bathtub from smoke inhalation, unable to move because of the drugs coursing through her system.

"Have you ever shot up Ambien?" Wogan asked.

Dean looked appalled. "Of course not."

"Yes. Did you know your hearing goes flat?"

"Flat?"

Wogan nodded. "Not deaf. Flat. Every noise, uniquely enhanced, has the same tone -- the same quality. A car accelerating down the road has the same sound as somebody sneezing. And while you think that might wake you up, or make you more aware, it's almost the opposite, because right after the sensory changes, the drug hits you like a train wreck."

"How?"

"Growing up, I knew a lot of guys into hallucinogenics --"

"You?" Dean blurted, surprised.

"Yes. It was the sixties. Everybody knew somebody in that scene. Some people knew many people." A rare smile spread across his face as memories passed through his mind. "Anyway, I once knew a guy who described one of his tamer acid trips. Of course we didn't have Ambien back then, but I did some research when Janice was first prescribed Lunesta, just to see what alternatives might be out there. The Ambien trip, while similar to acid, isn't exactly the same. It's sort of half-hallucinogenic, I guess, and it can vary from person to person."

"Odd."

"New science."

"Do you think Janice really injected it?" Dean asked. "Do you think she fell off the wagon?"

"If the FBI didn't find any trace of the pill in her GI tract, nothing in the stomach contents, it's certainly plausible. Evelyn mentioned fresh track marks on her body. It also explains why she didn't move. She couldn't."

"That bad?"

"It can be." Wogan looked down at his hands. "I'd thought we'd gotten her through it. Finally."

"The drugs?"

Wogan nodded.

Taking a deep breath, Dean said, "I think you and Mrs. Wogan did just about everything you could?"

"Just about?"

"Just about."

"What did we miss?" Wogan asked, his brow furrowed.

"Supervision while she was away."

"At school?"

Dean nodded.

"We discussed that before she left. After two sessions, and being clean for so long, it was time to let her go, let her out on her own. If she didn't make it then..." his voice trailed off, and he reached for his drink. After a long sip, he set it back down, but it wasn't for several more minutes before he was able to speak. "We did everything we could. She was sober for years."

"Doesn't that make you wonder, though?"

"What?" Wogan asked.

"The drug issue."

"Why? Because she was sober?"

"And it wasn't what she was prescribed. The doctor prescribed Lunesta, not Ambien."

Wogan studied him. "She decided to get high, not take her usual sleeping pill. I'm sure she was just blowing off steam from a long week of classes. That's all. Why do you keep pushing this? You've been talking murder ever since the plane trip out here the night we... the night we found out."

"Because I don't think she was killed by smoke inhalation."

"You heard Evelyn's report," Wogan continued, losing his patience. "It was there in black and white. There's no sense disputing it. Janice died from smoke inhalation."

"You know what I mean. That drug kept her in the tub while the smoke killed her, but it wasn't the drug she was prescribed. It wasn't what she would usually be taking."

"So what?"

"What if someone staged it to look like an accident?" Dean asked. "What if it was someone that knew her history with drugs?"

"The FBI doesn't agree. Evelyn doesn't agree."

"What about the woman that was seen walking with Janice into her apartment?"

"A friend," Wogan said, trying to dismiss it. "Evelyn didn't say anything. I even showed her the picture of Morelli."

"As I said, Evelyn's made mistakes before."

"I still don't understand why you're pushing this."

"Because I don't want you to give up. I was close to Janice, too, you know. I watched her grow up. I saw the agony she went through fighting addiction. She didn't deserve to die in that bathtub."

"I know that," Wogan said, very softly.

Dean stood up and looked down at the folder Morgan left on the desk. "Just don't take that FBI report at face value. Janice deserves an investigation."

"There was an investigation." Wogan opened the folder and scanned the cover sheet with his blue eyes. "No evidence of foul play. Death ruled accidental."

"And you believe it."

"It doesn't matter what I believe. Not anymore." Wogan ran his hand down his face and grimaced, noticing the stubble for the first time. "Janice is dead, and all the wishing in the world isn't going to change that."

"But if we could find justice --"

"No," Wogan said, shaking his head. "It's done."

"We could hire an investigator."

"No." Wogan closed the file and slammed it down on his desk. "It's over. It's done. Let her rest in peace."

Dean stared down at him, a look of sadness in his eyes. "So you'll accept Evelyn's report?"

"I will accept that my daughter died an addict in a bathtub. Now leave. Have the plane ready in an hour. I need to get back to Colorado and salvage whatever relationship I may have left with the only woman I've been able to keep around."

***

"I want to bring him here," Morelli said, closing her eyes and resting her head against the back of the chair.

They were sitting on the porch, each silently picking apart their actions earlier that morning. Everything worked out, but it was clear they were being hunted.

"Who?" Ben Iblis asked.

"Wogan."

"Why?"

"I want to be done with it. He won't stop hunting us. Surely you must see that."

"How does bringing him here finish anything?"

"You could kill him."

He chuckled. "Really."

"Why do you laugh?"

"Because you should know that it's never as simple as that. Did that episode earlier today really upset you that much?"

"I never thought he'd try to have me killed," Morelli admitted.

"Because you were lovers? You of all people should know better than that."

"Yes, I suppose I should."

"Besides, you do not know they were there to kill you."

"I don't think they were there simply to chat."

"No, but perhaps they have a capture order on you. That would explain the rather reckless pursuit."

She thought back to that afternoon in the hall of the church as she raised her pistol and pulled the trigger. The body collapsed behind her eyes and she was out the door in an instant. Wogan's man, the survivor of the pair, never reappeared.

"Of course," Ben Iblis continued, still gazing up at the ceiling of the porch, "that order may have been changed with this recent development."

"I doubt it."

"You do not think he would have you killed?"

"No," she said. "I doubt it was a capture order in the first place. Nobody does that these days. Too easy to screw up. Too many questions that I could answer, given the right amount of pressure. It'd be easier just to kill me."

"So why do you think he will come if you call and summon him?"

"Because I have information he desperately wants."

"What?"

"I know who killed his daughter."

"You are assuming he has not chalked it up to an accident."

"No," she said, shaking her head. "As I said before, he'll instantly suspect it wasn't an accident. My guess, he's trying to run everything down now. That's probably why he's so hell bent on catching me."

"There are easier ways to deal with women, as you said."

"And when have you ever dealt with a woman?" she asked, amused. "Other than Morgan."

He paused briefly, his breath catching in his chest, but it was out almost as quickly, and he replied, "Many, many years ago."

"Was she pretty?"

"More than that."

"Tell me."

"Why?"

"Tell me about her beauty," she repeated.

Silence enveloped them for several minutes before he said, "It was similar to yours, actually. Your beauty. She was Turkish. Jet-black hair, lips like a blood rose, and the finest olive skin. We spent several months together on Cyprus...." His voice trailed off, and Morelli saw the muscles in his forearms tense and relax several times in a row. "Many wonderful weeks, all those years ago. It seems so very far away."

"What happened to her?"

"I shot her."

"Why?"

"Because she witnessed the murder of her parents." He bore his cold brown eyes into hers. "When I shot them."

"They had a contract?"

"Her father did."

"So you used the daughter to get to the father."

He nodded. "But I never thought it would go that far."

"How far did it go?"

Pursing his lips, he said, "Too far."

"Did you love her?"

"I think so."

"What was her name?" she asked, watching his eyes for any kind of emotion, any sign that there might be something there, but they remained cold.

"Astia."

"A beautiful name."

"As I said, she was a beautiful girl."

They fell into silence again, Morelli turning his admission over in her mind. Is that why he could not kill Morgan? "Do you regret it?" she asked after several minutes.

"Which part? Falling in love with her or killing her?"

"Either. Both."

"I regret I did not maintain my professionalism, and I regret she walked in when she did."

It took her a minute to digest that. Finally, she asked, "What if she hadn't walked in and seen it?"

"Then things might have turned out very differently."

"But her father would still be dead."

"Of course."

They lapsed into silence again, the crickets in the fields the only sound. "Would you kill him?" Morelli asked after several minutes.

"Wogan?"

"Yes."

He thought about it. She could almost hear the gears whirling in his head, weighing the options, and the consequences. "He is a dangerous adversary."

"That would suggest he should be removed."

"There's no profit in it."

"No profit?" She sat up in her chair. "Are you kidding? We'll be free and clear from surveillance. We won't have him chasing along at our heels like some dog in heat."

He stared at her, but did not say a word.

"You'll have your retribution," she pressed.

"Revenge is an ugly business. There's very little profit in it."

"But it can be necessary."

"No," he said, shaking his head. "There, you are wrong. There is no place for revenge in this business. It is best that you learn that early. Emotion does not belong here, and there are few stronger than revenge."

"But there were... questions in Wogan's dealings with you."

"Wogan was professional," he said, as patiently as possible. "This is a business. As long as he remains professional, then there's no room, or reason, for revenge." He looked over at her again, his eyes switching between hers. "Tell me. Did that episode in the church today really scare you this much?"

"No," she said with a smirk. "Not at all."

"Then why all this talk?"

"Because it would be easier with Wogan out of the picture."

"Easier how?"

"Easier between you and me."

"What do you mean?"

She got up from her chair and walked over to him. Leaning forward, she moved her lips within inches of his, her eyes darting back and forth between his, searching for something behind their cold emptiness. "Just think what we could do together."

In an instant his right hand was on her hip, pushing her backwards against the porch's rail with such force she gasped and grabbed his wrist with both hands. As soon as her arms moved, he twisted, reaching around her neck, clutching a handful of hair, pulling and twisting her head back in the same violent motion.

She took a deep breath, trying to quell the initial panic, and what warmth was in her eyes disappeared.

"Listen to me," he said in a voice dark with malice. "If you want to kill a former lover, then that is your business. Do not try to control me with amateurish lines and your dirty twat. The only way a relationship will be built between two people like us is mutual respect, as you were so adamant to point out earlier, and your behavior at the moment leaves much to be desired."

"You agreed to train me," she said, her eyes not leaving his, her skin stretched painfully in his grasp.

"I agreed to mentor you and then retire. Based on the events of this past week, I don't believe you need any training, except, perhaps, in discretion. And I am planning on retiring sooner than originally expected."

He dropped her hair and pushed her back.

Twisting her head side to side she said, "I'm sorry. It was foolish to try to manipulate you that way."

He stared at her for several minutes, turning over the idea of killing Wogan in his mind. She did not avert her eyes, or back down under his withering stare. Taking care of Wogan would solve many issues, he agreed. "Are you prepared to kill your lover?"

"That's a stupid question," she spat. "Of course."

"As you said, it would clear up several problems."

They lapsed into silence as she watched him from the edge of the porch. She could see his mind working as it turned over the possibilities.

After several minutes, as the cold air overcame her adrenaline and her skin began to cool, he said, "Call Wogan. Invite him to meet you in Killarney."

"Where?"

"We will discuss it once we have had time to put the operation together. Tell him fly to Killarney. You will call him upon arrival with the details."

"So you'll kill him?"

He smiled. "One of us will."

Chapter 24

It was a terrible idea. Of all the things she had done in her life, of all the mistakes she made, and the lessons she learned, this one ranked way up there, easily in the top five. It was an awful idea. But, if Keller knew what happened to Janice, what really happened to Janice, she thought it might be worth the risk. It was evident he worked closely with Wogan. If he funneled money for one operation, it was reasonable to expect he funneled money for others, and she doubted any of that money could be tied directly to Wogan's company, WGI Systems. With that same conviction, she also knew Janice Wogan was clueless about her role in Odyssey Systems, and that was how Wogan was financing his black operations. Sloppy, yes, but if no one looked too closely, and the money was laundered through several corporations, it was easily hidden.

So she drove through a city bathed in twilight, the streetlights guiding her way. It took nearly twenty minutes to get to the Hoover building. Kloser and Keller were where she left them, Keller looking even more miserable, if it was possible. She paused in the anteroom, staring at Keller through the one-way mirror.

"Go home and get some rest, Brad."

"What?" Kloser asked. She spoke so softly, it was hard for him to hear.

Still not looking at him, she repeated, "Go home. Get some rest. I'll take care of Keller tonight."

"Are you sure?"

"Yes."

Without another word, Kloser left the room. Morgan took a deep breath, then walked into the room with Keller. She would have to play this very carefully, she knew. She needed Keller, and she needed the data on his laptop if there was any hope of proving her theory correct.

"You wanted to see me," she said, stopping just inside the door.

"I did," he said. "I did some thinking."

"And?"

"Your friend, Nichols. Your lover. He, ah, he was a good man?"

"Yes."

"And he was killed during this investigation, uh, into the terror cell? Into Ben Iblis?"

"Yes."

Keller nodded and nervously tapped the table with his fingertips. "And you think you can catch him? You can catch Ben Iblis?"

"With help, yes. But I'm not sure he's the one you're truly afraid of."

It was easy to see the struggle behind his eyes. "Nichols. Did you love him?"

She turned her head to one side and gazed at him. "I could have."

"I was in love once."

"So was I."

With a nod, he said, "I know. I always hoped you'd find it again."

Blowing out a heavy sigh, her shoulders slumped, she closed her eyes. "Right now, all I want is to catch the man responsible. I'm so tired of hunting, of searching. You can help me, Ben. We've known each other a long time. You know I play by the rules."

"I've also known you to bend them from time to time."

"Not often," she said, opening her eyes and sitting in a folding metal chair across the table from him.

"But sometimes, if it suits your needs. That's ultimately why I surrendered to your agents, and why I asked to speak with you again."

"You reached out to me because you're out of options. Don't kid yourself. If there'd been another way, you'd of taken advantage of it."

"Maybe," he said noncommittally, "but if there's the slightest chance of getting out of this, it's through you."

"Now, maybe," she said, an edge in her voice. "But I wasn't your first choice."

"No."

She nodded. "So tell me. What do you know?"

"A lot, but I can't stay here. Give me your word I'll be free to go."

"My word?"

"Yes."

She looked at him, trying to gauge his expression. "Does it really mean that much to you?"

"In this town? Absolutely."

"No. I can't give you my word. Not yet, anyway. I need to know what you have."

"The laptop's full of stuff."

"On what?"

"A lot of people."

"In Congress? In business? Where?" She was growing frustrated. "I can't do anything for you if you're going to play games! Give me something, Ben."

"I know who killed Janice Wogan, and it's enough to get me killed the minute I step into the system. Anywhere into the system," he emphasized. "So I can't have you running to the Justice Department to set up some kind of immunity."

She watched him, surprised by the fear in his voice. "If it's as bad as you suggest, then let me talk to the U.S. Attorney's office. We'll get you debriefed and into Witness Protection. You've been working at that level for a very long time. I'm sure we could come up with something and get you a new identity."

He shook his head. "No. I won't trust my life to the government. You either tell me you're going to arrest me now, in which case you get jack, and I get killed in the next forty-eight hours, or I give you what I've got, and you let me walk. That's the deal, Evelyn. Decide."

"Why do you think Janice was murdered?"

"It's not a matter of thinking. I issued the contract."

She nodded. Now they were getting somewhere. "Through Janice Wogan's company?"

That shocked him, and he stared at her in surprise. "How did you know that?"

"It's not important," she replied. "Tell me about the company. Who set up its financing? I can't believe it was actually Janice."

"No," he admitted. "I doubt Janice even knew she owned a company. It was just a shell corporation to transfer money. The person who set up the company, who financed everything through it, just needed some way to mask the financial trail."

"Andy Wogan."

He shrugged and arched his right eyebrow. "If you think so."

"What the hell have you gotten yourself into?"

"Let me go tonight," he repeated, "and you'll have everything."

She folded her arms across her chest. "Let's say I believe you, but I need more convincing before I agree to this."

"What?"

She reached into her coat pocket, but stopped when he suddenly tensed. "It's ok," she said. "It's just a picture." She slowly removed it from her pocket and laid it on the table. "I think this woman was the last person to see Janice alive. A security camera caught her a few hours before the place burned to the ground."

"You couldn't find her in your database?"

"I haven't had a chance to look."

Keller picked up the picture and examined it.

"I also think Ben Iblis had something to do with all of this."

Taking his eyes off the picture, he looked at her.

"His original operation was finished a week ago," she continued. "But he stayed around for some reason. I think he stayed because of Janice."

Keller did not react.

"Do you recognize her?" Morgan asked.

"Penelope Morelli," he said without hesitation. "One of Wogan's. Interesting."

"Did she order the hit?"

"No."

"Why did you say interesting then?"

"Because she's not the one who took payment on the contract."

"Who did?"

He handed the picture back and looked at her pointedly. "The same handle who's done a number of jobs over the last thirty years, most of them never solved."

Her eyes narrowed. "Ben Iblis?"

"Yes."

"And you know how to contact him?" She was suddenly breathless, her heart in her throat.

"Yes."

She stared at him, her tired mind trying desperately to process the rush of emotions. She was right. Keller was the key. "All these years. We've known each other all these years, Ben. You know I've been hunting him. You know what I've been after all these years! Why didn't you say something?"

"I wouldn't be a very good businessman if I did," he said with a note of sympathy, "and I doubt I would've lived long enough to enjoy your success."

"All these fucking years!"

"I'm sorry, Eve. I really am. And I'm sorry for your friend."

Rubbing her eyes, she stood and began to pace. It was obvious Keller knew far more than just who killed Janice Wogan. It was also equally obvious he knew how to play the game. Trying to force anything from him was not going to work, and if she did take him into custody, he would be dead long before they could get anything useful out of him. "Why would anybody want Janice dead?"

"Why does anyone want to hurt someone rich and powerful?"

"If they wanted to do that, wouldn't it be better to simply kidnap her and hold her for ransom? What's there to gain in murdering her?"

"I don't think they were interested in Wogan's money."

"Then what are they interested in?"

"Wogan."

It was plausible, she thought. A man that powerful had to have a host of enemies. "You said Ben Iblis collected the payment for Janice's contract, but he didn't killer her. I know that."

"How?"

"Because he was with me around the time of the killing."

If Keller was surprised, he did not show it. "Perhaps Ms. Morelli did," he said, tapping the picture on the table.

"He's never worked with anyone else," she argued, though her mind went back to their conversation in her townhouse. Ben Iblis did say he was going to retire. Was he training someone as a replacement?

"People change, Eve."

"Apparently," she said, her mind still lost in thought. "What I can't figure out is how does killing Janice get the financier closer to Wogan."

Keller remained silent.

"Who financed the contract?" she asked.

He simply shook his head.

"Christ," she swore. "Then how do you know whoever financed it is after Wogan?"

"Believe me. They're after Wogan."

"Who?"

He looked at her. "You'll let me leave?"

She stopped pacing. "The password to the laptop, and the name of the man who put all of this together."

"And you'll let me go?"

"Yes."

"Give me your phone," he ordered.

Handing it over, she watched as he typed several entries into a new note on her smartphone.

"That's the password to the laptop," he said, handing it back to her.

"One second." She sent an email, then dialed a number. It was answered immediately by one of the lab technicians working to break the encryption on Keller's laptop. "Paul? I've got the password. I just emailed it to you."

She waited several more seconds before she closed her eyes and said, "Thank you." She hung up the phone and looked at Keller. "Ok. The password worked. Now who financed Janice Wogan's company."

"Andrew Wogan."

"No," she said, shaking her head, the rage welling in her chest. She balled her hands into fists to keep from throwing up. It was several minutes before she could speak. She looked up and met Keller's eyes. "Andrew Wogan didn't kill his daughter. I saw the grief in his eyes. It was real. He knew nothing about the contract on his daughter's life."

Keller looked amused. "I didn't say he took out the contract on Janice. I doubt even Andrew Wogan would stoop to that level just to remove a potential liability. No."

"Then who ordered the hit?"

Morgan's legs went weak when he told her the name.

***

The farmhouse was dark and cold when she stepped out of the shower. She felt the need to wash herself after the encounter with Ben Iblis, not because he frightened her in any real way, she was with far too many men to have that little episode scare her, but because she really detested playing the whore, despite what she told Ben Iblis. Using her body to advance her prospects did not mean she had to like it. Of course, Ben Iblis fixed that. It was not much use anymore trying to pretend. Not with this man.

He had a strange sense of honor, if that's what it was. Or maybe he was just too smart, knowing that the last thing he should do was to get mixed up with her. She had been with hundreds of men, and she was having the most difficulty getting a handle on this one. With all of her experience, she knew it would be challenging, but she also thought it would be doable. Now, she was not so sure. Not that it really mattered.

She brushed her hair, skipped her makeup, and dressed simply in a pair of heavy duty black cargo pants, a black blouse, and an olive green vest. As she was sitting in a chair in her room, tying her boots, Ben Iblis opened the door.

"You smell better," he said.

"Your caretaker is very particular about her soaps," she replied without looking up from her laces.

"Killing Wogan may be harder than you anticipate."

"I don't expect it will be easy. He'll have security."

Ben Iblis nodded. "I think we can get around most of that by requesting a private meeting, or, at least, a private space. But this man Dean. He is always around."

"Yes."

"Is he dangerous?"

"Yes."

"I suspected."

"I was never able to dig into his background," she said. "Wogan keeps a pretty tight leash on Dean's personnel information, but he is definitely dangerous. An adversary who will need to be dealt with very carefully."

"He keeps information even from insiders?"

She smiled. "Especially from insiders. The whole organization is very compartmentalized."

"I see. We can talk about neutralizing Dean once the details are settled. First, though, we need to get you into town to make your phone call."

"Town?" she asked, confused. "Now?"

"Yes."

"But it's late. I was going to take a walk before bed. Besides, I thought you were sleeping."

He stared at her. "You cannot call Wogan from here."

"Obviously."

"So let us go." He gestured with his hand and walked out of the room.

She double knotted her boots, grabbed a jacket, and followed him to the barn. They climbed into the Land Rover and drove to Killarney in silence. Ben Iblis stopped the big SUV in front of a pay phone near the post office on New Street. It was dark, but the streetlights provided ample illumination. Morelli stepped down onto the sidewalk and into the phone booth. Withdrawing a credit card from her wallet, a card Ben Iblis had set up with a dummy account, she placed a call to Wogan's private number and waited.

***

Wogan lounged in one of the jet's leather recliners, his eyes closed against the setting sun, its amber rays filtered through the cabin's windows. The liquor he consumed earlier lulled him to sleep shortly after takeoff, but it did not keep him asleep for long. They were somewhere over Kentucky, judging by the in-flight status on the monitor mounted to the forward bulkhead, and he could not wait to land in Colorado. There was so much he wanted to do. Needed to do. He left his wife in the capable hands of therapists two days ago, but judging by his own grief and experience, there was not much they would be able to do for her. The only thing that would help her start to heal was his presence. He needed to be there to hold and comfort her. He knew that, but he also knew two days ago that he did not have a choice. Until he found out, conclusively, what happened, he would never be able to rest.

But now he knew.

He felt, rather than heard, the presence in the aisle next to his chair. Dean asked, "Is there anything I can get you?"

"No," Wogan answered, not opening his eyes. "Just solitude, and the engine noise."

"Of course," Dean said, and walked to the front of the cabin.

Before he took two steps, though, Wogan said, "She must not know."

Dean turned on his heel and caught the ice blue of Wogan's eyes. "I'm sorry?"

"Mrs. Wogan. She must not know."

"About Janice?"

"Yes. She must not know how she died. None of the details."

"As you wish."

Wogan watched him walk to the front of the plane and step into the galley. Then he closed his eyes again and leaned back into the recliner. Healing would not come easy to his wife, or to him, he admitted, with some reluctance. Despite Janice's issues with drugs, she had made a turnaround. She finally managed to get control of her life, and after graduation, he was prepared to make a position for her in the company.

But not now.

"Christ," he muttered.

On top of it all, he did not know what to do about Morgan. She was the only flesh and blood he had left, but she obviously did not want to have anything to do with him. If only he could make her see that he wanted to be a part of her life. But no, that would not do. She would not agree to that. Why should she, he asked himself. He abandoned her, and there was not an easy way to fix that regardless of how close he wanted to be to her. There were choices he made he could not undo.

The entire situation made him angry and frustrated. He would grieve for Janice in his own way, but it would not be at the wake and funeral he knew his wife was already planning. No, his was a much more private service. It always had been. But he would take care of his wife. That he could do, after neglecting his family for all of these years.

"Mr. Wogan," Dean said, coming down the aisle.

"Yes?" he asked, startled, his eyes jumping open.

"Ms. Morelli is on the phone."

"What?" he asked, shocked. "Pen?"

"Yes."

Wogan looked down and rubbed his chin. "Did she say anything? Did she mention what she wanted?"

"No. Only to ask whether or not you were available."

"And what did you say?"

"I thought that, for her, you would be available any time. I asked her to please hold while I located you."

Wogan nodded, slowly, almost solemnly. Penelope was one of the reasons he knew his wife felt so distant, and why he never really missed her on those long business trips. If it wasn't Pen, it was some other girl, or multiple girls. He knew it was a holdover from his days in the Navy, but only now did he wonder what it might have actually cost him.

"How did she know we were in the air?" Wogan asked.

"I'm sure she just called the locate number. It would route here."

Dean was right, of course. The highly sensitive number automatically routed to wherever he was in the world, be it an air phone, a mobile phone, or a satellite phone.

"Do you want me to tell her you'll call back?" Dean asked.

"No," Wogan said after several seconds. "I'll speak with her."

"Do you want me to trace the call?"

"Of course."

"She's on the first line," Dean said, motioning towards the phone on the table next to the recliner.

"Thank you."

Wogan looked at the phone and sighed heavily. His emotions came as a surprise. He thought he would look forward to this call. Now, however, he found himself dreading it. After being gone so long, nothing good could come of it.

"Hello, Pen," he said, picking up the phone and trying to keep his emotions in check. "We've been trying to figure out what's going on."

"Andy. Hello."

"How are you?"

"I'm well, thank you."

"We've been trying to find you."

"I know. Concerned for my welfare?"

"I'm concerned about many things," he said. "Your welfare is one of them."

"And the others?"

"What are you doing in Ireland, Pen?"

"Something came up."

"Was it Ben Iblis? Is he there with you? Is he the one that got you out of the country? Did he kill my agents?"

"No," she said, her voice cold. "I killed your agents. I thought maybe you'd get the hint after the first two, but apparently not. The third man, in the cathedral, was… careless. He should've known better."

"They were only following orders."

"Aren't we all?"

Wogan chewed on his lower lip. "Is he with you now?"

"C'mon, Andy. You know better than that."

"I could've used your help the last several days. Something... something dreadful happened. Janice is dead."

"I know."

His heart sank. "You do?"

"Yes."

"How?"

"I know who killed her."

"What? How? Tell me!"

"Meet me here. Come to Ireland, and I'll tell you. I'll tell you everything."

"No," he seethed. "You were there. What happened? Tell me! Who killed her? How did she die?"

"Killarney. Book a suite at the Park Hotel. I will contact you."

"Tell me, Pen!" he screamed, his face beet red, but the line went dead in his ear.

Wogan clutched the receiver in his hand, trying to crush the cheap plastic in his fist. Dean stepped from the cockpit and walked down the aisle. "Did it come from Killarney?" Wogan asked, looking up from the phone, malice burning his eyes.

"Yes. A pay phone."

"Alter course. Get us there now!"

Without masking his hesitation, Dean asked, "Are you sure that's wise? We don't have the means to provide security, at least not adequate security, on such short notice."

"We have a host of agents in Ireland. Lord knows they haven't done a damn thing to earn their salary. Put them to use."

"Of course," Dean said. "Anything else?"

"Stay off the phone. I have someone I need to call."

Dean looked puzzled. "Who?"

"Book a suite at the Park Hotel, Thomas," Wogan said, ignoring his question. "And hurry. Get them to change the flight plan and get this bird turned around. I need to be in Killarney as soon as possible."

"Yes, sir," Dean said, not wanting to press. The look in Wogan's eyes was all the warning he needed.

Chapter 25

Morgan sat in her darkened car, the lights of passing headlights flashing like bright ghosts across its interior, their waning paleness matching her complexion. She was ashen, her mouth dry, her palms sweaty as her mind chewed on the meeting with Keller. Every piece was there. It all fit. Nichols' death, Baker's treachery, Ben Iblis and his desire to have her removed, her father, the entire thing. The puzzle was done. The only question remaining was what she should do about it, because if she sat there too much longer, her father would be dead.

It was that thought, or rather the prospect, that kept her in her seat, immobile, her mind working through the possibilities. Ben Iblis killed Nichols. He did not pull the trigger, but he started the chain of events. He paid Baker. He killed Nichols.

Wogan could have stopped it. Then and there.

But that did not suit his needs. Did he know Baker was after her? Did he know Baker's ambitions? Baker's nature?

Did he even care?

When she learned of Janice's death, she had not felt any emotion. Janice was a woman she never met, never known. A sister by blood, yes, but not someone she ever felt any emotional connection with. Wogan was different, though even in his case she did not feel an emotional connection. Emotional reaction would be a better term. There was little, if any, connection left between them, and sometimes she wondered if there ever was.

Where the hell did she go wrong? What forced him to abandon her? Was it really his wife? Was it his job and the idea of a scandal? Did that force him away?

Did it matter?

She watched the headlights of passing cars, listening as the whoosh of their tires cut through her partially open window. The Washington Monument was a brilliant white in her windshield. She knew what she wanted to do, and she also knew what she should do. They were two very different things.

Her phone chirped and buzzed from its clip on her right hip.

"Christ," she swore, wiping a tear from her right eye as she reached down and grabbed it. "Morgan."

"Evelyn, it's --"

"Andy," she interrupted. "I did not expect to hear from you. In fact, I hoped never to hear from you again."

"I know," he said, resignation filling his voice.

"Then why are you calling me?" she asked, desperately trying to push what she just learned to the very recesses of her mind. The last thing she needed was something coming through her voice. Now was not the time to tip her hand.

"Because I wanted to ask for your help."

"My help?" she asked, nearly choking on the word. "You must be joking. Why the hell would I help you?'

"Because I'm your father."

"Could've fooled me."

There was silence on the line: a crystal-clear digital stillness that made her wonder whether he hung up.

"Do you know Penelope Morelli?" he finally asked.

Was he going to finally start telling her the truth, she asked herself. "Yes. I know the name. She works for you."

"Yes. Well, she did. She was one of my operatives. She disappeared two days ago. We believe she's gone rogue."

"So find her. Or pay someone to find her. That's how these things are usually taken care of, isn't it? I don't know why you're bringing her up now."

"She called me tonight," Wogan said. "She wants to meet."

"So?" Morgan asked, catching something in his tone. "What is she to you besides an employee?"

"She's my lover. Or she was, up until a few days ago."

"Why did she go rogue?"

"I don't know."

"No indication? Nothing?"

"No," he said, his tone even. "I even offered her a promotion, pending the outcome of her latest assignment."

"Did you plan to grow old together?" she asked, condescension dripping from her voice.

"Give me a break, Eve."

"Give you a break? Why? You got a break when you connived your way into the Director's pants and convinced him you needed federal resources to prove your daughter died under mysterious circumstances. You took me away from an extremely important investigation, an investigation vital to national security. For what? To placate your personal belief that there wasn't any possible way your daughter fell back into drugs!"

"I asked you this earlier, but you didn't answer me. Are you mad because Janice was my daughter, or because I cared enough to find out how she died?"

The question was asked so calmly, and in such a straight tone of voice, that it temporarily caught her off guard. She was ready for a range of emotions, but understanding was not one of them.

"You can't fix this overnight," she said, very quietly.

"I know, and I don't want to."

"You don't want to?" she bristled.

"That's not what I meant. Not at all what I meant." He sighed. "Look, Eve. You're the last thing I have to leave behind on Earth. God knows what my wife's going to do when I get back to Colorado. I want to fix this. I've wanted to fix it ever since Steamboat, ever since I walked away at the waterfall."

"It's not possible," Morgan said. Using the back of her hand, she wiped the tears from her eyes. "For as long as I can remember, I've felt nothing but anger, resentment, and hatred towards you. Now you come barging back into my life because you need a favor, and you expect me to simply put everything aside?"

"It's the truth."

"I don't believe you."

"What will it take?"

"What the hell do you mean, what will it take? This isn't one of those problems you seem to think you can solve with your checkbook."

"I can give you Ben Iblis."

It was like a thunderclap. "What? How?" Her mind switched gears rapidly. "You know where they are?"

"Where who are?" he asked, suspicious.

"I know what happened." She didn't want to give him everything. Not yet.

"Everything?"

"A lot. I know what Morelli was doing in Washington this week with the Senator. You think she's with Ben Iblis. I'd bet money on it. That's why she went rogue. Is he going to train her?"

There was silence on the line as he digested what she said. Finally, "I don't know why she went with him."

"But you think she did. You think she went and she's with him now."

"Yes," he said after a short pause.

"You hesitated. Is it because you don't want to believe she left you, or because you don't think she went with him?"

"I'm not sure it matters at this point," he admitted. "Not anymore. I believe she's with him. After Baker overstepped his authority, I think Ben Iblis recruited her, and they fled to Ireland. Her motivations don't matter. She wants to meet, and I plan on being there. If she shows up, Ben Iblis will be nearby. He won't leave her alone for long."

"She's luring you there."

"Yes, I know."

"Probably to kill you."

"The thought has crossed my mind."

Morgan worked on the possibilities. "Yet you're still going."

"Yes."

"Why did you lie to me about the picture of Morelli earlier in your office?" she asked.

"I don't know."

"I told you at lunch that I'd walk the minute you started playing games. I wondered if you'd actually try it, even with your own daughter's investigation." She shook her head. "Some things never change, do they, Andy?"

"No. Some things never do."

Closing her eyes, she leaned her head back against the back of the seat and let the tears stream down her face. Even after all these years and the death of his daughter, he hadn't changed. Would he ever? Could he? She thought about it. "You realize this isn't going to clear ten years of bad blood. Giving me Ben Iblis still won't square it with us."

"If it gets me in the door, I'll work on the rest."

"No more games, Andy."

"That was a mistake." He sounded almost desperate. "Let me make it up to you. I know you've been after him for a very long time."

Taking a deep breath, she asked, "What are you going to do with Morelli?"

"It's not your concern. I only offered Ben Iblis."

"Alright," she said, her eyes closed. "When?"

"I'm on my way now. Meet me there."

"Where?"

"Killarney. The Park Hotel."

"Ireland? How do you know Ben Iblis will be there?"

"That day on the bridge under the falls? Let me make it up to you. Here and now. He'll be there."

"The Park?"

"Yes. Dinner tomorrow. I'll be sorely disappointed if you're late."

"You'll be worse than that. You'll be dead."

***

Morelli stepped from the phone booth into the Land Rover. "It's done," she said. "I expect he'll arrive early tomorrow morning."

"You think he'll check into the hotel?" Ben Iblis asked.

"Of course."

"And you're sure he'll come."

A devilish smile curled her lips. "He'll come. I'm sure."

"After this is done, we'll need to check for additional assignments."

"You changed your mind about lying low?"

He pulled the SUV away from the curb, through Killarney's sleepy streets, and back on to the carriageway. "I should have clarified. You will check for new assignments. I am finished. After tomorrow's introductions, I will retire. With Wogan out of the picture, we should be able to move freely again."

"Are you forgetting the Americans? They'll want answers. There will be an investigation."

"I have not forgotten the Americans." He looked at her, trying to judge her emotions. "They will pose an immediate problem, but, I think, with time, they will lose focus. Morgan will lose interest with my retirement."

"How do you know?"

"They will not be able to tie assassinations to me, if you take over operations."

"You will really go?" she asked, somewhat surprised.

"With the cut I'll make from every operation you complete, I will be able to live handsomely, if I so choose. It's time."

"I am surprised."

He nodded. "I know. Now, there's much to do. I want to introduce you to the operational end of my empire. With Wogan scheduled to arrive tomorrow, it does not leave us much time to plan. But with both of us running down the details, I believe we may accomplish all of the necessary arrangements."

She continued to stare at him, trying to contain her surprise. Their arrangement was not even a month old, and already he was bowing out. "Can we do everything from the house? I didn't think we had a connection."

"No. We'll need to put everything together when we come back to town."

"Tonight?"

"Yes," he said, glancing across at her in the darkness. "We'll pick up some things from the house and then come back."

"You want to set all of this up from an internet café?"

"Of course not," he laughed, and she could almost see the smug smile plastered on his face. "We'll put everything together from the comfort of our suite."

"Our suite...."

"Yes. At the Park Hotel."

Chapter 26

The deli was mostly deserted when Morgan walked in. A wave of delicious aromas hit her, quickly replaced by an eerie sense of déjà vu which drowned a hungry growl from her stomach. She was surprised, when she called Vogel, to find he was planning on stopping here for a late dinner. Either by coincidence, or some awkward twist of fate, he chose the same delicatessen where Nichols enjoyed his last meal. So it was not without some trepidation when she crossed the dining room to Vogel's table.

As his security detail watched her approach, Vogel stood and offered her a chair. "Good evening, Eve."

"Good evening, boss."

"Have you eaten?"

"No."

"Why don't you grab something," he suggested, "then we can talk."

"It's important."

He appraised her, replacing his napkin in his lap. "I gathered by your phone call, but if five minutes were really going to make that much difference, I doubt you would have agreed to meet me here. Besides, you look like you could use something to eat."

"Aren't they closing soon?" she asked, looking over her shoulder at the deli counter as employees carried the food back to the kitchen.

"They'll make an exception," he said patiently. "Just walk up and tell them what you would like."

"Alright," she said, skeptical, as she stood and walked to the cashier at the end of the long counter.

"What can I get you, hon?" the gray-haired cashier asked.

"Are you all still serving food?"

"If you're a friend of Adam's, yes."

Morgan tried to hide her surprise. "Corned beef on rye, please."

"Mustard?"

"Yellow. Slathered."

"Comin' right up," the woman said and walked back to the kitchen.

While Morgan waited, she wondered why the deli seemed to bend over backwards for Vogel. Could he own part of the place? She knew an FBI executive-level salary was decent, but it certainly did not go far in the DC economy. An ownership stake probably was not realistic. What, then?

"Here, hon," the cashier said, handing Morgan a plate with a massive corned beef sandwich.

"Thank you," Morgan said. "How much do I owe you?"

"No charge," the cashier replied before disappearing into the kitchen again.

Morgan stared dumbly at the door for a few moments before turning on her heel and walking back to Vogel's table. "What did you do?" she asked when she arrived.

"What?" he asked, standing as she put her plate down and took a seat.

"No charge for the sandwich," she said, watching as he sat back down. "More than a pound of corned beef after closing time for free. What did you do? Do you own part of this place or something?"

"No," he said, putting the last of his spaghetti and meatballs in his mouth.

"Then I don't get it. You don't get free food just for being an FBI agent."

"Who said it had anything to do with the FBI?"

"I just assumed."

"You should know better than that," he said gruffly. "Now what did you want to talk to me about?"

She studied him. "So, part owner?"

He sighed and took off his gold-rimmed spectacles. Taking a handkerchief from his pocket, he gently wiped the lenses. "Eve, I like you. So drop it. What did you want to talk to me about? Something with the investigation? Have you been able to trace down that missing laptop?"

She didn't want to let it go, but she knew better than to argue with Vogel after a warning like that. "Yes. An hour or so ago."

"That's good news. I was afraid it might've been lost." He watched as she took a bit of her sandwich. "Did it yield anything?"

"I don't know," she said. "We just managed to get the password to decrypt its contents, but I suspect it's going to prove invaluable."

His eyebrows arched in surprise. "Why?"

"Do you remember Ben Keller?"

"Of course. Bradley's Chief of Staff."

"He's also good friend of mine."

"I know. What about him?"

"The laptop is his. That's why we couldn't find it."

"So he was the money man. He transferred those funds into Ben Iblis's account."

"Not Ben Iblis's account," she corrected him. "One of the accounts the terror cell used to fund their operation. But that's not the point."

"It's not?"

"No," she said, taking another bite of her sandwich, making him wait. When she finished chewing, she continued, "Keller isn't on Ben Iblis's payroll. He didn't have a clue where he was funneling the money. He was simply following orders."

"Who's orders?" Vogel asked. "And that doesn't excuse the fact that he's aiding terrorism."

"I agree. And it wasn't only money transfers. He also handled most of the contracts for industrial espionage, including assassinations."

"So who was pulling the strings?"

She told him and watched as his eyes went wide.

"Really?"

She nodded and took another bite. "He was the one delivering the orders."

"And Wogan?"

"I'm sure he's aware of some of what's going on. In fact, I'm sure he's giving the orders. But he's in the dark about some things. Could you see him putting out a contract on his own daughter?"

"No," Vogel said, shaking his head. "And I would also guess there's not a scratch of evidence tying Wogan to any of this. To any of the transactions he orders, I mean."

"I'm sure that's the case," she said, lying through her teeth. After her discussion with Keller, and the subsequent discussion with Wogan, she decided Vogel did not need to know everything.

"Where is Keller?"

"I let him go," she said, taking another bite.

"You what?" Vogel thundered, his face suddenly beet red. "You let him go? When? Where is he?"

"I don't know."

"What the fuck were you thinking?"

"I was thinking about bigger fish," she replied, matter-of-factly.

"How are we going to get them without Keller?"

"There's enough evidence on the laptop."

"How do you know?"

"Keller's never let me down before."

He stared at her, incredulous, as she calmly ate her sandwich. "That's a hell of a risk. It's also a decision way above your pay grade!"

"It's done."

"It's done?" he asked, his eyes wide. "Have you lost your fucking mind? You let a material witness just walk away, and you act as if it's the most normal thing in the world!"

"Trust me, it wasn't an easy decision."

"The consequences aren't going to be easy, either," he said, his anger rising. "You're suspended, effective immediately. I want you to see one of the counselors first thing tomorrow morning. I don't know if recent events have put you over --"

"Before you suspend me," she interrupted, "let me finish."

"Finish?" he asked, amazed she would have the gall to interrupt him. "Finish what?"

"What I came here to tell you."

He took a deep breath and leaned back in his chair. "Alright. I don't know why I'm going to listen to this, but alright." He laid his spectacles on the table and folded his arms across his chest. "Tell me what you have."

"Wogan called me a little while ago. That's why I asked to see you."

"What about?"

"Ben Iblis."

"In what context?"

"Have you heard the name Penelope Morelli?"

"No," he said, shaking his head. "Should I?"

"She is, or was, one of Wogan's operatives. He mentioned on the phone that he believes she's gone rogue. In fact, he believes she may have been recruited by Ben Iblis in the last week or so. Wogan wasn't clear exactly why it may have happened."

"Is she capable?"

"From everything I've heard, yes. She's on surveillance video coming out of Janice Wogan's apartment a few hours before it burned to the ground."

"An interesting coincidence."

"Yes, and that same camera went dead an hour before the fire started. Annapolis PD interviewed several of the staff at the bar where Janice was last seen alive. All of them observed Janice leaving with Morelli."

"Ben Iblis has always worked alone," Vogel argued, though he was growing more interested in Morgan's theory. "Why would he suddenly recruit someone? And why would he kill Janice Wogan?"

Morgan finished her sandwich and pushed her plate away. "Do you remember how he paid me a visit the morning after Nichols was killed?"

Vogel nodded.

"And you remember how I said he warned me to back off, that he was going to retire?"

"Yes."

"I think he picked up Morelli as a student."

"Why? To train her? To carry on his work? Like a legacy almost? Take over the business, so to speak?"

"Yes. I think that's exactly what he's planning."

"Do you have proof?" Vogel asked. "Anything concrete?"

"No. Nothing that would stand up in court, at least. The laptop will yield all the evidence we need. The lab's already working on it. But based on my conversation with Wogan, it seems plausible."

"Speaking of the laptop, why couldn't the techs simply hack into it?"

"With the level of encryption Keller employed, we would not have been able to crack it for many years."

Vogel thought about it. "Would Keller have been able to add anything to this? Anything concrete."

"Keller is gone. We won't hear from him again."

Vogel watched her carefully. He recruited her personally, and she was one of his top agents. Her instincts for ferreting out information about cases was uncanny, and he never regretted placing his trust in her. But her methods and maverick spirit got him in trouble more than once with the FBI's more established order. There was little doubt in his mind that he would catch hell over her decision to let Keller go.

He sighed, his anger subsiding. "Alright, Eve. Finish what you came here for. What do you have?"

"Wogan's headed to Ireland now to meet with Morelli. I believe he's walking into a trap."

"Why?"

"A number of reasons. Janice Wogan was murdered. Keller facilitated the contract on her life."

"Using Wogan's money."

"Yes," she said, not going into details about the shell corporation they set up under Janice Wogan's name. If Vogel knew Wogan paid Baker from that shell corporation, he would yank her from the investigation in a heartbeat.

"Did Keller say who drew the hit?"

"No, but Ben Iblis collected the money."

"He knows that for a fact?"

"Someone using Ben Iblis's handle collected it, at least. I think it's a pretty safe bet it was the man himself."

"But you said he was with you that morning."

"He was," she replied. "I think Morelli carried out the hit. Ben Iblis couldn't have done it based on the coroner's report. The timing isn't right." She thought about it. "Well, I guess he could've carried it out, but it would've been damn tight. Besides, we have Morelli at the scene just hours before Janice died. I think she did the dirty work."

"That's a damn frightening thought," Vogel said. "If she's already capable enough to fool our forensics, it's terrifying to contemplate what she may be capable of with the training and funding that Ben Iblis can provide. Without your investigation, Janice's murder would've been filed as an accident."

"Yes, Morelli seems quite capable."

"You said Wogan's on his way to meet her?" Vogel asked.

"That's what he indicated on the phone."

"Why?"

"I think he's going to try and bring her in. Or kill her."

"And he knows Ben Iblis is there?"

"He suspects," she said.

"Did you mention any of this to Wogan? Anything you learned from Keller?"

"No."

Vogel caught a glimpse of something behind her green eyes. "You're going to let him walk into that trap."

"Yes."

"They will butcher him."

She nodded. "Wogan's relationship with Morelli is complicating things. It's blinding him to the reality of the situation."

"Which is?"

"That Morelli is even more dangerous than Ben Iblis."

Tapping his fingers absently on the table, Vogel turned everything over. Morgan watched him closely. It made sense, she knew. Too much sense. She fed it to him on a silver platter.

He caught her green eyes and held them. "So why didn't you warn Wogan?"

It was a question she had been asking herself for the past hour. "He knows he's walking into a trap. But ultimately, I want Ben Iblis. He's responsible for Nichols' death."

"He's your father. You're prepared to let him walk into this?"

"He made his bed," she said, anger flaring behind her eyes. "Based on what Keller told me, and what I suspect we'll find on that laptop, Wogan's been shoulder-deep in this shit for a very long time. Either Morelli gets to him, or we let the courts sort it out after this is all over. It really doesn't matter to me either way."

He nodded. "Ok. What do you want to do?"

"Authorize a jet," she said without hesitation. "Let me go over there and get Ben Iblis."

"And the others? Morelli? Wogan, assuming he's alive?"

"After Ben Iblis," she said. "We need to get Ben Iblis."

"How?"

She just gave him a cold stare.

"Will you take your team?"

"No."

"That seems rather impulsive and stupid. Ignoring the danger of going into that kind of situation alone, your team's going to want to know where the hell you are."

"Put me on medical leave. Nobody will question that, not after everything that's happened this week. It'll solve a number of problems."

"And the jet authorization?"

She thought about it. "Do you know somebody in Interpol? Somebody you trust without question?"

"Interpol?" he asked, confused by the apparent change of subject. "Why?"

"It will solve a couple of problems. Classify the operation so its true aim will only be known to a select few, and then only after the fact. That will clear the use of the aircraft. Your man in Interpol can meet me in Ireland. That'll get me through customs, and he can provide backup. Plus, with as many ears as Wogan has around, the fewer people that know about this, the better."

"And your team?"

"I don't need my team for this. They've done the work to get us this far. Let them work on the laptop, and running down whatever additional leads it yields."

He thought about it, but was not quite convinced. "You said you talked to Wogan. If he told you about Morelli and Ben Iblis, it's a pretty good bet he also told Dean he was going to talk to you."

"I'll have to take that chance."

She waited, watching as Vogel continued to drum his fingers on the table, his mind churning. Finally, he said, "I know one man in Interpol that I would trust to that extent. I will contact him and get his thoughts. I doubt he would be much good offering any sort of physical backup, but I'll discuss that with him. In the meantime, get some things packed and put together, then head out to Reagan. I'll have a jet standing by."

"Thank you," she said, standing up.

"I'll give you until 1700 EST tomorrow," he said, looking up at her. "Then I have to contact Interpol and let them know what's going on. I hope you have him by then."

"So do I," she said. "Because otherwise I'll most likely be dead."

Chapter 27

They walked in to the Park Hotel early in the morning, the sun still far below the horizon, arm-in-arm after leaving the Land Rover with the valet. It was a beautifully appointed hotel, rich in charm and atmosphere, located in the middle of the town. The lobby was paneled in dark wood, and a fire crackled in the fireplace to their left, despite the early hour. Dressed as a wealthy couple on vacation, a bright, cheery receptionist greeted them warmly as they walked up to the desk.

"Good morning!" she said with a large smile, her Irish brogue delightfully cheerful, even to Ben Iblis, that early in the morning.

"Good morning," Morelli replied, flashing an equally charming smile. "We decided to make a last minute stop and we hoped you could accommodate us."

"Of course," the receptionist said, typing quickly and scanning her computer monitor. "For how many nights?"

"Two nights."

"We have a small suite with a view of the gardens available."

"That would be perfect," Morelli said, glancing at Ben Iblis before handing the woman a credit card.

The receptionist swiped the card, and while it was processing, she asked, "Do you need help with your bags?"

"Yes, please, though the valet said he would take care of it."

"Very good. Here are your room keys. Suite 301, if you'll just take the stairs back to my right. We'll bring your bags straight away."

"Thank you," Morelli said.

Ben Iblis led them around the reception desk, across the marble floor, and up the carpeted stairs to their suite. It was as magnificently decorated as the lobby, with dark wood trim, a fireplace, king-sized bed, a sitting area with table, couch, and two chairs. An expansive bathroom tiled in rich black and white marble completed the suite. Even Morelli, used to living the good life as Wogan's mistress, was impressed.

"A beautiful suite," Ben Iblis remarked in Arabic, closing the door behind them.

"We should vacation here," she exclaimed, admiring the large claw-footed soaker tub.

There was a discreet knock at the door. Morelli opened it and the valet walked in with their two suitcases. She gave him a small tip and showed him out. When she returned to the bedroom, she found Ben Iblis sitting in one of the armchairs. He had opened the French doors leading to the balcony, and sat entranced by the view. Spread out before them lay the beauty of Killarney National Park, and in the distance she was able to see the first of the sun's rays reflecting from Lough Leane, one of Ireland's largest lakes.

She wanted to talk to him about the operation, about removing Wogan, and what they would do after its successful completion. But he seemed so entranced by the country's beauty that she was not quite sure how to start. "I can take over the day to day activities. I believe I've proven that I can handle it."

"Isn't it peaceful?" he asked, ignoring her.

"Yes," she muttered, rolling her eyes.

He stared across the expanse of green. "Muckross Lake is out there, just beyond Lough Leane. There's a beautiful castle, too, on its edge."

Watching him, a small warning started to tickle the back of her mind. This was not the man whose reputation she feared. This was not the infamous assassin. There was a marked change from the man she met in the coffee shop two weeks ago. Had their episodes with Wogan's men changed him so much? "I saw the map back at the farm," she said, setting her concerns aside for the moment. "Muckross Road goes right by it."

"Yes, N71. A beautiful drive."

"Will you take me there after we've finished with Wogan?"

"If you wish."

She continued to watch him, staring at the back of his head. "You didn't answer my question."

"Which one?" he asked, finally turning to look at her. "I answered you."

"I said that I believe I've proven I can handle the operations."

"Yes, you did. What was the question?"

"Do you believe that's true?"

"Yes," he said, turning back to the scenery. "To an extent. You are still young, inexperienced, and, at times, petulant."

Catching the bitter anger in her throat, she continued, "Which will just leave planning and administration to you." She sat on the couch. "Once you feel more comfortable leaving those aspects to me, you can fully retire. You've given me the contacts, and the introductions should be concluded this morning, correct?"

He looked at her with his cold, dark eyes. "Yes, the introductions will be made this morning, as I promised."

"It's one more operation, Omar, and it should be an easy one at that."

"So you say."

She ignored him. "I look forward to meeting your contact."

"Yes, I'm sure you do." He watched her. "So you feel Wogan will be an easy target, despite his security?"

"I think we have a sound plan."

"Based on several assumptions, the first of which is that he will behave exactly as you expect him to."

She cleared her throat, forced a smile, and asked, "Have you thought about where you'll go?"

"No, not really. Perhaps somewhere in the Mediterranean. I have always found it beautiful."

"You talked about Cyprus before."

"Yes, though I have been just about everywhere. Spain, Italy, Sicily, Morocco, Tunisia, Turkey. They are all beautiful."

"I've only seen some of those countries. Greece was by far my favorite, though."

"Yes. Another beautiful country."

"I will see them all before the end." There was little his attitude could do to bring her down that morning. Things were moving. There was a plan, and soon, she would meet Ben Iblis's most important contact. It was what she needed. All she needed. Once she had that contact, it would not matter whether Ben Iblis continued to help her or not.

Standing from the couch, she walked to the door and threw the deadbolt. Coming back into the bedroom, she stood near the couch and began to slowly undress.

"What are you doing?" he asked, watching her carefully.

"I thought we could have some fun before Wogan gets here."

He stared as she dropped her bra on the couch and stood naked with her hands on her hips.

"Care to join me," she asked, "or should I do this myself?"

With a sigh, he stood and walked to the door. "I'm going to get a cup of coffee and something to eat. When you're done, why don't you join me? They make a wonderful Eggs Benedict."

"You know, Senator Bradley is particularly fond of Eggs Benedict." She spread her legs and began touching herself.

"So I've heard," he said, taking one last look at her breasts before walking out.

She watched him leave, then lay back on the bed. Obviously, seducing him was not going to happen, but that had not been her intention this time. This time she just needed a man. Or a woman, she corrected herself, remembering her time with Janice Wogan. Now she had to do it herself.

***

Morgan leaned back in her seat and closed her eyes, trying to force her mind to sleep as the small FBI jet rocketed east over the Atlantic. Despite her exhaustion, she found it was useless. Her mind would not slow down, let alone turn off. She had learned too much in the last several hours, but she did not have all of the details. Most of her deductions were based on what she learned from Keller, and the question she could not get out of her mind was whether or not she could trust him.

He was like a brother during their days at the Academy, and they stayed close in the years since. Despite her misgivings, it was impossible to think he would do anything to harm her, at least directly. But there was the lingering fear of what happened to Nichols. Keller was responsible for that, at least in some small part.

Turning on her other side in an effort to find a more comfortable position, she listened to the roar of the aircraft. Wogan would need to be dealt with once he led her to Ben Iblis. The question was how best to control that situation. There was no doubt in her mind that he would fight. After spending the greater part of his life building an empire, he would not let it go easily, regardless of what he tried to tell her.

She already made up her mind that she would let him walk right into the trap Morelli was setting. Everything would be easier if he simply did not survive. The question was whether or not she could live with herself, knowing she made that decision. Ultimately, it came down to justice for everyone he trampled in building WGI Systems.

Or did it?

She sighed. Did he deserve to die because of his actions as CEO, or because he abandoned her? Or for the combination? And regardless of whether he deserved to die, could she forgive him?

She rolled back onto her other side and prayed the nightmare would not return. The roar of the turbines lulled her to sleep, and the next thing she knew, a gentle hand shook her shoulder.

"Agent Morgan," the co-pilot said. "We're about fifteen minutes out. We'll be landing in Kerry shortly."

She was instantly awake. "Has Wogan's plane already landed?"

"I don't know. I'll check with the tower."

"Thank you."

She shuffled back to the lavatory, splashed some water on her face, and stared at the mirror. A ghostly, thin, exhausted mask stared back, and she realized that the four or five hours she slept was the longest stretch of uninterrupted sleep she had in over a week. Vogel was right. She needed a break. After today, after Ben Iblis, she told the face in the mirror, she would take a vacation. Maybe back to Colorado. There were great hiking trails around the Academy, or she could splurge and spend some time at a nice resort to relax and recover.

"Right," she said. If only it were that easy.

She shut the lavatory door behind her and walked down the plane's narrow aisle to the cockpit. The co-pilot was on the radio with Kerry approach, but he turned when she stuck her head inside.

"Wogan's plane is on the ground. He landed a couple of hours ago."

"Ok," she said.

"We also heard from Vogel's people while you were asleep. One of the Irish Interpol liaisons will meet the plane."

"Vogel give you a name?" she asked.

"Dana Brennan."

"Garda?" she asked, referring to the Irish national police force.

"He didn't say."

"Guess we'll find out soon," she said, picking out the airfield in the distance.

The pilot nodded and turned back to his duties. Morgan withdrew to her seat and waited. There was little turbulence as the jet descended, and she barely felt a bounce when the tires set down on Kerry's landing strip. They taxied for a few minutes before the pilot parked the plane and shut down the engines. Morgan stood as the co-pilot stepped from the cockpit and opened the door. A cool, crisp, fresh breeze drifted into the cabin, quickly replacing the six hour-old stale, recycled air.

"After you, Agent Morgan," the co-pilot said, ushering her to the door. "We have some paperwork we need to complete. Director Vogel told us to remain at your disposal for the next forty-eight hours, pending additional destinations."

"Thank you. Do you have hotel arrangements?"

"Yes, the airport authority's put something together for us." He handed her a card. "You can call this number to get ahold of us."

"Thanks," she said, taking the card. "I'll contact you this evening."

He turned and walked back into the cockpit as she smoothed her suit coat and picked up a small overnight bag. Moving down the few steps embedded in the back of the plane's door, Morgan was taken aback by the deep blue, azure sky and its gentle sun shining on her face. The fields surrounding the airport were a dark green, gently waving in the slight breeze. She noticed an athletic man leaning against a nondescript gray Volkswagen sedan about twenty feet away, and he stood up straight as she stepped onto the tarmac.

"Agent Morgan?" he called, approaching with his hand extended, his Irish accent elongating the vowels.

Morgan smiled and shook his hand. "Yes, I'm Morgan."

"Dana Brennan," he said, returning her smile. "Inspector, An Garda Síochána."

"Evelyn Morgan, FBI," she replied, studying him. He was tall, and lithe, nearly a head taller than she, and probably a little older, somewhere in his late thirties. His sandy blonde hair was rather long for a policeman, hanging just over his ears, tapering back to his neck. Idly, she wondered if anybody ever grabbed a handful in the middle of a fight.

"I've taken care of customs," he said, admiring her through hazel eyes. "Your Director's request was rather... unusual."

"Director?" she asked, surprised, her smile disappearing. Vogel would not have been so careless to let the news of her assignment slip out, unless he needed the Director's authorization for the plane. "The Director of the FBI called you?"

"My apologies," he said, catching the alarm in her eyes. "Maybe I have the terminology wrong. A man named Vogel contacted our Commissioner."

"Yes," she said, her smile returning. "Vogel's an executive assistant director. Not 'The Director.'"

"I'm sorry, then," he said, embarrassed. "I'm not altogether familiar with your command structure. As I said, I've taken care of customs. I'm a little hazy on the details, but from what I understand from the Commissioner, you're in need of some help."

"Rather desperately, I'm afraid."

"May I take your bag?" he asked, reaching with his right hand. "Then we can jump in and you can give me the details."

"Thanks," she said, handing him the small duffel bag. Pausing for a moment, she watched as Brennan walked to the back of the sedan and placed the duffel in the trunk. He had the look of an ex-soccer player, she thought while she waited for him: trim, athletic, a little fat replacing what was once ultra lean muscle.

"Did you ever play soccer?" she called.

Brennan closed the trunk. "Football, you mean?" he asked, smiling. "Years ago, at university."

"Were you any good?"

"Not really."

She glanced behind her as the wind danced across the top of a nearby green field, then she sat down in the car. "Did you enjoy it?" she asked as he took the driver's seat.

"I did, but it wasn't going to pay the bills. I needed something a little more permanent."

"A good choice."

"And you? Did you play any sports?"

"I was a swimmer."

"Oh?" he asked. "Which event?"

"Butterfly and freestyle."

"Any good?"

"Not really," she replied, shaking her head. It seemed like a lifetime ago. "I knew several soccer players."

"Yeah?"

"Yeah," she nodded. "They were assholes."

Brennan smiled as he looked out the windshield. "Maybe I'll change your perception."

"Maybe."

"So... I'm not real clear on the details of what's going on. I don't know a lot about your command structure, but I do know the FBI doesn't send agents on private planes across the Atlantic all that often, and not on less than twenty-four hours notice."

She opened her mouth to reply, but he interrupted. "Wait, one last thing. Did you bring a firearm?"

Turning slightly in the seat, she pivoted her right hip forward and tucked her suit coat back behind the Sig Sauer's holster. "Is it going to be a problem?" she asked, catching his eyes more on her hip than on the pistol.

"No, so long as you're judicious in its use."

"Judicious in its use?" Her brow furrowed. "That's an interesting way to put it."

"Most of our force doesn't carry firearms."

"You're going to want one today."

"Just why are you here?" he asked. "And why are we making special arrangements for you to carry a pistol? Customs about had my arse while I was filling out the paperwork. It's extremely unusual."

"Have you heard of Omar Ben Iblis?"

"Of course."

"That's why you're making special arrangements with customs."

"What do you mean?" he asked, confused. "I don't understand."

"We're going after him."

There was silence as Brennan digested the news.

"I know that some of the Garda carry firearms, Inspector Brennan," Morgan continued, watching him carefully. "Are you one of them?"

"Yes."

"Good. You'll need it."

"I think you'd better tell me what this is about."

She nodded. If they stood any chance in succeeding, she would need his help. "We have reason to believe Ben Iblis is in the area of Killarney. He's wanted for at least two murders in the United States, and we plan to extradite him after capture."

"You say that like it's already a foregone conclusion. From what I know of the man, or at least his reputation, it'll take far more than your force of will."

"Perhaps."

Brennan looked out across the airfield. "Your information is very good. We haven't heard a word."

"And I'd like to keep it that way. We believe he is travelling with a woman, Penelope Morelli. Between the two of them, they have access to a vast array of intelligence. Hence the somewhat roundabout arrangements."

"I see. Tell me about the woman."

"Five-eight, brown hair, cut short, usually worn in a pageboy. Mediterranean descent."

"Not much to go on."

"No," she admitted. "Though I do have a picture." She pulled the surveillance photo from her coat and handed it to him.

"Do you know where in Killarney they are?"

"We're to meet someone at the Park Hotel. He'll have additional information, including whereabouts."

"Who are we meeting?"

"Andrew Wogan."

"The defense contractor?" he asked, his eyebrows arched.

She nodded.

"You run in some illustrious circles, Agent Morgan."

An amused smile turned the right side of her face. "Hardly."

"Why are we meeting with Wogan?"

"He's the one with information on where to find Ben Iblis."

"What else?" he asked, picking up on her tone.

"Wogan's my father."

"Jesus, Mary, and Joseph. Seriously?"

"Yes."

He studied her. "There's more."

She nodded. "Morelli has lured Wogan here to kill him."

"And he came willingly?"

"She's his lover, or she was. But she left him."

"For Ben Iblis? And Wogan wants to win her back?"

"I think he just wants answers, to be honest. She destroyed his pride, and now he wants to figure out why. There's more, though."

"You put me in the middle of some fucked up love triangle and there's more?" He shook his head, the displeasure evident. "You have some nerve, Agent Morgan."

"Wogan's daughter was murdered two nights ago. I think Wogan believes Morelli had some hand in it. That's why he's here."

"You Americans don't fuck around."

"No. We don't."

"Is your plan to capture Ben Iblis? Do you think that's a reasonable goal, given his background?"

"No."

Brennan pursed his lips and stared out the windshield. "Thus the question about whether or not I carry a gun."

"Does that bother you?"

"I was rather hesitant when this first came down through Interpol and then the Commissioner. I wondered whose dog I kicked to end up on the short end of the stick." He turned and looked at her. "Things were looking up when I saw you walk down those air stairs."

She returned his gaze with a piercing stare, but did not reply.

"But now I'm back to wondering what private hell I've created for myself. Your identification of the target, and your honesty in prosecution makes it very clear how they must regard me at headquarters."

"Well," she said, still holding his hazel eyes. "I told Vogel to send me somebody I can trust. Somebody I can work with. Do you know anyone high up at Interpol?"

"Yes, a few."

"I don't know Vogel's contact, but my guess is your Commissioner was told who to assign, and that's a comforting thought."

"Perhaps you're right."

"How far to Killarney?"

He started the car. "Not far."

Chapter 28

Ben Iblis sat at a table in the hotel's bar, a white cloth napkin in his lap, and a cup of dark coffee in his hand. It was more like a nice restaurant than a traditional bar. Tall windows provided natural light and a wonderful view of the hotel's immaculate gardens. Like everything else in this country, there was a peace and serenity in just sitting he did not realize he missed for these many years.

"I don't believe I've ever seen you looking so pensive," came a voice from behind, in Arabic, and he felt the pressure of someone leaning on the back of his chair. "At least not for many, many years."

With a small smile, Ben Iblis stood and turned. "The last several weeks have proven very interesting."

"So I understand," the man replied. He was slightly taller than Ben Iblis, with the same dark complexion and jet black hair, though small strips of gray intruded over his temples. "I do hope I did not disturb you in some way."

"Of course not. I am always delighted to see an old friend," Ben Iblis said with a bow before motioning to one of the empty chairs on the other side of the table. "Please. You should know you're always welcome at my table. After all these years, I shouldn't need to invite you, dear friend."

"And yet you always do," the man replied, taking the seat with a slight bow of his own. "Ever since I started out on my own, you were always diligent in maintaining contact. Those early years, getting everything up and running, would have been difficult were it not for your support."

"It was my honor, Daeva Aban" Ben Iblis replied, smiling warmly. Nearly a year had passed since their last face to face meeting, and Ben Iblis found himself wondering where the time went. "I considered it an investment, and a prudent one, given my need for a man with your talents. You have proven invaluable all these years."

"Logistics have always been a nightmare. I certainly don't see that improving any time soon."

"No, and we've known each other a very long time. You're right. It won't change. If anything, it will get worse." Ben Iblis sat down and sipped his coffee. "Do you remember those days, outside of Kandahar, when it was so cold at night we had boys burning siphoned Soviet diesel oil to try and keep warm?"

"I do."

"And when we slept together, everyone piled next to each other, just to keep warm enough to survive the nights?"

"I do," Aban replied.

Ben Iblis thought back, his mind wandering to those nights, naked in the desert, the Soviets harassing them with rocket and artillery fire. He'd heard stories of Allied soldiers during World War Two sleeping together to keep warm during the terrible winters. He often wondered if they could compare to the winter nights he spent in slit trenches in Afghanistan, hunted constantly by Russian helicopters.

A waiter appeared, standing politely out of earshot until Aban motioned for him to approach. "May I offer you some coffee?" the waiter asked, walking up to the table.

"Yes, please," Aban said. Then, turning to Ben Iblis, he asked, "Have you ordered breakfast?"

"I was waiting for you."

"What may I offer you gentlemen?" the waiter asked.

"What is the special this morning?" Aban asked.

"Eggs Benedict," Ben Iblis replied. "I already asked."

"Is that what you will order?" Aban asked, his English heavily slurred.

"Yes," Ben Iblis said.

"Then two, please, and a pot of coffee," the Persian said, looking at the waiter. "Knowing my friend, we will go through it."

"Of course," the waiter said, withdrawing to the kitchen.

They were enveloped in silence, the hotel's guests still asleep at that early hour. "You are a different man, Omar," Aban said, switching back to Arabic as he picked the songs of several birds, their notes drifting through the open windows.

"Do you think so?"

"It's hard to tell after a few short minutes, but the last time I saw you stare into space like that, you just lost Astia."

"You mean I just killed Astia," Ben Iblis said, looking out across the garden again. "I see her from time to time. More often in the last week."

"Even after Cyprus?"

"Even then."

"In your dreams?" Aban asked.

"Dreams, nightmares..." Ben Iblis trailed off. "In my waking hours when my mind wanders and I do not need to concentrate, she comes. She is everywhere."

They lapsed back into silence as the waiter delivered Aban's cup and a carafe of coffee.

"I know you miss her, "Aban said, pouring a small amount of cream into the bottom of his cup, then filling it from the carafe.

"Do you ever see them?" Ben Iblis asked without turning from the garden.

"Them?" Aban asked, somewhat confused. "From Afghanistan?"

"Yes."

"Sometimes."

"What do you tell them?" Ben Iblis asked softly.

"Nothing," Aban said, sipping his coffee. "But then, I was never in love with them. You loved Astia. It is different."

"As you say."

They sipped their coffee and listened to the birds for several minutes. "What do you tell her?" Aban asked, watching his friend carefully.

"Many things," Ben Iblis said, frowning.

"Do you ever speak of regret?"

"I've never uttered the word."

"But the thought?"

Several minutes passed before Ben Iblis replied. There was so much he wanted to tell his friend, and so much he could not say. "I'm haunted by the thought. It wakes me at night, and it causes me to stare at open fields during the day." He shook his head. "I am finished with this business, Aban. I am ready to move on with my life."

"What life?"

"A new life," Ben Iblis said, conviction filling his voice. "The life I will make for myself."

"Will that bring her back?"

Ben Iblis looked at him sharply. "Does it matter?"

"Perhaps, for you."

"Am I that far gone?"

"I don't know, but I worry."

"There are days when I worry, too," Ben Iblis said. "I am tired of this life. The events of the last two days made that clear. It is time, dear friend."

"They say you have a new assistant."

"Not an assistant. Someone to carry on my work."

"What happened to Khalid?" Aban asked.

Ben Iblis sipped his coffee. "We no longer saw eye to eye."

"You killed him."

"I did."

Aban took a deep breath and shifted his chair to provide a better view of the garden. Without looking at Ben Iblis, he said, "I have never known you to do such a thing."

"Such a thing?" Ben Iblis asked, not quite sure what he meant.

"To murder someone so close! Khalid was your friend."

"Khalid was expendable."

Aban stared at him in disbelief.

"What of all those boys we killed?" Ben Iblis asked. "All of those children in Afghanistan maimed by the Soviets? No hope of recovery, no hope of life?"

Aban looked at him sharply. "Was that Khalid? Had he no hope of a life? Had he no hope of a future, after caring for you all these years? After everything he did? After all of the years he spent in your employ? Was he one of those maimed boys?"

"He grew reckless."

"You have changed, Omar," Aban repeated, leaning back in his chair and shaking his head.

"Perhaps."

"Tell me about this new assistant." Aban refilled their cups.

"They say she is stunning."

"What they say is true."

A wry smile spread across Aban's face. "And smart, too, I'm sure."

"Yes," Ben Iblis agreed. "Dangerously so."

"So tell me. What does she provide that Khalid could not?"

"She is not my assistant, for one."

"I don't know what you mean."

Ben Iblis finished his coffee and poured himself another cup. "She is a replacement, as I said."

"How is that different?"

"She does not assist me. She will take over my work, carrying on my legacy."

"This is not something Khalid could do? Despite what he did for you outside of Kandahar?"

"Khalid was my friend."

"And this woman?"

"She is...."

"A lover?"

Ben Iblis shook his head. "No. Do you think me as stupid as that?"

"Then what?"

"She is capable."

"Khalid was capable, Omar." Aban said, unconvinced. "Who is this woman?"

"She has become my heir."

"Your heir?" Aban tried to hide his astonishment. "Through force or will?"

It was a good question. Days ago, when he recruited her in that café in the Washington hotel, it seemed like a fantastic idea. Train someone, and have them take over his business, continue his work. An heir. Now, though, seeing her operate, learning her thoughts, her actions, her intentions, he was less convinced. What did he tell his friend, though? This man who shepherded him for so many years. "Through will," he finally said.

"What is her name? This woman?"

"Penelope Morelli."

"And she speaks for you?"

"No," Ben Iblis said, shaking his head. "She will speak for her own operation. I am merely passing on a legacy."

Aban's face was a mix of emotion. "Can you tame the cobra?"

"Is that what I'm trying to do?" Ben Iblis replied, studying his friend.

"She is a deadly adversary. It is but a fantasy."

"A fantasy?" Ben Iblis asked.

Aban nodded. "I have not met Ms. Morelli, but let me say this. You cannot tame a cobra, regardless of what the Indians think. And if you think you have tamed this woman, you are sadly mistaken."

***

Brennan parked their sedan in the hotel's lot. They got out and walked to a bench on the sidewalk, the early morning sun barely tickling the eastern sky. Taking a seat, Morgan adjusted the holster on her hip and looked around.

"Do you get a lot of tourists around here?" she asked.

"Yes," Brennan said. "Killarney's a great tourist destination."

"Just for Ireland?"

"No. For most of Europe. There are a lot of outdoor activities around here. The national park is just down the street." He nodded to the west with his head.

"Convenient that it's so close. You could walk there?"

"Yes."

"I grew up in Colorado," she said, admiring the large trees that lined the lawn. "There are many outdoor activities there, too. My mom and I did a lot of hiking. Even camping."

"Your mother?"

Morgan nodded.

"Andrew Wogan was not around much, I suppose," he continued.

"Well, yes, but not because he was running a business. He wasn't around much because he's never publically acknowledged me as his daughter."

"So your mother raised you," he said. "I suppose I'm lucky. My parents are still together. I try to see them at least once a month, but they live south, near Waterford."

"Do they approve of you being Gardaí?"

"You mean a garda?" he asked with a smile. "Yes, they approve. They are both very proud. You should've seen their faces when I was promoted from a student to a garda."

"I'm sure they were very happy."

He nodded. "Was your mother proud?"

"When I joined the FBI?" she asked. "I'm sure she would've been, but she didn't live long enough to see it."

"I'm sorry."

She shrugged. "She did get to see me graduate from the Academy, though."

"The FBI Academy?"

"No, the Air Force Academy."

"You were in the Air Force?"

She laughed. "Don't sound so surprised."

"I'm sorry. You're apparently a woman of many talents."

Continuing to smile, she looked over at him and said, "Yes. Many talents."

"Maybe tonight you'd let me buy you dinner?"

Her smile faded abruptly, and she looked away. Nichols' broken body, smashed by Baker's shots, floated before her eyes. "No," she said, "but I'd certainly enjoy some company at dinner."

"Fair enough," he said, a little hurt.

"Trust me. It's not anything personal. I just got out of a... well, out of a relationship. Jumping into another one probably wouldn't be the best idea right now."

"I see," he said, not convinced. "I understand."

The noises of the garden enveloped them for several minutes as they lapsed into silence. "Is there somewhere around here I could get a good steak?" she asked.

"Actually, there's a place just down the road that does a pretty mean sirloin. And their drinks aren't bad, either."

"My kinda place."

They sat in silence for a few more minutes, each scanning the street and sidewalks in all directions. Morgan was putting a plan together in her mind, and while she did not exactly mind Brennan's questions, she wished he would shut up for more than two minutes.

"How long were you in this relationship with your boyfriend?"

Her heart missed a beat and she took a deep breath. "Not long. He was killed last week."

Brennan looked down. "I'm sorry."

She nodded, her concentration completely destroyed. What was she supposed to say? How was she supposed to respond? It still did not make sense to her for people to say that. Why were they sorry? What did they need to apologize for? Certainly not for feeling sad. That was a normal reaction. And they should not apologize for her pain. They had not caused it.

"The plan we discussed in the car," she said, changing the subject, "is acceptable to you?"

"Yes," he said. "I think we can handle Dean and Wogan until the cavalry arrives. Once the Garda support team arrives, we can work on capturing Ben Iblis."

Offering him a small smile, she said, "You're optimistic about Ben Iblis. My guess is he will die before allowing himself to be captured."

"He may not have a choice."

"There you're wrong, Inspector. This man makes his own rules. It is best you remember that. He will do whatever it takes to avoid capture, and that includes going through whatever obstacles, including your police personnel, he needs to go through to ensure that."

The cold resolve in her eyes made him pause.

"Please remember that," she emphasized. "I will tell your team the same thing when they arrive."

"I will remember." He cleared his throat. "Do you really plan to offer your father up as bait?"

"I do."

He nodded slowly, then looked around the garden. "It's sometimes difficult to think about the consequences we could face in this job, especially when sitting in so lovely a setting with the sun warming my face."

The same thoughts passed through Morgan's head. Whatever the outcome, she was at peace with the decisions she made to get to this point. People would likely die in a few hours, but with some luck, at least one of them would be Ben Iblis. "We should head inside and set up for Dean and Wogan."

"Yes," he agreed, standing.

"Let's plan on dinner tonight," she said, offering him a small smile.

Looking at her with a sense of hope he wished he believed, he nodded. "I'd like that."

***

"There's a call for you," Dean said, walking into Wogan's bedroom in their massive suite in Killarney.

Wogan looked up from some papers he had spread on the desk. "Morelli?"

Dean shook his head. "An Inspector with the police. He asked for you."

"Did he say what it was about?"

"Only that he wished to speak with you, and only you. He wouldn't give me any information when I answered."

"Odd."

"That's what I thought. Shall I tell him you're busy?"

Wogan thought about it. There was nothing in Ireland which would require his involvement with the police, at least to his knowledge. They would not have gotten wind of Ben Iblis, and any trace he had to the dead agents was so remote as to be non-existent.

Could it be Morgan? He asked her to meet him, not call him, and the last thing he wanted was for her to have involved the authorities. She would know that, though, he was sure. This was something else.

"I'll talk to him," he said.

Dean nodded and withdrew. Wogan picked up the phone on his desk and pushed the blinking button. There were several clicks, then the digital circuit cleared.

"This is Wogan," he said tersely.

"Mr. Wogan, my name is Brennan, Inspector Brennan with An Garda Síochána."

The name did not mean anything to him. "Yes, Inspector. What can I do for you?"

"There's apparently a discrepancy with your customs forms. Would you have a few minutes to speak with me?"

"My customs forms?" Wogan asked, incredulous. "Are you serious?"

"Yes." The conviction carried through the circuit was so absolute it caught Wogan by surprise.

"I'm sorry to hear that, Inspector," Wogan said, "but my assistant usually handles these details. I'm a busy man, I'm sure you understand. It wouldn't be any trouble to get him and have him deal with whatever issues may have arisen. Let me find --"

"Actually, Mr. Wogan," Brennan interrupted, "This needs to be handled by you. Personally."

"I don't understand."

"If you could come down to the lobby, I'd be happy to fill you in."

"I'll send my assistant, Mr. Dean, down," Wogan said, growing angry. "He can show you up to the suite, and we can sort out whatever the issue is."

"Well, we won't be able to deal with Mr. Dean," Brennan said, and Wogan caught a hint of something in his tone. "If you must know the details, it concerns your daughter, and it must be dealt with in person."

"My daughter's dead, Inspector. I thought you just said something about customs forms. You mean to tell me --"

"Your daughter, Mr. Wogan," Brennan interrupted again. "I've arranged for a private room down here with the hotel staff. They were kind enough to accommodate the request. If you could please hurry down."

Wogan turned it over in his mind. There was something in the Inspector's tone.

"Personally," Brennan added, with emphasis.

"The lobby you said, Inspector?" Wogan asked, still chewing on the idea. It was most likely Morgan. If it were Morelli, trying to draw him out, he doubted the suggestion would be so subtle. "I'll be right down."

"Thank you, Mr. Wogan."

Wogan replaced the receiver. Looking at the clock, he grunted and shook his head. It was getting late. Dean walked into the room, pausing just inside the door's threshold.

"You heard?" Wogan asked.

"Yes."

"Is there anything we missed on the custom forms?"

"No," Dean said, shaking his head. "It's a ploy to get you down there."

"You think there's a security concern?"

"I always think there's a security concern. It's my job."

Wogan nodded. "And still nothing from Morelli?"

"No. Nothing."

"She mentioned lunch. Do you think this is her way of getting me down there? I expected something different."

"No, I think this is something else. It doesn't fit her style. She would've called directly."

Wogan pursed his lips and nodded. "Who else knows I'm here?"

"Not many. Some members of the company. Your secretary. But this isn't company business. They would have contacted me."

"So what could it be?"

"I don't know," Dean said.

Wogan looked at him and turned over the possibilities.

The phone rang. Dean went to the desk and picked it up.

"Hello?"

Wogan listened to half the conversation as his mind continued to chew on the call from the Garda inspector. He overheard Dean on the phone. It was Morelli. She wanted to meet in twenty minutes. "Tell her it'll be an hour."

"One second," Dean said into the handset before moving the mouthpiece away and pressing the mute button on the phone's base. "She wants to meet for lunch, as you said. But she wants to do it soon."

"Where?"

"Pub a little way down the street called Murphy's Broken Hand."

"Tell her an hour," Wogan repeated.

"She wants to do it now."

"So?" Wogan asked, his anger threatening to explode. "One hour. I want to get this Garda business done with first. He said it wouldn't take too long. We should still be able to make whatever time Pen wants to set. She just needs to be a little flexible. I'm sure she'll understand."

"She may be gone if we wait an hour."

Wogan stared at him. "You know what, Thomas? I don't really give a shit anymore. Tell that bitch to cool her heels for an hour. If she doesn't want to wait, then we'll go about our business. I'm at the end of my rope."

"What do you mean?"

"Tell her she can wait an hour, or the capture order becomes a kill order, and it will remain in force, globally, until somebody fills it."

"You mean that?"

"Yes."

"Ok," Dean said, unmuting the phone.

Wogan listened as Dean argued with Morelli. In the end, she agreed to an hour. It was obvious to Wogan, at least, that she would have waited much longer. There was something she needed to tell him. It had always been that way.

"She agreed to an hour," Dean said, setting the phone back in its cradle.

"Ok. Let's get downstairs and see what this cop wants. Then we'll head to the pub."

***

Morelli hung up the phone at the bar desk and smiled politely at the bartender. "Thank you," she said before she walked towards Ben Iblis's table. He was deep in conversation with a man she did not know. With a bright smile, she approached the table, and stood politely at its edge. "Good morning, gentlemen. I hope I'm not interrupting."

Ben Iblis and Aban jumped to their feet and returned her smile. "Ms. Penelope Morelli," Ben Iblis said, "please meet Mr. Aban, one of my oldest, dearest friends."

"I'm very pleased to meet you," Morelli said, extending her hand.

Aban gently took it, and with a slight bow, brought it to his lips and kissed it. "The pleasure is all mine, Ms. Morelli. Omar has spoken very highly of you, but his descriptions have not done your beauty quite the justice it deserves."

"You flatter me," she said, her smile growing.

"Will you join us for breakfast?" Ben Iblis asked, offering her a chair. "We have only just ordered. I'm sure they could arrange something."

"I would love to, thank you," she said. "As it turns out, I have a bit of time to kill before my next appointment."

"Excellent!" Aban said, motioning for the waiter. "There is nothing quite like a beautiful woman's company to brighten the morning."

They sat, and Morelli ordered coffee, fruit, and yogurt.

"Beautiful and smart," Aban noted. "I ordered the Eggs Benedict. Absolutely terrible for you, but they're hard to pass up."

"How did you two meet?" Morelli asked.

"In Afghanistan," Aban said. "Many, many years ago."

"Mr. Aban arranged our travel the other day," Ben Iblis said.

Morelli studied him a little more closely. "Then I am very pleased to meet you. I've never seen such efficiency."

"Thank you," Aban replied. "I believe taking care of my clients is my number one priority. I've tried to instill that belief in my staff. It's good to hear they are doing their jobs so well."

"I cannot imagine they would be on your payroll for long if they were not," Ben Iblis said.

"That's true."

"It's fascinating to me how you're able to arrange everything over the Internet," Morelli said.

"It's the best form of communication now, especially for something as simple as travel arrangements."

"But the details!"

Aban smiled patiently. "They can all be worked out online. Granted, it's not like going to an airline's website and having your pick of the various flights and options, but I think we get reasonably close, given the delicate nature of our business."

"I was certainly impressed when we travelled here."

He offered her a sly smile. "Perhaps I might impress you again in the future."

Morelli looked at Ben Iblis, then back to Aban. "What do you mean?"

"Omar tells me he will be retiring, and he won't be travelling nearly as much. I believe he mentioned you will be taking over his business."

"That is correct," Ben Iblis said.

"From everything he's told me about you, Ms. Morelli, you seem more than capable of stepping into his shoes, so to speak."

"Thank you," she replied.

"And based on that recommendation, I would be happy to extend to you the same courtesies I've extended to Omar. Unless, of course, you have one of my competitors in mind?"

"No," Morelli assured him. "I very much hoped you'd be willing to do business with me. It would solve many problems."

"Very good," Aban said. "I'm glad we could come to an agreement."

"Here's our breakfast," Ben Iblis said, watching as the waiter approached from the kitchen. "No more talk of business. Let's enjoy our meal. All of the details may be worked out later."

Chapter 29

Morgan watched as Brennan clicked off his mobile. "It's done," he said. "Wogan will head down to the lobby."

"Then let's go." She stood and opened one of the hotel's front doors. If she was surprised at how calm she felt, walking into certain danger, she did not let it show. Her face was a mask: steady, confident, and determined.

The hostess greeted them as they walked in, though her smile faded slightly when Brennan showed her his credentials. After a brief discussion, the hostess picked up a phone and spoke briefly with the manager, who promptly appeared in person. Another short exchange, and they were in possession of the location of Wogan's suite.

"C'mon," Morgan said, "we need to hurry."

Brennan nodded, and they crossed the lobby towards the elevator. The entrance to the hotel's restaurant opened to their right, and as they passed, Morgan spotted the woman from the surveillance picture. She was seated with two men near the windows opening on to the garden, and Morgan swore one of them was Ben Iblis. Keeping her face impassive, Morgan kept walking.

"Morelli's in the bar with Ben Iblis and another man," she said when they reached the elevator.

"Yes," Brennan agreed. "I saw her, too. Do you want to stick with the plan?"

"The restaurant was brimming with people. I don't want to cause a scene, and a lot of innocent people could get hurt if we try to take them now." She pressed the button for the elevator. "Let's wait for your team to arrive."

"Alright. I'll meet you upstairs."

"Good luck," she said, then turned and headed for the stairs.

***

Wogan led them down the red carpeted hallway before stopping at the elevator. Dean pressed the call button and they waited. There were only two elevator cars, and while the hotel was not very large, it took a little time. Wogan's mind was preoccupied with the call from the Garda Inspector. What the hell could he possibly want?

"Did the Inspector mention where to meet him?" Dean asked, looking around.

"The lobby," Wogan said.

The elevator finally dinged on their floor and the doors parted. There was a man inside the elevator car.

"Where will the security detail meet us?" Wogan asked as they stepped on the elevator.

"In the lobby. I called them before we left the suite." Dean positioned himself between Wogan and the man already in the elevator. He pressed the button for the lobby and noted the button for the second floor was already lit. Apparently, that's where the gentleman in the elevator was getting off.

"We should have time for a cup of coffee before we need to head down to the pub," Dean said. "After we deal with this issue."

"I hope so. I could use a cup. My head is still ringing from the scotch last night."

The elevator dinged its arrival on the second floor, and the doors parted. Dean turned slightly to allow the man to pass, but before he started to move, he caught a flash in his right eye. Dean's hands and feet were already moving to try and parry the blow, but he was far too slow.

Morgan charged into the elevator, smashing her left elbow into Dean's nose, shattering it just between his eyes. With a howl of pain, Dean reflexively grabbed his face and fell back. Still moving, Morgan continued her assault, ramming her right knee into his groin. Dean collapsed to his knees as Morgan sidestepped around him and slapped a pair of handcuffs around his wrists. The elevator doors closed behind them, and the man already in the elevator hit the 'call cancel' button.

"What the fuck is this?" Wogan demanded, too shaken to even move. He stared down at Dean's limp body.

Brennan held down the 'close door' button and turned to face Wogan. "Mr. Wogan," he said. "Inspector Brennan. I'm sorry to introduce myself like this, under these circumstances, but Mr. Dean is under arrest for customs violations."

"Customs violations?" Wogan asked, incredulous. "What the fuck are you talking about?"

"We're also having him extradited," Morgan said, her hands on her hips.

"For what? What are the charges?"

"Grand larceny, conspiracy, attempted murder for starters," she said.

"I don't know what the hell you're talking about, but I protest your handling of this in the most extreme way possible, Inspector! Is this how you treat guests in your country?"

Brennan smiled. "Not all the time, Mr. Wogan. Only under special circumstances. Besides, we need to speak with you about your daughter."

"Would your suite be acceptable?" Morgan asked.

"I don't see how," Wogan said, shaking with rage. "You just assaulted my assistant, and you have me trapped in an elevator! Why in hell would I invite you to my suite?"

"I'm afraid I must insist on this point, Mr. Wogan," Brennan pressed. "It's imperative we speak with you."

Wogan stared at him in disbelief. "Are you serious? Is this really necessary?"

"I'm afraid so," Brennan replied, holding Wogan's angry glare.

Wogan matched Brennan's intensity, hoping the Inspector would back down, but when he did not, Wogan resigned himself. "Alright."

"Thank you." Brennan punched the number for Wogan's floor. When the doors opened, Brennan motioned to Dean's still limp body. "If you wouldn't mind, Mr. Wogan, please help Mr. Dean. It looks like he could use some assistance."

Morgan stepped around Dean and led the way to Wogan's suite. Propping Dean up from behind, his forearms under Dean's armpits, Wogan dragged him down the hallway while Brennan brought up the rear. Using the keycard Brennan procured from the hotel manager, Morgan opened the door, and they filed in.

Wogan dumped Dean on the couch and stood staring at the two agents. "I'd offer you something to drink, but somehow that doesn't seem quite appropriate."

"Perhaps we should offer you something," Morgan said. "You look like you could use it."

"No."

"Are you sure?" Brennan asked, eyeing the small collection of liquor arranged neatly on a table to Wogan's right.

Wogan ran a hand down his face, his mind trying to catch up and process everything that just happened. "On second thought," he said, "I'd love a scotch. Neat."

Brennan arched an eyebrow. "Scotch? In Ireland? For shame, Mr. Wogan."

If Wogan was amused, he did not show it.

"Help yourself," Brennan said, motioning to the bottles.

Wogan walked over to the table and poured a strong measure into a glass. He downed it in one quick toss, then poured himself another. "You still haven't told me what this is all about."

"Please, have a seat," Brennan offered, motioning to one of the chairs.

"I'll stand," he said, looking first at Brennan, then Morgan. "I believe I've been more than patient, Inspector." He swirled the liquid in his glass. "What is the meaning of this?"

Brennan walked around the table and stood, his arms crossed, just behind the chairs. "I told you it was regarding your daughter."

"My daughter's dead. What is so damn important that it couldn't have waited?"

"I meant your other daughter, Mr. Wogan. The one that's very much alive."

Wogan turned to Morgan. "You told him."

"I did."

"Why?"

"Because we have a small crisis on our hands, and he needed to know in the interest of full disclosure. I don't like to lie to a man I'm going to ask to risk his life."

"I don't follow," Wogan said, looking at Brennan more closely. "How long have you been with the service, Inspector?"

"Nearly twenty years."

"All of it in Killarney?"

Brennan smiled. "I didn't say I was based here, Mr. Wogan."

"Interpol?"

"How's your scotch?" Brennan asked, ignoring him.

"Nearly gone."

"I'd offer you another, but I believe you'll need all of your faculties in the near term."

"Stop talking in riddles. What do you mean?"

"Dean and Morelli conspire to have you murdered," Morgan said, watching her father very carefully.

"Nonsense," Wogan said, but his mouth went dry. He glanced at his assistant, still lying on the couch.

"You have a meeting with Penelope Morelli," she continued. It was a statement.

"Yes," he said, glancing at his watch. "Soon."

"I believe they plan to kill you then."

"In the middle of Killarney?" he scoffed. "Why?"

Morgan was not in the mood to play games. It was clear Wogan was in over his head. "How closely did you work with Senator Bradley?"

Wogan finished his scotch, looking at her with disinterest. "Inspector, would you mind getting me another one of these? I find that it calms my nerves. Especially given what my daughter has just told me."

"Are you sure?" Brennan asked.

"Yes, I'm sure," Wogan snapped. "I'm not in the habit of asking for things more than once."

Brennan shrugged, walked over, and took his glass.

Wogan looked expectantly at Morgan.

"Dean has been running operations through Keller for many years, all of them under your nose." She folded her arms across her chest. They needed Wogan's cooperation, and the easiest way to get it was to simply tell him the truth.

"I find that hard to believe," Wogan said automatically, but he took another glance at Dean.

"Keller also told me about some of the operations you hired Morelli to handle."

"What do you know about Morelli?"

"A good deal," she lied. "But I asked you about Bradley. Tell me about him."

"What do you want to know?" Wogan asked.

"How closely did you work together?"

"Bradley was a tool. Someone to use."

With a heavy sigh, she leaned against a wall and looked at him in disgust. "And Dean?"

That caught him a little by surprise, and she could see a shift in the defiance behind his eyes. He looked over at the couch again. "Dean's worked for me for many years. That's why I don't believe he's working with Morelli. Not Dean. I might believe Bradley, or Keller, but not Dean."

"Dean contracted the hit on Janice."

The color drained from his face. "No," he said, but his voice lacked conviction.

"Ben Iblis drew the contract. Morelli filled it." She shook her head, amazed at how simple some people could be. "Keller put everything together. We have all of the details. Your lover and your assistant murdered your daughter."

"No," he hissed.

"And now they've lured you here to kill you."

Brennan handed Wogan the refilled glass. "Here."

Clutching it, his knuckles white, Wogan stared at Dean. "Is this true?"

Dean sat up and tilted his head back until it was resting on the back of the couch. Blood streamed from his broken nose. "You don't honestly expect me to answer that, do you? In front of two law enforcement agents?"

"Is it true?" Wogan repeated.

Dean did not reply. He simply closed his eyes and laid his head back against the couch.

"Why are you telling me this?" Wogan asked, turning back to Morgan.

"Do you know what else I found out in the past twenty-four hours?"

"No," he said, somewhat pathetically. "What?"

"We found the dummy corporation you set up in Janice's name." She watched him for some kind of reaction, but he appeared too stunned to process much of anything anymore. "The dummy corporation you used to pay Timothy Baker."

"Baker's long gone."

In three quick strides, she crossed the room and stood inches from him. Using all her will, she clenched her fists at her side instead of crushing his throat. "Baker's dead," she spat. "I killed him a week ago outside of Washington."

The ferocity of her anger forced him back several steps, but he could not tear his eyes away from her penetrating stare. "Why?"

"He killed three of my agents, including someone very close to me, someone I loved. The only reason I'm alive today is because of this man's actions. And you killed him."

"What?" Wogan asked, incredulous. "Who?"

"You killed him," she repeated, taking another step closer.

"Have you lost your mind?" Wogan asked, his eyes wide. "I haven't killed anyone!"

"Arnon Nichols died at Baker's hand, and you paid Baker."

"You're nuts! You've lost your fucking mind!"

Her right fist exploded into his sternum before even Brennan saw it fly through the air. Wogan collapsed in a heap, his mouth agape as he struggled to breathe.

"Evelyn!" Brennan shouted, and he moved to put himself between Wogan and Morgan.

Before he took two steps, though, she held up her hands and walked to the other side of the room. "It's fine. I'm done. It's done."

Silence enveloped them. Brennan knelt to help Wogan, as the older man sat up and slowly regained his breath. Several minutes passed. Morgan stood against the opposite wall watching with disinterest.

"After everything," Wogan finally said, looking across the room at her, "wouldn't it simply be easier to let them go through with it?"

She looked at him with loathing. "Who said anything about not letting them go through with it? You still owe me Ben Iblis. I showed up. I still want him."

"What do you mean?"

"I mean that I have every intention of letting them go through with it."

Wogan stared at her. "You're not serious."

"I am. I can't think of anything better than having an end to you, to everything you've done over the last fifteen years. I don't want you rotting in some jail cell back in the States. That would be too good an end."

"I don't believe you," he said, but there was fear in his voice.

She shrugged. "Consider it payback for abandoning me all those years ago."

"I apologized!" he shouted, his eyes searching her face for some sort of emotion.

"It's a moot point," she said, her face blank. "I know what you are now. Looking back, I can finally see that was probably the greatest gift you could have ever given me. And despite the misery, I was right in keeping my son from you."

He stood slowly, shaking with rage. "You won't use me as bait."

"I will."

"The Garda won't allow it!"

She smirked. "The Garda are in the dark. Inspector Brennan is the only one in on this, and he's already made it clear that he's at my disposal. Interpol wants Ben Iblis as badly as we do."

"He won't let you do this," Wogan stated, looking up at Brennan, desperation in his eyes.

Morgan glanced at Brennan, her eyebrows arched.

"I've requested two tactical teams to help us deal with Ben Iblis, but they won't be here for two hours," Brennan said. "There's another team en route to take possession of Dean."

"It sounds like Inspector Brennan has a plan," Morgan said, turning back to Wogan. "We spotted both Ben Iblis and Morelli downstairs in the hotel's restaurant on our way up to meet you. They were having breakfast."

"They're staying here?" Wogan asked.

"So it would appear," she replied. "What we will do is wait until Inspector Brennan's backup units arrive, then we'll arrest them."

"I'm supposed to meet her in a pub down the street."

"That won't be possible," Morgan said flatly. "We will simply need to negotiate another meeting when she calls back after you don't show up."

"What makes you think she'll call back?"

Morgan's eyes narrowed. "She called you in the first place. She'll call back."

"If you say so." Wogan looked at Dean, still prostrate on the couch. "You said Thomas put together the hit on Janice."

"Yes," Morgan said. "I did."

"Why?" Wogan asked, looking at Dean.

There was no response.

Taking a deep breath, and wincing as it caught in his chest, Wogan looked back at Morgan. "It's clear to me now I've made a number of mistakes, including how I treated you all those years ago. I truly am sorry for the pain I've caused you, Evelyn."

She stared at him, but did not respond. The sincerity of his apology caught her off guard, but she was wary. His duplicitous nature forced her to not take anything at face value, regardless of what she felt. But she could see the turmoil behind his eyes. Perhaps Janice's death had actually done something to the man.

"You said Morelli killed Janice?" he asked.

"Yes."

He nodded. "And Morelli's downstairs in the bar?"

"Yes."

Straightening his tie and jacket after standing up, Wogan walked around the couch and moved to the door. With his hand on the doorknob, he paused and turned back to look at Morgan. "Perhaps you will think better of me in the future."

"Where are you going?" she asked.

"To deal with Morelli. It's the least I can do for Janice."

"No," she said, moving towards him. "We need to wait for the Garda team. We can't risk trying to take them now!"

"I may be a broken old man, but I have a security detail down in the lobby. I'm sure they'll be more than adequate."

"Don't do this," she said. "We can catch Ben Iblis. We can catch them both! But we need the Garda assault team."

Wogan shook his head. "If you want to use me as bait, it's got to be now. I won't wait for Morelli. I won't take the chance she may not call when I don't make the meeting with her in an hour. If she killed Janice, I will deal with her now."

"I could arrest you," Brennan said.

"If you do that, you will lose any chance at Ben Iblis." Wogan turned to Morgan. "You know that. It must be now." He opened the door and walked out of the suite.

"Shit!" Morgan swore. She looked down at her feet and closed her eyes. Wogan was right. Morelli might bolt if Wogan did not show up to their meeting. On the other hand, they stood little chance of capturing Ben Iblis without more help. She turned to Brennan. "I'm going down there. You can stay and watch Dean if you want, but I have to go down there."

"This is a terrible fucking idea," Brennan said.

"I know."

He watched her for a brief moment while he made up his mind. "Fine. Let me secure Dean, and we'll see what we can do."

Chapter 30

"Mr. Aban," Morelli said, shaking the smaller man's hand as he stood to leave, "it was a pleasure meeting you."

"As I said earlier," he replied, "the pleasure is all mine. I look forward to doing business with you now that Omar is retiring."

Ben Iblis stood and smiled. "I'm glad I can continue to add to your bottom line."

Aban walked around the table, and they embraced. "Goodbye, my friend," he said quietly. "I hope you find the peace you are looking for. It will come." His voice changed to a whisper. "And be careful with this one. She is quite a bit more than she seems. Even for a man like you."

"Thank you."

They watched as he left, then sat back down.

"What did he say?" Morelli asked.

"He wished me good luck."

She sipped her coffee, not confident that was the whole truth. "He seems worried about you."

"He is a good friend. We have seen a lot. Been through a lot. I would be concerned for him if our roles were reversed."

"It seems like it's more than the typical concern for a friend transitioning to a new job, or a new lifestyle."

"Perhaps," he said, looking at her. "But it is not something you should worry about. Everything will work out. There is still our agreement."

"Ten percent, I remember."

Ben Iblis nodded. "Good."

Morelli watched him from the corner of her eye while they lapsed into silence. While only a brief week passed since their original meeting in Washington, she thought he had aged considerably. It was clear to her that Aban saw the same thing. She doubted that good luck was the only advice the logistics man conferred to Ben Iblis during their embrace.

"When are you meeting Wogan?" Ben Iblis asked.

"I should leave soon. He told me an hour when I contacted him before sitting down for breakfast."

"He told you?"

She shrugged. Their plan would work regardless of the time of day.

"Yes, it will take you ten minutes to walk down to the pub."

"The plan is still the same?"

"Of course," he said.

"Then I will see you when we've --" her eyes went wide as she caught sight of Wogan walking into the bar.

"What?" Ben Iblis asked, still turned to face the garden. He followed Morelli's stare, and his eyes narrowed. Wogan, flanked by two men, obviously security personnel, approached their table.

"Mr. Ben Iblis," Wogan said, stopping short and glaring. "I wish I could say it is good to see you again."

"As do I," Ben Iblis replied. He looked over Wogan's security personnel. "And your friends?"

"Simply a precaution."

"I'm sure," Ben Iblis said, an amused predatory gleam filling his dark eyes.

Wogan stared at him, hatred welling behind his eyes. "I wonder if you would excuse Ms. Morelli and I for a few minutes? We have several things to discuss."

"Of course," Ben Iblis said, standing slowly. Walking around Wogan's security, he sat down at an empty table on the other side of the room, his back to a corner, the entire room spread before him.

Morelli watched him go, then changed seats, putting her back to the garden. From there, she could see anyone coming into the room through either the front entrance or the kitchen. "I'd offer you a drink," she said as Wogan continued to stand at the edge of the table, "but I'm not sure you'd accept."

He stood there wrestling with his emotions, his face a jumbled mask in perpetual motion. Morelli sat there, watching him, waiting for it to end, waiting for him to come to some kind of decision. After what seemed like an eternity, he took a deep breath, composed himself, and sat down opposite her. The waiter instantly appeared.

"Coffee," Wogan said before the waiter could even ask.

The waiter shrugged and left, hollering something at the bartender in Gaelic.

"I'm sorry, Andy," Morelli began, trying to find some kind of opening, not quite knowing the best place to start.

"Sorry for abandoning me? Sorry for shacking up with Ben Iblis? Sorry for murdering Janice?"

She took a long, slow drink from her mug, draining it as she felt the color drain from her face.

"Which?" he asked in a calm, measured tone.

Setting her mug back down, she said, "I'm sorry it's come to this."

"You could've had anything, Pen. I would've given you the world."

The waiter delivered his coffee, and he took a sip, grimacing at the taste.

"How did you find out about Janice?" she asked.

"Morgan."

That surprised her. "How did she know?"

"Keller."

"Who is Keller?"

Wogan's eyes narrowed, and he looked down at his coffee.

Morelli nodded. It would not be hard to find out. It was one loose end she would have to tie off. Soon. "I suppose you want to know why."

"I deserve to know," he replied.

"It was a job," she said. "That simple."

"Bullshit!" he thundered, pounding his fist on the table, drawing the heads of every patron in the bar.

She leaned in to the table. "Getting upset isn't going to help anything, Andy."

"But it might make me feel better."

"I doubt it. You know how it works in this business. Janice was a target. Somebody wanted her dead. The question of why, when looking at who gets marked, shouldn't even come into the equation."

"It does this time. She was my daughter."

"Somebody wanted her dead."

"She was my daughter!" he screamed, spittle flying from his mouth, his eyes wide with rage.

"She's dead," Morelli said, leaning back in her chair. "Screaming isn't going to bring her back."

Wogan buried his head in his hands, trying to regain control of himself. "He's been teaching you well," he said, looking up.

She stared at his ice blue eyes. "He's a good teacher."

"Is he as good in the sack?"

"I wouldn't know."

"Probably not a whole lot of experience pleasing women." He looked at her pointedly. "When you fuck whores, you don't need to spend a lot of time pleasing them."

"Does insulting me make you feel better?"

"No, not really."

"I'd apologize...."

"But you're not sorry. I get it."

"Actually, I was going to say that I don't think it would do any good. Because I am sorry. I'm sorry Janice was the first assignment. I'm sorry you sent two assets to take care of Bradley last week. I'm sorry you felt the need to put a capture order on me. I'm sorry I wasn't able to fuck you away from your wife after two years." She looked at him with a measure of sympathy. "I'm sorry for a lot of things, Andy. But this is a profession. It's business."

"Bullshit," he repeated.

"It's not bullshit. It's the truth." She wanted to convince him, to make him see. "If it was your wife on that contract, she would be dead. Or Morgan. Or you. It's business."

"Did you even feel anything while you were doing it?"

She stared at him, a glimmer of pain in her eyes. "You should know better than to ask me something like that."

"Did you?"

She just stared at him, boring her brown eyes into his.

"And Dean?" he asked.

"Dean?" she asked, confused. "What do you mean?"

"Don't play dumb, Pen. I know. I know it all. Morgan put it all together, but I had my suspicions."

She did not have any idea what he was talking about. One more loose end to tie up, or, at the least, look into. "Is she here?"

"No," he lied. "Dean authored Janice's hit. Did he tell you before you left? Before you carried it out?"

"Morgan figured all that out?"

"As I said, she talked to Keller."

Her mind started to chew on Wogan's disclosures. One thing became immediately clear. Morgan was an extremely dangerous adversary. If she was able to put all of it together, including the fact that Dean authored the contract, she needed to be taken care of. Quickly. "Where is Dean," she asked.

"I don't know," Wogan lied again. "He left a message for me at the hotel saying he went ahead to meet you. He wanted to make sure you didn't leave before I had a chance to speak with you."

"I haven't seen him."

"Apparently."

Morelli poured herself more coffee and thought more about Morgan. Ben Iblis wouldn't kill her. That was clear. But she needed to be dealt with. What was the best way to do that? If Ben Iblis discovered she killed Morgan, there was little doubt in her mind he would come kill her, retirement or not. It was a sobering prospect. She held no illusions how long she could survive against a determined Ben Iblis. That was something else she would need to deal with, if she hoped to take care of Morgan.

"Did you ever love me?" Wogan asked, breaking into her thoughts. "Do you now?"

"It's hard to rationalize love," she said, switching gears rapidly.

"Love is an emotion. It's hard to rationalize any emotion. That's why they're emotions."

She searched his eyes. "Did you love me?"

"I think I could have. But it's hard to love what you own."

That should have hurt. Crushed her, even, but she learned long ago, been forced to learn long ago, that it did not matter. That was how it worked. "That first night you took me into your bed, I knew what had to be done. I did what I needed to do, because you were the one signing the checks. You were the one making all the decisions. You determined who would be put in what program, who would run which division." She sighed. "You think I didn't see that? You think I did all those things because I enjoyed it? I knew that if I wanted to make something of myself, you were the meal ticket. You were the one footing the bills."

He looked at her across the table, loathing in his eyes.

"So tell me," she continued, her voice low, her eyes cold. "Who's the one fucking whores now? Who's the one paying delicate little women to lie down and take it? Who's the one training people to take orders? To do what needs to be done and not ask questions?"

He just stared at her.

"How many more do you have in other cities just waiting for the opportunity to prove themselves?" she asked, a sneer curling the right side of her face. "Are they all even women?"

She saw his hand out of the corner of her eye as it flew up from beneath the table. Slow. Sloppy. Catching his wrist in mid-air, she forced it down to the table and, half-standing, she leaned over, her face inches from his. "The one thing I learned, years before I ever met you, Andrew Wogan, was that you can always count on men for one thing, and only one thing. It's fantastically easy to manipulate them once you learn that."

"You're a dead woman, Pen."

"We're all dead people," she said, very calmly, a slight smile on her face. "It's just a matter of time." Out of the corner of her eye, she saw his security people stand. She did not care. With a lightning movement born from years of practice, she drew the small Walther from its holster at the small of her back and shot Wogan twice in the chest.

Her shots were followed by the bark of two double taps, two separate groups of two shots. The sounds crashed through her ears, and she dove to her left, under the table, before Wogan's bodyguards crumpled to the floor. Chaos erupted as people jumped from their seats and ran for the nearest exit.

With the pistol in her hand, she crawled to her left, trying to find better cover behind a bench lining one of the windows overlooking the garden. Wogan's body slowly dropped from the table to the ground to her right, his sightless eyes staring at her. Silence filled the room, mixing with the sweet stink of cordite and blood. Chancing a glance around the bench, Morelli checked for movement. The room appeared empty, chairs and tables strewn haphazardly across the space, shattered glass, plates, and food spread over every surface. She saw three bodies. But where was Ben Iblis? He had disappeared.

"Omar?" she called, risking her position.

No response. He either fled, or he suspected someone else might still be in the room and remained silent. She could not stay there. The police would pull up in moments, and escape would be impossible. Bug out, her mind screamed. Get up! Meet Ben Iblis at one of the alternate rendezvous locations. Escape and evade!

She counted to thirty, willing her heart to slow. At thirty-one, she chanced one more glance around the booth and jumped into a squat. Moving quickly, she stayed hunched and ran for the bar, nearly twenty feet away. Before she took two steps, though, she heard Ben Iblis yell from her right, followed by a searing pain as something punched through her left shoulder. The bullet whipped her around, throwing her back behind the booth, shielding her from any further fire from the bar. Blinking rapidly, her breath coming in ragged gasps, she heard the crackle of additional gunfire from her right. She needed to move, bullet or not. She knew that. With effort, she picked herself up on her right elbow, her left arm useless, and looked to her right in time to see Ben Iblis move across the room, his pistol held at the ready, aimed at some unseen target behind the massive mahogany bar.

He was leaving, she realized, as he moved up the steps and disappeared through the bar's front entrance.

Out. She needed to get out, but there was no way she would make it to the front without getting hit from whoever was behind the bar.

The windows!

She willed her foggy mind to function. They were floor to ceiling, no screens, opening right onto the gardens. One was open, a few feet away, fully hidden from the bar by the booth. Moving slowly, cradling her left arm, her pistol still in her hand, she followed the back of the booth and went through the window.

***

"Watch the right," Morgan ordered, poking her head over the bar to get a sense of the destruction. "I think she might be down behind that booth. I hit her at least once."

"Ok," Brennan replied, watching for any movement, a small pistol in his left hand.

"Ben Iblis went through the front." She scanned the room. There was no movement.

"Is he hit?"

"No," she said. "I didn't have a shot when he moved."

"I'll cover right. Let's move."

"Right behind you."

They shuffled around the bar, Morgan covering the entrance, Brennan keeping his gun trained on the booth where Morelli went down. "Clear," he said, rounding the back of the booth and following a light blood trail through one of the open windows. "It looks like she made it into the garden. There's a very light blood trail here. It gets lighter where she goes through the window."

"Ok," Morgan answered, her mind racing. She wanted Ben Iblis, but Morelli was wounded. She would be easier to run to ground.

"I don't think you hit her very hard. Probably more of a shock wound than anything."

Morgan nodded. There was not enough blood on the ground to signify a major wound. She made up her mind. Before moving, though, she knelt next to Wogan and checked his pulse. "He's gone," she said after a few moments, closing her eyes.

"I'm sorry."

"I'm not," she shot back, surprising herself. Maybe she did care. Now was not the time for self-reflection, though. "Follow me. We'll stay on Ben Iblis."

They moved to the entrance, taking cover behind the doors and scanning the lobby. Nothing. Walking quickly, they pressed forward, no one in sight.

"Which way?" Brennan asked, shifting his gaze between the stairs and the hotel's doors.

"He went up the stairs," a voice called from behind the receptionist's desk.

Morgan looked at the woman, little older than a girl, huddled under her desk, tears streaming down her face. "Thank you," Morgan said, and she charged up the stairs, her pistol in front of her, Brennan covering their rear.

As they came to the first floor, Morgan poked her head around a corner and glanced down the hall. She was rewarded with a shower of plaster and the stinging bite of a bullet as it disintegrated in the wall next to her cheek. Seconds later, she heard the bang of the door to the emergency stairs slamming against its stops.

"Go back downstairs and circle around," she ordered, blinking several times to try to clear the dust from her eyes. "He's headed down."

"You're bleeding," Brennan said, looking at her.

Absently, she wiped blood from her cheek. "Get back downstairs!"

"And split up?" he asked, incredulous.

"We'll come at him from two directions. Go! I can take care of myself!"

He did not move, still staring at her, undecided.

"If he gets to one of those cars in the parking lot, we'll lose him again. He'll be out of the country in no time. Go! I'll meet you down there!"

"Be careful," he shouted over his shoulder as he turned and headed back down the stairs.

Taking a deep breath, she rounded the corner and ran down the hall. The emergency stairs were just a short sprint away, and she threw open the door without a thought, running down the stairs, her heart pounding in her ears. There was no time to think about the consequences. The desire to get to the bottom of the stairs as quickly as she could overcame every other impulse, every caution her brain screamed at her. This was the closest she had ever been! She could catch him. She had to catch him.

Bursting through the bottom door, her breath was kicked from her body by two hammer blows to the middle of her chest, just above her heart. They stopped her momentum completely. It felt like her lungs collapsed, and her eyes went wide as she staggered backwards into the door. Stumbling, trying to force her mind to command her body, she fell to her left as two more shots splintered the hotel's stucco where her head was a scant second before.

A row of low hedges provided some cover from her shooter, masking where she was, but they would not stop incoming fire. There was a low wall just to her left which would give her better cover. Taking slow, deliberate breaths, she tried to ignore the searing pain where her vest stopped the bullets. Her vision cleared and as she crawled to the wall, she heard someone's footsteps, moving quickly, to her left. She picked her head up, and raised her pistol.

There!

He was running down a garden path, his shoes pounding the stone pavers leading to the parking lot. Aiming quickly, she fired six quick shots in three groups of two, hitting him on the third shot, spinning him around, and knocking him down. The brief spray of blood told her he was not wearing a vest, but she lost sight of him when he fell back behind a small rise in the path.

Picking herself all the way up, she rubbed her chest with her left hand and tried to take a deep breath. Her vest was a class III, rated for most handguns, but whatever Ben Iblis was firing, it did some damage. At least a couple of broken ribs, she thought, wincing as she moved down the path, changing her magazine as she jogged.

Crossing the rise, her left arm clutching her ribs, her pistol in front of her, struggling to catch her breath, she heard the distinct crack of two more gunshots, farther off, probably on the other side of the hotel. Maybe Brennan found Morelli, she thought as she caught sight of Ben Iblis. He had picked himself up, and was nearly twenty yards farther down the path than where she expected. It took her a precious second to adjust her aim. In that brief moment, Ben Iblis pivoted on his left foot and fired. It went wide, though.

Adjusting her aim, she squeezed the trigger and watched the bullet plow into his left breast, high, near the shoulder joint. It was not a great shot, but it was all she needed. The forty caliber bullet from her Sig Sauer packed a punch, knocking him back and down. With a grimace, she ran forward, kicking the pistol from his hand, then taking a few steps back.

"I always wondered if you would do it," he said in his heavily accented English, his head back, his eyes lost in the clouds.

"What? Shoot you?"

"No, kill me."

"How do you know I haven't been trying?"

He picked his head up and looked at her. "Because your aim's not that bad."

"You didn't have any problem shooting me," she said, still holding her ribs.

"Armor?"

She nodded.

"I warned you not to come after me."

"You were foolish to think I'd stop. After everything that's happened, you were stupid to think I'd ever stop."

"Because of your lover?" he asked. "What was his name?"

"Nichols."

He laid his head back and looked up at the sky. He could not feel the blood pouring out of him so much as the cold invading. "Astia," he said, closing his eyes.

Her face softened as she thought about the poor girl. "Would you have killed her, had you known?"

"Known what?"

Stepping closer, she looked down with some measure of sympathy. "Known that you'd be bleeding to death here in the dirt, calling her name."

"Everything must end. Even us."

"Morelli," Morgan said, watching him grow weaker by the second. "She was in the bar. Where is she?"

"I don't know."

"Where were you to rendezvous?"

A small smile spread across his lips and he opened his eyes to look at her. "I always thought you had the most beautiful eyes, Evelyn Morgan."

As she stood there looking at him, a warning bell exploded in her mind, but it was too late. Far too late. Her head started to swivel left, to pick up the threat that suddenly crested the small rise, her right hand already moving to bring her pistol to bear.

She never made it.

Morelli's first shot erupted in both her eyes, and she felt the hammer blow of the round as it punched down into her left shoulder, blowing it back and exposing the damaged vest to the nine millimeter rounds of Morelli's Walther. The second round hit her just above her sternum, in almost the same location as Ben Iblis's shots, and her legs buckled. It was like someone hitting her square in the chest with a sledgehammer, shocking her entire system into a state of abject collapse, and when she tried to stand, she found she was no longer able to control her legs.

The third round hit her somewhere in her right side, and the entire area went numb. It was hard to tell where, exactly, as her vision was dark and her mind began to shut down. The last thing she wondered, before she succumbed to the blackness, was whether or not Morelli felt anything when she pulled the trigger. But that was a stupid question.

Chapter 31

Morelli ran down the path and stood over Morgan. Taking careful aim, she pointed her pistol at the back of the FBI agent's head and was about to squeeze the trigger when she heard Ben Iblis say, "Don't."

"Why not?" she asked, looking at him. "This woman knows everything! She's traced you everywhere! With her gone, we don't need to fear anything anymore! We can operate across the globe without repercussion."

"There are always repercussions," he said weakly. "Every time you accept a contract, every time you go out, every time you act, there are repercussions."

Morelli took a step to her left and stood over Ben Iblis, her shadow casting his face in darkness.

"What happened to the other guy Morgan was with?" he asked, trying to see the clouds past her face.

"I shot him."

"Help me up," he said, lifting his one good arm. "We need to get out of here. There's still a chance. Kill Morgan, and we have no hope of getting out of the country."

But she did not move. "I realized something this morning," she said. "After speaking with Aban, and then Wogan, there are certain things I need to do before I'm able to set myself up in this business.

With any hope of success, I should add." Walking over to Morgan's body, Morelli holstered her pistol and picked up Morgan's Sig Sauer. She quickly dropped the magazine and replaced it, ensuring there were still rounds in the gun.

"When you recruited me in Washington, I thought it would take years before I would be capable enough to take over your operations. After this past week, though, I know differently." She stood over Ben Iblis again, and she met his eyes. "We are not all that different, you and I. Only I know what must be done, and you are unwilling to do it."

Nodding weakly, he closed his eyes and took a deep breath. "One day you will realize the foolishness of your choice. It may be thirty years, if you make it that long, but one day, you will realize what a waste it was."

Without a word, she raised Morgan's pistol and fired, hitting him in the forehead. Then, conscious of how much time she wasted, she quickly wiped down the pistol using her blouse and dropped it next to Morgan's right hand. She knelt and felt Morgan's neck for a pulse, but finding none, she stood and jogged down a path perpendicular to the one they were on.

Emerging from the hotel's garden, she crossed a street and moved rapidly down the sidewalk. The feeling was starting to return to her left arm, a dull ache that she suspected would turn into a raging firestorm once her nerves fully recovered. After the emotionless front she put on when speaking with Wogan, though, it was good to be able to feel something again.

It took her several minutes to find the Land Rover, walking down one street before turning the corner, finally spotting it halfway down the next. Morelli knew she needed time to get away from the city, and she could not trust the security of the farm for long. The police would turn the countryside upside down.

***

A gray haze covered her eyes as she tried to open them, and when she ordered her arms to move, to bring her hand to help wipe her eyes, they would not respond. The whole left side of her body felt numb, like it was not even there, while the right side erupted in an excruciating burst of agony unlike anything she ever felt before in her life. Despite all her efforts her limbs would not move. As she blinked over and over and over to try to clear the misty haze from her sight, she moved her head side to side, frustration mounting as her brain tried desperately to process all the disparate emotions and memories that flooded back.

There was a vague memory of five or six people huddled over her, poking, prodding, cutting away her clothes. Then there was the memory of a helicopter, the sensation of flying a good distance, then more people, all of them faceless as they shouted and stabbed. Then nothing. Blackness. An inky, dark curtain that she was crawling to escape; more than anything else, she needed to get away from that velvet swath.

"Shhhh," came a voice in her ear, and for the first time, a sensation; a touch. Somewhere along her right arm. Contact.

"Where am I?" she mumbled, her lips dry and chapped. She was not even sure if those were the right words, not convinced that someone would even be able to understand her.

"Queen Elizabeth Hospital," came the male voice. "In Birmingham."

"Vogel?" she asked, her mouth like cotton swabs. A name. From before. Something she remembered. She licked her lips, trying desperately to get any kind of moisture to her parched tongue.

"Here," he said. "Drink this."

She felt a hard plastic tube being pushed gently into her mouth, and she drunk greedily.

"Not too much," he said, and the delicious elixir was pulled away far too early.

"My eyes. I can't see."

She felt, rather than heard, the sound of tape being pulled from the sides of her temples, and suddenly the diffused, grey haze was transformed into a brilliant blaze of white light so bright she crushed her eyes closed to block it out.

"They said it would be bright, at first."

"It's terrible," she said, trying again to bring an arm up to shade her eyes from the light.

"The doctors will be here soon," Vogel said. "They must know you've come around by now, just from your vitals."

She remained silent, his features finally coming into focus.

"They were afraid you weren't going to make it," Vogel continued, "when they first brought you in. The EMTs in Ireland were able to get your heart restarted at the hotel, and they flew you over here once you were stable."

"I'm glad," she croaked, not sure she actually believed that.

"And there's a running bet on when you'd come around."

"What were the odds?"

"Not good."

She laughed, a short almost cough-like exhalation that racked her entire body in the same terrible agony she felt when trying to move her limbs. "Christ," she swore. "Don't make me laugh."

"Alright," he said, though now her eyes were adjusting to the light and coming into focus, she could see the large grin plastered on his face. "I need to tell them you've come around."

"Ok," she said. Then, "Wait."

He stopped at the foot of her bed and turned around.

"Why can't I move my arms?"

The smile on his face disappeared, and he looked down. "They've got your left arm immobilized. The bullet went through and through, but it played dirty harry with your shoulder. Bad news for the tendons and soft tissue."

"And my right arm?" she asked, almost afraid of the answer.

"The bullet that went through your back...." His voice trailed off.

"What about it?"

"The vest failed," he said with a sigh. "Too many rounds."

"So?"

Their eyes met. "They don't know if you'll be able to move it again."

She looked up at the ceiling, but couldn't bring herself to say anything.

"I'll tell them you're awake," he said, withdrawing.

It was difficult for her to contemplate the idea of dying, the finality of it, but those few times she had thought about it she came to the realization that if it was her time, when it was her time, it would probably be quick and painless. She would not linger. It never crossed her mind that she might be paralyzed; that she would be forced to go through life crippled, re-learning how to do everything, teaching herself anew. It was a terrible prospect. One she wished… she closed her eyes.

A low voice cut into her thoughts. "How're you feeling?"

"Not well," she replied, her eyes still closed.

"We're worried about you."

She opened her eyes and moved her head down and to the right so she could see him. The doctor was older, and it was difficult for her to determine his age. Over fifty, she thought, watching as he examined her chart. "Would you mind tilting me up a little bit?" she asked. "I can't seem to operate the damn bed."

"Sure."

"Thanks," she said, after the bed pushed her torso and head into an upright position. "I must have so many drugs going through me. It's hard to tell which way is up sometimes."

"They were the only thing keeping you alive for a while," he replied with a small smile. "I've got some things I need to check on. It's good to see you're awake. I'll be back in a bit."

Morgan watched him leave, and Vogel walked back over to her bed. She looked at him, strangely diminutive sitting in the cheap plastic hospital chair. "You said you were worried."

"Did I?" he asked, feigning surprise.

"Yes."

"You must've misheard."

"I don't think so."

Vogel smiled half-heartedly, his lips barely turning at the corners. "You died, Eve. When I got that call two weeks ago, they said you died. I got on the plane thinking I was going to have to bury another agent."

"It may have been better that way," she said, looking down at her right arm.

"No."

She pursed her lips. "I've been out for two weeks?"

"Yes."

She thought back, trying to remember that day. "The shots. I didn't hear her come up. I didn't even know she was there. I heard gunshots behind me while I was chasing Ben Iblis, but I thought they were Brennan's. I thought he finished her." She paused, her memory cloudy. "I was talking to Ben Iblis. He was dying… and then I felt that round in my shoulder."

"Did you see the shooter?"

"Yes. Morelli."

Vogel nodded, watching her.

"Brennan," she said. "He's dead, isn't he?"

"Yes."

A deep sigh blew through her lips. "And Morelli?" She forced herself to push the Garda Inspector to the back of her mind. "She was hit in the bar. There wasn't much blood when I saw her in the gardens, but there was some."

"We don't know. Gone."

"Ben Iblis, too?"

"Ben Iblis is dead," Vogel said, still watching her closely. "You put a round through his head."

Furrowing her brow, she tried to remember, but nothing came back. "I remember shooting him, putting him down, but the rounds went through his chest, not his head. He was alive before Morelli shot me. I talked to him."

"Are you sure?"

"Yes," she said, though she was not convinced. It was too fuzzy.

"I don't blame you for killing him."

The drugs made it impossible to concentrate, but she knew she did not put a bullet through his head. Despite everything, it was not what she wanted. Conscious of Vogel's stare, she looked away and closed her eyes.

"We found Wogan in the bar," he continued.

She nodded. "I knew he was gone before we went after Ben Iblis in the garden."

"Who shot him?"

"Morelli. Brennan and I came around and hid in the kitchen. I could see most of what was going on through the doorway into the dining room. They were talking, and it looked like he moved to hit her. She caught his fist and put two rounds in his chest before I could even move. She was fast. Damned fast."

"What about his security detail?"

"Ben Iblis," Morgan replied. "It all went to hell. Brennan and I wanted to wait for the Gardaí, but Wogan insisted on confronting her when he learned she killed Janice."

"Who told him that?"

"I did."

Vogel looked like he wanted to say something, but he bit it down and simply nodded his head.

"Did she get out of the country?" Morgan asked.

"We think so."

She nodded. It made sense. "I assume you found Dean?"

"Yes. He's back in Virginia at a safe house. Interrogation has him."

"They won't learn much."

"About Ben Iblis?" Vogel asked, taking his spectacles off and wiping them with a handkerchief. "I'm afraid you're right. But he may be able to give us something on Morelli. Something to help us catch her."

"She's long gone," Morgan said, disappointment palpable in her voice.

"Probably."

"What has Dean said about Wogan?"

"Nothing."

Morgan looked at Vogel, her eyes searching his. "He's lying."

"You trust Keller?"

"I don't have to. The laptop should give us everything we need."

"It's given us a lot." He cleared his throat, replaced his spectacles, and stood. "Did your mom ever tell you the story of the dinosaurs?"

Puzzled, she said, "No."

"Suddenly, an asteroid hit the Earth and killed them all. The end." He walked to the end of her bed and looked at her. "They don't always have happy endings, Eve. Get better. We need you back."

Morgan watched as he walked off. He stopped briefly in the corner of the ICU, spoke with the doctor, then left. She looked down at her right arm and tried to lift it again. The same shooting agony rocketed up her side and nearly caused her to black out. After several minutes, as she lay there panting, trying to get her heart rate under control, she tried again. And again. She would be back. There was a new enemy to hunt.

Acknowledgements

Thank you all for your generous support! *Muckross Folly* would not have been possible without your skills.

My wonderful wife Jennifer, whose selflessness is an inspiration, and without which this book would not exist.

Mrs. Kris Salo, for forcing the reexamination and consideration of details which otherwise may have slipped through the recesses of the editing process.

Mrs. Barbara Johnson, for her constant moral support, editing, and attention to detail. I'm particularly grateful for the three glaring issues she discovered in the final draft.

Mrs. Julie Montieth, for her questions, ideas, edits, analysis, and the reconsideration of certain descriptive terms.

Matt and Sapna Skinner, for their thoughtful, no holds barred analysis.

About The Author

J.L. Austgen was born in 1979 in Indianapolis, Indiana. He attended a Jesuit high school where his love for writing fiction took root. After graduating college in Colorado, he took a job in IT and stopped writing fiction.

Several years passed before he realized how much he missed writing, and with excitement, he sat down and created Evelyn Morgan.
J.L. spends his spare time reading, listening to music, and enjoying time with his family. He is married with two kids, two dogs, and currently resides in Colorado.

www.ingramcontent.com/pod-product-compliance
Ingram Content Group UK Ltd.
Pitfield, Milton Keynes, MK11 3LW, UK
UKHW041415180426
11947UKWH00007B/147